HEIRS of EMPIRE

ALSO BY EVAN CURRIE

Odyssey One Series

Into the Black

The Heart of Matter

Homeworld

Out of the Black

King of Thieves

Warrior's Wings Series

On Silver Wings

Valkyrie Rising

Valkyrie Burning

The Valhalla Call

By Other Means

Other Works

SEAL Team 13

Steam Legion

Thermals

EVAN CURRIE

AUTHOR OF THE ODYSSEY ONE SERIES

HEIRS of EMPIRE

Published by 47North, Seattle

www.apub.com

ISBN-13: 9781503946903

ISBN-10: 1503946908

Cover illustration by Chris McGrath

Cover design by Jason Blackburn

Printed in the United States of America

HEIRS of EMPIRE

PROLOGUE

The supply train was just over three hundred chains in length, barreling along the open plain and outpacing sound by threefold. Ahead of the bronzed bulbous head of the floating engine, a crackling blue shimmer of lightning was all that showed the energy field that kept the bow shock wave from destroying everything. The linked machine passed silently, a ghost in the night as it swept toward its destination.

The third car of the train was dark, mostly empty, with only a handful of people standing watch, and most of them were barely able to focus on the blur of the landscape as it sped past. Toward the front, however, one woman stood with eyes glittering in the night, alert and active as she watched. The touch of silver gleaming from behind her irises was the only hint that she was running enhanced at the moment, but it was all a careful observer would need.

"Have you seen anything, my lady?"

Mira Delsol half turned, the silver fading from her eyes, and shook her head.

"Only the heat fog in the distance, Stephan," she said. "Nothing else moves along the great bowl."

Stephan El nodded.

Nothing, not even the greater viewing lenses, could penetrate the permanent heat fog that hid details from sight. Only remote viewers had a chance, and they were finicky beasts at best.

"Well," he said, "that is no surprise, my lady. No one knows of this run, not even the royals. There are no leaks to be found."

"Air escapes through solid steel, Stephan," she said darkly, eyes turning back to look out over the landscape that was blurring past. "Count only on that."

"There is a half century of men-at-arms aboard with us, plus a knight and—"

"Two knights. Never forget it."

"You are too humble, my lady," he said, but smiled nonetheless.

If it was a slightly bitter smile, Mira said nothing. Stephan was a knight, yes, but she was Cadre. They were a cut above, legends in their own lifetimes, so calling herself a knight was almost irritatingly humble of her.

"The point is, my lady," he said softly, "what force stands a chance against a half century and us?"

Mira shrugged, knowing that he was right in a very real way. Few forces in the area could be mustered that would be a serious threat to the train, not with its air screens fully charged while it tore across the desert at hypersonic speeds. Add to that the strength of the half century posted on board, and then Stephan and herself.

No, he is right. There's no force for a thousand leagues either crazy or stupid enough to meet us head-on, and nothing for even farther that could catch us from the back. I'm being paranoid, thought Mira.

In that, at least, she wasn't alone.

Someone had assigned a Cadre member to guard duty, something that just didn't happen without cause. So, paranoid or not, she reached inward and cycled her enhanced senses again before looking out the great window to the dark landscape as it flashed by.

The silver hint returned to her eyes as her vision shifted, growing sharper and more defined. It let her spot details in the blur of the closer terrain as well as pick out the occasional animal padding through the flat bowl of the Great Desert. Beside her she noted Stephan pick up a pair of portable field viewers and join her.

She felt some pity for Stephan. He was a good knight, but he'd never managed to qualify for a Cadre slot despite near constant attempts. It wasn't a shade on his record. Fewer than one in a hundred made it into the Cadre, and that was from the one in five hundred who successfully earned their helms as knights. He'd already beaten the odds just making it to where he was. It was nothing to feel shame about, but she knew that he felt just that.

Mira didn't pity him for not achieving his goal. She pitied him for not realizing just how high he had already climbed.

Some men could fly to the Great Islands, and still it would not be high enough.

Mira leaned forward and glanced both ahead and up, noting the laser-straight line of light cracking open the skies ahead of them.

"We'll shortly ride into the new light," she said. "Nanna's Great Island moves past."

"Aye." Stephan nodded, looking out as well. "So it does. The heat will be on us soon too. The fog will worsen."

He had a point, of course. When the Great Island moved from between them and the sun, things would grow hotter quite quickly. There was little rain and no cloud cover in this region and, as far as anyone could tell, the environmental wards had grown less and less over the years. That was why they had put the testing range so far out this way, where few people cared to go and where there was next to nothing to destroy.

The heat fog was a minor issue, really. It never went away after all. It just waxed and waned, so while it would be a problem, it was really just a matter of degrees. Still, she wouldn't care to be caught out in that heat, not without the environmental controls of the train to cover them.

It would be a trial to endure, of that there was no doubt.

"Wake a squad of the men-at-arms," she said. "Double the forward watch. Let us be sure that the field remains solid. It would not do to lose shielding now."

"True enough." Stephan nodded, stepping back. "It will be done, my lady."

She snorted, half smiling as she turned to look at him. "How long have we known one another, Stephan?"

"Almost five years," he admitted with a bit of a grin.

"I've never known you to call even nobles by those old titles," she said, "so why have you begun with me?"

"Those soft-ass fools never earned a thing in their lives," he told her simply. "You made Cadre, my lady. That's worthy of a little respect."

She laughed softly, shaking her head. "Call me my name, Stephan. You need not do more than that."

"Yes, well," he said as he stopped by the door to the next car, "that too is worth a little respect . . . You're still too damned humble for your own good, though."

The door slid back and he stepped through before she could respond, the low hum of the levitation system filling the cabin until the door slammed shut again.

"Never did know the difference between humility and pragmatism, Stephan," she said to the empty car. "Some of us just don't like the attention."

That was something she knew that he would—no, likely *could*—never fully understand or appreciate. Some people lived for the glory; some just lived for the challenge.

*

Wakened, the reinforcing squad of men-at-arms moved forward on its orders to better secure the train. Mira left them to their concerns as she continued her watch, thinking about what they were carrying and their destination.

They had been traveling fifteen hours already and had another ten remaining at their current speed. That would solidly put them in the center of Lanthan Imperial Territory, defended not only by the might of the Imperial forces but also by the sheer inhospitality of the Great Desert.

It will have to do, I suppose.

The shadow of the Great Island was racing past, and she could now see the sky ahead of them. It appeared out of the heat fog, a little over fifty degrees up, and only came to sharp clarity at about eighty degrees. As always the sky was mostly white, with occasional swirls she knew to be distant cloud formations. Some slates of gray and even occasional blobs of blue were defined as well, but the most visible features were the other Great Islands that could be seen as they moved slowly around the distant sun.

"My lady . . ."

"Report," Mira said softly, not turning around.

She heard the man-at-arms salute, his open hand clapping to his chest, palm faced up.

"The prisoner is secure. All systems on board remain at their nominal state. We arrive in nine hours, forty minutes."

"Very good. Dismissed."

The man saluted again, then retreated, leaving Mira to her thoughts as the train burst out of the final shadow of Nanna's Great Island and into the open heat of the desert sun. With full light now, and a double duty of guards posted around the train, Mira stepped back from the post and made her way back through the cars.

The remaining men-at-arms assigned to the train were camped out in the troop cars. She walked through quietly. Many of them had just finished a double shift and were still on emergency call, so they needed what rest they could get. Her objective was three cars back, barricaded by four men-at-arms who barred her way as she approached.

"Stand at rest," Mira ordered, tilting her head and gesturing them out of her way.

They moved.

She walked into the secure car, a long empty expanse with a single cell in the center and a lone man sitting within.

"We can't be there already," he said as she approached, "not unless they've improved the train's speed a bit since my day."

"We have another ten hours," she said, her tone cool. "But I'm sure you knew that."

"Of course. Mira, I believe . . . Delsol?" he asked, raising his head to look at her for the first time.

Mira nodded. "I am."

"I saw you test for Cadre. Impressive. Pity you didn't test a few years earlier. I'd like to have recruited you."

She snorted. "I am no traitor."

"Is that what they call me?" the man asked. "I believe that I really need a better image coordinator."

"I think you missed a few," she countered. "Monster, I believe, is the most popular."

"Well, slaughter a few thousand people and you do get a bit of a reputation," he said, standing up. "I honestly should have killed more. No one really seems to mind if your kill list tops a million for some reason. The difference between a *murderer* and a statesman, don't you know?"

"Statesman? You led a revolt against the lawful government, using chemical warfare as your lead weapon. That's not statesmanship; that's a psychotic break," Mira told him. "What troubles me most is just how many knights you got to go along with your insanity."

"Ah, insanity." He smiled. "The fun thing about insanity is that it is often so very hard to tell it apart from brilliance."

"Outcome would be one way to tell them apart," Mira said.

"So very true," he agreed. "So I suppose we'll find out shortly which it is."

She was about to respond but froze, eyes narrowing as she turned to look at him sharply. "You are in a maximum-security cell on a train bound for the most secure facility in the empire."

"Yes, yes, I am." He smiled at her. "Tell me that you don't really believe that's a coincidence?"

Mira chuckled softly, shaking her head. "Don't try your mind games with me. I just wanted to know how a disgrace like you ever made Cadre in the first place."

"Please, love . . ." He smiled. "You're young yet, still filled with all that lovely idealism."

He walked over to the field separating them. "I suppose you still believe in all that 'corps is mother, faithful forever' nonsense. Took me a long time to shake the mind molding and see the way things really are."

"And just look where that got you," Mira said, shaking her head. "A failed coup."

"It's only failed if I'm not sitting on the throne when it's over, love," he countered, smiling, "and it's so very far from over."

A siren blaring in the distance stopped the conversation. Mira half turned, looking forward, then glanced back at the prisoner, who was now looking far too smug for her comfort. She lifted a link to her ear and touched it on. "Delsol. What is it?"

"My lady, there is an ambush ahead of us. Men flanking the tracks with weaponry we can detect from here. Should I send more men-at-arms to the front?"

"No!" she snapped. "If they have weapons to bring down the shield, we'd lose every man standing. Call back our forces from the engine and have them arm for siege."

"Yes, my lady."

Mira cut the link and looked back at the prisoner.

"As I said, we'll see when the game is over," he said.

"If they bring down the shield, they'll crash this train. That'll put everyone on board at risk," she said as she walked across the compartment and opened an electronics panel, violently ripping out a group of wires. "Some more than others."

"What did you just do?" he asked, his tone suspicious.

"I am not stopping this train," she told him, eyes meeting his. "If they want to stop us, they'll have to do it . . . catastrophically . . . and you will have to endure it *without* inertics to cushion the blow."

"You can't do that . . . ," he said, his tone almost wondering. "That's against all regulations."

She opened the door and stepped out, her voice wafting over her shoulder. "Do what? That was clearly battle damage."

The door slammed shut behind her, leaving the prisoner alone in the dark once more.

*

The siren was wailing as Mira strode through the train, heading for the front of the long line of speeding cars. She reached up with her right hand to tap the trinity emblem on her left shoulder, not breaking stride as she activated the device with a thought and motion.

A shimmering iridescent field flowed around her body as she moved, expanding until her entire form was covered in glowing energy, and solidified into a gleaming white shell. In full armor now, Mira paused between cars, climbing up and knocking open the access hatch before pulling herself up.

"Delsol," she said, speaking over the comm line in a calm voice. "Report."

"Enemy ambush is three minutes ahead, my lady."

"Clear the front car," Mira said softly as she planted her feet on the roof of the train. "Everyone brace for impact. If they can take out the shield, this is going to be a rough ride."

Mira didn't bother acknowledging Stephan's reply. She was too busy focusing on running forward along the moving train cars. The magnetic levitation of the vehicle was quite smooth, but enough vibrations passed back from the forward energy shield to keep her plenty busy when combined with the buffets of wind sweeping around. Through the display floating in front of her face, she could already see what her men had reported.

The ambush looked professional, two lines set up with an elevated cross fire clearly intended to catch the train as it passed. She didn't know if the enemy had enough firepower to do the job but had to assume that if they were this far out in the desert, they had probably come prepared.

"Stephan, have you broken out the heavy weapons yet?"

Stephan's voice came back almost instantly. "We have, my lady. What are your orders?"

"Stand by to engage from the second car," she ordered. "They might get the first shot. But let's be sure to get the last."

"As you say, my lady."

Confident that Stephan and her men had things well in order, Mira hopped the space between the second and first car. Now she was almost directly behind the forward energy shields, sheltered from the rushing wind and all but the heaviest weapons. Unfortunately, she was quite certain that whatever weapons the enemy had, they would not prove to be lightweight.

Mira settled to one knee, eyes examining the track ahead as they roared on into the ambush.

This could be a problem.

Even though it was outfitted with holding cells, the train was not made for heavy fighting. For better or worse, it was designed to be a sleek high-speed transport, and what little shielding it had was intended primarily to protect the vehicle and its occupants from the sonic shock wave it produced. While some defense would be provided by the systems, they wouldn't hold up for very long against a concerted assault.

"Where are you, my lady?"

"I'm on the roof."

"What?" Stephan's voice was incredulous. "That's insane! You're outside the protection of the train!"

"That was implied when I said I was *on* the roof," she answered with a wry smile. "Hold position—I'm tracking the enemy position now. We're seconds from contact."

"Understood."

Mira smiled a little wider, noting the distinct lack of honorifics in the sullen words. Apparently she'd finally found a way to get him to stop kowtowing to her.

Should have done something recklessly foolish hours ago.

Her information overlay glared warningly as weapon signatures began to show, and Mira set her jaw. It was showing distinct signatures for weapons designed to counter combat armor.

"They're better equipped than I expected," Mira growled low in her throat. "Delsol here. Targets have combat armor rated weapons. Engaging now," she said over the comm line.

"Delsol? Mira!" Stephan yelled back. "Don't be a fool! We'll stop the train! They likely want the prisoner alive. We can use him as leverage!"

"No," she said tightly. "That murderer is not leverage, and we're *not* stopping this train. Delsol out."

She mentally nudged her projective combat armor and drew her Armati Elan from her thigh holster.

It was time to show the rabble just why she'd been made Cadre.

*

Projective combat armor was composed primarily of photons entangled into a crystalline lattice, resulting in a "solid light" projection. The system provided for excellent ablative armor, since the projector automatically replaced any sections that were dislodged from the lattice, doing so at the speed of light while also allowing for some other tactical advantages.

The shimmering iridescent wings that erupted from Mira's back were just one of many such tactical surprises, and she only paused for a moment to anchor herself to the train before leaping up into the air and letting the airstream snap her up and away as she activated her Armati.

The stubby handgrip came to life as she lofted over the train, flying on borrowed power and wings of light, both ends of her Armati extending out on either side of her fist as she haloed the first target in her mind and saw her armor information overlay mirror her thoughts almost instantly.

A line of light pulsed into existence as her fingers caressed the formerly invisible line between the two arched ends of the weapon, and she drew it back with a practiced motion until a bolt of force appeared under her touch. The issued weapon of the Cadre wasn't, perhaps, the most efficiently designed, but by the time you reached a skill level high enough to be Cadre, almost any weapon would slow you down. The Armati was probably the most versatile weapon she'd ever trained on, quirks and all.

She loosed the photon trigger that cast the force bolt away, already haloing a new target.

Not anything as simple as a laser or focused light, the bolt was composed of linked photons similar to her armor. When they slammed into the ambush emplacement with the speed of light behind them, the lattice holding the densely packed bolt together exploded in all directions with intense radiated and kinetic power. Dirt, steel, and flesh were thrown in all directions as Mira again brought her paired fingers to the catch line and drew a new bolt from thin air.

What the weapon perhaps lacked in ergonomic efficiency, it made up for in combat capability.

Sometimes traditional and elegant didn't mean old-fashioned.

*

He supposed that the first sign that things had taken a turn was when the light appeared above the oncoming train, suddenly rising up into the sky. The train was still a long way off, however, so he wrote it off as a flare and put it out of his mind. There was no one within response range, just the train itself and his team. They were halfway between the closest population and the facility, days' travel for anything short of a hypersonic transport.

The explosion tearing into his ranks, however, made it clear that whatever he was looking at wasn't a flare.

"Take cover, damn it!" he ordered. "Take cover!"

He didn't know what was firing on them, but it was clear that they'd been spotted. The train was still a few seconds out of their range, but now it was clearly a race to see whether they'd last long enough to snap the trap shut or be finished by the trap snapping shut on them.

"Sir! It's a Cadreman!"

"What?" he snapped, turning to the speaker. "Are you sure?"

"Yes, commander, seen them in action before," the soldier said, nodding to the light above the train. "Not too many see that armor from this side of the fight and live to tell about it."

He swore, still pushing men to cover.

A Cadreman.

There was only supposed to be one on that blasted train, and he was on *their* side.

The Cadre were ghosts, monsters that haunted the dreams of the enemies of the empire, and they were vanishingly rare. To have two in one place was almost unheard of. Given that the prisoner they were here to extract was a Cadreman himself, it hadn't been expected that another would be assigned as a mere guard, of all things.

Any other traitor to the empire would be guarded by anyone other than his former comrades-in-arms.

The fact that there was a Cadreman on the train spoke sheer volumes of the emperor's confidence in their loyalty and was, of course, a clear political statement of the same.

"The train is almost in range!"

"Hold steady, then! Ready yourselves to fire!" he ordered.

Cadreman or no, they were still just dealing with a human being. There were limits to human beings, and not even the Cadre could shatter *all* of those.

The hypersonic shock wave of the oncoming train blew through the markers they'd established days earlier to show range, definitively putting the train into the kill box.

"Open fire!"

*

Mira swore as the antiarmor bolts slammed into the forward shield of the train. The shield held briefly, but it wasn't intended to hold against military power, let alone real armor killers. The plasma spikes tore through the forward shield with lethal effectiveness and went right on to punch through the powerful engine that ran the whole system.

They were clearly using precision weapons in an attempt to take out the locomotive with as little damage as possible. Mira was glad she'd ordered her men back a few cars, however, because she was well aware that tactic was doomed to fail.

A miracle shot, one that took out the primary coolant system, for example, *might* result in a controlled decrease of speed, but the odds of such a strike were infinitesimally low, and they'd have to do it without taking down the shield entirely.

Not going to happen, Mira thought.

She could see the shield flicker and start to overload as she pulled back her draw and loosed another photon bolt into the attackers. The train was only seconds from the ambush when the shield failed catastrophically, the hypersonic shock wave rebounding back off the desert floor and throwing the train clean off its quantum-locked rail.

Mira cut her line and flew free as the train wrecked beneath her, trusting the inertics to save the lives of the people on board.

Well, most of them.

Her mission now was to preserve her men and the crew of the train and ensure that the ambush earned the attackers *nothing* for their efforts.

The wings of light that had erupted from the back of her armor now tightened in close as she leaned into a dive, preparing for what was to come. No longer shielded by the train as she blew through the sonic and hypersonic barriers, the shock wave nearly threw her ass for ankles to the figurative and literal winds, but she held.

She could feel time slowing down, her perceptions amping up as the thud of her heart roared in her ears. Adrenaline and a host of other wonderful crisis chemicals flooded her brain, but not in the uncontrolled manner that civilians or even knights endured. For her and the rest of the Cadre, everything was about self-control.

She moderated the influx of chemicals, bringing herself to the edge of her abilities without sacrificing the calm steadiness that allowed her to act with firm forethought.

Wings aside, actual flight was out of the question, even with all the miracles built into her armor. The sort of manipulation it would take to make the hardened photon field move to provide lift and propulsion would require computing cycles and power beyond what could be packed into the armor discs.

Gliding, however . . . that was well within its capabilities.

She dove hard over the train wreck while it was still in motion, angling ahead of the engine and the cars rapidly piling up behind it. The inertics on board would keep her men alive, but they were going to be badly shaken . . . literally . . . and would need time to gather themselves.

As she cleared the engine, she saw the bulk of the enemy forces break cover, already running toward the wreck.

Let's buy some time.

Mira reconfigured her armor midflight, wings snapping back to full extension and flattening out. The wind drag snapped her feet downward, and she started bleeding speed as fast as she could. Preparing for a hard landing, the armor automatically extended from below her and prepared to absorb as much impact as it could.

Mira wasn't interested in her own safety at the moment, however, and had no intention of softening her landing. She curled her legs up tight, balling up as her wings continued to slow the descent from suicidal to merely insane and nudging her trajectory with minute changes. The Cadre warrior slammed right down in the middle of the lead contingent.

Mira snapped her legs out straight and nearly tore the head from the unfortunate man she struck and then continued on to hit the ground and crumple to one knee as her projected armor did everything it could to both keep her alive and in fighting trim. Pain tore through her frame, but she ignored it. Pain was merely information to her, and right now it didn't have a priority feed to her brain.

There was a shocked moment while everyone nearby just stared at her, not quite believing what had just happened. Mira took that time to straighten up to her full height and flick her wrist to change her bowed weapon.

The Armati Elan snapped out straight, the bow vanishing in an instant, leaving her with a six-foot staff in hand. She flipped it up, snapping it under the chin of the closest man, sending him tumbling to the ground with a loud crack. The weapon flipped casually over her shoulder, rolling behind her back and up into the crook of her other arm as Mira looked around, her expression hidden by the ethereal helm covering her face.

Her voice, however, was crisp and clear as she spoke. “You’re going to pay for wrecking my train.”

*

Stephan groaned as he picked himself up off the deck of a train car. He gently shook his head in an attempt to clear it but regretted the action as a spike of pain tore through his skull. He took a couple deep breaths and quickly walked through the centering exercises he’d learned in order to become a knight. The pain faded, not vanishing but becoming less important as he got to his feet and took stock of the situation.

The car he was in was apparently half buried in the desert, clearly on its side, if he were to judge from the sand and dirt that had scoured the armored glass. The men-at-arms were groaning to their feet and he walked among them, pulling them up and getting them clearheaded and ready to move.

“Come on, to your feet, men!” he ordered. “We’ve got enemy forces incoming!”

He grabbed a comm helm from where it had been bounced around the interior of the car and pulled it on roughly, ignoring the pinching pain as it hooked his ear on the way down. The system came online automatically, searching and finding friendly signals from around him, interpreting what it saw.

There wasn’t much to interpret, as the men-at-arms were all inside the cars. Some had systems online but most didn’t, and he paid little attention to the lot of them as a series of harsh red points lit up his display, surrounding the green signal representing Cadre Commander Delsol.

He swore, seeing that she was surrounded, and started to work faster, slapping the men around him on the shoulder as he called them up and got them moving.

"Get your patterns in gear, you sorry lot. We've a woman in the heat out there!" he snarled, grabbing a pulse carbine from the rack it was still hanging in.

"Sir," a man said, "calm down."

Stephan growled, turning toward the voice. He noted idly that the door to the next car back was open and figures were pulling themselves through.

"She may be Cadre, but she needs backup. Get moving," he ordered calmly.

A pained voice caught his attention from the open door, and he turned to see an injured figure being helped into the car.

"You don't need to worry about that, knight," the man said. "That one is going to get everything that's coming to her."

Something in his voice caused Stephan to pause and look closer, his eyes widening as he finally recognized the figure. His carbine was still coming up when the men-at-arms opened fire on him.

*

Mira ducked, twisting clear of the line of fire as the pulse carbines roared around her.

They were using Imperial technology, restricted weapons, she noted in the back of her mind as she continued to move. Snapping up into a jump that brought her over the closest figure, she hooked the crook of her leg around his neck and twisted hard as she yanked him down. The audible crack was satisfying, but she didn't have time to pat herself on the back.

The carbines roared loudly. The chemical cartridges in their breach were consumed in a fiery blaze of self-annihilation. Coherent, bomb-pumped gamma bursts emerged, capable of blowing through her hard light armor as if it were nothing but air and faery dust.

Water was one of the few things capable of stopping the bursts, and since she was surrounded by many ambulatory bags of the stuff, she grabbed the nearest attacker and held him as a human shield while his comrades pelted him with enough radiation to kill a man a hundred times over. She wasn't entirely spared. Gamma particles were extremely high energy and a single human body wasn't going to entirely stop them, but these were coherent bursts intended for field combat. They were designed to kill one target, not keep on going until they'd irradiated a dozen.

The man's armor and his body's water were enough to slow the particles down, break up their coherence, and leave enough energy behind that her own armor could deal with what was left. Still, she needed to keep moving, and as useful as the human shield was, it wasn't mobile.

Mira planted a foot in the small of his back and kicked off hard, sending the nearly dead man flying into his comrades. Blood was pumping from a dozen festering black boils, his heart still pumping, his brain still registering the horror of the situation, his death completely assured all the same. She didn't watch him strike; she was already in motion the instant she'd kicked out.

She swept the next closest man with her Armati, the length of the staff taking his ankles out with brutal ease, and then dove aside as another round of fire tore into the sand behind her. She hit the sand in a roll, collapsing her Armati back to two feet in length and shifting her grip as she surged back to her feet.

Her draw was lightning quick, and the slim weapon in her hand parted smoothly to expose twin curved blades that swept across another foe's armor, slicing through it like paper. Hot blood spattered the desert sand as she pivoted and swung around with the intent of making another charge.

Mira's motion was checked by a familiar voice from behind her. "Hold!"

She swung around, eyes widening behind her helm as she recognized the speaker.

General Corian looked somewhat worse for wear, standing on one leg and leaning on an armored man-at-arms, as his other leg was clearly missing. His face was a mess, one eye completely obscured by dried blood. Perhaps most obvious of all, however, was the fact that he did *not* look happy with her.

"Cadrewoman Delsol," he snarled, "you and I have a discussion to finish."

Mira snorted, already calculating what she'd have to do to close the distance, eyes flicking to the men-at-arms standing behind him.

The treason runs deeper than anyone suspected, she thought.

"I think we covered the highlights, *general*," she said sarcastically. "Don't you?"

He sneered, mostly on the left side of his face, as the right didn't seem capable of much movement. "Indeed. I'll have your weapon now."

"My Elan dies with me," she said firmly, shaking her head. She would part her own flesh and bleed out on the desert floor before she handed her Elan over to a traitor. Her blood tie to the weapon would ensure that it ended with her. Few others would go so far, she knew, but her Armati was the very soul of her being.

Despite his injuries, Corian laughed.

"A traditionalist to the end?" he asked rhetorically. "So be it. Men-at-arms!"

The entire squad snapped to attention as their armaments came up and locked onto her. Mira tracked all the weapons around her for a moment, calculating how many she could evade, block, and endure. The numbers didn't come up in her favor.

She lowered the blades of her Armati, letting the tips gently trace tracks in the sand below her.

"Watch for cross fire," Corian ordered.

Mira looked up and took a deep breath.

"Fire!"

The order was only halfway out of his mouth when Mira dropped her weapons, letting the points dig into the ground. The swords quivered in place as she threw her arms out to either side and overcharged her armor. The white flash exploded out even as men's fingers started to close on the firing studs of their carbines, and for a moment the world turned white and echoed with the explosive sounds of bomb-pumped gamma bursts blasting across the desert.

Corian was yelling over the noise, even as he tried to clear his one good eye so he could see again.

"Check fire! Check fire! You'll shoot each other, you fools!"

A few moments later silence finally reigned as men blinked the spots from their eyes and looked around them.

Where the defiant woman had stood, there was now nothing but desert sand. They scanned in all directions, but no trace of her was left.

General Corian swore under his breath but pushed off the fury he was feeling.

"Leave her be. We're several weeks' march to the closest civilization, and there's neither food nor water for at least two of those in any direction." He couldn't afford revenge; he had an empire to claim.

That and, more importantly for the moment, medical attention to seek.

I can't believe that bitch turned off the inertics, he thought angrily, though just a little admiringly.

It was practically something he would have done.

They cleaned the train of anything useful and were on their way in the waiting transports within fifteen minutes. Behind them the wreck of the transport engine and its cars were left, still cooling as the shadow of one of Nanna's Great Islands passed over.

In the darkness of the shadow of night, a spot on the desert floor shifted as the sand bulged upward and then fell away.

Mira sat up from where she'd concealed herself and determinedly got to her feet.

Battle rage was a wonderful thing, but when it was over even a Cadrewoman felt everything she'd been able to ignore while in its embrace. Mira limped slowly to the train, taking stock of what had been left behind, which wasn't a whole lot. The weapons from the armory were gone, of course, but so was all the water and food.

The only thing of value left by the traitors was apparent to her when she broke into the third troop car.

The body of Stephan was lying crumpled where he'd fallen, with over a dozen festering black holes burned through him.

CHAPTER 1

The Imperial capital was a metropolis of thirty million people on an island barely large enough to tax an average citizen's fitness if they were to cross it in a day. Once upon a time it had made sense. The wilds that were now civilization had been so untamed that even the hardest of men and women would consider carefully before venturing out. In the modern era of the empire, however, from wall to wall of the explored world, such things were no longer serious threats.

At the center of the island, the black palace of the Imperial family towered above even the tallest buildings around it. Royal legend had it that the castle predated the empire, even predating humans in the area.

The palace was built of metal plates, blacker than the darkest hues, and said to be impenetrable to assault from the outside—which was clearly legend, since no such attack had ever been attempted within living, or recorded, memory. Cut from shadow, the palace was a symbol of the empire's might, absorbing heat and light from the sun to provide power for the city's inhabitants. Despite the edifice's height, there were no spires or towers, just a sharp, angular construction that seemed out of place in comparison to the smooth skyscrapers surrounding it.

But even with its reputation of being impervious, the palace was no stranger to blood, violence, and intrigue.

*

William Everett marched stiffly down the corridors of the palace, not glancing either right or left as he reached the end of the long hall and paused before pivoting on his left heel and rapping three times on the door.

"Enter, Will."

The door swung open of its own accord, allowing William access. He stepped over the threshold and glowered at the young man standing at the far window looking out. Dressed in casual Imperial colors, the crown prince was a tall young man with sandy blond hair and the angular features of his father. Too young yet for much facial hair, he contented himself with a rough shoulder-length haircut that William suspected one of the palace maids had told him looked "manly."

"Sire . . . ," William started, sighing audibly.

"Yes, yes," Kayle Scourwind said. "I'm standing in the window, and there might be an assassination threat. Relax, Will. The armor is active, and there have been no threats reported for fifteen days."

"A good assassin—"

"Is patient, yes." Kayle turned, looking William over with a very slight smile that appraised the older man. "I often wonder, you know, how it is that you learned so much about 'good' assassins."

"Ask me when you're king and emperor, sire," William countered mildly, "and I may just tell you."

"May?" Kayle asked, amused but almost pouting. "Only that?"

"When the time comes"—William shrugged—"ask and see."

"Of course." Kayle sighed. "As always. I have classes shortly. What is it, then?"

"Classes will wait," William said. "Your father wishes to speak with you."

Kayle grimaced slightly but nodded without complaint.

One did not refuse a request from Emperor Scourwind, not even if you were his son.

*

William walked dutifully behind the crown prince as they negotiated the dark metal corridors of the palace. Over the generations the Imperial family had brought in touches to soften the hard feeling of the place, but you couldn't quite get away from the cold steel that surrounded you.

Historically it was difficult to keep people in the palace, in truth. The Imperial family was known to be of sturdy stock, but even they were occasionally driven from the structure by mysterious happenings. Lights where none should be. Voices and music from the ether. On occasion, things would shift and move as though someone were there when no one possibly could be. The halls felt a little too squat for comfort, the doors a little too wide. None of the proportions were exactly what people felt they should be, even after lifetimes and generations had passed.

For all that, however, the palace was the symbol of the empire and never remained unoccupied for long.

It had been decades since the last vacancy. The current emperor refused to be pushed from his seat of power, and perhaps as a sign of his strength of character, the palace seemed to concur, becoming kinder and gentler in its moods and offerings. However, even without major incidents to terrify the occupants, it occasionally proved difficult to retain staff.

William had never encountered anything he couldn't explain, but he knew the feeling of something being off as you moved through the metal halls.

Kayle had grown up in the palace, and like a true Scourwind he didn't seem to notice the discomfort his home caused others. William suspected that he, like most of the Imperial family, actually enjoyed the notoriety the structure evoked.

"Did you look in on my sister before coming to fetch me, Will?" Kayle asked, barely tilting his head to see the Cadreman walking a half step behind him.

"Yes, my lord," William answered immediately, his thoughts about the palace vanishing in an instant. "She is in science class at the moment."

"We'll check in on her, then," Kayle said. "It's on the way."

William merely nodded, knowing that his opinion wasn't being sought on the matter. Nor would he care to offer it.

*

Lydia Scourwind was staring at the display at the front of the class, her eyes slightly unfocused as her mind wandered from the lesson. She *knew* all this—really, she did. Why did they have to keep making her review it?

"My lady . . ." The attendant sighed. "Please describe the nature of the observed universe."

Lydia sighed as well, but her eyes refocused on the attendant as she began speaking. "The observed universe exists as a sphere that is measured in the length of time light takes to cross from one side to the other," she said simply. "Due to some variation in the speed of light, and the difficulty of getting a direct reading through the celestial flame, the precise measurement is under some debate, but most people accept that the universe, as we know it, is between two and three hours across at the speed of light. Of course, that speed is impossible to reach, and no expeditions have returned from more than three days' travel beyond the world walls, largely due to lack of fuel, it's speculated."

"Very good." The attendant nodded. "However, why did you say the 'universe as we know it'?"

Lydia sighed again. "Advanced research speculates that there is more to it than that, and the math behind our understanding of physical laws seems to agree."

"Excellent, though somewhat advanced for this class." The woman smiled. "Now, if you could please try to pay attention from now on?"

"My apologies," Lydia replied, not looking particularly apologetic.

The attendant took what she could get. Teaching members of the Imperial family could be a frustrating exercise, despite the fact that she had dispensation from the emperor to discipline them.

Lydia was, quite possibly, the worst of the lot.

The girl was frighteningly intelligent—there was no question of that—but she was a terrible brat who knew just how smart she was. It made for a bad combination with the privileged life she lived, but there was little to do about it than continue on.

A noise at the door caught the attendant's attention, and she saw the uniform of the Imperial guard standing there as a familiar figure in royal colors stepped in.

"I do hope I'm not interrupting anything important?" Kayle asked with an easy smile and a tone that made his question sound far more like a statement than a question.

"No, sire, please . . ." The attendant gestured with a smile as the emperor's senior Cadreman just smiled wanly in her direction.

"Brother!" Lydia squealed, leaping at Kayle.

Like her brother, Lydia had inherited the sharp features of their father, but her body was clearly inherited from her mother. Lithe, with only a hint of the curves that she was sure to grow into in a few short years, the young girl had long raven hair that contrasted her brother's sandy blond as the two embraced.

"I didn't know you'd gotten back. When did you get in?" she asked as he set her down.

"Late last night," Kayle explained. "Just a training mission, Lyd, nothing to be concerned about."

"You're never around anymore." She pouted, a look that rarely failed to get her whatever she wanted, even from those who were familiar with her tactics.

Kayle, however, just laughed at her.

"A few more years, Lyd, and you'll be doing the same. The flag must be flown."

She sighed, shaking her head. "Yes, yes, I know."

He smiled at her. "You'll understand. I just wanted to check in and say hi while I was here. Father called me in. I'll try and meet with you later."

The teen pouted at her older brother, only to look immensely frustrated when he just laughed at her again.

That just made Kayle laugh even harder, much to her growing ire, as he backed out of the room and waved to both his sister and the attendant.

"Pay attention in classes, Lyd. They're important," he told her as he closed the door behind him.

Lydia glared at the door, wanting to shout out a comeback but knowing full well that he wouldn't hear her.

He always gets the last word.

*

The Imperial throne was located in the largest hall of the palace, a place that always felt dark and foreboding no matter how many lights were on or how it was decorated. The dark metal that made up the entire construction of the palace felt more deeply black and otherworldly here than anywhere else.

Kayle personally felt that it was mostly psychological, but the size of the space also played a part. The sheer scope of the hall alone would have absorbed a majority of the area's light, but the dark walls gave the empire one of its most enduring nicknames: the Throne of Shadows.

His father was sitting on the throne as Kayle walked down the length of the hall, the sound of his footsteps echoing steadily as he approached. He came to a stop twenty yards from the throne and inclined his head as the guards examined him for weapons. Only when he was cleared and the emperor had waved him forward did he approach.

"Father," Kayle said as he came to a stop at the base of the metal throne, "you summoned me."

"I did."

Edvard Scourwind was neither an old man nor a particularly impressive one to look at. His thick beard was well maintained and his voice rumbled slightly as he spoke, but sitting on the large throne, he looked almost younger than his son.

"We lost contact with a supply train a week ago," he said. "It was going to the Redoubt."

Kayle stiffened, his mind racing.

Few things went to the Redoubt.

The facility was the single most secure station in the empire, with the sole possible exception being the palace itself. Most likely the palace was number two, given that it was situated on an island with thirty million people surrounding it. The Redoubt was literally in the middle of nothing but sand—which made it ideal for storing some of the most dangerous items in the empire . . . and, very occasionally, the most dangerous people.

"The general, Father?"

Edvard sighed, then nodded. "We sent him there, in hopes of removing him from his supporters. Quite likely, we should have had him executed."

Kayle grimaced, thinking about the chaos it would have caused. "The riots alone, Father . . ."

"I know. That's why he was spared, at least until memories have faded. Corian also knew things we'd have preferred not to lose. Now, however, we may have lost more than that."

Kayle nodded. "I can take a team to investigate the situation."

"I dispatched a high-speed skimmer three days ago. They found the wreckage of the train about halfway out. Clearing the track alone will take weeks." Edvard sighed. "We couldn't locate any survivors, but Corian's corpse was nowhere to be found either."

"Damn him to the fires above."

If Edvard took offense at his son's swearing, he didn't show it. Instead he merely nodded and went on.

"There was a full crew on the engine, a half century of men-at-arms, and two . . . knights."

Something about how his father slowed at that moment caught Kayle's attention, and he looked up sharply.

"Two knights, Father?"

"One knight," Edvard corrected, "and one Cadre."

Kayle blinked, shocked. The Imperial Cadre were currently under a rather dark cloud politically, given that Corian was one of their number. For his father to assign a Cadre to the train was a bold statement, no doubt, but now that this had happened, it was certainly going to turn on the emperor. It would turn on them all.

"Bodies?"

"The knight was buried, his weapon at his side. No signs of the men-at-arms, nor the Cadre. We found evidence of combat, military pulse carbines, blood, and clear signs of fire from an Armati."

"So he fought. We just don't know on what side?"

Edvard nodded, though with a correction. "She. Mira Delsol, newly promoted to Cadre. She came up after Corian, should have been outside his influence."

Kayle nodded unhappily, remembering the woman in question. The problem was that Corian's influence could best be described as a sea beast, his tentacles stretching well beyond the matters he had any business with.

"What do you want of me, Father?"

"Go to the Cadre. See if you can learn where they stand and what their feelings are on this," Edvard said. "This will blacken their reputation."

"It will be done." Kayle saluted, fist coming up to shoulder level as his father nodded and waved him away. Kayle turned on his heel and strode back out.

William met him at the door to the hall.

"Were you briefed?" Kayle asked as he passed, not breaking stride as William stepped into pace behind him.

"Yes, my lord."

"We have work to do," the crown prince said. "The Senate will not like this."

William had nothing to say to that. It was a clear and blatant truth after all.

The Imperial Senate was made up of representative members from the eighty different precincts of the empire. Before unification, most were their own kingdoms or feudal baronies, but they now submitted to the empire. It didn't mean that they were entirely without power, of course. Even with the Imperial Army answering to the Scourwind legacy, the precinct forces were strong enough to be reckoned as significant, and they all held economic and political sway as well.

One thing they all feared, however, was the Imperial Cadre.

This was going to give them a chance to blacken the name of the Cadre with the public, and Kayle was well aware that while he had no need to fear any other noble in the entire kingdom . . . the common men and women, they were a potential force that nothing the empire had could stop.

*

The Imperial Cadre were officially stationed at the Redoubt, though it was mostly a political fiction designed to keep the various lords, barons, and nobles from screaming about the empire's "trained killers" sitting right in the middle of the capital.

In actuality, there was an entire wing of the castle for Cadre bunks, stores, and training.

It was there, in that familiar wing, where Kayle found himself just a few minutes after meeting with his father. The men on guard at the doors saluted as he walked past, his focus such that he barely gave either of them any notice.

Behind him, the two Cadre members exchanged silent glances, and as one they cleared the clips on their holsters. It was a subtle motion, but between two blooded warriors it was unmistakable. They'd just reduced their draw time by about a third of a second. A knife's edge's advantage, perhaps, but many warriors had lived and died by thinner edges.

If Kayle Scourwind was stalking through the palace with that much focus, something was up.

Once inside the Cadre wing of the palace, Kayle cut a straight line through to the administration offices, walking past the commandant's personal assistant as though he weren't there. The man was halfway to his feet when William put him back down with a hand on his shoulder.

Unlike most other sections of the empire, only Cadremen worked inside Cadre-controlled sections, and a face-off between Kayle and an annoyed administrator looking to burn off some energy after being stuck doing deskwork for a few weeks was something William felt was best avoided. They had enough trouble without having to renovate the Cadre's administration offices.

General Paul Beuforte barely bothered to glance up at Kayle's entrance, opting instead to continue working while he gestured to the empty chair across from him.

Kayle just smirked slightly and took the seat. "I take it you've heard."

"We lost one of our own," the general said. "I've heard."

"Did we lose her or did she turn?" Kayle asked, his voice dead neutral.

That got him the full and undivided attention of General Beuforte, who leveled an even gaze at him that stopped just short of being a full glare.

"Mira Delsol is no traitor."

Kayle just spread his hands, shrugging slightly. "No sign of her was found, other than evidence of her Armati being fired. That will put suspicion on her, no matter how you cut it."

"Someone buried the knight with field honors," Beuforte countered.

"Guilt?"

"Why no sign of the armsmen, then? No bodies, nothing," the general growled. "Think for a moment."

"I," Kayle said calmly, "am not the one you need to convince. Corian was a high-ranking Cadre officer. His shadow has already tainted the reputation of the entire Cadre. This may be enough to kill it."

Beuforte grunted but had no response.

"Fine. What are you saying?"

Kayle looked across at him evenly. "I'm saying that the Cadre needs to ready itself to weather a storm, the sort of storm you don't fight with weapons or martial skill."

"Pity. We're not much good at that sort."

Kayle smiled slightly. "Some of us are better than others, general."

"Now you offer some respect, you little pup." Beuforte laughed. "Takes something like this for you to visit?"

"I've been on mission until recently," Kayle said with a sigh. "I had been hoping for some time to relax with family."

The general nodded. A young Cadre officer, particularly one of the Imperial line, didn't get much time to rest. "Anything interesting?"

"Nothing I can share over drinks." Kayle smiled.

"Very interesting, then."

The crown prince shrugged. "It depends. Some of it could be, but for now it's just . . . well, you know the game."

Beuforte nodded. "I do at that. So what does the emperor command concerning this situation?"

"Call in the Cadre teams. Anything less than red-level priority is suspended," Kayle said. "Stand down *everything*. Go dark."

"That bad?" The general sighed.

"Yeah," Kayle said. "It's that bad."

"All right. It's done. Anything else?"

"One thing," Kayle said, standing up. "I need a team sent to the Redoubt."

"Red level, I presume?"

"White."

The general nodded slowly. "I'll see a reactor transport off the grid within the hour."

"Thank you, general," Kayle said, standing up. "With your leave?"

"As though you need it." The general snorted. "Go on, pup. We'll speak later."

"As you say."

Kayle smiled, saluting before he turned to leave. He wasn't required to, strictly speaking, but he'd learned through hard knocks that it paid to be respectful to people capable of taking your head off with a thought. The fact that they weren't technically permitted to do so really didn't matter as much as most people seemed to think.

Outside, William was waiting for him.

"What now, sire?"

Kayle sighed. "Take me to my brother."

CHAPTER 2

Reaction craft were the fastest transports in the empire, capable of acceleration and top speeds that were unequaled by almost every other method of transport available. They were also obscenely expensive, however, since they relied on consumables to provide thrust. Since those fuels were extremely costly in both time and money to synthesize, only the military generally had access to them.

The Cadre jump ship punched out of the capital under the shade of night and topped out at a hundred and twenty miles over the surface, moving just over fifteen thousand miles per hour. The curve of the land climbed up in all directions around the craft, soon blending into a distant haze.

The haze itself continued up for a ways, then cleared to expose the mottled pattern of the sky's blues, greens, browns, and other colors. Still, the Cadre pilots had other things on their minds than the view as they increased the speed and hammered their passengers around roughly in the hold.

The Redoubt came into sight within two hours, and they fired reverse thrust to kill their speed, dropping back into the firm grip of gravity.

"Redoubt Control, this is Cadre Flight Aleph on approach. Clearance is requested."

After several long moments with no response, the pilot glanced over his shoulder. "No contact from the Redoubt, sir."

"All right. Land us hot."

"At your command."

Interface projections in front of the pilot altered as the ship began its descent, atmospheric friction blinding the visual display in spectacular fashion as armored sections closed over all sensitive systems. For a little over three minutes they were flying entirely on internal dead-reckoning systems as the extreme heat and friction rendered external sensors useless. The heat faded, leaving the armor of the jump ship still glowing dull red as the craft reached the lower atmosphere and decelerated to supersonic speed.

The protective armor retracted, bringing visual and external sensors back just before everything went to the upper reaches.

Alarms wailed, cockpit lights went dark and red, and the pilot instinctively leaned the whole ship hard left and stood on the thrusters.

"What's going on?" the Cadre commander demanded from behind, struggling against the sudden force that slammed him into his harness.

"Respectfully, sir, *not now*!" the pilot screamed, putting the ship into a powered dive that quickly climbed back to hypersonic speeds and caused the sensor shielding to snap shut again as friction once more made its power felt.

In the back of the jump ship, the Cadre team could do little else besides hold on for their lives as the ship began to buck and twist in every possible direction.

Plummeting for the ground, the pilot kept the ship moving in an effort to dodge what he'd glimpsed briefly before he'd been forced to accelerate again.

Mindful of his altitude, he pulled up hard as the jump ship came within a few hundred feet of the desert floor, bleeding speed as quickly as he dared. Once the exterior cooled enough for the armored panels to open up again, the pilot got his visual instrumentation back.

Alarms sounded through the jump ship as he stood on the thrust again, lancing the ship straight up. Targeting scanners from the Redoubt were locked onto them, and bursts of energy were exploding all around.

"Prep for emergency drop!" he yelled over his shoulder. "This is your stop!"

The Cadre commander started to say something as he slammed his hand down on the controls, but it was lost as the wind howled through the interior of the jump ship and the ejection systems did their job. The Cadre team was launched into the air, fired down with enough force to throw them hundreds of feet from the ship before they recovered from the sudden acceleration.

The pilot turned his focus on his attacker now, leveling the ship out and lining up for his last run.

"Faithful forever."

*

The six ejected Cadre squad members got their fall under control, stabilizing in the air and finding one another after the initial shock of being ejected without warning. They brought their projection armor online with a tap, the rushing wind going quiet as they got communications back.

"What the hell was that?"

The unit commander, Seph Meynard, twisted in the air until he could find the jump ship, not answering the question. The others followed suit, mostly ignoring the spinning ground below as it lunged up toward them. The jump ship was in the midst of a star storm of fire, its own weapons roaring in return as the Redoubt's formidable defenses lanced out in an attempt to strike it from the sky.

"Emptiness above," he swore. "Someone's taken the Redoubt."

It was painfully obvious as one of the shots holed through the leading airfoil of the jump ship, rocking it to one side. Then, once they'd bracketed the ship and gotten its range, another flurry of shots from below turned it into a fiery rain of scrap and shrapnel.

"Dive," he ordered. "Get on the ground fast, before they get our range."

The squad tucked their arms and legs in, pitching forward, and dove like their lives depended on it.

Moments later it was clear that their lives likely did depend on it as fire from the Redoubt was re-aimed in their direction. Explosions tore the sky asunder, shaking the squad members to their core even through their armor.

"Go stealth!" Seph ordered, triggering his own system as he did. "Spread out, meet up on the ground!"

The team banked hard away from each other as the photons that made up their armor color shifted randomly out of the visual spectrum. Latticework photons had many properties, but there were limits. They were, in effect, frozen light. That meant that they *constantly* emitted some waveform of light, so they couldn't go completely stealth against high-technology scanners.

What they could do was shift to less used frequencies and lower the power rate of their output. It wasn't perfect. Those frequencies could still be picked up by a skilled operator, and at lower output levels their armor was significantly weaker . . . but it was what they had to work with.

Invisible to the naked eye, and hopefully invisible to the scanning beams from below, they dove for the deck, slowing their descent until the last possible moment. The continued fire from the Redoubt exploded around them, but quickly became less focused as the team broke up and proceeded to evade.

Within a few dozen feet of the ground, the commander activated his armor's wings, turning his plummeting dive into a fast, swooping curve. He was late in slowing his fall, however, and hit the ground moving too fast for a safe landing. With the armor keeping him from breaking bones, the crash landing was operationally survivable . . . that is, he not only lived through the impact but he didn't injure himself beyond his ability to continue the mission.

It still hurt like hell.

After several long moments of trying to get his breath back, the Cadre squad commander finally spoke. "Sing out," he ordered over the comm line. "I'm down and intact."

Slowly all but two members of the team checked in, and he called them in. Once they'd regrouped, the four of them took a moment to try to locate their missing members, but considering the density of the air-defense fire, it seemed likely that they were officially two men down. The survivors' armor had a dull sheen to it, masking their location as best it could, and each had his weapon drawn as they gathered.

"The Redoubt is over those dunes"—the commander nodded—"and I suppose it's safe to say that it's currently held by unfriendly force."

The other three Cadre warriors laughed dryly, though there was little to find humorous in any of it.

"The way I see it, we're pretty much screwed," Cadre Commander Meynard admitted cheerfully. "We're weeks from any source of food or water, as this entire region is a dead zone for a thousand miles, except for the supplies in the Redoubt. Fair bet Corian has control of it now, so unless we get a miracle, I doubt we're cracking that nut with four men."

The others nodded in agreement, but the choice between dying of thirst or going out in a blaze of glory wasn't remotely a difficult one.

"Have a plan, chief?" asked Sergeant of Arms Birk, the largest of them.

"Well, we could try being sneaky and infiltrate," he said, no thought of backing down or surrender entering the conversation, "or just launch a head-on assault. End result will be the same."

"My ego says let's go with the head-on assault, boss, but my head says we'll cause more havoc if we infiltrate."

The commander looked around at his remaining men and nodded. "All right. Split up, pick your ingress points, and I'll see you on the inside. I'll be the one with my hands around Corian's throat."

"Not if we beat you to it, chief."

*

"Scanners in sector three just went dead."

Corian shook his head and rubbed the bridge of his nose as he considered the news from where he was sitting. He was more than a little disgusted. *They could have at least been subtle about it.*

He didn't know who was attempting to sneak into the Redoubt, but if it were any of the Cadre officers he'd trained in the past, he was going to make their death painful and longer than it needed to be. There was no excuse for that sort of incompetence.

"Pull the men back from sector three," he ordered. "Have them converge in sector . . . eight."

"Yes, general."

That should be far enough back, just in case someone is getting a little clever and attempting to lure my men into a reverse ambush.

Unlikely, he thought. Cadre officers tended to be a little less complicated than that in the field, since simple actions were less prone to failure. There were a few who enjoyed toying with lesser foes, however.

"Help me up," he ordered, extending an arm to the closest man-at-arms.

"General, you should be at ease, we'll—"

"Help me up."

One look from him ended the discussion, and one of his men helped him carefully to his feet and put a brace under his arm. His injuries had been bandaged up, the worst of the bleeding stopped long past in the field with rougher methods than he'd have preferred. But even if everything from this point forward went to plan, he would still be down a leg and an eye.

Prosthetics would handle the former, but even the best Imperial technology wouldn't replace an eye torn from the socket as messily as his had been.

*

Commander Meynard shifted the grip on his Armati, eyeing the corridors of the section of the Redoubt he'd been able to infiltrate. As empty as they were, he'd be suspicious of a trap under normal circumstances, but without knowing just how many men Corian had to his credit, it was entirely possible that the Redoubt was nearly deserted.

It would take significant forces just to man the defenses appropriately, so patrols might be few and far between.

We may have just gotten lucky.

He flicked his wrist, the Armati in his hand flowing out slightly as it extended for medium-range engagements. The Cadre Armati were unique devices, no two precisely alike just as no two Cadremen were precisely alike. His was about a 70 percent link, a very high match for the ancient weapon.

To even qualify for Cadre, you had to be able accomplish a 20 percent link to an Armati and your projection systems. No active Cadremen, as far as he knew, operated with less than 40 percent. It was one of the advantages the Cadre held, being the only organized group of humans with that level of interface capability.

There were, of course, others with the capacity throughout the population. Flyers were the most common, as interface capacity was important to their lives, but most were never tested. Even then, however, only the Cadre had the resources and capacity to recruit, train, and outfit men and women to the level they enjoyed as the elite of the empire.

Of course, that was partially due to the empire controlling every single known Armati and most of the projection technology available.

Meynard's own Armati Turo felt warm in his grip as he slowly made his way down the corridor, pausing by a pair of sealed autodoors. He laid his fingers on the door, using a sensitive photon field to pick up vibrations and convert them into sound.

Quiet. Too damn quiet. Corian can't have this few people here, not if he took the Redoubt.

He smirked.

Ambush.

Seph knew Corian's playbook. Ambush was the only thing that made sense. That left him with two options that he cared to consider. He could avoid conflict, fade away, and come back from another route. That would be the best option if he were alone, but he wasn't. Or, he could . . .

Trigger the trap. Get Corian's attention focused on me. Give the others a better chance.

Decision made.

Seph stepped back, twisted around, and then mule kicked the doors right at the locking mechanism. As they exploded outward, he turned and strode calmly into the room beyond.

He made it about twenty feet, right into the center of the kill zone, before Corian made his move. The men with carbines popped up from the elevated catwalks, their weapons aimed down at him, but Seph only had eyes for one person in the room.

"You've seen better days, general," he said amiably, looking up where the familiar man in a dark-blue uniform was standing. "Someone took a liking to your flesh, I see."

Corian smiled crookedly, only half his face seeming to respond. "I underestimated the bitch they assigned to watch me."

"Delsol?" Seph asked, amused, as he counted the heads he could see. "She kick your ass?"

"Crazy bitch turned off the inertics in my car before the crash." Corian laughed. "Just about the only thing I hadn't planned for. Can you believe that?"

Seph didn't know Delsol personally, but that told him a lot about her. "She saw you coming. Impressive."

"Yes, it was," Corian said, almost sadly. "I almost regret leaving her to die in the desert. I'd have still recruited her, even after . . ."

"You never were one to waste talent, I'll give you that much," Seph acknowledged, shifting his grip as he finished his head count.

"No, I never was. You don't need to die here, Meynard," Corian offered. "The emperor is a weak-willed, sadistic piece of filth, and you know it."

"I serve the empire, not the man."

"So do I." Corian leaned forward, bracing his hands on the rails. "It's time for new leadership."

"You, I suppose?"

"We are Cadre. We are the best of the empire," Corian said, his tone rising. "Who else should rule? Who else deserves to rule?"

"I've served in the Cadre for over ten full cycles of the Great Islands," Seph answered, his tone pensive now. "I've seen kingdoms rise and fall, brought more than one into the empire myself. You know what I learned in those ten years?"

Corian looked evenly at him for a long moment before answering. "Enlighten me, O veteran of so *many* years," the sixty-three-year-old general said sarcastically.

"In all my time," Seph said, as though he'd not heard the sarcasm, "do you know how many nations I've seen that came out better for a violent overthrow of the government? In forty years, not a single one. How many in your sixty-three?"

"I'm not like any of those fools!" Corian snarled. "Rank amateurs. We carve through them like they're *nothing*. You know that."

"You're *exactly* like those fools," Seph countered. "Arrogant, self-aggrandizing, egotistical. You think you're better than everyone, just like them. You know what you really are, Corian? Do you?"

"Why don't you tell me?"

"You're a superb warrior and a general whose leadership skill in battle is nearly unmatched," Seph said, tensing, "neither of which make you competent to lead the empire in anything other than a war."

"And *he* is? That imbecile we call emperor is?"

The cool, collected figure was gone. The man above him was spitting as he spoke now, and Seph smiled slightly as he finished marking off his targets. Corian was legendary for his calm under fire, but almost equally so for his lack of patience with the orders of those he considered fools. Pushing his buttons was as easy as implying that those he had so little respect for might just be correct.

It was the opening he was waiting for. Seph fell into the projection link and made his move.

He made it eighteen feet before the first shot was fired reflexively.

Seph's Turo flowed out to full extension as he swept it up, already in motion before the shot was taken. The flat of the blade swept into the path of the gamma charge, slapping it away and splattering it across the room behind Seph as he continued his charge.

More carbines fired, most of the shot tracks cleanly missing as Seph powered his armor to the highest levels and planted a foot on the closest wall and kicked off. In midair he swept two more blasts aside, his armor tracking every single blaster aimed in his direction along with their trajectories. Before each shot he got about a tenth of a second warning as weapons ignited their rounds, just enough to let him intercept the attacks with his own weapon.

Gamma bursts could tear through his armor easily enough, but there wasn't much of anything that could damage an Armati.

Of course, once the ambushers got their act together and started firing together, they'd easily overwhelm his ability to defend against them. That's why he had to close the range as quickly as he could.

Seph hit the catwalk in a slide, turning it into a roll that brought him to his feet right underneath one of the shooters. He reversed his grip on the Armati, running the man through as he knelt low, and then sheltered behind the body.

"Sloppy, Corian," he called out. "I shouldn't have gotten more than ten feet!"

Corian sneered from where he'd taken cover. "This isn't exactly a Cadre deployment, Meynard. You still aren't getting out of this alive."

That's not the plan, Seph thought as he took the weight of the now cooling body across his shoulders. The temporary lull in the fighting was only a brief respite, but for the moment he could feel the uncertainty as the men-at-arms balked at shooting through one of their own. That wouldn't last much longer.

"Fire!" Corian ordered. "He's dead, just fire!"

Seph drew his back up as he powered to his feet, throwing the body up and through the air. He twisted under the airborne corpse, extending his sidearm and firing.

Unlike the carbines, his sidearm was older tech and less lethal. The lasing rounds loaded in the 1796 blaster burned in the high ultraviolet range, not hot enough to perforate Cadre armor projectors but more than enough to turn flesh and blood to expanding plasma.

The closest man-at-arms took the first shot dead center in the torso. The burst of coherent UV superheated the flesh, blood, and bone of his sternum with enough force that the resulting spray of hot plasma lifted him off his feet and threw him back over the rail. Seph stayed low, sprinting under the body he'd thrown, leaving that cover behind.

As he straightened up, he slashed with his Armati, half slicing through the next man as he hit his stride. The men-at-arms weren't more than a distraction to him. Lined up along the catwalk, they couldn't mass their fire and one on one they fell like leaves from a tree.

Seph didn't give a damn about them.

He wanted Corian.

The blaster in his off-hand roared, lasing rounds seeking out their targets almost as fast as his Armati sliced through those in its path. Seph bulled through, sending men flying in both directions . . . over the rails and hard into the wall as he focused on his target. Corian had to die. Taking out the head of the snake would end everything, and the general's arrogance had put him within reach.

Seph was two-thirds of the way to his target before the first gamma burst holed through his armor and into his body. He staggered, straightened, and slashed his Armati into the shooter. Blood splattered the rail as the man fell aside, and then another burst took Seph in the gut. Four of the men-at-arms got their act together as he stumbled back, leveling their weapons and clearing enough space so they could coordinate their fire.

Those still on their feet watched as burst after burst of coherent gamma blasts burned through Seph Meynard. He staggered forward, his sidearm roaring twice more. For the first time, Meynard missed a shot, the laser glancing off the wall and barely scorching the metal. He swiped with the Armati, barely connecting, and threw his weight forward.

He broke through the four men, eyes falling on Corian as he fell forward to his knees. Seph lifted his Armati, willing the shift. The weapon morphed as he tried to focus, with Corian's image changing to two, then three, then back to one.

The general stepped forward and pulled the Armati from Seph's hand with a calm composure that belied his earlier rage.

"Walking dead," Corian said, "and you're still trying to kill your target . . ."

He sidestepped the sidearm and plucked it from Seph's hand as well. "Careful now. Wouldn't want to have that go off accidentally."

Seph didn't answer as he slumped back on his heels.

Corian turned the Armati over in his hand for a moment, shrinking it back to its standard form and casually tapping it against Seph's projected armor.

"Very impressive, commander. I applaud your target focus," he said pleasantly, shaking his head as he turned away. "Too bad you wouldn't work for me. Such a waste."

"Burn in the skies, you traitorous . . ."

Corian whipped back around, the Armati in his hand extending out into a blade that slashed through the projective armor as though it weren't there. Meynard's body hit the ground a moment later as Corian turned the Armati over in his hand, considering the feel of it.

"Not bad," he said. "Not quite as good a match as my own Turo, but not bad."

He looked over at his remaining men. "He didn't come alone. Find the others. Kill them." He paused. "And for the sake of the depths, don't let them get as close to you as he did," the general continued. "I'd rather not lose all my men before the revolution even starts. Idiots."

CHAPTER 3

Mira Delsol paused at the crest of a dune, checking the power rating on her armor projector. Without the armor protecting her from the sun above, she knew she wouldn't last three days in the desert, let alone the weeks it would take to get back to civilization. Unfortunately the charge was already down by 70 percent, and she only had a couple chargers left from scavenging the wreck of the train.

And it didn't really help that she wasn't heading toward civilization.

The Redoubt was a few more hours' march from her position. She was close enough that she'd been treated to an impressive light show when the air-defense systems cut loose an hour or so earlier. Mira wasn't sure what that was all about but could only hope that loyalists were still holding the Redoubt against Corian's forces.

She only wished she were that lucky.

Not having many other options, however, she pushed on through the desert sands. There was a trick to walking on moving sand, a rhythm to the motion you had to follow to avoid wasting energy and time. She wasn't a master, but she could dance to the tune, and Mira was making decent speed as she wound her way through the dunes rather than climbing every one.

It was almost the break of first light past Siden's Great Island when she came into sight of the Redoubt. With the cover of darkness just about to be taken from her, Mira settled down below the peak of a dune and shifted her projected armor to match the sand around her. With the sun perpetually above, there was no shade to seek save for that of the Great Islands, and it would be another twelve hours before Zaius's Great Island floated past.

I should be able to sit out the day on my current charge, Mira believed as she considered her options. *Use one of my chargers as the shadow passes and move on to the Redoubt, then.*

It wasn't much of a plan, she was all too aware, but it was what she had to work with. Her armor and her Armati Elan were the only tools she had to her name. For all that, Mira couldn't have asked for better tools, even if she might have wished for more.

The Armati was one of the most versatile weapons every devised, a weapon of a bygone era that none quite knew how to replicate. Her armor wasn't quite so unique, but mobile projection of latticework photons was restricted to military use by nature of how much it cost to build a projector that small. Well, some civilian applications existed, depending on your definition of mobile, but the Cadre projection emblems cost more than a year's worth of squadron reaction fuel.

If she had to choose only one weapon and one defense, Mira had no doubt she had the best she could have asked for.

She just would have liked a few more options when tasked with assaulting an entrenched fortification like the Redoubt.

Like an army, perhaps?

Of course, while she was wishing for things, she might as well ask for a tactical strike.

The Great Island had moved on, leaving her in the sunlight for nearly a full hour as the heat climbed steadily and quickly. Her armor could quite effectively keep her cool, but its primary mechanism for that was to reflect the light and heat away, and as that would reveal her position, it wasn't an option. The sand itself reflected away a fair degree of the sun's light and energy, but it still absorbed enough heat to leave her sweating away irreplaceable water and salt.

She ignored it as best she could, not moving to brush the sweat from her eyes as it could expose her position. This was unlikely, given that the heat shimmer from the desert itself should mask any shift in her own armor, but with someone like Corian leading the enemy forces, it was best not to take chances.

She hadn't been watching for long when a flash from the Redoubt startled her, the rumbling echo of an explosion reaching her several seconds later.

Someone's kicked off a party.

Mira took a few moments to decide what to do, but there wasn't really much of a decision to make. No matter how she cut it, she could use the chaos of the explosion to mask her own infiltration. She might not get another one, and she really *wanted* just one clean shot at Corian before her life came to an end.

With that firmly in mind, Mira leapt from the shallow pit she'd dug into the side of the dune and broke into a loping sprint.

*

Mira loaded one of her last two chargers into her armor, powering it up to full as she approached the smoking Redoubt.

The structure's angled black metal was similar to that of the palace, though considerably smaller overall. The Redoubt was nearly indestructible, though it was apparent that whatever had happened to it had pushed those limits nearly to the breaking point.

Scorched earth tactics. Corian took what he wanted, torched the rest.

She stepped over a still-smoking piece of shrapnel and paused at the gaping hole where a large pair of doors had once been.

Overpressure wave blew them halfway across the desert from the looks of things.

The Redoubt might be intact, but with a blast wave like that she doubted anything inside it would have survived in one piece. That meant that even if Corian had left anything inside, it wasn't likely she'd be able to use it.

She found the first bodies a short distance inside the Redoubt, curling her lips up as she recognized them as some of the men-at-arms she'd been assigned for the transport operation. They were scorched and blackened, still smoking slightly and giving off a chemical smell from the remnants of the explosive, but it wasn't the explosion that had killed them.

Mira recognized the gaping wounds caused by a blaster and the deep slashes that were distinctive of a Cadre Armati.

She walked through the scene, eyes seeking something she knew would be there—knew in her gut.

The burned projector emblem caught her eye and she paused by another smoking body, but this one hadn't been killed with a blaster or an Armati. She knelt by him and pushed the body over, looking for features she could recognize.

Other than the black holes burned into him by the gamma burster carbines, she couldn't find much of anything she recognized. The explosion had done a good job of masking any obvious evidence of identity, and she didn't have the time or resources to look for the less obvious.

The Redoubt, even in its current state, would shelter her from the sun and provide water. Even if the well were damaged, she was confident she could harvest condensation from the interior of the Redoubt's shell. So she wasn't about to die anytime too soon, though without food she still had a turning clock to worry about.

First thing, Mira thought, *is to see to the bodies.*

There was a pit in the dunes not far from the entrance that would be suitable for the men-at-arms, but she had at least one body here that deserved a bit more.

Nothing to do but get to it, Mira supposed. This would be the second good man she put in a hole since the operation had begun.

*

The shadow time was half past before she was done. Nearly a half century of men-at-arms were piled four deep in the pit, and three individual markers rested on holes she'd dug by hand. It had taken her hours to clear the Redoubt as best she could but only minutes to be certain that she'd arrived too late to do anything. That left her with the duty of burying the dead, instead of saving the living.

She knew one of the Cadremen she'd found. He'd been in her graduating class at the academy, and they'd both been offered a shot at Cadre just out of school. Only the top ten got that offer, and Cadre had only accepted two of those that time around. She hadn't known him well, but he'd been the more sociable of the two, although that wasn't saying a lot.

You didn't get through academy by being a party type.

For all that, however, he'd been a comrade, and his body here told her that he'd been loyal to the end.

"Faithful forever, friends," she said, lips twisting slightly, as she straightened up and made her way back into the soot-coated interior of the Redoubt. Mira almost couldn't even think the words of the old oath now, not after her own men had tried to kill her. What sort of faith was that? Who was she supposed to be faithful to? The people who tried to kill her? She'd trained those men, lived with them, laughed with them . . . and they still tried to burn her down.

Mira had to force down the anger, not for the first time, and turn her attention to the job at hand.

As he took his leave, Corian had used an overpressure explosive, a type of weapon that filled the structure with a flammable gas that was ignited when the mixture was ideal. Against anything less than the ancient construction of the Redoubt—or the palace—the resulting detonation would have left nothing but a crater and the faint smell of chemicals.

The Redoubt, however, had been built long before humans settled the Imperial Sector.

Corian was in a rush, or shorthanded, she decided as she made her way deeper into the Redoubt and found some of the doors stubbornly shut. Mira considered the bodies she'd deposited into the single large pit. *Probably both, I suppose.*

If he'd had more time or men, she was certain that he'd have opened all the internal doors. That would have caused a more complete destruction of the facility. As it were, with some of the heavy doors sealed, the explosive chemicals wouldn't have been able to penetrate the Redoubt completely. The shock wave too would have been blunted or even stopped in certain places.

Behind those doors, once she'd gotten the mechanism working again, Mira found supplies intact.

Just foodstuffs, water supplies, and basic gear, of course. As best she could tell Corian seemed to have taken everything of real value, or destroyed it in place. She wasn't about to complain, however, as some superweapon wouldn't keep her alive. Food and water would.

The destruction of the command center had been, unfortunately, complete.

No way to fix any of this, she decided as she looked over the communications equipment. *I'll not be calling for help or sending any warnings ahead of that bastard, not this time.*

She turned to leave the wrecked center but paused when a single blinking light caught her eye.

Mira made her way over to the station, kicking a burned and blackened chair out of the way, and crouched near the light. She brushed some of the ash away from the console, but the display and projector there were beyond repair.

Bringing her own armor back with a flick of her fingers across the projector emblem, Mira took her time and felt out for the active circuit through her armor. The empire primarily used photonic systems, which made her armor and its technology ideally suited to linking into Imperial data services. It was handy if the service in question wasn't half blown to the furnace above, but as long as she could find a live optical link, Mira was confident she could get in.

Alarm on the detention level.

Mira was tempted to pass it off as an artifact of the blast; in fact, normally she probably would have. However, she didn't have much else to do, certainly not until the next shadow pass. She left the command center and made her way down through the facility to the detention level. According to her briefing, it was probably the second most secure section of the Redoubt, not intended to hold many prisoners . . . just those that couldn't be risked in the empire's normal prisons.

The door to it was sealed, which likely meant that the area beyond was at least partly intact.

Whether that was a good thing or not, she couldn't say. She hadn't been briefed on who, if anyone, was currently being held at the empire's premier black site. The entire system was in emergency lockdown, but that actually made it easier to access the area. She only needed valid officers' codes to open the doors from the outside, likely on the belief that anyone already inside the Redoubt who was trying to get into the detention level was probably authorized.

The doors caught as they opened, and Mira had to brace against them and push, sliding the heavy metal back into the wall. *The explosion probably tore out the pressure valves,* she thought.

Mira made her way through the level, glad not to be picking through destroyed material and walking across carbonized bodies. Her footsteps rang out on the metal deck. She made no attempt to mask her presence. Her armor was up, blazing bright in full Cadre uniform, and given the mood she was in, she'd be pleased to encounter anyone who cared to pick a fight.

Unfortunately, perhaps, no one was there to take the challenge.

She found the cells and walked down the hall at a deliberate pace, taking only a moment to check each one before moving on. She reached almost the end before she stopped, finding one that was occupied. The reason for the alarm became apparent when she spotted that the cell's environmental system was damaged. There was no immediate rush, but given another hour, the occupant would have been suffocated by his own carbon waste.

Mira sighed, then linked into the system through her armor and popped the door lock.

"Step out," she ordered, "and identify yourself. I'd warn you not to try anything, but the mood I'm in right now, I think I'd be happier if you did."

A slightly pudgy man with dark hair slowly made his way out of the cell, hands clearly showing.

"Name's Gaston Rouche," he said slowly. "Imperial engineer, assigned to the Redoubt."

She checked her briefing files and nodded. The name and face matched.

Apparently Corian didn't have much use for him.

"Mind telling me how you got yourself locked in the detention cells?" she asked dryly.

Gaston snorted angrily. "That bloody traitor is how."

"Corian?"

"Who? No. Commander Jessup. She was assigned command of the Redoubt. She's been shifting assignments for months, getting her own people into position. The rest of us never stood a chance."

Jessup. Bethany Jessup, commander, Imperial Army. Clean record. Mira consulted the files on her personal data system while keeping an eye on the engineer. *No links to Corian in her files. No surprise. If there had been, she'd have had her command pulled before he was sent here.*

Every time she learned something more about this mess, Mira thought it stank of conspiracy far beyond what she'd been led to believe.

Corian is good, but this is more than a military coup. He's got backing from inside the Senate, at the very least.

That probably didn't narrow the field as much as she'd have liked, however, given that the only thing the Senate hated more than its own members was the Imperial Family.

The empire balanced on three powerful forces, each not entirely in opposition but certainly not in alliance with one another: the Senate, the Corporate Alliance, and the Imperial Family. Militarily, the emperor commanded enough forces to make the other two submit, but using that power had cost. The Alliance could subtly bleed the empire, and did so when given half a chance, while the Senate was made up of the various lords, barons, and other assorted nobles, who weren't much of a force as individuals but together could present a credible threat.

In practice, the corporatists were too focused on their profits to play the long game, and the nobles were too busy fighting each other to ally against the Imperial forces. That left Emperor Scourwind largely in charge, but exceptions had happened in the past and, it seemed, might just be happening now.

"Do you know what they were after?" she asked the engineer.

He shook his head. "Jessup locked me up from the start. Didn't even bother trying to recruit me . . . Should I be insulted, do you think?"

Mira laughed humorlessly. "I don't know. Maybe she just didn't like you much."

"There's truth in that," he grumbled. "Never got along with her from the start. She was always a little too interested in my project . . ." He trailed off, his eyes losing focus.

"What?" Mira asked, recognizing that he'd just thought of something.

"I need to get to secure storage," he said. "Flight deck."

"Knock yourself out," Mira gestured, following him after he started to walk quickly away. "Don't expect to find much."

Gaston stopped, turning back to look at her sharply. "Why not?"

"Corian—I'm guessing it was him . . . It's his kind of move—" she said idly as she caught up with him, "used an overpressure bomb to clear the Redoubt. Not a lot left in one piece up there."

"That wouldn't have destroyed my . . ." Gaston shook his head. "I have to check."

Mira just gestured again, then followed when he ran off.

*

"Oh, burning skies!" Gaston swore as he looked over the large flight deck. "It's gone."

"What's gone?" Mira asked from behind him, still debating how much to trust the man.

"We were working on a prototype ship," he said. "The *Caleb Bar*. It's . . . it's one of a kind."

"That's often what prototype means," Mira said, now tensing up. "What kind of ship?"

"The *Caleb* is a strato-cruiser, heavily armed," he said. "She's got some of the heaviest armor projectors we've ever built, but that's not what makes her so dangerous."

"Don't keep me in suspense, Rouche," Mira growled. "What the hell did Corian fly out of here?"

"The *Caleb*'s equipped with a prototype quantum-rail drive," Gaston said. "You know how those work?"

Mira nodded. "Sure. You lay a quantum rail by linking subatomic particles. Slow acceleration, unbelievable power, very efficient for super-atmospheric transport over long distances."

"Right, but with a quantum tractor drive you can't go anywhere there's no rail, so the rails have to be linked by a strato-ship or a reaction vessel."

"So?"

"The *Caleb* can link its own rail as it goes," he said. "She can travel above the atmosphere and strike from any angle, like a reaction ship, but the *Caleb* is hundreds of times the mass of a reaction ship and can do it without a thermal signature. It's unstoppable."

Mira closed her eyes, half turning away, as she tried to keep from swearing.

"We need to get back to the capital," she finally said, "while there still *is* a capital to get back to."

*

The open foredeck of the *Caleb* was awash in the wind of the upper atmosphere as General Corian walked stiffly to the large wheel mounted on the center platform. His missing leg had been replaced with a temporary prosthetic that was ill matched, but he didn't have time to do things the right way just then. For the moment he'd eat the pain and walk on fire and plasma if that was what it took to finish the job.

The wheel was a throwback, a nod to a bygone era of Imperial greatness, but it did the job. He gripped it tightly, easing it back as he felt the ship respond under his feet. They were at full sail, with long runners reaching high up above the ship into the strato-winds, pulling hard for the Imperial capital.

He heard steps behind him but didn't bother to look back.

"My compliments, commander," he said, a smile flitting across his scarred face. "She is everything you said she'd be."

"The best engineers in the empire worked for half a decade on design alone to make her so, general," Bethany Jessup said as she came to a stop on his blind side.

"I'm shocked that something so purely beautiful could be made under the corrupt fools that control the empire," he said, rolling the wheel to the right just enough to feel the big ship shift underfoot and dip her starboard side, showing the ground far beneath them as he finished adjusting the course and leveled out. "Magnificent."

"I'll take that as a personal compliment." Jessup let the roll lean her into his side, careful not to put too much weight on him for fear of aggravating his injury.

"You should. You oversaw the construction of something that will change history," Corian told her, turning his head so he could see her with his good eye.

He tilted his head down, his lips capturing hers for a long, deep kiss before Corian looked back over the foredeck of the ship.

Jessup just smiled. "What now?"

"Now we take the empire," Corian said with a smile as he locked the wheel and stepped back. "Time to go belowdecks, love. Call down to the engines; tell them to warm up the tractor drive."

"Of course, Corian," Jessup answered.

"Seal all ports. Dog the hatches shut," he ordered as he stepped down through the heavy door that led below. "We're taking the *Caleb* clear of atmo. Next stop," he said as the door swung closed with a heavy clang, "the capital."

CHAPTER 4

Brennan Scourwind whooped as he landed his skimmer, glancing along the roof of the palace and sliding sideways for a dozen feet or so before bringing it to a stop a scant few feet from the edge of a straight hundred-foot drop. He grinned and peeled his skullcap back as he hopped clear of the craft, planting his boots on the rooftop.

He stomped a few times, dancing from the heightened adrenaline rush he was still on, but came to a stop when he recognized the two people standing across the rooftop waiting for him.

"Brother," he said, feeling like he was crashing as his brother and William walked across the rooftop toward him.

"Brennan . . ." Kayle Scourwind nodded politely. Kayle always did everything politely. "That was . . . impressive flying."

"I'm the best." Brennan smirked.

"You're also reckless and stupid." William glared at him. "One mistake and you'd have pitched to your death on that landing, to say nothing of those maneuvers."

Brennan rolled his eyes and made a rude gesture, one that would have gotten him belted if he'd tried it with his father. William merely glowered but said nothing further.

Kayle, on the other hand, cuffed him lightly behind the head.

"I taught you better than that, flying *and* manners, you little fool." Kayle chuckled. "Stop baiting William when you know he's not going to call you on it."

"You haven't taught me anything about flying since I was seven, and you know it," Brennan told him cockily. "I can outfly you any day you choose."

Kayle smiled fondly at his younger brother, memories briefly eclipsing his annoyance. "You're a natural flyer, Bren. I told you that the first day I took you up in my skimmer. You're also a spoiled brat who's been a pain in my ass ever since I qualified you on your own."

Brennan shrugged. "What else is new?"

"I hear you can't find a flyer to qualify you on reaction craft or heavier skimmers."

Brennan looked away. "I'll find someone."

Kayle shook his head. "I'm not going to put my reputation on the line for you again, not when you're flying like that. If I won't, no one else will."

"I'll pay someone." Brennan sneered. "There're flyers out there who need cash."

"None with reputations worth a damn," Kayle countered. "Until you get a grip on your ego, Bren, you're going to stay skimming the bottom layer."

"As if," Brennan snorted, waving dismissively.

Kayle sighed deeply, but there wasn't much more he could say. Brennan hadn't listened to him the first dozen times he'd made that speech, and the kid wasn't about to start now. While Kayle loved both his siblings, his sister came across as a darling, while his brother was an egotistical little child. If it weren't for the family name and his bloodline, Bren would either be out on the streets or dead after some daredevil stunt on his flyer.

"Hey, William," Kayle said, glancing over his shoulder, "leave us for a bit, will you?"

William looked evenly at him for a long moment, then out across the open skyline beyond the palace.

"I know, William." Kayle smiled chidingly. "But we're on top of the palace. There's no sharpshooter alive who can hit me up here, and you know it."

William hesitated for a moment but then nodded. "I'll be inside."

The Cadreman went back inside, leaving Kayle and his brother standing out in the open. Kayle looked around. From where he was standing there wasn't much to see really. The other city buildings were nowhere near as high as the palace, which was already sitting atop a hill in the center of the island. He could see the surrounding countryside, but it was all fifty miles away if it was a foot.

As he'd told William, not even a Cadre sharpshooter could make that shot.

So Kayle turned his attention to his little brother, eyeing the fourteen-year-old for a long moment of silence.

Brennan shifted uncomfortably under the steady gaze of his brother. "What?"

"I want you to watch out for yourself, and Lydia, Bren."

"What are you talking about?" Brennan asked, clearly confused.

"Just stay close to Lydia for a few days," Kayle said. "Maybe it's nothing . . ."

Brennan shook his head. "Kayle, you're a dick, and a pain in my ass . . . but you don't try to scare the hell out of people for no reason. What's going on?"

"There's just some things happening," Kayle said. "I can't talk about them. I just want you to stay close to Lydia for a few days. Do that for me, all right?"

Brennan reached out as Kayle started to turn away, roughly pulling his brother back around. Kayle didn't resist, though he could have easily.

"No. You don't get to drop something like that and then just walk away from me, damn it. What the hell is going on?"

Kayle shook his head. "I don't know. I really don't, Bren. Just do what I ask, all right? For once in your life, just do what I ask."

He turned again, and this time Brennan let him walk.

"You know what, screw you, Kayle. Go drop that turd on someone else!"

Kayle sighed, stopping in his tracks. He turned his head, seeing his brother's turned back. "Do what I ask, Bren, and I'll qualify you for a strato-skimmer."

Brennan spun around to stare at his brother, but Kayle was already stepping through the door to the interior of the palace.

*

Kayle and William made their way down the halls of the palace, heading back toward the Imperial Family's residential wing.

"Has there been anything new from the team the general dispatched to the Redoubt?"

"Not since we lost contact with the reaction craft," William answered. "I think we have to assume we lost them."

Kayle swore, shaking his head. "A Cadre team just got dusted so clean we didn't even get a call for help. Tell me why the whole empire isn't on alert, William? Why is my father sitting on this?"

"I haven't been informed," William said simply.

"Get me an *audience*," Kayle growled. "Father knows something, or every unit for five hundred miles would be standing at alert by now."

"I'll put in the request, but you know how the emperor is," William warned.

"Yes, I know my father all too well. Just do it. He'll pay more attention to a request from you than from me."

His father would, likely as not, ignore a request from his children during a crisis. Family was there to be seen, not heard.

Even a family member who wore a Cadre emblem.

*

Brennan Scourwind made his way toward his residence, still thinking about his brother's rather insistent request. It wasn't like Kayle to ask anyone else to watch over Lydia, as their sister was the real princess of the family. A real overachiever, everyone's favorite, even if she was as spoiled as everyone thought Brennan was. Few people knew just how much trouble she could get into, mostly because Lydia was more than capable of getting right back out of it on her own. Kayle knew that.

So why is he worried?

He made a choice on a whim, turning toward his sister's rooms.

"Lyd, you in?" Brennan asked, tapping on the side of a door as he leaned into the room and looked around.

"What do you want, Bren?" Lydia appeared from her private rooms, stepping into the common area.

"Just checking on you," Brennan said, hesitating a bit. "Look, did you see Kayle earlier?"

Lydia nodded. "Sure. He visited me in class."

Brennan blinked. "In class? Really?"

"Yeah. Why?"

"You don't think that was odd?"

"Kayle always visits when he's home."

"He interrupts classes?"

Lydia pouted a little, causing Brennan to roll his eyes. She might be everyone's favorite princess, but she was such a drama queen.

"No," she admitted, "usually he drops by here."

"Yeah." Brennan nodded. "OK. Thanks, Lyd."

Brennan stepped back and started to leave, but Lydia called out after him. "What's going on, Bren?"

"I don't know," Brennan admitted, three words he didn't often utter, whether they were true or not. "Just . . . don't go anywhere too far for a couple days, OK? Kayle's acting weird, and you know what it takes to get one of those soldier boy types up in arms."

Lydia smiled, giggling a bit. "Yeah. OK, I'm not going anywhere anyway."

"Good. I'll be around, sis."

"Bren," Lydia called, smirking in his direction. "What did Kayle promise you to get you interested in what I'm doing?"

Brennan sighed. "He said he'd qualify me if I watched out for you for the next couple days."

Lydia giggled at him. "You're so easy to buy off, Bren."

Brennan rolled his eyes as he left. "Just remember what I said, OK? I'll be in my rooms."

"Speak with you soon, brother . . . ," she called after him, her voice taunting him slightly in singsong fashion.

Brennan frowned as he got out of there, wondering how it was possible that almost everyone else saw his sister as the perfect princess but somehow saw him as the brat.

Life sucked.

*

"Course and speed update."

The words were delivered quietly, but with no chance of being missed by those standing their stations on the *Caleb*'s enclosed quarterdeck.

"We just crossed eighteen times sound, groundspeed, captain," a man answered. "Course holding en route to capital."

Corian nodded, absently scratching the patch that covered his damaged eye. *This itch is driving me insane. Damn that woman.*

"Arrival time?"

"Within the quarter hour, captain."

"Good. Sound combat alarms and bring everyone to their stations," Corian ordered, taking a seat at the large chair that backed the room. His armor projector instantly connected to the ship's systems, linking him into all available information, but for now he ignored it all.

Until they were in a fight, in his experience, it was better to keep the crew involved with their commanding officer. Asking them for information ensured that they were in the moment as well and not being lulled off to some dreamland of distractions.

Once the blasters started lasing, then he'd lean on the projection systems, but not until then.

"Beth"—he leaned to port, where Jessup was standing—"strike coordinates?"

"Entered, checked, and confirmed," she answered professionally, "just as you ordered, captain. We can end this before anyone even knows we're there."

"Don't get too confident, Bethany," he chided lightly. "They still have a full regiment of Cadre down there. We have to end the fight before they know what happened, or we'll be cut to ribbons."

She nodded, knowing that it was the simple truth. The Imperial Cadre were a fighting force unmatched in the empire, lavished with the highest levels of training and equipment and culled from bloodlines that could fully interact with projection systems and those damned Armati.

"Are you certain you can contain them afterward?" she asked softly, a hint of concern in her voice.

Corian nodded. "The Cadre can't act . . . *won't* act without direct orders from the emperor. It's not only in the charter; it's the oath they swore. If the general orders them into action against that oath, he'll have a civil war on his hands."

She nodded uncertainly but didn't question him.

"No, love," he went on, drawing a smile from her, "we're on a high-risk operation, but have faith in my plan. There is a true victory condition here, not the illusionary ones we've been fighting for over the past few years."

"I have faith, captain."

"Good," he said, glancing aside at a bit of data floating near the corner of his eye. "We're approaching the launch window. Speed?"

"Almost twenty times sound, captain," the man standing the helm called out automatically. "Launch velocity will be reached on schedule."

"Stand by, weapons!"

"Launchers standing by."

"Locks loose! Fire as she bears!" Corian ordered.

The *Caleb Bar* sailed on for a moment, seemingly without response to the order, and then a shudder ran through the ship as they reached the first launch point.

"First rack away, captain. Trajectory looks good—impact in three minutes."

Corian leaned back in his chair and closed his one good eye. "And so history marches on. The emperor is dead . . ."

Jessup placed a hand on his shoulder, whispering, "Long live the emperor."

*

Launched at twenty times the speed of sound from over two hundred miles above the surface, the weapons were simple kinetic projectiles. Initially they fell unchallenged through the thin atmosphere that high up, eventually plunging into the thicker gasses below. Guidance fins came into play as the weapons locked onto their targets from a hundred miles above and three hundred out.

Moving twenty-eight times the speed of sound by the time they stopped accelerating, having reached equilibrium with the air and gravity, the projectiles crossed the distance from the ship in the blink of an eye and were inside the capital's air-defense system before the warning alarm sounded. Air-defense systems were still moving to track when the first projectile slammed into the palace with the force of a small atomic weapon.

The missiles were made of the same material as the palace, a metal formula beyond the ken of Imperial science. No one knew where the alloy had come from, but it was one of the hardest materials they'd ever discovered.

It was that alloy that made the palace, Redoubt, and few other such fortresses nearly impenetrable.

It was also that alloy that turned conventional bombardment weapons into fortress busters.

The impacts rocked the capital, shaking things to the foundations as shock waves rolled out, but where the missiles struck, the penetrator tips blasted right through walls and continued on to tear into the interior of their targets.

The Imperial hangars took three hits, alloyed penetrators punching holes through the roof and then proceeding to ricochet around the interior. Men and machines were torn to shreds with equal ease in a split second of nightmarish chaos. When it was over, less than a minute had passed, but for those who'd been miraculously passed over by the angel of death, a lifetime had passed, and they felt aged a thousand years.

Across the capital and the palace, similar strikes continued unabated over the next three minutes, and then everything went silent.

*

"All weapons away, captain."

"Stand down bombardment," Corian ordered. "Send the signal to the others, then rig us for atmospheric braking and take us down."

"Aye, captain. Rigged for air brakes, reversing tractor drive. We're losing altitude."

The *Caleb Bar* began to shudder slightly as it dipped down into ever thickening atmosphere, the air brakes helping the slow but powerful tractor drive begin to claw inexorably at the fabric of the universe as it slowed the ship's forward rush. Ahead of them, the capital could now be seen, smoke from the kinetic strikes billowing over the city with the first flashes of weapons fire.

*

Edvard Scourwind scowled deeply as he pushed off the wall and rushed down the long corridor that led to the strategic command bunker of the palace. He reached a bend in the hall and came to a skidding stop as he saw what lay beyond the turn.

The command bunker had taken a strike. Smoke was pouring through the wrecked blast doors, and without progressing farther he could tell that there was little point in trying to utilize the space.

There was only one weapon that could have made that strike, and if it weren't for the urgency of the situation, he'd have been forced to laugh outright at it being used against him. The fortress busters should have secured the empire for all time against the Senate and its mix of traitorous and ambitious nobles.

Damn you, Corian. You were the best of us.

He turned, running now as he dodged through the confused men and women pouring into the corridors. With the command center eliminated, strategic command would fall to the Cadre general. However, reports had already singled out that area as having been struck as well. That meant that the defense of the capital and the palace would be fractured, likely confused, and almost certainly not as efficient as it should be.

He needed to get to a system he could use to coordinate the response. Even if they beat back the attack, the cost could cripple the empire for cycles to come.

*

Outside, across the capital, the shock of the attack had just begun to set in as the rumble of the explosions was surpassed by a deep vibration that shook everyone to the core. Citizens, militia, and emergency workers all paused what they were doing and looked around for the source.

No one could quite tell who spotted it first, but a scream went up and people started pointing to the skies, and in seconds nearly everyone was watching as a massive ship slowed to a crawl over the city and came to a stop a few hundred feet above the skyline. The vessel was black, without the peculiar shimmer of plated metal.

No, it was the same color as the palace, a black that sucked in the light and didn't let any of it go.

No flag could be seen, but movement was clear on its decks as the capital held its breath as one, waiting to see what the unknown ship would do.

Assault lines were flung from the *Caleb Bar* a moment later, and city dwellers had their answer as soldiers began to drop along the ribbon cables to the ground, even while the ship opened fire to cover their descent.

Shock turned to panic then, and few people remembered much else from that point on.

*

"Squads deploying, captain. We've heard from our allies in the Senate. They've ordered their own forces forward."

Corian nodded. "Good. That will keep any units outside the city from responding. They'll be too busy with them. Have our men secure the air defenses first. I want to call in our backup."

"Aye, captain."

Corian was standing on the foredeck again, looking over the smoking city below as the wind plucked at his coat and hair. He was keeping his weight on his good leg, the prosthetic now a deep irritation that he would be glad to be done with once he had time for proper care.

Until then, however, he would endure.

"You should be belowdecks, captain," Jessup said softly at his side. "You can command the action from there."

"No, I'll stand where I can be seen," he said simply. "If there's a sharpshooter on the other side capable of making a kill shot on me here, they've earned it."

She shook her head, clearly disapproving, but said nothing more.

He turned from the scene, stalking toward where the defense guns were firing. "Let me know when we've taken the city. I will lead the assault on the palace personally."

CHAPTER 5

Kayle held his issued blaster in his off-hand as he waved to a squad moving into position to reinforce the primary access to the Cadre facilities.

"Set up the squad heavies to catch the door in a cross," he ordered. "Bastards have to come through here if they want to secure our command center. We've got a call out for reinforcements. Stop them here. Make them pay for every inch!"

The Cadre nodded, backed up by dozens of men-at-arms for each one of them. They were putting heavy weapons into place so as to hammer to atoms anything that dared stick its head through that passage.

While the heavy weapons were being set up, Kayle turned to where William was following his example and coordinating another group.

"Does anyone have any idea what the hell happened?" Kayle demanded, hoping that William had heard something.

Anything would do.

William just shook his head. "Nothing. Looks like a precision kinesis strike, but I didn't think anything existed that could do this."

Kayle nodded grimly, understanding what William was talking about.

Until only minutes earlier, he'd have personally sworn that there wasn't a weapon in existence capable of the damage whatever had hit the hangar had done. The palace was next to invulnerable, the same as all the ancient Redoubts that dotted the Imperial Sector.

Someone just shifted the balance of power in a big way.

"General!"

Kayle half turned, noting an armsman running up to the general as the man was trying to coordinate responses as best he could.

"What is it, son?"

"We've reports of fighting all through the palace, but it's not coming our way!"

The general scowled. "That makes no sense. If they want to take the command and control, now that they hit the primary, they have to come through us."

"Sir, the Imperial Family isn't within our lines."

Kayle felt like a hammer had just struck him between the eyes when he heard the exchange, his throat running dry as he looked around.

"William," he croaked out, a plea evident in his pained tone.

"Go. We have this," William said. "I'll have a squad on your heels within five minutes."

Kayle nodded gratefully and broke into a run as he sprinted out of the Cadre facilities and headed for the Imperial residency as fast as his feet would carry him.

*

Brennan picked himself up off the floor of his room, shaken almost as badly as the room itself had been a few moments earlier.

What in the burning sky was that?

He didn't think anything could shake the palace like that. In fact he was pretty certain that nothing *should* be able to. He walked to his window, looking out, and his jaw dropped when he saw the smoke and fires burning.

Is that shooting? What's going on?

Brennan checked the information broadcasts, but they seemed to be just as confused as he was. He shut off the projector and took a few breaths, trying to treat this like a situation in his skimmer.

Fear is good; panic is not. Be afraid, but address the fear.

He thought back to his perfect older brother's request.

What the burning sky did Kayle know about this?

For the moment that didn't matter.

Lydia.

Brennan burst out of his rooms and skidded as he turned down the corridor, heading for his sister's suite at a dead run. Kayle was a pain in the ass, but one thing Brennan knew was that his older brother didn't joke around when it came to family safety.

The halls were chaotic, but he recognized most of the faces. People with clearance to be in the residency wing were relatively few, so Brennan and Lydia got to know the new staff as they showed up.

Brennan ignored them. He was almost to his sister's suites when another explosion rocked the floor, sending him crashing to the ground for a second time.

Smoke poured into the hall, rolling over him as he struggled back to his feet. Coughing, Brennan covered his mouth and nose as he staggered the rest of the way, half-blind in the smoke, until he shouldered open the door to Lydia's suite and stumbled inside.

"Lyd!"

He looked around for his sister as he kicked the door shut and rubbed the smoke out of his eyes. "Lyd!"

"Bren?" Lydia peered around the door from her private rooms. "What's going on?"

"I don't know, but we have to get out of here. There's a fire or something," Brennan said. "The halls are filled with smoke."

"Bren, you know a fire's impossible," Lydia told him, confused. "Nothing in here burns!"

That wasn't strictly true, of course, as there were tapestries and furniture that might burn. In general, however, Brennan knew that his sister was right. The walls were metal, as were the floors, ceilings, and hell, damn near everything. There were no systems in the palace that could cause a fire, except possibly the armory or the hangar where they kept reaction craft and fuel, but those were on the other side of the structure.

But there was damn sure a fire around the corner that he'd seen with his own eyes and choked on with his own lungs.

"Just trust me, Lyd," Bren growled. "We've got to find a safe place. Kayle will know what to do."

"We're going to Kayle? He'll be in the Cadre wing." Lydia perked up. "I'll just grab a cloak."

Brennan rolled his eyes but didn't object as his sister ducked back into her rooms for a moment. She reappeared seconds later, wrapping a dark cloak around her shoulders.

"Ready? Good. Come on," he said, taking her hand.

The smoke in the halls was subsiding, much to his relief, but the air was still acrid and smelled of chemicals he didn't recognize. Brennan led his sister down the direct path to the central part of the castle, where they'd be able to head for the Cadre wing. They hadn't gotten far before odd sounds started to echo back through the halls to them.

"What are those sounds?" Lydia asked, puzzled.

"Blaster cartridges, lasing," Brennan answered, having heard the sound more times than he'd cared to in the past.

Like his brother, Brennan had been trained by some of the best martial trainers in the empire. Blaster courses had been fun, at first, but they eventually just boiled down to mind-numbing boredom. He was a decent hand with a blaster, on the training field at least, but Brennan never had much interest in or use for them.

Now, however, he rather wished he had one.

"Come on." He nudged his sister. "We need to keep moving."

Lydia let him pull her along, heading down another path away from the lasing blasts. A few dozen feet from the central hall, they were stopped when the doors to the hall blew open. Brennan stumbled back, surprised by the sudden movement. That surprise likely saved his life, as a lased blast vaporized a chunk out of the wall where his head had been just moments before, hot plasma scorching his face.

"Bren!" Lydia screamed, yanking him back and to the ground as more blasters fired.

Men poured in through the door as Brennan and Lydia scrambled back, lasing blasts filling the air above them. The siblings twisted, clawing at the ground as they scrambled in the other direction, only to find another group of men coming from that way as well, firing their blasters.

Caught in the cross fire, the two teens crawled to a doorframe.

"What's going on?" Lydia screamed.

Normally Brennan would have cringed at the volume of her voice, but at the moment his ears were ringing so badly that he barely heard her as it was.

"We're under attack!" he shouted back.

Lydia slapped his arm, annoyed. "I *know* that much, idiot!"

"Don't hit me, damn it! I just answered your question. We have to get out of here!"

He got the door beside them open, and they fell into the room beyond as the fighting intensified behind them.

"They're between us and the Cadre wing," Brennan said, peering back out. "I think we need a new plan."

*

Corian limped with each deliberate step he took into the palace. The prosthetic taking the place of his leg was just a fraction shorter than it should have been. He ignored it, focused on making each step as certain as possible as he followed the assault teams through the halls.

"Sir, heavy fighting in the residency wing."

Corian nodded. That was expected. The guards assigned there were the most strictly vetted people in the empire. Subverting them hadn't been worth the risk associated with such an endeavor.

"Remember, we need at least one of the family," he said, his voice deadly calm, "alive. The girl would be preferable."

"Yes, sir."

The Senate would be just as happy, happier probably, if the Scourwinds simply ceased to exist, but that wasn't his game plan. Killing the entire family would have its own perils, not to mention the near criminal loss of their bloodline. Politically the name had power, and it was power he could use.

Corian had few delusions that the Senate would be his ally forever. They were backstabbing, self-entitled fools without the slightest clue as to how the real world worked, or should work. They only thought about their own short-term benefit, and not one of them was smart enough to even consider how his actions would affect himself more than a cycle or two into the future.

The instant one of them thought it would get him a quick shot of power, Corian knew they'd betray him, just as they were now turning on the Scourwinds.

To maintain the power balance, albeit nudged more than a little in his own favor, Corian needed one of the younger Scourwinds on his side . . . in appearance at least.

"Reports from the Cadre facilities?" he asked, glancing at the aide walking alongside him.

“Our infiltrators have kept them from proactively moving on the rest of the palace, and the emperor has been cut off from them,” the aide confirmed. “Last reports put him on his way to the throne room.”

Corian nodded. “He’s going for the master communications panel. Predictable.”

“Yes, sir.”

“Let’s pay our respects to the emperor then, shall we?”

*

Edvard Scourwind was sitting calmly on the massive throne as the doors blew open, sending several of his guards scattering like leaves in a hurricane wind. Gamma carbines and lasing blasters roared back and forth, but the fight was never in question as more and more men poured into the hall.

As the blasts faded and the fighting ended, the invaders split to allow the approach of a man clad in a long, dark coat and heavy combat gear, a man who Edvard recognized without any strain, even considering his rather shocking appearance.

Corian limped to a deliberate stop, well within the point where he would normally have been checked for weapons. The calculated statement was clear and brought a smile to Edvard’s face.

“Not one for subtlety, are you, old friend?” the emperor asked mildly, ignoring the armed men to focus on the man he’d known for so long. “You’ve looked better.”

Corian laughed softly. “Thank your pet guard dog for my new look. I have to hand it to you, Edvard, that one was as ruthless as any I’ve seen.”

Edvard’s expression didn’t waver as he shrugged. “And what, if I may ask, happened to Cadrewoman Delsol?”

"By now? Dead of thirst in the Great Desert," Corian said with a calm gesture. "I didn't get to kill her personally, unfortunately, but then I'd have been cleaner and more merciful than the desert."

"Ah . . ." The sound rattled dryly from the emperor's throat. "That does answer some questions I had concerning the scene. She managed to cause you this much injury and escape into the desert? You must be getting old, Corian."

Corian snorted, rolling his eyes. "Crazy bitch turned the inertics off in the prison car before the train was derailed. I never got a chance to cross arms with her."

Edvard snorted and then slowly began to shake on the throne, finally laughing out loud at the man who was pointing a dozen blasters and carbines at him.

The former general just sighed, nodding his head. "I know. I know."

For those present, the sight of the emperor laughing near helplessly at the man holding him at gunpoint was a scene that would not be forgotten, nor spoken of without looking over their shoulders, for the rest of their lives.

Corian, however, didn't seem particularly put out by any of it. In fact he just waited calmly for the other man to stop, an expression of mild chagrin on his face.

"If you're quite finished?" he asked as Edvard slowly stopped laughing and took a few deep breaths.

"Ah, Corian, how many times did I tell you? You underestimate people, old friend. It's your fatal flaw," Edvard said calmly as he took another breath.

"And you overestimate them—that's yours," Corian said, his affable posture and tone gone now.

"Perhaps," Edvard conceded. "I certainly overestimated you . . ."

"Enough," Corian snapped. "It's over, old *friend*."

"I suppose it is," Edvard said, his hand dropping to an object on the arm of his throne. "I believe this is what you came for?"

Corian's eyes twitched to the object and flickered in recognition.

"You didn't reassign it?" he asked softly.

"Who would want an Armati tainted by what you did? By what you are?"

Corian seethed, but did his best to keep it under control. Few people could push his buttons quite the way Edvard did.

"I am what you and the empire made me, and I'll take that back now," he said calmly.

"Will you?" Edvard asked. "You know, in training I never could take you. You were the best of us, but you're not looking so good right now."

"You have over a dozen carbines and more blasters aimed at you." Corian shook his head. "Give it up, Edvard. You're still worth a little more alive than dead."

"I think we both know that if this little coup works, I don't keep breathing."

"It doesn't have to be like this," Corian said, shaking his head.

Edvard smiled slowly. "I think it does."

The emperor moved so fast he seemed to blur. The men covering him opened fire, but they were aiming at where he used to be, not where he was. He swept the Armati up as he moved, the weapon responding to his link automatically. It lengthened, flowing outward from the hilt, blade beveling and curving as he brought it around.

At the end of the arc, a fraction of an instant after he started to move, metal met metal and sparks erupted into the room as the Armati in the emperor's grip slammed dead into another Armati wielded by his target.

Corian met Edvard's eyes over the crossed blades and smirked slightly. "You sent a Cadre team after me, Edvard. Did you really think I wouldn't replace what you stole?"

*

"They're everywhere," Brennan hissed softly, ducking back from where he'd been looking around the corner.

Lydia stared, wide-eyed and fearful. "What do we do?"

Brennan looked helplessly about, not wanting to speak the truth—that he had no clue whatsoever.

"I don't know," he finally admitted, not able to come up with anything else. "Just . . . we have to get away from them."

She nodded, not having any better idea herself.

The two worked their way back from the men searching the wing, trying to find a way around them and out into the main part of the castle. But the infiltrators seemed to have every route covered. Brennan was feeling more and more desperate, knowing that he had to figure out a solution or bad things were going to happen to them both.

I can't believe I'm trying this hard to keep a promise to Kayle.

Normally he'd make it a point of pride to disappoint his perfect older brother, but that line of thinking seemed more than a little petty at the moment, even to Brennan.

"My skimmer," he finally said.

"What?" Lydia looked over at him sharply.

"They're between us and every path out," Brennan said, "but my skimmer is on the roof."

"I am *not* getting in that thing with you flying, Brennan Scourwind!" Lydia hissed angrily. "I've not forgotten—"

"We don't have a choice! Look, I'm sorry I tried to freak you out, OK?"

Lydia shot him a look that probably would have killed a man in a just universe. "Oh, *now* you admit you did it on purpose?"

"Yes, all right? I did it on purpose." Brennan groaned. "Look, there's no choice unless you want to take your chances surrendering . . ."

Lydia grimaced but finally nodded.

Brennan managed not to sigh in relief, instead grabbing his sister's hand and running in the opposite direction from where they'd been heading before that. All the fighting was focused around the entryways, and so far the roof access was clear.

*

Kayle Scourwind led with his Armati Bene, cutting down three of the attackers from behind before they even knew he was there. The blaster in his off-hand barked a dozen times, filling the air with the smell of lase chemicals and superheated blood. The six-man squad he'd found hit the ground at the same time, but he had no time to give them a thought as he stepped over the bodies and entered the residency wing with purpose.

Bodies littered the floor, both those of Imperial guardsmen, the dedicated branch of military that protected the emperor and his family, and those of the attackers. Kayle didn't have the time or inclination to bother identifying them, though he had his suspicions.

They're using gamma burster carbines, he noted wearily. *The only way they could have gotten those weapons in significant quantity is with major backing from the Senate.*

The bursters were relatively new technology, still restricted and quite expensive. Despite being designed with combat in mind, they had a tendency to overpenetrate targets. That made them, perhaps, exceptional weapons for an open battlefield but poor excuses for gear in situations when you might have mixed environmental situations.

Perfect for killing Cadre, if you don't care for the lives of anyone else.

His armor was cycling slowly through the nonvisible frequency ranges as he soft-stepped through the halls he'd once called home. As he got deeper in, it seemed that the fighting was wrapping up, and it appeared that the guardsmen had not been on the winning side.

"Any sign of them?" Kayle overheard an invader ask, while he leaned quietly against a wall and didn't move.

"A squad thought they saw the girl and maybe the younger brother heading up for the roof. They're in pursuit," another responded.

Good man, Bren.

Kayle left them be, padding quietly for the roof himself. He didn't need to kill all of the invaders.

Just the ones threatening his family.

*

"Everyone back up! This is between us," Corian ordered, stepping back from Edvard as he swept the attacking blade aside with an almost casual motion, deflecting the emperor's Armati blade.

Edvard tilted his head, shifting the blade up to a guard position. "Just like old times, then?"

"One last old time." Corian nodded once, shifting his footing. "Your last."

"You've got one leg, one eye, and you look like you just picked a fight with a freight hauler." Edvard snorted, eyeing the armed men shifting around them. "And you wonder why we all considered you an arrogant son of a—"

Corian snapped his blade up, slashing at the emperor's head with lightning speed. Edvard ducked back a half step, letting the blade pass, then countered with a lunge to Corian's torso.

Corian pivoted, letting the blade pass by him as he turned, using the momentum of his initial strike to speed his turn as he tucked in his blade and stepped past the emperor's lunging form. He flipped the Armati around in his hand easily and completed the move he started with the initial feint as his blade slid smoothly into Edvard's back.

Edvard's hand went limp, his blade dropping to the metal floor with a clatter.

Corian stepped in behind him, propping him up with the blade as he clamped his free hand onto the emperor's shoulder and spoke softly into his ear.

"I'm not arrogant, Edvard," he said simply. "I am just that damn good."

Corian jerked the blade out, letting go of the emperor's robes, and Edvard dropped to his knees as blood flowed freely and his clothing ran dark and wet with his life's fluid.

As Edvard Scourwind slumped forward onto his face, Corian looked around the room.

"The emperor is dead. Long live the emperor."

CHAPTER 6

"There they are! Get them!"

Brennan shoved Lydia ahead of him as they broke out onto the roof, pausing only to slam the door shut behind him and seal it with the palace codes. He hoped that their pursuers didn't have those same codes, but he knew that he couldn't count on that.

He pushed off the door and bolted in the direction of the skimmer, hearing pounding on the door behind him as he did so.

"Get strapped in!" he ordered, grabbing the tie lines that secured the skimmer against wind gusts.

Brennan got the ties undone and tossed the lines aside, then grabbed the nose and pulled the light craft about, checking the first cloud layer carefully as he did. He didn't have time to get proper bearings, so he'd have to get the launch right by dead reckoning everything.

Lydia was struggling with the harness in the backseat of the skimmer, fumbling with the unfamiliar clasp as he twisted the craft around.

"Left over right," he called, "then flip the catch shut and pull the harness tight."

The snub-nosed skimmer settled into position as he quickly checked the primer on the launchers and then pulled off the safety catches. With the craft ready to fly, Brennan ran back around to the front and rotated the flyer's seat in front of his sister, locking it into place.

"Almost ready," he promised. "I just need to . . ."

The door behind him burst open, and he looked back with wide eyes as men started running out across the roof.

"I've got to clear the end of the strip or we'll hook up and crash before we get clear!" he said. "As soon as it's clear . . . launch the sails!"

"What? Bren, I can't fly this thing!"

"Yes, you can, and you know it!" he snapped over his shoulder as he ran. "Don't worry about me—just do it!"

She nodded shakily, not that he could see her as he bolted across the rooftop to the far end where the catch nets were deployed. The nets were intended to keep someone from overshooting the roof, as he'd come close to doing, and crashing down into the courtyard below.

Of course they did require that you approached your landing on the expected trajectory, which Brennan rarely did. He hit the switch to drop the nets just as the first of the men grabbed him. Brennan hit him with an elbow, then kicked out his knee just like in training. As the man went down, Brennan turned and waved wildly to Lydia.

"Go! Go now!"

Lydia had her hands on the secondary controls, and he could see her face as she stared wide-eyed back at him. He knew she'd been scared of flying ever since he'd pulled that idiot stunt when they were younger, but he was still taken back by the stark terror in her face right then.

The distraction cost Brennan as he was tackled to the ground from behind, still yelling at his sister to take off.

He struggled underneath the weight of the man who'd tackled him, but there was no getting loose, and Brennan's stomach sank into a deep pit as he saw three more men run up to the flyer.

Damn it, Lyd . . .

With men holding the flyer down and locking the safeties back, there was no way for it to take off. Brennan flinched as he was hauled to his feet, struggling a little, but it was mostly for form since he was out-massed more than twice over and had his arms pinned behind his back.

"Hold still, brat," the man holding him ordered. "You're not going anywhere. The new emperor has requested your presence."

Brennan twisted around. "New emperor? What new emperor? What happened to my *father*?"

The man just laughed, shoving him forward.

"Move it, kid. Cry about your daddy later."

The men pulled Lydia from the skimmer kicking and screaming, and roughly pushed her toward Brennan and the rest. The two young teens were shoved together as the men regrouped and checked the rest of the roof.

"Clear, sir."

"Good," said the man who seemed to be in charge. "Looks like we got them both. The general will be satisfied."

"You said something about our father," Brennan growled. "What happened to him?"

The men glanced at one another and smirked, leaving Brennan with a sick feeling in his stomach.

"Worry about yourself, kid," the leader said, turning to another of his men. "OK, call for a larger escort. Tell them we have the kids and are coming down from the roof."

"Yes, sir."

Brennan kicked out at the man holding him, but didn't accomplish much other than annoying him. The armsman shook him roughly, growling as he did.

"That's enough out of you! Come on—get moving."

The two teens were shoved across the rooftop toward the broken open door they'd come through. Neither of them had any ideas about what they should do next, and fighting didn't seem like a reasonable option, so they went along without further protest. Brennan's mind was still caught up trying to work out what they meant when they said that there was a new emperor.

That means father is . . .

He closed his eyes tightly for a moment, only opening them when he was again shoved forward.

Neither of them, nor even their older brother, had been particularly close to their father, but not even Brennan had ever wished the man dead. He was a distant figure in their lives, who spent more time as the emperor than as their father, but they all had memories of his presence.

Brennan had come to resent the man's absence. He suspected that both his siblings had as well, though they masked their emotions better. The idea that he could be even more absent had never really occurred to Brennan, and now that it had, the prince felt a coldness inside that he'd never experienced before.

His mind was still whirling with those thoughts and feelings as he and his sister were pushed through the door and into the palace again.

A brush of motion raised the hairs on his skin, but Brennan had no time to react before a hot splatter of liquid hit the back of his neck and a blaster lased a round off right behind him. He flinched, twisting out of the suddenly slack grip of the man who'd been holding him, and saw the armsman fall with blood gushing from his throat.

The man holding Lydia had taken a lase round at point-blank range to the head, and without much blood to absorb the energy, it looked like his head had popped like an overripe melon. A glimmering hand dropped over Lydia's eyes and turned her away from the sight as a second matching hand gripped a blaster, lasing off several more rounds.

It was over in a second. The four men who'd taken them were cooling on the ground as Brennan stared at the glowing Cadre armor standing there, holding his sister.

"Kayle?"

The armor faded, and his brother nodded. "Come on. We have to get you two out of here."

"Kayle, they said that father . . ."

"The reports are that father was killed by Corian," Kayle said. "I know. Come on."

He got them moving, heading down the stairs, only to stop as the sound of heavy boots came up to them from below.

"They called for an escort when they caught us," Brennan said.

"Damn," Kayle swore, turning them around. "OK, back to the roof."

"There's no way off the roof!" Lydia protested as they ran back out onto the roof and the private landing platform.

"There's the skimmer," Kayle corrected, nodding toward the flyer as it came into sight. "Wasn't that your plan?"

Brennan nodded. "Yeah, but, Kayle, the skimmer only takes two people."

"I know," Kayle said as he ran them over to the skimmer. "That's why you're going to get in it and fly your sister out of here."

"What about you?" Lydia protested, fighting him as Kayle pushed her into the rear seat.

"Don't worry about me," Kayle said. "Bren, do it."

Brennan grimaced but finally shoved the flyer's seat into position, locking his sister in before he dropped into place and pulled the restraints down over himself.

"Take this," Kayle said, handing him the compact weapon Brennan recognized as Cadre issue. "My Bene will protect you."

"Kayle? This is your Armati?" Brennan was confused.

The Armati were deeply secretive weapons of the Cadre, and they were the one type he'd never been tested on. Brennan didn't know much of anything about them, but he knew that a Cadreman didn't just hand his over to anyone, not even family.

"I've enough weapons to do what I need to do," Kayle smiled easily, handing his blaster back over the seat to Lydia. "Now do as I said and get your sister out of here. Find William, if you can, or one of your old teachers."

He stepped back, pulled the shielding cover down over Brennan, and slapped the clear visor twice as he stepped back.

"Go on!" he ordered again, turning around and running back to the door.

Brennan gripped the controls in both hands, thumbs on the launcher studs, but his eyes were glued to where his brother was kneeling near the door and picking up one of the fallen armsmen's carbines. He started firing down into the hall beyond almost instantly, and ionized traces could be seen flying back in return.

"Bren? We can't leave him there!" Lydia objected.

Brennan's grip tightened around the twin sticks, knuckles whitening as he stared unblinking.

An explosion rocked the door, throwing Kayle out and back. The armored Cadreman hit the roof in a skid that brought him halfway back to the skimmer. Brennan threw off his restraints and popped the canopy, but before he could get out Kayle turned over and waved violently at him.

"Get out of here!"

As men came pouring out of the door, Kayle flipped back over to his feet, charging them with his armor glittering brightly from internal light. Brennan winced as carbine blasts shook his brother's form, barely slowing his charge.

At the last moment before Kayle reached the armsmen, blades of hard light erupted from every facet of his armor and he dove into them. The blood spray was nightmarish as the fight turned to extremely close combat, brutal in ways that ranged fighting never could be. Men fell to the roof, sometimes minus limbs, losing life's blood with alarming speed.

In the middle of it all, Kayle seemed untouched by any of it. His armor gleamed, clean and pure as the sun. Blood couldn't stick to hard light projections, and any damage he'd taken had already been repaired . . . on the outside at least. He spun, tearing a man's throat out with a bladed elbow, then snapped a kick into another.

A carbine blast from behind the men took Kayle in the shoulder, driving him back a step, then another holed through his armor and lower abdomen. The moment of lessening pressure was enough, and the armsmen regrouped.

The flurry of blasts drove Kayle back to the ground, and men poured out of the palace onto the roof, one of them pausing to put a single round from his carbine into Kayle's head before turning to the waiting skimmer.

Brennan didn't remember saying anything, though he could hear someone screaming. Maybe it was him, maybe Lydia. He couldn't tell. It might have been both.

He jabbed his thumbs down on the launch studs and the twin rockets on either side of his skimmer roared, launching the sail line into the air. A thousand feet up the rockets activated their projectors, casting a light sail across the sky; far below it the skimmer twisted with the wind and began to slide along the rooftop of the palace.

Men ran after them, but no one seemed to be firing as Brennan drew in the line and lifted his skimmer into the air.

*

On the rooftop, a squad leader skidded to a halt and held out a hand demanding a radio.

His sub handed the device to him, and he quickly got in contact with the strike coordinators.

"A skimmer just launched from the palace . . . No, do *not* fire on it. Track it and force it down," he ordered.

There was a pause and a mostly garbled response.

"Because the Imperials are on it! The general wants them *alive*!"

Another rapid exchange, some garbled sounds from the box, and he growled and took a breath before replying.

"Just *do* it."

He shut the radio off and handed it back to his sub, shaking his head before looking back to the fallen Cadreman who'd held the door. He sighed, "Find out who that was and locate his Armati. The general wants them all under his control."

"Yes, sir!"

*

"Bren . . . ," Lydia whispered weakly. "Kayle . . . he . . ."

"I know. I saw," Brennan croaked back, hands working the controls of the skimmer automatically.

He was riding the low winds, a river of air that moved a little over a hundred miles an hour between seven hundred and thirteen hundred feet above the surface. They were generally predictable and easy to navigate, mostly because they'd been mapped for over a century. Brennan continued to winch in the line, dragging the skimmer up closer to the sails, which increased his altitude and speed as he reduced line drag.

"What are we going to do now?"

"I don't know," Brennan admitted. "I just don't . . ."

A shadow crossed his canopy, causing him to turn and spot a military skimmer coming in hard from his left side. He could see the lights flashing, a signal code ordering him to put the skimmer down.

"Lyd," Brennan said, his voice and mind going cold. "Hold on."

"What?"

The military skimmer had sails three times the size of theirs, but with weapons and armor it probably massed five times more at least. Bren jerked twin sticks in opposing directions, and his skimmer keeled over and banked to the right as he climbed for the first wind layer, trying to eke out as much speed as he could.

The military skimmer followed suit in short order, but its maneuvers were not quite as sharp as his had been.

Both craft clawed for altitude, shortening their sail lines and drawing themselves up into the lee of their own sails. That cut down on air resistance, and in short order the two were flashing through the skies at just over a hundred miles per hour.

"Not going to lose anyone here," Brennan mumbled to himself, his head moving on a swivel as he tried to keep the military skimmer in sight.

So far it wasn't shooting, so he figured that they'd gotten orders to force him down.

That's good. Getting shot down would suck.

"Bren, there's another one."

Brennan looked back, then up to where she was pointing. He let out a curse as he spotted it.

"What?"

"They're in the median layer, Lyd," he said. "I can't lose them."

"What do we do?"

Brennan looked around and then down as he considered the situation. Military flyers could go a lot higher than his skimmer could. They carried bottled air and stronger sails, which would allow them to breathe in the upper atmo and deploy sails into winds that would tear his baby apart.

"Sorry, sis," Brennan said, wincing as he reached for the controls. "Have to do it."

"Have to do *whaaa—*?" Lydia's question turned into a wail as he killed the sail projectors and wound them back in, the skimmer suddenly nosing forward and dropping like a stone.

*

"Burning skies!" the coflyer of the skimmer swore. "He just killed his sails."

"He what?" the flyer demanded, looking down. "Where?"

"Overwatch just lost him. They're moving too fast and overshot the dive point. They'll come around, but it'll be a couple minutes."

The pilot killed speed as fast as he could, letting out the sail line. The drag of the line and the weight of the skimmer against the air would eventually pull them out of the sky, but there wasn't much else he could do.

"Did you see where he went?"

"Down into the skyline on the north sector of the city," the coflyer answered. "He's in an unpowered dive. We'll never be able to follow."

"Not in these buckets," the flyer agreed. "I'll circle around, try and keep overwatch. Maybe we can spot him when he comes out of the dive."

The military skimmers were heavily armed and armored, which made them great in a fight but gave them a distinct disadvantage if their prey was willing to go unpowered. Civilian skimmers could glide, after a fashion, being built with lightweight composites and projectors. A sky fighter, however, was designed to take—and dish out—a beating.

They curled back around, keeping an eye out as they tried to locate the missing skimmer, but nothing came to sight after several long minutes.

"Damn. Those were the Imperials too. The general is *not* going to be happy."

CHAPTER 7

"We're losing ground, Everett!"

William nodded. The fighting wasn't going well. The invaders had greater numbers than they should have, and the initial strikes had destroyed the coordination of the palace forces. Even knowing something was brewing hadn't prepared him, or anyone, for what had actually happened. It was all so unthinkable.

"Hold the line," he ordered grimly, shifting his grip on the Armati he'd lived with for the last forty-odd years of his life. "We'll do our duty to the end."

"The end might be closer than you think, Everett."

William half turned to see General Aleksander approaching. "Sir! What?"

"We just got confirmation. The emperor is dead."

William felt like he'd been struck by a skimmer. "Are you sure?"

"I said we got confirmation. He's gone."

William shook his head, trying to wrap his brain around that bit of information, "The heirs, we have to . . ."

"The squad you sent after Kayle just reported back," the general said, shaking his head.

"Brennan, then, or Lydia . . ."

"Reports suggest they escaped by skimmer."

"Brennan is a natural flyer," William confirmed.

"Well, we can only hope that they got out clean. For now we have a larger problem," the general said grimly. "We'll try to track them down, but it's clear that the invasion had far more support than anyone thought possible. There are currently three legions outside the capital sector. They're not doing anything yet, but we didn't call them in."

William closed his eyes for a moment, considering that.

Three legions would be enough to lay siege to the capital, but he doubted that was the plan. They already had enough forces inside to break a siege defense if they wanted to, which meant that the legions were a threat, a message to the Cadre.

It was a good threat too.

Fight us, and we'll level the capital.

"We can't give up that easy, sir."

"We're not," the general said darkly. "But we can't win here. I'm going to signal a withdrawal, but Everett . . . I have one more operation for you."

*

Brennan pulled up hard on both sticks, leveling out the skimmer within a couple hundred feet of the ground. Buildings rose up on either side of them as they flashed through the fabricated canyons, heading for the great walls at the city's edge.

"Bren!" Lydia yelled. "I'm going to *kill* you!"

"Sorry, Lyd, I know I promised, but it was the only way."

He jammed the left stick forward as a building came too close to one side, throwing the skimmer into a sharp bank even as he fought the motion with the foot pedals, trying to keep the trajectory straight.

Before they could lose too much altitude, he threw the stick back and leveled the skimmer out as the building flashed by them.

The walls of the capital were manned, but he didn't see anything out of the ordinary. In fact, the patrols there seemed a little light. Brennan hoped that meant that these were the normal guards and some had been called away due to the fighting at the palace or the destruction of the initial strikes. If they were, then they'd probably just flag his skimmer ID and send him a fine.

It wouldn't be the first time.

If they were part of the invasion of the capital, though, they might just shoot them down.

Brennan was praying as he hit the inner perimeter of the wall and then as the wall flashed under them. They were well past the wall before he took another breath and started to relax.

"I think we made it out," he said over his shoulder. "I'm going to get as much distance as I can before I launch the light sails again."

Lydia nodded quietly behind him, but her eyes were focused elsewhere.

"Bren, look out to your right."

Brennan did, and his eyes widened at what he saw.

"There shouldn't be a legion this close to the capital, Lyd. We'd know if they'd been called in for any reason."

"I know," Lydia whispered. "The Senate must have summoned them."

"To help?" Brennan asked, confused.

"Bren"—Lydia shook her head—"they'd have had to cut those orders *weeks* ago."

Brennan swallowed. "You're saying that the Senate is in on it?"

"Some of them, yes."

He pushed the right stick forward, pumping the pedals to match, and banked the skimmer away from the assembled forces of the Imperial legion. In moments they were out of sight, and the skimmer was running low to the ground and a lot faster than even he felt comfortable with at that altitude. Still, Brennan hesitated with launching the light sails, since his skimmer wasn't equipped with the stealth tech of military aircraft. Once their sails went up, he knew that he and Lydia would have effectively sent up a flare.

Need to run as long as I can. I might be able to get out of their range before they spot us.

Just a little longer.

*

The fighting had intensified around the Cadre wing. Now that the invaders had apparently accomplished their primary goals, they were moving in force against the biggest remaining threat to their actions. The volume of fire from the embattled sections of the wing was truly impressive, particularly considering that it was being mounted by very few volunteers.

Most of the Cadre personnel had already evacuated the wing, scattering to the winds. You didn't serve the Cadre for long without learning to have fallbacks—and backups for your fallbacks.

William Everett walked unhurriedly away from the sound of fighting. He had orders of his own to complete, and then if he were lucky he'd be ready to vanish into his own little bolt-hole.

An explosion behind him told him that the defenses had fallen. He didn't look back. William stepped into a large room filled from one end to the other with gleaming metal boxes, half as tall as he was, each of them whirring with restrained power and guided intent. He walked down the length of the room, pausing only to attach small devices to each of the boxes in turn.

At the far end, William stopped and pushed a seat out of the way as he activated a projection interface and sent a few quick commands into the main computer system of the empire. There was only so much he could do from the Cadre systems, of course, but he could make things a little more difficult for Corian and the Senate.

He could also make things a little easier for himself, since he was about to become an outlaw and all anyway.

The door behind him was kicked open and men stampeded through the doors, running toward him. They stopped well out of his reach, weapons leveled on him as the officer in charge stepped forward.

"The Cadre have been disbanded, by Imperial edict. Surrender yourself and your weapon now, or I will authorize lethal action."

"Emperor Scourwind is the Cadre's most ardent supporter," William said, still working without turning around.

"The Scourwinds are no longer in control of the empire. Stop what you're doing and turn around, or we'll fire!"

William entered his last command and straightened up, turning slowly with his hands visible.

"My oath is to the emperor," he said. "If Edvard Scourwind is no longer the emperor, then my oath goes to his heir."

The men relaxed a little as he showed no weapons, and the officer actually lowered his sidearm.

William shook his head almost imperceptibly.

Amateur.

"Surrender your weapon. Slowly."

William reached down, slowly, and tapped the blaster on his hip. "This one?"

"Your *weapon*. Now."

"Ahhh"—he breathed out slowly—"*that* one. Sorry, never going to happen."

"Then you die here."

William locked eyes with the officer and smiled. "You talk too much."

The room exploded, engulfing them all in flames as the bombs he'd put on every computer mainframe in the room detonated on his command, taking the identities of every Cadre officer in the empire with it.

*

Trees were whipping by mere feet below the skimmer as Brennan scanned the skies for any sign of military flyers.

"I can't risk it any longer, Ly," he said. "I need to set the sails now."

"OK."

He thumbed the firing studs on the rockets, launching the projectors into the sky. Redeploying sails in flight was tricky business, something only daredevils tried. Luckily, the prince was a noted daredevil.

The light sails snapped into place a thousand feet over their craft, just as they were skimming treetops. The instant he had tension on the lines, Brennan hit the winches, bringing in the line and dragging the skimmer up into the skies again.

"Keep an eye out," he said over his shoulder. "Let me know if you see anything coming our way."

Lydia nodded, not that he could see it, but he knew his sister well enough to know she'd done it anyway.

Spotting military skimmers wasn't easy. They used light sails in the nonvisible or sky-matched spectrum and didn't leave contrails like reaction craft. And considering the paint scheme most of them used—a neutral gray underneath and earth tones from above—spotting them by eye was a distinct challenge.

As he gained altitude and speed, Brennan started to breathe a little easier.

Flying was the one part of his life he'd felt real control over. When he was at the sticks of his skimmer, there was no one who could tell him what to do, how to act. He was free.

Freedom was, perhaps ironically, something a scion of the Scourwind blood didn't get to enjoy very often.

"I don't see anything," Lydia said from behind him. "I think we're OK?"

Brennan twisted slightly in place, turning to look out behind them. The smoke was curling up in the distance, blacking out the skyline of the capital.

"No, Lyd, I don't think we're going to be OK for a long time," Brennan said as he tightened up the lines, bringing his skimmer up into the first wind layer.

*

Corian walked through the debris, stepping casually over bodies as he made his way to the front of the room.

"Disappointing" was all he said aloud.

"The Cadre elected to destroy their records rather than let them fall into our hands, sire."

"Yes, it was a risk," Corian said. "We never had enough assets inside the Cadre section to secure their mainframes. How many Cadre can we confirm dead or captured?"

"None captured. Perhaps fifteen dead? No more than that."

Corian laughed bitterly. "Fifteen. And now they've gone to ground. This will get bloody."

He turned and walked out of the Cadre computer mainframe room, shaking his head.

"So very damn bloody."

*

The city was looming in the distance as an old, ramshackle skimmer skirted the edge of the detection perimeter. It was a wind craft that had seen better days, and in fact barely seemed to hang in the air behind ephemeral light sails.

"I see major damage to the city and the palace, my lady."

Mira Delsol sighed as she worked the controls, bringing the cobbled-together skimmer around so it wouldn't trip perimeter security.

"So we're too late."

Gaston nodded from where he was standing on the deck, observing the capital through powerful lenses. "It would appear. The damage appears days old at least, perhaps longer, and the *Caleb Bar* is holding position over the city. It is not flying the Scourwind colors."

Mira nodded, thinking hard. "New plan. I know a few drop sites and secure communications systems. We'll go to ground, see if we can figure out exactly what happened. I'm not going anywhere near the capital until I have that information and a plan."

Gaston nodded, setting the lens down.

"I rather believe that is a damn good idea, my lady."

Mira tightened the sail lines, bringing the skimmer up into the wind layer, and turned away from the capital.

CHAPTER 8

The cloaked figure made his way through the crowds, occasionally pausing to rest. The city was one of the outlying metropolises of the empire, only a few hundred miles from the nearest God Wall. In the distance out past the walls of the city, you could see the God Wall rising to tower over everything, reaching out past the atmospheric envelope and into the cold emptiness beyond.

In the city, however, that symbol of the unknown had long since been relegated to everyday scenery, and it was the God Wall that the cloaked figure was looking at as he rested. After each brief rest, he once again pushed his way through the crowds of the market bazaar, finally ducking into a narrow alley and knocking on a doorway deeply shadowed within.

The door opened silently and he stepped inside, waiting until the door closed before throwing off his cloak.

"Did you find anything?"

"No," William Everett said, shaking his head as he took a seat. "The rumors seem to be false."

His contact nodded, unsurprised. It wasn't the first time in the weeks since the coup that they'd tracked down rumors of the missing

Scourwind heirs only to find nothing at the end of the search. The only good side of it was that the forces of the new emperor weren't having any more luck than they were.

Every semiclandestine unit in the empire had orders to be on the lookout for the Scourwind twins, but so far nothing but rumors and ethereal stories had appeared since the day Edvard had died. None of it was common knowledge. Regular police and guardsmen couldn't be informed without spreading rumors across the surface of the world in an instant, but the directives should have been enough to catch even the wiliest of criminal fugitives.

Had anyone asked prior to that day, no one would have bet that Brennan and Lydia Scourwind of all people would have a chance in the burning skies of evading an empire-wide search, and yet they'd done just that. William himself couldn't believe it, and he knew them better than most.

Brennan was an overly pampered troublemaker and a dedicated pain in the ass to anyone in authority. His rebellious period against his father had started when he was barely thirteen and had still been going strong. Lydia was just as pampered, though her personality couldn't be more different. She had embraced the cute image of her as a princess and acted it at all times. It won her few close friends but many admirers willing to do almost anything she asked.

The two of them should have been captured within a week of escaping the palace, though, in his mind, reports of Kayle being killed on the roof where Brennan's flyer had been stored explained their escape.

"Thank you for your help and hospitality, my lord," William said.

Lord Baron Kennissey waved off the honorific. "The Scourwinds were allies for a long time. They deserved more support than they received."

"I believe this." William nodded soberly. "However, it is difficult to hold for allies when you're being ambushed."

"We should have seen it coming." The baron sighed. "Now Corian is moving to solidify his control over the Senate. The fighting has spilled out of the capital. We have reports of confused resistance being slaughtered by Corian's legions. I do not believe that those who support him in the Senate expected Corian's brutal response to relatively minor defiance."

The baron laughed bitterly. "More than one of those fools is learning just who they backed. Scourwind may have been a hard man, but Corian has no inkling of how to manage the empire. He only knows how to command armies."

"I know." William nodded.

Corian was noted for the near fanatical loyalty of the soldiers under his command, but the man didn't know how to manage allies. If you weren't one of his soldiers, you were a nonentity at best . . . an enemy at worst. He'd begun by quickly taking the forward Scourwind allies out of the Senate with brutal efficiency. Baron Kennissey had only avoided this so far by virtue of being more interested in managing his own lands than spending time in the Senate and the capital.

Eventually, they both knew the new emperor would turn his focus to the fringes of the empire, even this far out.

"How are things looking?" William asked finally, though he was far from certain he wanted to know.

"The old group are stocking for a fight," the baron admitted with a sigh. "They know Corian won't leave well enough alone. It's not in his nature. He'll insist on military discipline in government, and we both know that's never going to happen."

William laughed darkly, shaking his head. "Not without a lot of blood spilled."

"Not even then," Baron Kennissey countered. "Bloodshed will get him the appearance of discipline, but it'll also start the conspiracies running, if they're not already."

"Are they?"

Kennissey shrugged. "I haven't made plans yet, but there are others not as forgiving as I am, and Edvard had friends. I don't know. What about the Cadre?"

William was silent for a moment as he considered that question.

"Scattered," he finally said. "The Senate limited our numbers, but Scourwind had the last laugh on them in that deal."

"How so?"

William grimaced. "The limit was one century of Cadre, the elite of the empire."

Kennissey nodded. "I know. What of it?"

"We never had enough men to fill half that, and the Scourwinds knew that we never would when they agreed to the *limit*," William said.

"Men come from all over the empire to take a shot at a Cadre slot," Kennissey objected. "How is that possible?"

William glanced around, but the room was empty. It was a reflex gesture more than a sign of real suspicion. He parted his cloak, exposing the Armati where it rested strapped to his thigh.

"These. They're our Armati, our sworn weapons," he said. "A symbol of office, if you will."

"I know. The Senate was briefed . . ."

"No"—William shook his head—"you weren't. I've probably already told you more than I should, but given the state of the empire, I can probably tell you a couple things even Corian isn't aware of. The Armati aren't manufactured weapons. The empire didn't create them."

Kennissey stiffened. "Then who?"

"They're from the Atalans."

"That's a myth," the baron countered, disbelieving. "No one believes they really existed."

"They existed," William said confidently. "The Scourwind histories go back far into the pre-empire history. The Atalans most certainly existed."

"Then where did they go?"

William snorted. "Where do you think? They founded the empire."

"Scourwind . . ." The Baron breathed out, shocked.

"And half a handful of other bloodlines"—William nodded—"and only those bloodlines can link to an Armati, or even neural projection interfaces. Today there are millions in the empire with some hint of the blood, probably tens of millions, but most of it's thin. Scraping together enough men to fill a century of linked wielders? Effectively impossible, and growing harder with every passing generation. Another handful, and there won't be a single person left in the empire who can link to an Armati. Be thankful that projection links are far less stringent."

William paused, considering his words, then pressed on.

"Further," he said, "of those who *can* link to an Armati, only a fraction are physically and mentally capable of serving as Cadre."

Kennissey fell silent at that, wondering if his young friend and ally quite understood just what that meant, in political terms.

"This is explosive, William. You know that, right?"

"There is a reason Edvard, not to mention his predecessors, chose not to make it known."

Kennissey nodded, understanding the former emperor's thoughts on the matter. The Cadre were the arm of the empire. The ideal they represented was arguably the iron core that held the kingdom upright. While Imperial forces controlled the explored world, for all practical purposes, many of the outlying territories were under the Imperial flag in name only, and some weren't even that. Oh, they still bowed to the empire when the force of the legions were brandished in their direction, but like petulant children they pretended loudly that they held no fear even as they shook in their boots.

The legend and, yes, the reality of the Cadre—warriors worth a century of men and women on their own—and the idea that anyone in the empire could one day become such, was more powerful than a legion. The empire didn't have nearly enough legions to cover the known world, but legends? Those had no limits.

"I'll not speak of this," Kennissey swore. "I think maybe you should not have told me."

William nodded. "I know."

"So why then?"

"Because if Corian isn't stopped soon, the empire will begin to unravel . . . and you need to plan for a very different future."

"Understood." Kennissey sighed. "So what is next for you?"

"My oath makes that clear," William said wearily. "I have to locate the Scourwind heirs. But until I have another lead, I have a secondary task."

"And that is?"

"I need to ensure that there is an empire waiting for them when they're found," William said. "This idiotic fighting has to stop. The loyalists can't be facing Corian's legions in a battle line. Damned fools."

Kennissey merely nodded, having nothing in particular to add. Any commander who thought he could face a legion with a century or less should be so lucky to be considered a fool, and he would most certainly be damned.

"Well, good luck in your endeavors, my friend . . . and speedy travels."

*

"Brennan? Are you here?"

Brennan looked up as Lydia stepped into sight. "Hey, Lyd."

Lydia sighed, relieved, as she saw her brother working on the skimmer they'd escaped from the capital in. She winced at the same time, however, because he wasn't going to be happy with her.

"I brought food and a few supplies," she said.

Brennan stiffened, eyes snapping to look at her and the bundle she was holding in her arms. "You didn't."

"We needed food."

"Lyd, we're on the run from the empire," he said, exasperated. "Literally *everyone* is trying to get us. We can't just stroll into towns and get supplies."

He paused, confused. "Where did you get the money to pay for everything?"

She shot him a look, one that he'd long ago interpreted to mean *Don't ask! You won't like the answer.*

"Lyd . . ." He groaned. "What did you do?"

"It's not like they needed it," Lydia defended herself. "The guardsmen's stores had plenty for such a small garrison."

"Oh God, you *didn't*!" he hissed, shocked. "Lydia, that's insane! They monitor those stations! We have to move—"

"Please"—she rolled her eyes—"do I look like a technical illiterate? I looped the monitors before I walked in. They haven't changed the codes in over a year."

Brennan closed his eyes, groaning again.

While he was the natural flyer of the family, Lydia was something of the family criminal. Not that anyone was supposed to *know* that, of course. Oh, she preferred to think of herself as a security or technical specialist, but some of the things she'd done that he knew about made his delinquent acts pale by comparison. There were few secrets that she got the scent of that remained secret from Lydia for long, in his experience at least. More than one time in the past she'd narrowly avoided being caught stealing data from palace servers by expertly playing the bratty princess card to whomever came looking.

He only wished he could get away with half of what she managed.

"Lyd, we need to keep low. We've been getting by—"

Lydia rolled her eyes again. "On the survival pack in your skimmer and what pocket change we had when we ran? We were days from being starved out of your little cave here, Brennan, and you know it. Besides, we're far enough from the capital. No one here cares about the orders to take us in."

"Don't kid yourself, Lyd," Brennan said with derision. "There's nowhere far enough that they won't care about the orders to take us in. With father and Kayle . . . gone, we're the Scourwind heirs. Everyone is going to want a piece of us."

"Look, do you want to eat or not?" Lydia demanded, now quite put out. "I'll be happy with double rations."

He scowled and held a hand out. "Fine."

Victorious, Lydia smirked at him and dropped a ration pack into his hand. Brennan turned it over, noting that not only was it Imperial issue but it had the quartermaster's stamp on one side.

"Honestly"—he shook his head—"I can't believe that I'm the one everyone considered a delinquent."

"I always was the smarter twin." Lydia shot him a grin.

Brennan, well used to comments like that, just sighed. "I suppose that I'll have to settle for being the better-looking one."

The glare of pure death shot in his direction cheered Brennan up immensely as he thumbed the autoheat switch on the pack and set it down while it warmed. He had a few things left to do to his skimmer before he ate.

"How is it?" Lydia asked after a moment, knowing that the skimmer was about the only thing in the world they still owned.

"Ready to fly," he answered. "I just pulled the identification systems and blasted the numbers off the side. I'll paint some fake numbers on it, if I can find some paint. They won't stand up to a scan, but it's better that than the alternatives."

"I'll see if they're stocking any paint in the local stores," Lydia offered.

Brennan closed his eyes, taking a breath. "Please don't get caught, Lyd."

"Aw," she cooed at him, "are you worried about me, bro?"

"Less and less every time I talk to you, but yeah," Brennan said, drawing another glare from her. "We're in this together, Lyd. Stand or fall."

She nodded slowly. "Stand or fall."

"All right, tell me what I have to do," Brennan said, taking a breath.

"What?" Lydia looked puzzled.

"Lyd, I'm not letting you go back into town alone, and besides, two can carry more than one."

*

They left the skimmer in the cave they'd stashed it in, hiking the few miles to the edge of the small settlement. The two of them were moderately disguised, though they weren't too worried about being recognized. The empire was a big place, and the Imperial family—such as it was—didn't photograph as often as one might expect. Still, Lydia tied her dark hair up, and Brennan wore his flight cap and tinted goggles. He looked like a skimmer groupie, which was fair enough, he supposed, and she could pass for any of ten thousand young girls in the area.

They hoped, at least.

A commotion caught their attention, and the twins pulled back as they watched a long column of bedraggled men, women, and children come to a halt near the edge of the town, where tents were already being set up.

Brennan wanted to head back to the skimmer and preferably take flight before any more people arrived, but Lydia ignored his entreaties. Instead she grabbed the first person she could, one of the townsfolk who was watching the scene with morbid fascination.

"What's going on?" she asked.

He didn't look back at her. He was too intent on the people and the tents. "Refugees from the fighting out near the capital."

"I thought that was over weeks ago." Lydia blinked, genuinely confused.

"That was then, wasn't it?" He shrugged. "Word is that some senator or another thought the emperor was weak after the attempted coup."

Attempted? Lydia hardly knew what to think of that.

"The new high general put an end to that thinking, though, I'd warrant." The man grinned widely. "Corian's not one to lose a trick. I marched with him before I retired, about fifteen cycles back. He was just a captain then, but one look at him and you knew he was destined for better things."

High general? There's no such position . . . Lydia just nodded, affixing a fascinated look onto her face. *What in the burning skies is going on?*

She allowed Brennan to pull her away, withdrawing to a safe distance from all the commotion, where they could observe it for themselves and still be able to escape if anyone took note of them. It didn't seem likely that anyone would, however, as the attentions of every living soul were on the refugee column.

"Something's gotten out of hand," Brennan whispered. "This sort of thing won't sit well with anyone, not so close to the capital."

Lydia nodded absently, eyes flicking across the sea of dirty faces.

Conflict was commonplace along some of the empire's borders; it was almost expected in certain areas, even inside the empire. Father had once told them that some areas were like that by design, lawless and violent. People who desired to be lawless and violent had somewhere to go, a place with fewer laws and fewer lawmakers.

The best of those people were on the frontier, expanding the empire and adding to the wealth of the whole. The worst tended to congregate in the pits, isolated sections of the empire that no one in power cared about. Deaths in these regions were used to distract people, to remind them of just how well they had things. She'd thought it horrible, but knew that those who died in places like that weren't considered people by many in power, just numbers to be manipulated.

What she was seeing here, however, was something else. She wasn't certain *what* it was just yet, but it was certainly something else.

"We have to find out what happened," Lydia hissed back. "We *have* to."

"Why?" Brennan scoffed. "Not our problem anymore, if it ever was. Father played his games, and Kayle did too. Look what it got them. Kayle shot dead like an animal, and Father . . ."

He trailed off, shaking his head. "It's not our concern."

Lydia slapped him.

"Brennan Scourwind!" She glowered at him. "People are *dying*! Our family—"

"Is dead," he hissed angrily back, one hand to the side of his face that was glowing with heat, "because they served the empire and it turned on them. Do you really want to be next?"

Lydia took a deep breath, closing her eyes against the tears that threatened to fall. Not sadness, not anger. She didn't know how to describe what she felt, other than a great frustration at the world and its treatment of her family and everyone else within it.

"Do you remember what Father said about the strong and the weak?" she asked.

Brennan snorted. "Which thing he said? He spoke about such matters all the time. Don't tell me you want to protect the weak because we're *strong*, Lydia. We're two teenagers with only a skimmer and some stolen provisions between us. We're the definition of weak."

"No. We *are* strong," she said passionately. "We're Scourwind. Our family has stood against the storm for generations. We earned our name in flesh and blood. You and I may be the weakest of our family, but that still makes us *strong*."

She paused for a moment. "Father once told me that it is *not* the duty of the strong to protect the weak. Our duty is to take the weak and make them *strong*."

Brennan looked to her for a moment, shaking his head. "I'm not going to turn you from this, am I?"

"No, you will not."

"All right. What's the plan?"

The stumped look on Lydia's face was so profound that Brennan started laughing at her there and then.

The teen angrily stomped her feet, glaring at her brother. "Stop laughing at me!"

*

Corian sat stiffly on the throne, glowering at the projection display floating in front of him, furious with what he was reading.

"I want the military commanders we captured *shot*," he ordered. "Any sane man would know to bow against the force we marshaled. I don't care if they did believe they were being loyal to the empire; I won't tolerate that level of stupidity."

"Yes, sire."

For the most part his plan had progressed very nearly perfectly, but there were ugly shadows in the tapestry. Several officers had escaped the palace after the initial strikes, apparently with the intent of retrieving reinforcements. He could appreciate their determination, and was even thankful that they hadn't elected to go for the much more damaging option of forming an underground resistance, but the sheer waste of personnel and equipment they were fomenting was enough to drive him mad.

Over the weeks since the coup, Corian's forces had destroyed several centuries of men. Mostly mere guardsmen, certainly not people in any short supply, but the principle of the matter was absolute.

For the moment he'd been forced to maintain the illusion that a Scourwind still lived and sat on the throne of the empire, if only for the common fools on the streets. The Senate and the military ranks of consequence were well aware of who now wore the crown, and they were the only ones who mattered for now.

His day in the light was coming, sooner than some of his erstwhile *allies* would believe, but first he had to end this damnable waste.

CHAPTER 9

Field Marshal Groven sat tiredly in his command tent, staring at the projection display floating in front of him and willing it to change. Not through the link. Had he done that it would have changed on command, but that wasn't the sort of change he desired.

The damned traitors who'd taken the empire seemed to control far too much of its military resources. There was no way some jumped-up tyrant should have been able to take as much as had been lost, let alone control it, and yet the legions smashing his fellow loyalists spoke volumes about just that.

His fellow field marshals had done their best to stem the treason, but it was like attempting to blot the heat of the sun in the burning sky without the aid of one of the Great Islands. It seemed like for every square foot you succeeded, there were many square miles where you didn't.

The forces under the control of the mad general were blanketing this entire section of the empire faster than he'd have believed, cutting the resistance off from supplies and sanctuary. The fact that the *new* emperor had managed an effective disinformation campaign made it all the worse, confusing many regiments into staying quiet and leading others to brand the loyalists as traitors.

Groven was at a loss, but one thing he knew was certain: he and his fellows could *not* let this stand.

That lunatic will be the end of the empire if we don't stop him here, now.

He reached for a panel to open communications with his adjutant but froze as he felt a cold point dig into his throat.

"Just what do you think you're doing?" a voice demanded coldly in his ear.

"Wha—?" Honestly, Groven had a hard time thinking, given the blade at his throat, and barely understood the question.

"You're wasting Imperial resources and getting Imperial subjects killed with your idiocy," William Everett growled, stepping around so he could be seen and recognized.

"Everett! What are you—*urk*—"

William cut him off with a slight jab of his Armati, keeping the field marshal in his seat. "You don't have the forces to face Corian in open combat, you imbecile."

"We can't just let him take . . ."

William ignored the strangled sound as he again jabbed the marshal in the throat. "Shut up. Listen."

He sighed, flipping the Armati back as the blade withdrew into the contoured grip.

"Corian holds the high ground," he said. "His position is unassailable at present. If you'd been halfway intelligent, you'd have gone to ground yourself and played the part of a loyal little minion, all the while networking and readying yourself for a proper resistance."

He stepped back and turned around, eyes falling on the tactical map of the region that Groven had been examining.

"That, unfortunately, is no longer an option."

"So what do you suggest—"

William spun back, hand coming up in a sharp gesture. "Shut up. Listen."

Groven fell back, silent.

"You are going to pack up camp tonight. Fade," William ordered. "Like a bad dream Corian doesn't want to remember. Take your men, every piece of gear you can lay your hands on, and just . . . fade."

Groven glared at him, still silent. William sighed. "You can speak now."

The field marshal continued to glower, but slowly stood to look evenly at William.

"And just what, pray tell, do you intend to do while I . . . fade?" he asked distastefully.

William turned back to the projection, ignoring the question. He pointed out a dot on the map. "What's this?"

"Refugees," Groven answered, "from the fighting. We sent them to a neutral township outside Corian's direct influence. I considered sending them to an allied duchy, however . . ."

"No point attracting Corian to allies before it's time," William said with a nod. "For the same reason, you need to go somewhere similar. Don't hide with people who oppose Corian. We don't want to draw his attention until we're ready."

"Ready for what?"

"For the heirs to the empire to take their rightful place."

Groven stiffened. "You have a Scourwind? One escaped?"

"Two."

"Two?" Groven looked puzzled, then winced. "Not the twins. Burning skies. They're contemptible, spoiled children."

"They're Scourwinds." William was in no mood to debate the actions of two teenagers he had enough doubts about himself. "The last two in the direct line."

"There are cadet lines of the blood. Surely . . ."

"They. Are. Scourwinds."

Groven held up his hands. "Fine. It's on your head, then. Where are they?"

William grimaced, shaking his head.

"You don't know?" Groven snorted. "We might be in luck after all."

"Don't," William warned, gesturing with his fingers. "Just don't."

Groven shrugged. "As I said, fine. So you're going to be looking for the brats while I *fade*, then?"

"Among other things," William told him, extending a metal card to him. "These are the coordinates of a place you can get lost in. There are . . . supplies there. I'll send your fellow marshals—the ones who survived this idiocy, at least."

Groven glared at him again, but William ignored him and turned to leave.

He paused near the exit, glancing back. "Don't get any more people killed before we meet again. Corian is bad enough. We cannot afford to be our own worst enemies as well."

Then the Cadreman was gone and Groven collapsed back into his seat, taking a deep breath.

Burning skies. I hate dealing with those bastards.

Cadremen were nearly untouchable in the empire, and not merely for political reasons. When one went rogue, as happened from time to time, you either sent other Cadre after him or you prepared yourself to bury a lot of your police force. Certainly they were neither immortal nor invincible, but they were beyond the ken of most mortals.

Surviving the experience of having one of them *annoyed* with you was enough to shave a few years off your life all the same.

*

A few days had passed since the refugees had moved into the area, and for the Scourwind twins, they'd not been pleasant ones. It was easy to slip into the new mass of people, hiding their identities and listening to what had happened. Lydia, in particular, was horrified by what they'd learned.

In the aftermath of the coup at the palace it seemed that several centuries of men had openly opposed the new regime, but they were seen as rebels rather than loyalists. The general consensus among the populace, so far as they could tell, was that a Scourwind had survived the attack . . . though no one could say which it was.

So the men, women, and children of the refugee band all believed that they were on the run from the retributive attacks by the empire, on command of a Scourwind.

As bad as that was, however, what Lydia was seeing firsthand was almost worse.

"These people are starving," she hissed to Brennan as they toured the camp. "They don't even have enough water for everyone."

Brennan nodded. "I don't understand why. There's a garrison not three miles from here. Maybe they don't have enough food, but the moisture condensers should keep a legion served indefinitely."

Lydia was quiet for a moment before she spoke. "I think the empire recalled the garrison. When I broke in, there was barely a token guard."

Brennan shot her an amused glance. After he'd gotten over the fact that she'd put herself at risk when she'd broken into the garrison for rations, he'd asked her about how she did it. Lydia had told a somewhat more dashing story than "there was barely a token guard."

"All right," he said. "What can we do about it?"

"I'm not sure," she admitted. "We can't exactly tell anyone who we are—"

"No, we *can't*," he cut her off, putting his foot down.

Brennan was willing to entertain a lot of his sister's ideas, but he drew the line well before *that*.

Lydia just nodded, showing no notice of his tone. "And without our name for credibility, I don't think anyone is going to listen to a couple of teenagers."

Brennan shrugged but didn't argue. She wasn't wrong, though he'd heard enough rumors to wonder just how much credibility the Scourwind name would really hold. "For the record, I vote we take my skimmer and find someplace quieter."

That caught her attention, but a glare was the only answer he got.

"All right"—he sighed—"then all I can say is what we were always taught, Lyd. If you've got a huge problem, break it down into pieces and solve them one by one."

Lydia nodded slowly. "Right. We can't solve it all at once, so let's deal with what we can . . . Come on, I want to look around a bit more."

Both twins had learned from a young age how to fade into crowds, to appear as if they belonged but not like they were particularly important. It might seem an odd skill set for a pair of pampered kids from the emperor's blood, but neither of them had been particularly interested in wandering around with bodyguards surrounding them at all times, so they'd had to figure out a way to keep said guards from finding them after they'd ditched their escorts.

So the twins inconspicuously made their way through the refugee camp, watching everything with eyes glittering.

Men, women, and children were collapsed along the side of the makeshift roadway, most clearly injured or exhausted beyond reasonable measures. Neither of the twins had medical training, but they could recognize blaster burns and shrapnel injuries, the sort of thing you only saw in a real fight.

They'd both seen their fair share of those, which often struck people not close to the Imperial Court as surprising. Both of the twins had survived several assassination attempts in their young lives, and though most seemed to believe that the attempts were more likely warnings than real tries to see them in their pyres, it didn't lesson the injuries to those who had been sworn to protect them.

Death was an old friend to any Scourwind, but normally it came quickly on the beam of a blaster, not from the slow descent into starvation.

A scuffle ahead of them caught their attention, and they made their way quietly toward it. A single young boy, about their age, was standing over a weak figure of a girl. Five others surrounded them, trying to steal the girl's blanket and a small bag that the twins presumed contained what little she still owned. The boy they'd first noticed was fighting viciously, but it was clear he wasn't going to last much longer.

Around them a few others looked on, some with concern and some with varying degrees of disinterest. No one had the energy or, apparently, the desire to intervene, much to Brennan's disgust.

"Bren . . ." Lydia softly spoke up.

"I've got lead. Follow me in and watch for stragglers."

Lydia nodded firmly. The two stepped up their pace and angled their approach to close in on the attackers' uncovered flank.

Under other circumstances, Kayle would have been disappointed in them for getting into a fight, Lydia reflected as Brennan launched his attack. He snap kicked the knee of the closest attacker, then followed through with a palm thrust to the shoulder that sent the man hard to the ground. There was a cracking sound when his knee met dirt, probably a dislocation, thought Lydia as she stayed close to Brennan but let him take the offensive actions.

They'd been trained in the basics of fighting most of their lives, but Kayle had always told them to never call attention to themselves. Enough attention rained down on them as a matter of course; anything else was superfluous and could actually give their enemies information that could be used against them.

Before the others could react, Brennan swept the next man with enough force to take him off his feet, then dove at two others and got them in a headlock as he drove them to the ground with all his weight. Lydia casually snap kicked the second target as he struggled to get up, putting his lights out with the edge of her foot. She stayed focused on the last attacker, who was rushing in to help his two compatriots as they struggled on the ground with Brennan.

She met him with a heel kick, launched straight out from her core and braced directly to the ground via her other leg. The air rushed out of his lungs and he collapsed, curling up on the ground and only moving to gasp and moan.

Lydia looked around and then down to where Brennan was still struggling with his last pair. "You good?"

"Sure," Brennan gasped as he winked at her. "The hard part is not snapping their necks when they struggle, Lyd, you know that."

Lydia smirked very slightly as the duo went very still at those words, and she shook her head slightly. Brennan was always a better master of wordplay and psychological games in fights than she was. Normally he used it to drive his minders mad, of course.

She turned her attention to the two they'd stepped in to help, appraising them carefully. They were both clearly hungry, like everyone else, but their dehydration was obvious. Water wasn't exactly hard to come by in the empire, but it wasn't precisely easy to get either. Rains habitually swept most regions, even the deserts, but there were few natural sources available.

Water that fell from the skies just . . . vanished into the ground.

No one really knew where it went, and people had dug hundreds of feet down without finding any hint of moisture. In fact, past a couple hundred feet it was like there had never *been* any water.

Unfortunately that meant that there were few streams, lakes, and the like, and if you didn't have a condenser or a good aquifer available, then you could easily go thirsty waiting for the rains. Imperial garrisons were all well equipped, of course, and every town had both emergency supplies and a reasonably outfitted aquifer for their needs. But the closest town to their current location was far too small for the number of people present, and the garrison had been locked down with only a token number of low-ranking guards remaining, who were unlikely to do anything without orders.

The legion should be here already, but if these people are running from battles, then they could die before things get under control and anyone has time to wonder what happened to them, thought Lydia.

"Thank you," the boy croaked out, collapsing to the ground and just sitting there as he panted for breath.

Lydia nodded simply. "Are you OK?"

"I'll live," he said tiredly, "for a while anyway."

His eyes darted to one side, to the girl, and he moved to her in a flash.

"I'm fine," the girl mumbled, pushing him back.

Lydia could hear the dry rasp in her voice. She pulled a waterskin from under her cloak and tossed it to the duo. "Here."

They held it between them, stunned and disbelieving, transfixed by the flexible synthetic pouch holding the liquid. Lydia let them take turns drinking, turning back to Brennan, who was just now getting up and dusting himself off.

"That took you long enough," she said dryly.

He tried to look nonchalant. "I wasn't kidding about it being harder to leave them alive than otherwise," he said as he watched the attackers straggle off.

He looked around, noting the stares they were now getting, and grimaced slightly.

"We'd best be moving, Lyd," he said. "Too many folks eyeing us up."

Lydia looked around and saw that some of the refugees were also eyeing up the young duo they'd just saved. She knew instantly that if they left them here, the pair would be considered easy pickings.

"You two shouldn't stay here," she finally said. "Join us, if you like."

Brennan shot her an incredulous look, hissing softly, "Lyd . . ."

She didn't look at him. Lydia had seen what she needed to see in this mess. The good, the bad, and the apathetic. The bad she would see on their knees, the good at her back, and the apathetic would awake or they would end here. She didn't much care which.

She turned to Brennan and nodded, and the two of them started to walk away as the pair on the ground glanced at each other and then scrambled to their feet to follow.

*

William was a tired soul as he made his way back toward the capital. Since the coup he'd been running doggedly around the empire, both searching for the twins and fleeing pursuit. The new emperor—for that was certainly what Corian was—was no fool. He knew just how dangerous the Cadre would be to his rule, and he put every loyal man he had to task hunting down people just like William.

Between fleeing pursuit and hunting for the twins, William was trying to get some manner of organization into place for the resistance. It was rough going, for few people really understood just what had happened. If things continued as they were, then Corian would soon have full command of the empire and all the power held within.

Honestly, William wasn't certain that Corian wouldn't secure command no matter what happened. He'd managed to gain too much of an advantage in his opening move. Too many people flew to his banner. The Scourwind emperor and his true allies hadn't realized just how much people had chafed under Edvard's rule.

William expected that it had been the corporatist lobby that had thrown the final edge of weight to Corian's side. Edvard hadn't liked the way they did business, and he suspected that reopening the Imperial manufacturing group to handle military orders had been a step too far.

Edvard was possibly too much of an idealist for the position he'd held, though William found the idea of anyone considering the emperor an idealist to be almost hilarious. When he had a conviction, however, all the fires in the skies couldn't turn him from it. William had himself argued with Edvard many times. They rarely saw perfectly eye to eye, but he'd served the family loyally because he knew that Edvard did what he believed best, damn the cost.

This time, perhaps, the cost had been his life.

And now William was left to pick up the pieces and perform at least one last service to the family.

First he had to figure out where the resistance was getting their supplies from. Someone was feeding them enough foodstuffs, water, and munitions to keep legions on the march, and they were doing it on extremely short notice.

Where are they getting all the legion specification ordinance? Corian must have locked down all the major supply depots. I would have.

CHAPTER 10

"The Four Nineteen is inbound, tracking hot and normal on skyway nine."

The station commander nodded as he lifted his drink to his lips and took a quiet draw on the hot liquid. The Four Nineteen was a regular commuter and transport train coming in from the capital—three hundred freight canisters, fifty-odd passenger capsules, and half a handful of mail and live cargo capsules all pulled by a single quantum-tractor rig.

The system wasn't the fastest ever devised, but a q tractor would pull almost *anything* without flinching. The vehicle was locked into the skyway through subparticle entangling, and it would take a major act of the universe to shift it from its path.

Perched on a narrow spire that reached down to the ground, the tower was the local control hub for all traffic for three days' travel in all directions. Situated just above the atmosphere from his station, the commander could see the world's curve as it wrapped around him until finally vanishing into the haze.

The commander glanced over the numbers and nodded absently, starting to turn away to focus on other things, when a warning sound caught his attention.

"What's that?"

"Proximity warning. We have a ship on a converging track, commander."

His eyes flicked up, looking out the thickly armored translim shields that surrounded the control tower, searching for the intruder. "Warn them off."

"Sent. No response."

"Lens," the commander ordered, hand out expectantly.

A slim chromatic glass device was dropped into his palm without hesitation, and he lifted it to his eyes, letting it seal itself to his face as designed. The internal optics went into action, picking up and highlighting traffic around the tower, but he was only interested in one craft.

There it is, he thought as the lens locked in and magnified the desired signal. It was a skimmer, a high atmo vessel that rode the extreme wind currents that existed about thirty miles above the surface of the world.

He swore, annoyed. "Get those fools on the box, damn it. They've deployed for full sail. One gust will send them right into someone else up here."

"There's still no response, commander."

"Best call up emergency stations," he ordered, "and contact the Guard. I want that damn fool's head on a platter when this is over."

"Yes, sir."

He turned his focus back outward, wondering what the fool was playing at. Flying with full rigging into controlled aerospace was the height of stupidity. Even Guard flyers weren't insane enough to try something like that.

Hathe below. It would take a Cadre pilot to even . . .

His thoughts trailed off as he looked up sharply, a sudden stab of genuine fear running through him as he strode forward and slammed a hand down on the station alert.

"Commander! What?"

"I want every guardsman converging on us, *now*!" he ordered. "Only two types of people fly like that. Cadre . . . and *former* Cadre."

*

"The station just lit off their alarms."

"Too late by far." The captain smiled as she nodded. "Signal borders, they're clear to go."

"Yes, ma'am."

On the command deck of the high-atmo craft, she rose from her station and stepped back and out of the shelter of the partially enclosed cockpit. They were high enough over the world to require breathers, their ship skimming near the edge of the empty beyond where only ships with reactor or q-traction drives could go.

Her skimmer, the lovely *Andros Pak*, was a medium-size high-atmo bird. With her rigging deployed below to catch the eternal winds, the ship was damn near as fast as any reactor vessel and had the wings to leave them sucking vacuum when their fuel rods failed.

On the open deck, men were readying themselves for the deployment as ordered. The captain would have had their heads if they'd done anything else, but it was still a good feeling to see everything going to plan.

The traction drive they were converging on was entering the upper atmo. She could see the long train extending air brakes to help bleed the velocity off. It took so long to accelerate using a traction drive that they generally preferred to use friction brakes to slow down.

It also served to keep the long train of capsules and canisters from bunching up and snarling if the tractor itself attempted to slow.

"Intercept in ten mikes!" she called as the warning tone sounded in her ear. "By the numbers, people, you know what we need."

The suited men waved. The low pressure wasn't suited to speaking, and no one wanted to transmit, not with the empire listening.

The tractor train was in full view now, heat bleed making the leading edges of the formation glow red hot. The men prepped their gear in the last few moments before the range closed, then the order went out and the time for preparation was done.

Lines lanced out from the *Andros*, arcing only slightly in the low air pressure and low gravity of the upper atmo, impacting the closing train with precision. Using filament lines was a little old school, the captain supposed, but she was doing what she could with what she had.

"Tension the lines!" she called, gesturing with her hand.

The *Andros* leaned slightly away from the oncoming train, bringing the lines taut with a twang that could be heard even in the high atmo. She nodded curtly to the men, and they threw themselves over the side.

She watched them glide across, flying on almost invisible lines, then smiled to herself as she stepped up to the side and casually flipped her blaster from her belt and glanced over her shoulder.

"Your ship, old friend," she called before leaping off herself. "I'll see you when we're done."

*

The commander of the tower swore under his breath, using words that would make even a guardsman blush as he recognized, too late, the situation for what it was.

"Pirates," he swore, almost more angry at himself than at the criminal swine flying outside his station.

In the months since the regent took over the empire, piracy had been on the climb, malcontents looking for any sign of weakness in the armor of the state so they could act. There was no weakness, but some of them would still succeed. Most would be stamped out, but as he watched their actions and checked the network for the guardsmen's response time, he didn't think this bunch would be among them.

Not yet anyway.

That's former Cadre all right. No one else coordinates like that.

He'd been a guardsman himself in his younger years, but though he'd taken the aptitude tests for Cadre—everyone did, at least once—he'd never been considered for a slot.

He'd heard that some of the group's former members had bought into the conspiracy bullshit about the regent overthrowing the Imperial Family, but he'd thought they were just rumors. No one with any sense believed that nonsense for an instant.

There was nothing more dangerous than an insane Cadreman with a cause, however, and the Cadre was composed of men and women like everyone else. No matter how skilled and powerful they were, they still made mistakes, still believed nonsense.

"What do we do, commander?"

"Do?" he snorted. "Nothing to do. We hit the alarm. Now all we can do is watch the brazen bastards and hope they don't kill anybody."

*

"Get that disrupter into position," she ordered. "I want all the passenger capsules off this line in three mikes, or you'll have to answer to me."

The men didn't respond, bending to their task as she jogged along the line of cars, easily hopping the space between each car despite the gap being over ten times her own height. The lesser gravity of being forty-plus miles up came in handy sometimes.

She slowed as she arrived at the traction engine, giving one last hop and tucking her arms and legs in close as she dropped between the cars and came to a stop on the engineer's landing at the back of the engine. The hatch unlatched without a fuss, and she wrenched it open. It was easier than it should have been. The interior was pressurized, and she had to twist out of the path of the door before it could knock her out into the clear skies beyond.

It was a long way down.

The engineer and mate were scrambling for breathers when she stepped in, and she gently tapped the pommel of her blaster against a wrought handgrip to get their attention.

"Gentlemen," she said, "a moment of your time, if you please."

The two looked at her, clearly out of their depth and likely wondering where the hell she'd come from.

It wasn't often that someone boarded an engine in flight, especially just after it had breached atmo. She wasn't planning on giving them time to come to terms with these new circumstances.

"Retract the air brakes," she ordered.

"We'll crash into the tower!"

Her grip shifted slightly on the blaster, and the gaping maw of the weapon turned toward the engineer. She rested the tip against his throat. "Did I ask for your expert opinion?"

"N-no."

"Then pull in those brakes," she ordered again. "And let me worry about what we'll crash into . . . or I can toss you off right here and pull them in myself. You choose."

The cold delivery of the statement probably convinced him more than the words, but whatever it was, the engineer only hesitated a moment longer before nodding and dropping back into his seat. A tap on the controls unlocked the system, and then he pulled the big hydraulic levers back one by one until they were in the closed position.

Fearfully, he looked back at the woman. "N-now what?"

She smiled, which would have almost made her beautiful if it weren't for the sardonic twist of her lips and the cold gleam in her eye. The captain leaned in as she reached over him and tapped commands into the controls. "Now watch and learn something they don't teach you at your little engineering academy."

*

When the air brakes retracted on the Four Nineteen, the commander almost needed a new pair of pants. Things didn't get any better when his scanner tech spoke, his voice shaking and unsteady.

"Commander, the Four Nineteen is accelerating again."

He didn't curse this time, but only because he was too caught up in visualizing the results of the tractor engine slamming all that mass right into his tower, accelerating all the way. The tower was constructed of crystallized carbon in chain molecules, one of the hardest and strongest materials in existence, but even that wouldn't stand up to a traction sled with thirty million tons of material backing it.

The skyway ended before impact, of course, but that much weight would jump the quantum fold in space-time with almost no effort. At hypersonic speed, the tower would be decapitated before they could even begin evacuations.

After that, well, it was a long way down to a *very* abrupt stop at the bottom.

*

Quantum-locked states made for interesting and spectacular visuals on the smaller scale, particularly as a demonstration of quantum levitation.

For a traction rig, the effect was largely similar. A superconducting system with sufficient power running through it could actually bend space-time sufficiently to create an artificial "track." Once that existed, then all you had to do was lock a traction rig into it, and you could generate propulsion of immense power by "crawling" along the twisted section of space-time.

Acceleration wasn't impressive, but low-end power truly was. A traction rig would effectively tow anything that wasn't itself locked into place, either via a quantum lock or a vast enough gravity field (which was, in many ways, the same thing).

That made the system ideal for bulk transport and a low-cost passenger service. Since initial acceleration was slow, however, it was really only useful for long distances where velocity could be built up gradually to incredible speeds, with braking applied rapidly toward the end of the run.

Few people, other than some of the designers of the system, were aware that it was possible to make a traction-engine jump track. That was mostly because there was so little point to it. Once free of the quantum track, the traction engine no longer had any, well, *traction*. Without the track to crawl along, it would spin its proverbial wheels.

Of course, even fewer people were aware of certain other minutiae of the system.

*

The traction engine jolted slightly, and the captain smiled. The passenger cars had been disconnected, and they'd slow to a stop before the end of the skyway. She had nothing against, nor any use for, the peons traveling from the capital to work their dead-end jobs.

Her interests lay elsewhere.

A figure dropped in the back of the engine, but she only bothered to tilt her head slightly in acknowledgment.

"We're clear and cut, skipper."

"Excellent," she said with a thin smile. "Hold on. This is going to get a little rough."

"We're going to crash! We have to get off this thing or we're dead!" The engineer was panicking.

The captain calmly backhanded him out of his seat, entering another command into the console. "If you really believe that, you're a sorry piece of work. You should have died rather than set those air brakes back."

The traction engine and the rest of the train continued to accelerate to the end of the line as she braced herself, withdrawing her Armati Elan back to its compact form and holstering it at her side. She planted her feet wide, gripped the back of the engineer's chair, and grinned wildly as the train struck the end of the line at ten times the speed of sound . . . and accelerating.

As the engineer predicted, they jumped the space-time fold like it wasn't there. There was barely a bump as the traction engine bore on through, heading for the tower with thirty million tons of material hauled right along behind it.

A moment later, however, the engine suddenly jerked hard to the right as it locked into another skyway and continued to do what it was told.

Accelerate.

In the engine room, the engineer and his mate were flung against the wall, not having braced, and lay there, stunned, as they looked at the woman with the flowing red hair who'd hijacked them. The wind from the open hatch blew her hair and loose clothes about as she laughed wildly, holding on as the entire train redirected away from the tower and headed back up into the empty vacuum above.

*

He'd flinched.

He didn't mind admitting it.

When the engine jumped the skyway track, he'd thought it was his last moment of life. When nothing had happened a few seconds later, he'd reluctantly opened one eye, and then the other popped open wide at what he saw.

The engine had apparently locked onto another skyway and was happily pulling up and away from the tower as it headed out into the clear vacuum above. He stared for a long moment as canister after canister of invaluable cargo just sailed right past his tower and then glanced back at the now slowing capsules containing passengers; he swore as he realized what was happening.

"Find out what skyway they're on *now*," the commander ordered, still a little numb and unbelieving, "and get rescue flying. I want those people off the capsules before they lose q lock. Without the engine powering them, we don't have more than a few minutes."

"Yes, commander!"

The pirate skimmer was now under full rigging, dropping low behind its wind turbines as it tightened up for speed and angled to follow the departing engine and train. He focused in on its markings and swore again—loudly.

"Commander?"

"It's the *Andros*."

"What's the *Andros*, sir?"

"The skimmer," he said. "It's the *Andros Pak*. An Imperial yacht stolen from the emperor's own hangar last month."

His subordinate stared at him, wide-eyed. "Who could do that? Who would be *crazy* enough to even try?"

He didn't blame him for wondering. If you wanted to steal a yacht, there were easier ones to grab—hell, there were easier *military* vessels to grab.

"Cadre Commander Mira Delsol," he said, shaking his head.

*

Mira hopped the short distance from the traction engine to where the *Andros* was edging alongside, accepting a hand from her mate to steady her as she landed.

"Any problems?" he asked.

"Smooth as silken sheets, Gaston," she said with a sly smile. "A perfect mission."

"Good. Next time, perhaps you'll stay on board? You are the skipper."

Mira shrugged simply, uninterested in the debate.

"I'm the skipper of a pirate skimmer, Gas," she said, smirking just slightly. "Fuck the rules."

Her mate just sighed and clapped her on the shoulder as she passed.

"Hot tea is ready in your stateroom. I'll oversee the rest."

"Just make sure they jump tracks a few times, or the guardsmen will get them," she warned.

Gaston rolled his eyes. "I may not be your grandpa, Mira, but I know how to pluck a grapha fruit. Go get some food and leave the menial work to the people who do it best."

She snorted. "You're one of the empire's top engineers, Gas. Pull the other one."

"If they get you, I'm a smear on the wall," he told her seriously, "which is why I'd appreciate it if you showed a little more caution."

"If you wanted safe, you should have stayed with the empire."

He watched her go, shaking his head.

"No amount of safety is worth selling my eternal pattern, Mira."

*

"Letting them come with us is a risk, Lyd."

Lydia shrugged as she and Brennan walked with the pair they'd saved, who were currently struggling to catch up. The twins adjusted their pace carefully so that it wouldn't be too hard for them to catch up, but they wouldn't make it too easy for the stricken teens. If they were the sort to give up, neither Scourwind wanted them at their back.

"Hang on," the boy said as he reached the siblings first. "My sister's not in great shape."

Lyd and Brennan exchanged glances and nodded slightly, slowing almost imperceptibly in response.

"I'm Mikael," the boy said, breathing hard from just the short rush. "This is my sister, D—"

"Dusk," the girl said, catching up. "I'm Dusk."

"Good to meet you," Lydia said neutrally. "I'm Lydia. This is Brennan."

"Thank you both," Mikael said tiredly, Dusk nodding beside him. "Both for helping and for . . ." He held up the waterskin and shrugged.

"Don't worry about it," Brennan said curtly. "We're leaving the camp, so if there's anyone you want to go back to, you may want to do it now."

"We don't have anyone," Dusk said softly. "Our family was caught in the cross fire . . ."

She stopped, looking down, and the other three teens found that they didn't have any words to fill the silence. Brennan and Lydia both flashed back to watching Kayle as he went down under fire from the soldiers who'd invaded the palace.

"Yeah . . ." It was Lydia who finally spoke. "We lost ours too."

"Look, I'm all for sentiment," Brennan lied, "but we've got to get moving."

"We're not allowed to leave," Dusk whispered, eyes rising to where the perimeter of the camp was being patrolled.

Brennan snorted. "We snuck in. We can sneak out."

The two other teens stared at them both with a sort of horrified awe.

"Why in the burning skies would you sneak *in*?" Mikael asked, his tone hushed.

"We have our reasons," Lydia said. "Now come on. If you're with us, you're going to need to learn to move quickly and quietly."

CHAPTER 11

Cadrewoman Delsol glared over the table at the man in a legionnaire colonel's uniform, though she knew damn well he had no right to that rank. The chaos left in the aftermath of the coup had splintered the ranks, and field promotions were flowing quickly in the loyalist camps as well as more than a few self-given bumps in rank.

That wasn't why she was pissed with the fool sitting in front of her, though.

"The empire is grateful for your aid in the war effort," he told her, a smarmy smile on his face. "However, we simply don't have the available funds to complete the agreed deal. You'll have to wait until the next—"

"Listen to me, you smug, hopped-up piece of sky shit," she growled out slowly, cutting him off. "I'm loyal to the Scourwind empire. I've pledged my blade, my blood to them. My men are loyal to the empire as well, but they are *soldiers*. Soldiers get *paid*. They don't fight for the honor, and duty fills no stomachs. If you want the shipment, you're going to pay for it. Burning skies, man, it's not like I'm asking for even a third of the value of the lot!"

"Be that as it may"—the hopped-up colonel shrugged, smirking at her—"you'll just have to wait."

"How long are you planning on making my men wait for their pay?" Mira growled.

"Could be some time. This is a war after all."

Some time my ass. Mira scowled. It was clear that the rumors she'd been tracking were, in fact, true. The loyalists were *losing*. Badly.

Everything she'd heard said that the Scourwinds were no more, that the Cadre were scattered to the wind, and that Corian was solidly in power and gaining ground with every passing day. She'd continued to funnel whatever aid and supplies to the loyalists that she could, partially out of loyalty to the empire she'd pledged to serve but mostly because it was a way to stick a blade into Corian's eye.

Someday she wanted to do that personally, but for now she was willing to settle for living her dream vicariously through others. But that ended *now*.

"No payment, no supplies," she said, her tone flat as she let her temper flow from her body like dross from a metal forge.

The "colonel" smiled superiorly at her. "Need I really remind you just how many troops I have in the immediate area, and just how few you have?"

"You only live so long as I allow it," she countered. "None of your troops are close enough to save you from me."

His face twitched as that struck home, but surprisingly he didn't back down.

"Yes, that's true enough," he told her. "Unfortunately for you, the colonel was well aware of that."

She twitched as she realized that the reason he was wearing a rank he hadn't earned was for an entirely different reason than she'd thought. Her head cocked slightly to one side as she heard the distinct clunk of a blaster round loading into the combustion chamber.

"Now, Cadrewoman, if you value your crew, you'll surrender peaceably," the fake colonel said, his voice only slightly shaking to betray the nerves he felt. "The bounty on you is such that—"

Mira's blaster practically leapt into her hand, roaring once as she started to spin. The lased blast took the fake colonel midsternum, vaporizing flesh, blood, and bone the size of a fist from the shocked man's body. The explosive ejection of the plasma from the vaporized material pitched him back over his chair and to the ground as she finished her move, dropping to one knee as her free hand closed over her weapon grip to steady her shot.

The blaster roared three more times, mowing down the guards who were rushing in to take her with a clean efficiency. Before they hit the ground, Mira activated her comm line back to the skimmer.

"Gas, report."

Gaston's voice came back. "I'm seeing movement around the *Andros*, skipper."

"Betrayal, Gas," she said in a dull tone that sent shivers down the back of the man on the other side of the comm line. "Raise the black flag."

"Aye, skipper."

Mira Delsol rose from her kneeling position, blaster in hand, and strode out of the legion tent. Beyond the synthetic fabric walls, she could hear the guns of the *Andros* open fire. A dark smile was pasted on her face against a dull bored look. She was already running enhanced, deep in her own mind as her body walked out and into the chaos.

*

On the command bridge of the *Andros*, Gaston looked over the field they'd landed in and noted just how badly things had turned on them. The loyalist forces numbered no more than a few companies, but that was a few companies more than the crew of the *Andros*.

He swore, slamming his hand down on the console to send up the black flag as ordered.

The light-sail projectors erupted to life, putting a rippling image above the ship of a black flag with a crossed Armati and blaster over the skipper's own Cadre emblem. It wasn't subtle, but it made a point, and the *Andros* was moving to battle stations instantly.

They'd hijacked the *Andros* from an Imperial yard. The little luxury skimmer had originally been commissioned by the Scourwind family for their personal use. Unlike almost every other vessel of its class, the *Andros* was more than a pretty face. Gunports slammed open along port and starboard, the ship-mounted blasters roaring almost in unison.

That should set the bastards back on their heels for a moment, Gaston thought with satisfaction. *Come on, skipper, get your ass back here.*

*

Mira was walking on the balls of her feet, a light feeling making her almost bounce like a giddy schoolchild. Anyone experienced with the Cadre would have given her a wide berth just on seeing that stride alone, but none of those nearby knew this.

The first attack came from her left. She watched it from the corner of one eye with an almost disappointed feeling. Mira reached out at the last moment, grabbing the arm of the attacker and yanking hard enough to lift the poor man off his feet. She held him aloft like a shield as a barrage of blaster bolts rained down, tearing his armor and back to shreds, and watched the life fade from his eyes before letting him drop.

A part of her mind knew that when she came out of enhancement, she'd feel bad about that.

For the moment, however, she merely answered the shots with blasts of her own. The blaster in her hand bucked as the explosively lased material was ejected from the barrel. A hand blaster was controllable on rapid fire, but only just, and there was a trick to it. The weapon had been balanced to drive the force directly back, so if you held it precisely right, you could keep on target with little trouble.

Few managed it, but she was Cadre. She could do it in her sleep.

She walked through the confusion of the battle untouched, as if nothing could harm her in all the world. Anything that got too close met its end at the impact of a bolt from her blaster, but honestly, few even seemed to notice her once the black flag snapped into being above the *Andros* and the big skimmer began to shift in the soft dirt.

The sails caught the winds a thousand yards up, pulling the *Andros* along and leaving a deep furrow in the ground behind her as the big blasters roared from her gunports. A luxury yacht suddenly turning out to be a heavily armed gunship tended to attract an inordinate amount of attention.

The *Andros* was picking up speed, heading in her direction, when it took off. Barely three yards off the ground, it flashed over her head and she casually jumped up and caught a grip on one of the lower ports. The shock was nearly enough to dislocate her arm, but Mira ignored it as she pulled herself up hand over hand. She tipped her head to the surprised face of one of the gunners, and then heaved herself over the foredeck and landed in a sprawl.

Footsteps approached, but she ignored them for a moment as she came down from enhancement.

"That was shaving things a tad closer than I'd like to see in the future, my lady," Gaston told her as he helped her to her feet.

"Wasn't the plan."

"Aye, and that's the problem," he countered dryly. "We should have known one of those types was going to turn on us once the tide was clearly in Corian's favor."

She sighed, nodding.

It was a glaring oversight on her part to believe that the loyalists would be . . . loyal.

"Well, we know better now," she said tiredly. "We'll do better."

"True enough, but it's a pity they got the shipment."

A white flash erupted behind them, and a moment later a thunderclap rocked the *Andros*. Gaston was thrown about, but Mira stood firmly planted on the deck. She straightened her back and lifted her jaw.

"I may not have seen the betrayal coming, Gaston," she told him, "but I was prepared in the event of Corian's forces overtaking us. Those traitorous bastards will not profit off our blood and sweat."

Gaston and the crewmembers who were in earshot looked back at the cloud rolling across the sky and then at the skipper as she began her march back to the *Andros*'s bridge.

"What now, my lady?"

Mira didn't look back to see who'd asked the question. In this case it didn't matter. It was what everyone wanted to know.

"Now we sail," she said, "and we do what we do. Our empire may have fallen, but we haven't. If we're to be outlaws in this new world . . . then we will be *legendary* outlaws."

She climbed up the steps to the flying bridge and stepped behind the wheel.

They were at a thousand yards and climbing. The wind was whipping across the deck as the gleaming light sails rode higher up into the stronger winds and the rippling black flag rolled out behind them.

She spun the wheel, and the *Andros* keeled over in instant response. "Let them all go to the burning skies. We'll see to our own."

*

"We really shouldn't be here," said Mikael.

"Shouldn't?" Dusk whispered to her brother. "Forget that. *How* are we here?"

The twins just smiled and didn't respond as they led the way into the quiet facility.

The garrison warehouse was about as empty as Brennan had ever imagined one could be. The large facility only had a token guard at the front doors, but that was wholly inadequate to keep out ruffians, to say nothing of an experienced system slicer like his sister and a dedicated troublemaker like himself. It didn't hurt that they had the advantage of growing up among the military; knowing their routines made slipping past almost too easy.

Half their tutors had spent goodly portions of their lives in buildings just like this.

"We're going to need transport," Brennan said as he glanced down one wide aisle inside the large storehouse. "We couldn't carry a condenser between us, not far anyway."

"I know. Vehicle storage is that way." Lydia gestured, leading the way.

The other two glanced at each other helplessly, then followed their new . . . compatriots? The word didn't seem fitting, but nothing else worked either. They walked deeper into the warehouse.

The four stepped through a small door and into a massive room with vehicles parked in lines. Brennan whistled softly, grinning as he recognized some of the models he was seeing.

"These aren't current issue, are they?"

"No, this isn't an important township," Lydia said. "They only stock reserve equipment here. Why?"

He pointed to a mottled green skimmer with stubby wings and a garishly snarling open mouth with long jagged teeth painted along the line where the canopy fitted to the front.

"That's a Fire Naga. They haven't flown those in twenty-odd cycles," he said. "A stripped-down Naga holds the skimmer speed record, just under the thousand-mile-per-hour mark."

That wasn't the fastest speed anything had ever reached, obviously. Reactor craft could triple that easily, and some vessels could manage much faster above the atmosphere. Quantum tractors could also hit incredible speeds, but for a light-sail skimmer, that was an amazing speed, especially since skimmers didn't run out of fuel in a couple hours. Nor did they take several days to reach their maximum speed.

The empire currently fielded the heavier Kosa Warrior in the place of the old Naga, but there weren't too many skimmer flyers alive who didn't want a Naga certification, in his book.

Lydia rolled her eyes. "Put your eyes back in your head, Bren. That's more than a little too flashy for our needs, not to mention light on cargo room."

Brennan sighed, knowing it was the truth.

"This is just about perfect," Lydia said as she walked up to a squat, ugly ground car that made Brennan groan.

"A Mule, Lyd? Really? I can run faster!"

It was a slight exaggeration but not by nearly as much as Brennan wished. The legion Mule was a workhorse of the service, but hadn't been seen in the field for far longer than even the Naga. Brennan racked his mind for what he could remember about them, but really only came up with the fact that they used some of the very first power capacitors to push the rig.

It was all power, no speed, and built to haul mountains, if that was what you wanted to do.

"I bet it's been sitting here more than fifty cycles." Brennan sighed, sliding the engine access panel back so he could have a look in.

"Can you get it running?"

"First generation power capacitors . . . nothing leaking." He shrugged. "Hit the power switch."

Lydia hopped behind the controls of the old Mule and did as he'd told her. Lights in the panel in front of her snapped to life immediately. "I have power here."

"Still holds a charge," Brennan muttered. "Either they've kept up the maintenance or, more likely, those old caps were built to last."

In the early days of the empire, there hadn't been much of a defense industry. The emperor owned the factories and employed the workers.

Since then things had changed, and one of the benefits of more competition was that modern gear was usually topped within a few years by someone else with a better product. Unfortunately, a side effect Brennan was well acquainted with was that more modern gear had a built-in obsolescence factor.

You rarely got even ten years out of the new capacitors, though they held far more power than what the Mule was working with. He shook his head, more than a little impressed despite his distaste for the old ground car.

Fifty cycles if it's been here a day, and it still holds a charge. Amazing.

He supposed that was what happened when the production team had no reason to design obsolescence into the device. They were paid much the same either way, and the emperor certainly wasn't interested in charging himself for the same thing twice, unlike the companies currently supplying materials to the services.

Of course, Brennan couldn't bring himself to be really regretful of the new way of doing things. Some of the fastest technological changes in the empire's history had been in the last hundred cycles or so, since production had opened up in various duchies and they'd begun competing against one another.

For the moment, however, he had other things to concern himself with.

"It'll do," he finally said. "Let's get a condenser on board, then figure out what we're doing with the damn thing."

Lydia nodded.

They had real work to do.

The other two siblings, standing forgotten behind them, looked at one another and then at the twins and spoke in near unison.

"Who *are* you?"

*

William grimaced as he looked over the sheer devastation in front of him. He didn't know what had gone down here, and it was clear that the empire didn't know much either.

Corian's forces were swarming the area. The huge blast cloud had drawn every free squad within a hundred miles, but they were clearly confused and looking for evidence. Since he'd been directed here by information he'd *lifted* about the location of a major supply transfer to a loyalist brigade, he supposed that the destruction wasn't good news for him.

Still, if Corian's forces don't know what happened, then something very strange is going on here.

He settled in to wait for shadow fall. When the next Great Island passed over the region, he would sneak into the area and gather more information.

*

Mira glanced up as the shadow of the Great Island crossed over her face, noting the time and the position of the *Andros*. They were all belowdecks now, with the ship sealed tight against the cold and air loss of the higher altitude they were cruising at.

The third-level wind streams were blowing nearly a thousand miles an hour; the drag of the lithe vessel they were flying dropped their cruise to a little under seven hundred. They were headed upturn, into the flow of the Great Islands and away from the capital and Corian's strongest force. After the betrayal, she knew that her crew needed a respite, but that wouldn't last too long.

They needed to eat as well, and the payment they'd received for the last clean delivery would run thin soon enough. She needed another score to keep the *Andros* flying and all of their necks out of Corian's nooses.

It was time to take a gamble.

"Gas," she called, gesturing the engineer over.

"Yes, my lady?"

"Set our course for here." She tapped the map.

He glanced at it, puzzled. "Of course, my lady, but why?"

"We need a score, and frankly I don't want to take the *Andros* in against another train this soon," she said. "Corian will be using them for bait after the last one."

The engineer permitted himself a proud smile. "We took a full supply train in sight of a tower, my lady, and we didn't have to fire a shot to do it. He'll have to put on a show of strength. He's lost too much face already."

"I know it. That's why we're going here." She tapped the map again.

"An old supply depot, my lady? There won't be much there worth taking. However, if you want . . ."

She smiled, teeth glittering in the half light of the shadow, and corrected him. "A Cadre stash is under the depot."

Gaston froze. "Really?"

"Yes, and Corian probably doesn't know about it." She was rather proud that she hadn't flinched at the word "probably." "No one knew them all, and it was opened just after he . . . well . . ."

Gaston nodded, knowing she was referring to Corian's first attempt at an uprising, which had resulted in several thousand people dying horrible deaths.

"At any rate, he won't have known about this one," she said. "So we're going to see if we can't liberate it."

"Won't he know of it by now, from the servers, my lady?"

She shook her head. "I've been watching his movements. There are . . . other targets he would have struck, had he taken those servers intact. No, Corian failed to take the Cadre's database."

"That's good news for us, then, I suppose."

She snorted. "That's good news for the empire. Not everything in those servers was as benign as the location of weapon and supply caches. Some of the things I personally added in my first cycle as Cadre . . ."

She trailed off, shaking her head.

"No, it doesn't bear thinking on Corian having access."

Gaston looked at her, clearly curious. "What do you mean?"

She glanced at him, a haunted look crossing her face. "Don't ask me for answers you truly do *not* want to learn, Gaston. Let me just say that this world within which we live is . . . more than it appears."

Mira shook away the old memories and nodded to her engineer and the ship's primus. "Have our course changed. Let's see if that cache is still intact."

He nodded. "But you said Corian doesn't have the location?"

"Corian is hardly the only former Cadre running around, Gas," she said with a laugh, "and I know of half a handful of others who know the location as well. Most likely it'll be intact, however. The closest caches to the palace would have been raided that same night, but none of our number would risk trying after Corian secured the palace, for fear that he captured the servers."

Gaston nodded, understanding.

"Very well, my lady. I'll change course immediately and tighten to the wind. We'll be there before light fall."

*

Imperial patrols were moving all around him as William knelt in the center of the carnage, wreckage strewn all about him. He picked up a small device and turned it over, considering what it meant.

Someone had wired the stolen weapons to blow, that much was clear. It hadn't been a single explosive that sent up that unmistakable rolling cloud, but rather the cumulative detonation of an entire cargo train's munitions shipment. He was relieved at that, as it meant that the explosion hadn't been a warning that tactical weapons were now in play and might be used against the capital or other cities.

The device in his hand, however, told him a great deal more than just that.

The explosion had been set off using a Cadre trick, something not many people knew outside the ranks and even fewer would be able to actually pull off.

Apparently not all of my comrades took the orders to keep their heads down seriously.

That certainly put an interesting wrinkle in the situation.

A rogue Cadreman could certainly tear the living hell out of things, but William doubted that he'd do more than merely tighten the support Corian had with the Senate. He pocketed the device and stood up, looking around.

The destruction of this much material would slow Corian slightly, of course, but it would make the Senate and the corporations deliriously happy as well. Corian would need to replace it, and that meant the corporations got a big order and the senators got their kickbacks.

In the end, the only people who'd suffer would be the citizens of the empire, who'd wind up paying for it . . . in one way or another.

William gritted his teeth.

Now he had to track down the rogue and set him straight. The timing was delicate, and you couldn't just wage a war of attrition with the entire *empire*, damn it. Sure, if you weren't caught and executed you might eventually bring the empire down, but you'd crash the *whole* system. That would destroy everything they needed to preserve. This war had to end with a clean decapitation, a surgical strike against the traitors. Anything else would just be too damned costly.

CHAPTER 12

It had taken the teens almost the entire passing shadow of the Great Island, but they'd finally loaded a condenser and as many emergency rations as they could pack onto the Mule. Lydia and Brennan were worn out, and their new friends were in even worse shape.

Lydia was impressed, though. Neither Mik nor Dusk had given up or begged off. Despite almost collapsing twice, Dusk had even managed to continue working through the shade time as much as could be expected. Given the shape she'd been in when they'd found her, even the light help she provided was more than they'd have asked, and Lydia was growing more and more satisfied with her off-the-cuff decision to include the duo.

She herself had spent more time watching for guard patrols than handling the heavy work, something she felt a little guilty about, but Mik and Dusk wouldn't have known what to look for, and Brennan was far better than she was at running the gear they were using.

She couldn't help but smirk as her brother shot another longing look at the Fire Naga parked across the storage hangar. She resisted the impulse to roll her eyes at him.

"If we get out clean," she said softly, "we can come back for it."

Brennan shot her a look, a mix of pleasure and concern. "Are you sure, Lyd?"

"They won't be able to check the inventory the way things are. It'll be months before anyone notices it's missing."

Brennan scowled. "Not if someone notices a legion-issued condenser in the refugee camp."

Lydia nodded, admitting that was an issue.

"We can scrub the serial number off and beat up the plating a little," she offered. "It'll look like an old rebuild unless someone looks really close. Should buy us time."

Brennan grinned. "All right. Let's get moving, then."

Boys. Lydia rolled her eyes and exchanged a looked with Dusk, who smiled weakly back at her. Lydia walked over. "Are you OK?"

"I'll be fine," Dusk said firmly, only a little shake in her voice. She glanced at the Mule as Brennan hopped into the seat behind the controls. "We're really bringing all this back to the camp?"

Lydia nodded firmly. "It should have been issued to them already. Everything's in such a mess. Things never should have gotten this bad."

"Good," Dusk said with surprising firmness. "It's horrible for people there."

"We saw."

Dusk shook her head. "No. No, you didn't."

Lydia thought to ask what she meant, but something in the girl's expression made her reconsider. *Maybe later, if she wants to talk.*

"All right," Lydia finally said, tapping Mik on the shoulder. "Grab that bag of tools. We'll work on the road."

"Right." He nodded, grabbing the satchel she'd pointed to before hopping into the back of the Mule.

Lydia helped Dusk get in first, then climbed in beside Bren. "Let's go."

The Mule barely groaned as it began to pull out of the hangar through the crack they'd made between the big doors. The electric drive whined just barely as they started to move, lights pouring out into the still shadowed dark.

"OK, just a few more minutes and we'll be clear," Lydia said, motioning Brennan to stop so they could close the doors to the hangar.

The twins hopped out, motioning the other two to remain in place, and were halfway to the doors when a sudden barrage of blaster fire sent them diving to the ground.

"What the hell was that?" Brennan demanded, his arms covering his head.

"Forget the door," Lydia said. "Sorry, Bren, but you'd better forget the Naga too. Come on!"

She tugged at his jacket, pulling him around as they scrambled back to the Mule.

"Crank it," she ordered as they both pulled themselves into the vehicle, and she drew out the concealed blaster she'd been carrying since Kayle . . . well, since Kayle . . .

"It's a *Mule*, Lydia," Brennan growled as he shoved the accelerator forward. "It doesn't crank. It barely creaks!"

Nonetheless the old hauler was doing its job, doggedly taking both cargo and passengers to the gate as quickly as could be expected. They could see lase blasts lighting up the dark skies.

Unlike true lasers, the light lased from a blaster had a great deal of particulate from the minibomb that pumped the blast to lethal levels. The particulate was hot and glowing plasma and also reflected off some of the laser light from the blasts. They cast traces of light along the blast path and threw shadows all around as the fight progressed.

Lydia and Brennan didn't know who was fighting, but it didn't seem to be aimed at them, so the siblings were happy enough to use the distraction to get the hell out of the area.

About halfway to the gate a new shadow was cast over the Mule, and they looked up to see a large skimmer settle into a controlled hover over them and the base. One part of Brennan's mind admired the control it took to steady a ship that size with nothing but light sails and the winds far above them, but the more urgent part of his brain was cursing the situation as assault ribbons were cast from the skimmer and men began to drop around them.

In seconds they were surrounded. The four teens slowly lifted their hands in surrender.

*

Mira Delsol casually stepped off the plank, dropping a few feet to the ground, and waved off the *Andros*. The ship tightened up its sails and was pulled up into the sky, out of sight for the moment, as she looked around.

The head of her assault team, a former legion captain named Kennick, headed in her direction as soon as she landed.

"Site secured, my lady," he reported. "You were right, the local guard was nothing but a token patrol."

Mira nodded. "Casualties?"

"Minor injuries, no fatalities," he said, adding as an afterthought, "on either side."

"Excellent."

You didn't make Cadre if you couldn't compartmentalize your morals. While she was far from squeamish about killing, Mira was more than happy not to dispatch Imperial soldiers. Even those who answered to Corian probably thought they were doing their duty.

"What about the Mule?" she asked, eyeing the ancient vehicle and the four teens standing beside it under guard.

"Thieves, my lady," Kennick said with an ironic smile. "They were almost out when we hit the gate."

"Unlucky for them . . ." Mira chuckled lightly. "What were they stealing?"

Kennick's expression grew a little more somber. "Food and a water condenser."

Mira glanced at him, surprised. "Oh?"

He nodded. "There's a refugee camp not far from here. According to them, conditions have gotten rough."

Mira considered that. "All right. Make sure they're fully loaded and let them go."

"My lady?"

"You heard me."

Kennick nodded, smiling slightly. "Yes, my lady. Oh, one other thing."

Mira paused, having half started walking toward where she knew the target cache was. "Yes?"

"One of the girls had this on her," he said, handing her a blaster.

Mira took it, surprised that he'd mention it. A blaster wasn't legal for most people, certainly, but it wasn't uncommon. And if they were stealing from a military depot . . . She paused as she turned the weapon over in her hand and noticed that it had been inlaid with precious metals and had an Imperial seal on the pommel grip.

She looked over to the teens. "I'll have a word with her."

"Yes, my lady," Kennick answered, waving a hand to the guards. "Bring the girl!"

The guard holding her pushed the girl forward, not particularly gently but hardly overly roughly either. He said something as well, but Mira couldn't make it out. Whatever it was, one of the boys took offense. Mira saw the sudden decision in his eyes and body and knew with a sinking feeling that he was readying to do violence.

She started to swear under her breath, already bringing her hands up, but what happened next shocked even her.

"Leave my sister alone!"

His voice carried clearly, the desperate snarl cutting the air like the blade that had suddenly appeared in his hand. The blade grew as he swung it, flashing in the shadowed air and coming to a rest under the guard's chin.

Blasters all around them made clear clunking sounds as cartridges were loaded into chambers and the weapons were aimed at the four teens. The girl that had had the blaster was frozen, still in the grip of the guard, though much less so than before. Behind them, the other two teens had pushed off their guards and were now holding what looked like tools from the Mule as crude clubs.

She admired their spirit, but for the moment she was entirely focused on the Armati wielded by the boy.

"Everyone *hold*!" Mira snarled, hands out as she strode forward.

She locked eyes with the boy. "If you even slip with that, and hurt my man, it *will* be the last thing you . . . or your sister . . . ever does."

He looked between her and the now motionless guard, the Armati glowing just slightly in his hands. Part of Mira's mind wondered at that, recognizing the glow signified a particularly strong link to the ancient weapon. Stronger than she had with her own Elan, in fact.

Who is he? Who are they?

"Lights," she ordered, waving.

Two men stepped forward, holding up bright spotlights that they leveled on the teens. Mira squinted, her eyes still accustomed to the shadow of the Great Island, trying to determine just whom she was dealing with. They looked familiar, but . . .

"Burning skies," she whispered. "Turn the lights off. Now!"

The lights snapped off as Mira stood there in the temporary dark, considering the two she now knew to be the Scourwind twins.

"Secure arms," she ordered, then set her gaze on the boy. "That goes for you as well. You've no need of killing my man, and I've no need of hurting you or your sister. We didn't come here for you."

She saw him take a shuddering breath and slowly slide the Armati back and away from her man's throat, retracting it back to its nondescript pommel.

"Everyone back on task," she ordered. "Go on, Kennick, I'll speak with them alone."

"My lady . . ."

"Go. I'll be along shortly to show you where the cache is," she said. "See if there's anything else worth taking."

He nodded unhappily but followed orders. Mira nodded to the guards. "You too. Go on."

They hesitated, perhaps to their credit, and didn't move. Unfortunately, Mira didn't have patience for them at the moment. "Unless you think that four teenagers are a serious threat to me?"

There really was no good way to answer that, and finally they reluctantly broke rank and left her alone with the four teens. Mira looked them over slowly, then handed the blaster back to the girl she now recognized as Lydia Scourwind.

"You'll probably need that," she said gruffly, not sure if she should be offering them allegiance, or if she even wanted to.

They may be the heirs of the empire, but the twins were notoriously spoiled and generally acknowledged to be full of mischief. She gave them some credit for not flinching much, and for raiding an Imperial depot for food and water to give to refugees, but the Scourwind empire had fallen. They were just a pair of children in over their own heads, even if part of her longed to see them prove her wrong.

"Thank you," Lydia said softly, accepting the weapon and sliding it out of sight.

Mira looked over at Brennan Scourwind, her eyes falling to the collapsed form of the Armati in his hand. "Your brother's, I assume?"

He nodded jerkily, clearly unhappy with the memory she'd evoked. Mira wasn't surprised. The only way his brother would have given up his Armati would be if he expected to be dead shortly thereafter.

"My condolences," she offered.

It wasn't much, but it was what she had to give.

"Who are you?" Lydia asked.

"Mira Delsol, formerly of his Imperial Majesty's Cadre," she answered. "I'll see you two out of here safely, if you like."

Lydia's eyes skipped up, looking to the sky. "Your ship could carry far more food."

Mira almost laughed out loud. *Oh, this one has nerve.*

"I'm not a delivery service, nor am I Cadre any longer."

"People are starving," Lydia countered, "and it wouldn't take you far from your path. The camp is only a few miles from here."

Mira considered that for a long moment, shaking her head.

I am going to regret this; I just know it. Mira knew that feeling all too well, but she'd never quite mastered how to resist the urge to walk right into the trap she saw springing.

"Come on, then. I'm not letting either of you two out of my sight," she scowled. "I've heard about the trouble you can get up to. Never believed it 'til now, but I've heard stories."

The twins just shrugged, unrepentant, while their companions exchanged confused looks.

"They don't know?" Mira nodded over the twins' shoulders, entirely unsurprised by the shake of their heads. "Probably for the best. You all may as well come with me. We've work to do before the empire figures out that this place is being raided"—she laughed dryly—"again."

*

Corian looked over the central table display of the Imperial war room, noting the disposition of available forces carefully. While the issues with the rapidly dwindling "loyalists" were still pressing, he was more concerned with the far reaches of the empire at the moment.

The Scourwind legacy had left the empire as the undisputed top power in the known world, but it wasn't the only power, despite many attempts to remedy just that, and the unknown world was calculated to be much, *much* larger than the empire by many times over.

That meant that he had to be careful with his available forces, particularly those on the downspin of the Great Islands, where the empire had an open border with several smaller kingdoms that occasionally erupted in disputes. Mopping up any one of them would be easy enough, but they banded together quickly whenever the empire showed an aggressive stance, so Scourwind had been happy to set up a large buffer area between the empire and them and leave them to their own devices.

It had been a surprisingly effective strategy, Corian noted. He'd have been impressed if he really believed that the old man had planned it that way. In the absence of an Imperial foe, the kingdoms had largely turned to squabbling among each other and kept their strength solidly in check. None of them at this point, even all together, were a threat to the empire.

However, what lay beyond them on the downspin was largely a mystery.

On the upside, the empire was secure. The immense God Wall that composed the final border of the empire went for thousands of miles in either direction and climbed up beyond the atmosphere itself. Nothing could breach it. Generations of Imperial explorers had tried, and so it was as secure as could be imagined.

To the north the empire was bordered by the Great Desert, a wasteland so large that despite traveling for months with some of the best equipment available, no explorers had found the other side . . . or returned if they had. The only reason anyone had constructed a track into that forsaken place was due to the valuable Redoubt discovered there.

Three navigation points, all secure.

Corian had spent thirteen cycles in deep cover infiltrating the south, and he knew that beyond those squabbling idiots there was a foe that even the empire needed to respect. Edvard hadn't listened, no matter what evidence Corian had brought back. He'd been satisfied with posting pickets and tripwires and leaving the kingdoms as a buffer.

Edvard, you blasted fool. What you've forced me to do in the name of the empire . . .

Corian pushed away the momentary regret. He had set his course and he would now sail it, whether to the salvation of the empire . . . or to its ruin.

CHAPTER 13

"This isn't on any of the plans."

Mira snorted, amused at the very idea, but didn't turn to look at Lydia as they stepped into the concealed lift and the doors closed.

"Wouldn't be much of a secret cache if it were, now would it?" she quipped.

"I suppose not," Lydia conceded, exchanging glances with her brother.

They went down four hundred feet in a few seconds. The doors opened and they stepped out onto a familiar metal surface. Brennan made a noise of surprise.

"This looks like the palace."

"Same metal," Mira said as they walked down a rough-hewn corridor, rock on all sides save the floor. "It's everywhere, roughly three to five hundred feet under the empire, depending on where you're standing. Deeper if you're on a mountain, shallower in some low-lying regions."

"But . . . it's naturally occurring? I thought . . ." Brennan scowled, honestly not knowing what he thought.

"Of course not. It's an alloy and it's been worked," Mira said, stopping in front of a large vault door. She brushed a section of air and a projection interface appeared in front of her. She quickly began entering data.

"Who worked it? The empire?"

The Cadrewoman laughed. "The empire doesn't have the ability to work this metal, child."

Brennan glared at her when she called him a child, but he'd been condescended to enough during his palace days to ignore it and let her keep talking.

"Or at least, we didn't have the ability." Mira shrugged, shutting the projected display and standing back. The vault door groaned as it began to pivot, dust shaking from the walls and ceiling as it opened. "Still, even with what we can do now, the whole empire working as one couldn't have placed that much metal that deep under our feet. So to answer your question, we don't know who put it there. It was here before we were."

"Why weren't we told about this?" Lydia asked softly.

"'We' as in you two, or 'we' as in the rest of us?" Mira asked, amused, glancing at the other two quiet teens standing in the back. "Most people don't know because it doesn't matter. It's never technically been a state secret. It's just largely irrelevant. We don't know how to cut the metal. We can't even scratch it for the most part, and it's perfectly seamless. The empire has people working on it, trying to figure out where it came from and all that . . . but the research mostly dead ended before either of you were a gleam in your daddy's eye."

"Dead?" Lydia felt mildly outraged by that. "How can it be dead?"

"How many holes can you dig and find the same thing before you run out of ideas?" Mira said as the big door finally swung open. She lifted a hand, waving to her men. "All right, you lot . . . go shopping."

Compared to the hangar up top, the room inside wasn't particularly big, but it was large enough and seemed stocked from floor to ceiling. The crew of the skimmer quickly and professionally began breaking all the supplies down and packing them back up for transport. Mira walked the teens in and paused by one large stack of cases.

"Are you all interface rated?" she asked.

Lydia and Brennan nodded instantly, while Mikael and Dusk hesitated a bit before nodding as well. Mira noticed but continued.

"We'll get you rated," she said after a moment, breaking open the case and handing two pieces of a small broken emblem to each teen. "Projection armor. Join the emblem and seat it on your body somewhere. Most of us choose the shoulder or chest. Even if you're not rated, this will stop blasters and give you a chance to escape."

She dropped one in each of the teens' hands, noting with amusement the wide eyes of the two who so obviously had no idea what they'd stepped into.

"As I don't know either of these two," Mira went on, gesturing to Mik and Dusk while looking at Lydia and Brennan, "I have to assume you picked them up either during your escape or after?"

"After," Lydia answered. "Just recently, at the camp."

"Ah." Mira nodded, understanding. "Well, we'll drop supplies there. I know of people who are looking for you both."

Lydia and Brennan both stiffened at that.

"Not those people," Mira chuckled. "William Everett is *scouring* the empire for you."

"Will?" Lydia smiled suddenly. "He made it out?"

"Most of the Cadre did, as I understand it," Mira said, "with instructions to go to ground and stay there until they got new orders. The surviving leadership didn't want to chance a real guerilla war that had the potential of tearing down the empire before it was over. Can't say that I really agree, but what's done is done."

She picked up a carbine and looked at the quiet teen duo. "You know how to use one of these?"

Mik nodded. "Our dad had a flecher. Same thing, right?"

Mira snorted and tossed him the weapon. "That's a different breed from your daddy's flecher, kid, but it works the same. It's a gamma carbine. Don't point it at anyone you don't want to die a horrible death. It'll burn big nasty holes in damn near everything except people. You don't want to know what it'll do to people."

Mik caught the weapon awkwardly, nearly fumbling his hold, but finally getting a grip on the carbine and cradling it in his arms. "Why give us these?"

"You're hanging around these two," she said, jerking a finger in the direction of the twins, "and these are rough times, kid. Shoot me or mine with it, and I'll see you hung up by your entrails. Got me?"

He gulped, then nodded.

"Not that I'm going to let you load it anytime soon, but get used to carrying it." She looked them over, a sardonic grin on her face. "I need to oversee the looting. Stay close and don't get in any trouble . . . and I mean you two." She finished her statement with a scowl in the twins' direction.

Lydia and Brennan gave her a look they'd practically patented during their previous life, a combination of affront at the accusation and complete innocence that would have fooled anyone not acquainted with them or as naturally suspicious as Mira had recently become.

She just gestured between her eyes and them, indicating that she was watching them, and then headed off to oversee some of the more deft requirements of the looting.

There was a silent moment before Mik and Dusk both turned toward the twins, faces a combination of high curiosity and severe annoyance.

"Who *are* you two?" Mik spoke first, being the brasher of the two. "Sneaking into the depot was one thing, but . . ." He just gestured around.

Lydia sighed. "Sorry. We intended to deliver the food and water and probably be gone before anyone asked that. We're . . ."

"Lyd . . . ," Brennan said warningly.

"Please, Bren," she scoffed. "It won't be that hard to figure out. Even if they can't, anyone they tell would work it out in a second. So there's not much point hiding it now."

Brennan sighed but said nothing, indicating that he objected no further.

"Hello," Lydia extended a hand. "I'm Lydia Scourwind. This is my brother Brennan."

Mik took her hand on reflex, before being frozen dumb in shock.

"Scourwind?" Dusk asked softly. "Really? Then why are you hiding your identities? Your father—"

"Is dead."

Brennan's flat delivery brooked little more comment on the subject, but Lydia closed her eyes for a moment.

"The rumors of a coup are true," she said. "We don't know much, but we know that our father died that night . . . as did our older brother. We've been running ever since."

"Well . . . damn." Mik felt as though he needed a seat, but there weren't many places to sit in the vault, and frankly he was scared of what he might be sitting on if he tried.

They'd all known that something had happened, something bad, of course. The empire didn't make a habit of waging full-scale battles in the middle of populated places for no reason. Few had guessed that the most unbelievable of the rumors, that a coup had succeeded, would be the truth.

Mikael glanced at his sister, reading the look in her eyes when she looked back.

They'd lost their parents to some damned power play so far above their heads as to be entirely out of sight.

It felt almost worse, knowing that, than it had when they'd been in the dark. At least in ignorance they could pretend that there was some greater meaning.

*

"Careful with those," Mira Delsol said as she walked the aisles.

The men checked the crates they were manhandling into a hand truck. "Are they dangerous?"

"No. Fragile. Those are server blades," she answered, "backups for key data normally held only in the palace servers. Corian would murder every soul in the region for just one of those. Do *not* damage them."

"Yes, my lady."

The operation was moving swiftly, as she'd planned and hoped, but Mira wasn't going to be happy until she and the *Andros* were well clear of the region. With a refugee camp in the area it was only a matter of time before the empire's forces were turned in this direction, and the fact that the guards above wouldn't be checking in anytime soon just upped that clock significantly.

The stores and other gear they were gathering, however, would make the risk worth it.

Since they had time, they'd also take a fair chunk of the regular stores from the depot above. Most of it was hopelessly outdated, but it would sell well on the civilian market or even to one of the pocket kingdoms that existed around the periphery of the empire. Many of those were technically Imperial provinces, but they were so far from the capital that they were effectively independent entities.

They were always slavering for Imperial military tech as well, even if it were massively outdated.

No one built gear like the empire used to.

*

"Sire."

Corian looked up from the reports of his private pet project, noting for the first time the aide who'd stepped in and waited by the door.

"What is it?"

"You asked to be informed of any regimental redeployments?"

Corian grimaced but nodded. He didn't want to waste time with such matters, but as things were he needed to know where every regiment of the legion was operating. "Who and where?"

"Colonel McReady is taking the Bulls north to the Kiran Sector, sire."

"Kiran? What's up there?" Corian asked, frowning.

The name meant something to him, but he couldn't place it.

"Most recently a refugee camp from the last set of battles with the rebel legions," the aide answered swiftly.

"Ah." Corian nodded. That was where he'd heard the name recently. It was basically the backwater of the empire, very little of value and of no strategic importance. He'd thought that they had elected to leave them be for the moment. "Why is the colonel taking his legion and support there?"

"Two reports, sire, or rather one report and one report that wasn't made when it should have been," the aide answered. "First, we have reports of a skimmer matching the *Andros Pak* in the area. It was discounted at first as an unlikely event given the region . . ."

Corian nodded. There would seem to be little reason for Delsol to take the *Andros* there on the surface of things. "And the report that should have been made?"

"The local supply depot had a minimal garrison," the aide answered. "They're overdue to check in. No contact can be established."

Corian scowled.

That didn't make any sense. A depot that far north wouldn't have anything of value to Mira, just outdated military equipment. The sort of things you could get on the black market across the empire for bargain rates at best. Going that far out of their way to raid a worthless depot made no sense.

Unless . . .

His eyes widened and he let out a vile oath, shocking the aide who was used to his former emperor being calm, even under fire.

"Sire?"

"Send backup for McReady," Corian ordered.

"Sire? Why . . . ?"

"She's Cadre," Corian snapped. "We're all entrusted with the location of one or more special cache locations. No one knows them all, but we all know some of them. The ones I knew of were decommissioned after I was . . ."

He left that unfinished, not wanting to discuss his court-martial.

Instead he just waved it off. "Suffice it to say, if there's a cache there, I *want* it."

"Yes, sire. I'll have the *Leo Francas* moved to backup the Bulls."

Corian nodded, calling after the man as he started to leave. "And have the *Caleb Bar* prepped for flight."

"Yes, sire."

Corian turned back to the map and couldn't help but smile ruefully.

"You are a credit to your emblem, Cadrewoman Delsol," he said finally. "Even after I've beaten everyone else, you're still haunting my steps."

*

"William."

The Cadreman looked up from his work, trying to track the location of the Scourwind heirs again as the uniformed legionnaire slipped into the room.

"Kell." He smiled. "What is it?"

"An answer to one of your questions, and maybe something important," the woman said. "The Cadrewoman you've been asking about appears to be Mira Delsol."

"Delsol?" William straightened up. "I had thought her dead."

Indeed, once Corian showed up again, given what they knew of how the man operated, it seemed likely that Delsol's body had sanded over somewhere in the Great Desert. The fact that the woman was not only alive, but also one of the major causes of his headaches—and, admittedly, Corian's as well—was, well, surprising.

He barely had time to parse that, however, before Kell went on. "Corian just ordered two legions to the north. He seems to believe that she's raiding a little-known supply depot out there," Kell said, appearing to be confused. "Not sure why. I checked the inventory. There're a few small fortunes' worth of antiquated gear, but nothing worth the effort and risk she'd be taking."

William closed his eyes. "It's a Cadre cache."

"What?"

"She's not raiding the depot. She's raiding the cache hidden under it," William said with certainty. "I need the location."

"It's here." Kell handed him a data shard. "I don't know what you think you'll be able to do with it, though. Corian has sent *two* legions, William."

"I can't let him get what's in that cache," William said, shaking his head, "or *any* cache. I destroyed . . . Never mind. Thank you, Kell."

"You never have to thank me for this, William. I'd better get back."

He watched her leave, considering his options for a moment, and then gathered up his belongings and rushed out, heading for his skimmer.

*

Crates of supplies, armor, weapons, and enough Imperial dinars to purchase a small warship were quickly moved to the lift center and then carefully shuttled up to the surface and out to the staging point. The lift was the bottleneck in the system, slowing their efforts considerably, but even so Mira was cautiously optimistic about how things were proceeding as the vault room was swiftly emptied.

The *Andros Pak* was on close orbit, circling the depot at fifteen thousand feet, watching for any sign of movement as the shadow of the Great Island moved fully past and the bright burning sky returned in full force. She would have preferred to have had at least another skimmer for backup and overwatch while they were loading the *Andros*, but needs must when the fires fly.

She had the teens back topside, keeping an eye on the twins, particularly Brennan, who was working on one of the old military skimmers stored in the depot. From what she'd seen, it was in decent enough shape for being an obsolete hunk of material, but she didn't know much about skimmers beyond how to fly one. The boy had the reputation as a fanatic flyer and, if the rumors were to be believed, a natural sail hand.

For all their notorious reputations, Mira was well aware that the twins were also rumored to be competent in what they did. It was just that most of the time what they did was cause no end of trouble for their guards, many of whom were cycled through from the Cadre ranks.

She'd never pulled that duty, thank the burning skies, but that didn't stop those who did from bitching loudly and often about the siblings.

Mira did know, or *had* known, she supposed, Kayle Scourwind. Really only in passing, but they'd met and exchanged more than a few words in their day. Kayle was from the academy class just ahead of hers, and one of the youngest to ever make Cadre. Some whispered that he'd been coasting on the Scourwind name, but she didn't buy that for a moment.

Honestly, the only thing that interested her about the twins was Kayle's Bene. The Cadre Armati was a tricky beast to master. To get one to link to you was basically the prerequisite to be *considered* for Cadre training. If an Armati wouldn't accept you, you were done right there, no point in further training.

Beginners were generally a bigger threat to themselves than anyone else, and yet the Bene had responded smoothly to Brennan and with a precision she'd only seen with a badged Cadreman before.

She could see the prince twitch occasionally, glancing around. Mira knew the symptoms.

The Cadrewoman walked over slowly, silently, and came to a stop right behind Brennan.

"Hear something?"

"What?" Brennan asked sharply, glancing at her warily and then looking around again.

"Whispers in the back of your mind? An itch where your skull meets your neck?" she asked.

He instantly reached up to scratch the very spot, then yanked his hand back guiltily.

"What do you know about it?"

She glanced down at the Armati on his belt. "Bene is speaking to you. Listen. Do not ignore your Armati. She's been fighting longer than your family has been in existence."

He gripped the ancient weapon instinctively, and looked up and around sharply.

"I don't understand . . ."

"You've no training, so of course you don't," Mira answered, considering him for a while. "Stick around, though, and I'll see about fixing that."

"Why?"

Mira chuckled at the suspicion dripping from his tone. "At least you've some brains in that damn skull of yours." She paused for a moment, then continued, "And as to why? Because I owe your brother one."

She was about to say more when Gaston's voice rang loud and clear over the comm line from the *Andros*.

"My lady, we have movement on the haze," he said, "*large* movement."

Mira swore.

She knew she'd been poking the fates with a sharp stick when she'd started feeling optimistic.

"Clear. Gas," she responded instantly, backing away from Brennan, "we've a team in the vault. I'll recover them. Get down here and loaded."

"On my way, my lady."

"Everyone," Mira called, circling her hand in the air, "we are *leaving*! Get packed and ready to load. Prioritize the selection, food and survival kit first. We may have to leave some of it! I'm going to get the below team."

Everyone snapped into action, and Mira sprinted for the lift, cursing her luck with every step.

CHAPTER 14

The four teens watched the sudden furor of activity erupt around them for a single moment before Brennan turned to his sister with a questioning look. "Lyd?"

"I don't know," she answered uncertainly. "If we stay with them, it's a risk. On our own isn't much better."

Brennan nodded, putting it out of his mind for the moment as he turned back to the Fire Naga. If they had to run, or fight, he intended to have something better than an ultralight skimmer on his side this time around.

"I want the weapon pods loaded," he said firmly. "Can you find them?"

Lyd smirked, turning to the local interface and calling up the depot's database with a flick of her hand. It only took seconds for her to locate the munitions section. "Grab a hand truck. We'll need it."

"Right," Brennan said, then glanced at Mik and Dusk, who were still looking on with a bit of a stunned countenance. "You two in? You can just leave, you know. They're not after you."

The other two siblings exchanged glances, then instantly shook their heads. They didn't have anything to go back to.

"We're in," Mik said.

"Grab another hand truck," Brennan ordered. "We can load this thing in one trip, working together."

The foursome all grinned and quickly rushed across the depot, weaving in and out of the other workers who were hurrying about on their own.

*

Gaston deftly let out the slack on the light sails, settling the bulk of the *Andros Pak* to the ground in the middle of the cleared area around the depot. Men were already rushing out to drop the lower plank and fill the corsair's holds with the latest haul from their raids.

On the ground, he no longer had line of sight to the approaching signals, but he had a good idea of how fast they'd been moving and how far away they still were. He was worried, though, as the legion had more than a few skimmers that could outrun the *Andros* if push came to shove, and many of those were armed fighters that could easily drop the larger ship in a fight.

They were on a schedule now, and it was tightening around their throats like a noose.

He rose from the controls of the interior command deck and stomped out to the topside deck, leaning over the gun rails.

"Hey, you lot, pick it up! We've a legion inbound, and they don't look like they're here to sightsee!"

He didn't bother waiting for a response, instead pushing himself back upright and glowering around at the deck crew. "And that goes double for all of you! I want our projectors checked and all the rigging eyeballed for any snags. When the *Andros* lifts off, we don't want any delays."

Men and women scrambled in all directions, seeing to the maintenance of the ship under Gaston's watchful eye. He couldn't help but smile at just how overqualified he was for the job he was doing. He'd been in charge of the most secret operation the empire had conducted for generations and designed the deadliest warship anyone had ever conceived. Yet here he was, overseeing a rogue corsair and honestly enjoying every moment of it.

A skimmer the size of the *Andros* was no small matter to keep aloft. Her eight sail projectors were each three times the size of a normal military skimmer's, and that introduced the complication of keeping the lines from crossing during maneuvering. Even at best, after each flight you had to check every single line, projector, hard point, and several dozen other potential points of failure.

They'd been doing it for generations, however, and the empire had ship handling down to an art and science.

The crewmembers Mira had managed to scrounge up were among the best people he'd ever worked with, even though most of them would never have made it on the empire's dinars without facing a firing squad. He sometimes wished that he knew where she'd met them all. Most of them were former empire military, of course, but the few that weren't were a strange bunch.

Gaston wasn't one to press, but he was almost certain that three of the *Andros*'s crew were rather notorious pirates from *before* they'd joined up. He supposed that being Cadre meant walking in some dark places, but actually *seeing* evidence of it shook him a little.

Not enough to object, of course. They were able ship handlers, and the *Andros* needed every able hand it could get.

Especially with what was bearing down on them.

*

"Crank that pod up into place." Brennan pointed as he maneuvered the hydraulic lift into place under the other side of the old Fire Naga. "It should click into place with a little shove."

He did the same on his side, putting the weapons pod up and shoving it hard until he heard the audible click of the hard point locking it in.

"What are these anyway?" Mik grunted as he shoved as hard as he could on his own side, struggling to hear the click to little avail.

Brennan strode over, gripping the pod beside him, and between them they shoved again and were rewarded with the telltale sound.

"It's a MAC cannon," Brennan said. "Not in issue anymore, mostly because the lase blasters are cheaper. The MACs use magnetic accelerators to fire chunks of metal downrange. I trained on them in the simulation systems back home. Nasty, but heavy and expensive. Not enough usable metal lying around to throw it at people, mostly."

"So why are we loading it?"

"Because we've got more than enough for a full load just sitting around here," Brennan said. "And no one ever mounted a lase blaster on a Naga, so there's none in storage that would fit."

"Oh."

Brennan patted the side of the machine. "Believe it or not, it actually packs a bigger punch than a lase blaster. Especially against modern legion armor. These days, no one expects to be hit by a two-inch-diameter chunk of metal moving at hypersonic speeds."

"I wonder why," Mik said dryly, shaking his head.

Brennan just smiled, a hint of the fear and nerves he was hiding showing through, but he distracted himself quickly by turning to where Lydia and Dusk were working on the Naga's flight systems.

"Lyd, everything check out?"

Lydia looked up, nodding. "Brennan, you're not going to believe how good Dusk here is with an interface . . ."

Brennan raised an eyebrow, glancing at Mik questioningly. Interface compatibility wasn't exactly rare in the empire. In fact it was fairly common. But for Lydia to describe someone as *good* meant that they had to have a particularly high natural aptitude.

Mik just shrugged. "Ma was a systems engineer for the local water and food reclamation center. She taught Dusk everything she knew . . . Sis, well, on her own she went on to figure out a lot more that Ma didn't know."

Brennan nodded. "Nice. So, are we green?"

Lydia nodded. "I just gave Dusk the specs and code from your skimmer, and we're using it to bring the operations system up to date. You'd never be able to fly this the way it was. Everything was automated with the *worst* control system I've ever seen."

"Thank the legion for that." Brennan chuckled. "It must have been wiped and set back to factory specs before it was stored here. Most pilots wrote their own operational code back in the day."

"I can see why. You'd fly into a hill if you tried to run this thing on the code they put in there."

"Just bug test it as much as you can, all right?" he asked, a little more agitatedly than he would have preferred.

"Relax. We just pulled most of the code from your skimmer," Lydia assured him. "It's almost identical, physically."

"It should be," he admitted. "My skimmer was based on the Naga frame. The same design firm built skimmers for popular use after the war."

"It shows," Dusk said, entering the conversation without looking up. "Just watch out for the weight. It's going to pull differently on the sails."

"I know. I've flown heavy craft before," Brennan said. "Leave it to me."

"Going to have to. I don't know anything about flying."

"Stick around, and I'll teach you." He grinned, winking at her when she glanced up.

Dusk turned several shades darker, sticking her head back down to avoid his eyes. Brennan just shrugged off Lydia's glare; he was used to his sister not approving of his interactions with others. Mik's matching glare, however, made Brennan hold up his hands and shake his head.

The other teen boy kept up the glare, clearly warning Bren off his sister. Brennan, while certainly not opposed to flirting with the dark-haired, dark-eyed girl, decided to back off.

They had other worries to deal with.

*

"Everyone grab what you've got, leave the rest," Mira ordered as she stepped off the lift and walked into the vault. "We are leaving."

"But there's more here—"

"We've a full legion heading our way!" She cut off the man with a sharp gesture. "And we already packed everything we had to grab. Unless you want to be hosted by Corian and his empire for the rest of your natural lives, be on the *Andros* before I fire the projectors up. I won't wait."

That shut them all up, and they grabbed whatever they could and bolted for the lift.

Mira herself picked up two cases and marched calmly but quickly behind them.

*

"Skipper, the long-range recon team think they spotted a skimmer in the distance, but we lost it when it dropped below the wind shear."

Commander Horace Kim of the Imperial destroyer *Elemental* nodded, taking a long lens from the holder next to him and using it to scan the mist ahead. "Location?"

"Right over the target depot, skipper."

Kim sighed, considering his potential actions. The target skimmer, if it were the *Andros Pak*, would certainly have spotted them. He might have been able to sneak his own destroyer in under their spotters, but a whole legion on his tail would be impossible to miss.

"Signal the squad to spread out. Keep the *Elemental* in the center of the formation, but I want flankers ready in case they try to bolt."

It wouldn't do much if they decided to run into the Great Desert, but he'd worry about that if it happened. At least in that forsaken wasteland there was nothing for Delsol to raid or steal, and though hunting her and her compatriots down in that mess would be a truly grueling affair, it would also be a quiet one.

"Aye, skipper."

The destroyer squadron under his command was the vanguard of the Bulls. Behind him rode fifteen hundred men and women, armed to the teeth, looking to slam any enemy of the empire into the ground like the garbage they inevitably were. It was likely overkill, since even a single destroyer like the *Elemental* would be more than a match for the *Andros*.

He'd seen the specs on the stolen Imperial skimmer that Delsol now commanded. The *Andros Pak* was heavily armed for its size and armored to a degree that should have been impossible save for the fact that it was the emperor's—*former* emperor's—private skimmer. As it was now a corsair in the command of a pirate . . . well, it was unlikely to find itself redeemed to honest duty.

Kim doubted that Delsol was going to surrender peaceably.

Even with all the advanced armor and weapons, the corsair could only take a destroyer of the *Elemental*'s class perhaps three fights in ten. Against a squadron, well . . . Kim smiled. He just hoped it wasn't over too quickly.

Nor too drawn out. His smile was replaced by a frown. If they ran, and they likely would, of course, there was still that blasted desert to hide in.

The eternal mist that marked the edge of sight was less predictable in the desert. It could close on you in an instant, swallowing vision like a beast gobbling up everything it could, or the mist could morph into the vision of an impossibly large body of water glinting in the sunlight. The image of that had driven men mad in the past and likely would again in the future.

It was a fate that Kim would prefer not to tempt.

That choice, however, lay in the hands of the disgraced Cadrewoman.

"Lay in the sails, tighten us to the wind," he ordered. "Bring the squadron up to full speed. We'll take her while she's on the ground."

"Aye, skipper!"

*

"That's it," Brennan said, satisfied as he checked the control surfaces and the twin sticks from the pilot's seat of the Naga.

Unlike his personal skimmer, the pilot sat in the rear seat in a Naga, leaving room for a gunner up front. It would take some getting used to, as it did cost him some of his forward- and lower-angle visibility, but all the same the setup felt natural.

He flipped a half-dozen switches, bringing systems online one at a time, checking them off in order. Power was still flowing through the old beast, and all the systems cleared the checklist.

Burning skies, they built these monsters to last, Brennan thought admiringly. He'd been trying to get Kayle to check him out on a Naga for so long.

His thoughts must have shown on his face, because Lydia touched his shoulder a moment later. "Bren?"

"I'm OK," he assured her. "I was just thinking of . . ."

"Kayle," she answered. "I know."

"He would be *so* pissed with us right now." Brennan forced a grin.

Lydia nodded, smiling as well. "He would."

Brennan let out a long breath, blowing until his lungs were empty and burning. After he'd filled them again, he looked once more to his sister. "Do we trust her?"

"Delsol?" Lydia frowned, uncertain. "She's Cadre."

"Former Cadre. So is the man who murdered our father."

Lydia nodded, though she couldn't help but smile just slightly as well. "I suspect that she would be somewhat . . . put off by the comparison."

"Boohoo for her," Brennan retorted. "I'm not interested in her mental problems. Do we trust her?"

Lydia considered the question a little more seriously, but honestly, she wasn't sure if they had a choice.

"I think we have to," she said finally. "For a while, at least. We can't outrun a legion, Bren."

"Like hell we can't," Brennan said, nodding to the gunner's seat. "You hop in there, and I'll have us clear before they can even spot our sails."

"What about Dusk and Mik?" Lydia asked gently, nodding to the other two. "It's a two-seater, remember?"

Brennan looked apologetically at them. "Sorry, guys, but you're not the ones they're chasing."

The duo shifted uncomfortably but nodded in understanding.

"We understand," Dusk said softly. "We don't really know each other much, and we already owe you."

"So where would we run to, Bren?" Lydia cut in. "To what?"

"I don't know, but I'm just not sure that this woman is the answer to those questions."

"Neither am I."

"Good."

The new voice startled both of them as they jerked around to see the woman in question standing off to the side with an amused look on her face.

"If you were sure," Mira told them, "I'd question your sanity."

They shifted uncomfortably, uncertain what to say.

"Look, if it were up to me, I'd give you all the time in the world to decide," Mira said, "but that legion approaching, they have other ideas. The *Andros* is lifting off in ten mikes. Your call."

She pivoted on her heel and marched away.

"Well," Mik said, amused, *"awkward."*

"Shut up, Mik," Dusk growled, actually raising her voice for the first time Lydia or Brennan could remember.

"Yes, ma'am." Mik chuckled.

The look his sister shot him would have likely melted steel, and even Brennan—as used to annoying Lydia as he was—was rethinking any future plans to tease Dusk in the same way. Instead he refocused on his own sister and restated the question hanging between them.

"Lyd, you've been calling the shots since we escaped," he admitted. "Say the word now and I'll fly the two of us out of here. We can hide out in the desert, skirt the dunes along the edge, and pop out downspin of here. They'll never find us."

"I know," she said. "I know, but then what? She offered to show you how to use Kayle's Bene, remember? It's the last thing he gave you."

"I don't care." Brennan shook his head. "This is about more than that."

"We have to trust someone."

"Yeah, maybe," he admitted, "but why her?"

Lydia just shrugged. "Why not her?"

That response was perhaps one of the few that Brennan didn't have an answer for. So far, though it was a limited sample of time, Delsol had been upfront and had treated them with respect, which was better than what they'd dealt with most of their lives, their brother aside.

"OK, fine. I'm still taking the Naga," he said firmly.

Lydia laughed, stepping back as she slapped the side of the military skimmer. "Get in the air, Bren. We'll follow."

Brennan blinked. “You’re going with her now?”

“May as well,” she said, shrugging. “Why?”

“I need a gunner,” he said, thinking hard.

Lydia blinked and considered it as well. She didn’t think she could do the job even if she wanted to.

“I programmed the systems,” Dusk offered quietly. “I might be able . . .”

“No.” Lydia shook her head. “You’ve never flown like my brother flies. If he’s serious about this, he needs someone with experience. Wait a moment.”

She strode across the ground to where Mira was overseeing the last few crewmen loading crates into the waiting skimmer.

“Make your decision?” Mira asked, not looking back as she approached.

“Yes. My brother needs a gunner.”

Mira blinked.

That wasn’t what she’d been expecting. She was about to ask if he could actually fly the old fossil that the kids had prepped but then remembered his reputation in that field. He was considered better at flying than troublemaking, which was saying something.

She considered it for a moment, then nodded sharply. “The Scourwind heir needs a gunner! Any volunteers?”

A long silence echoed until Kennick stepped up. “I’ll fly with him.”

Mira nodded. “Go, then.”

“Ma’am.” He saluted her, fist closed, and then headed toward the waiting Naga.

“You’d better get your other two friends on board the *Andros*,” Mira said to Lydia. “We’re leaving.”

*

Kennick nodded to Brennan as he stepped up on the stirrup set in the nose of the fighter, twisting around to drop back into the gunner's seat.

"Hope you can fly this thing," he said, hitting the switch that brought the canopy down.

The Fire Naga was laid out practically like a civilian skimmer, with almost complete forward visibility available through the canopy. For the person in the front seat, it was a little light sitting in midair with nothing around you but the sky. The only major difference was that the canopy had a very slight green tint, visible only because it was over four times thicker than the civilian model and composed of a considerably tougher material.

From Brennan's position, however, he was getting used to the slightly limited visibility of having someone sitting ahead of him. Passengers sat in the back in civilian skimmers, but there were no passengers in a Naga, and the gunner got the hot seat.

"If it has sails, I can fly it," Brennan said as he punched in the code to bring the circuits live and began to roll the Naga out of the hangar.

"That's what I hear," Kennick said. "Otherwise I wouldn't have volunteered for this gig. Name's Kennick, by the way. Jaymes Kennick."

"Brennan. You know the last name. We don't need it in here."

"Right you are," Kennick said with a smile, checking the instruments. "Been a while since I checked out on one of these."

"You certified on a Naga?"

"Back in my legion days," Kennick confirmed. "They were still using them as trainers then. You?"

Brennan shook his head. "Nope. First flight. Did all my time on Meridian model nines."

Kennick shrugged. "Better than I thought. Almost the same airframe, just a lot lighter with smaller sails. Watch for that. Sometimes the Naga will be sluggish, and sometimes the larger sail will hook better than you'd expect and you'll accelerate like nothing you'd ever believe."

"Thanks for the advice," Brennan said genuinely. "I can handle it."

"You better," the former legionnaire said as he glanced out to one side and whistled. "You loaded us with MACs?"

"They had enough in storage here to load a squadron." Brennan grinned.

"Damn. I wonder if the skipper knew and had time to steal some."

"Dunno." Brennan shrugged. "I was surprised to find them."

"I'll bet. They phased the MACs out decades ago. Metal is too precious to waste throwing at the enemy."

They were out in the open then, and Brennan found himself looking at the *Andros* as it was locked down for flight. The *Andros Pak* was a skimmer only by technicality in his opinion. Sure, there were some military ships that were larger, but any skimmer that used eight sails just *had* to be a nightmare to keep running. The software on a two-sail bird like the Naga or his own skimmer was complicated enough.

"Wait here for the *Andros* to lift off," Kennick advised. "We'll follow the skipper's lead."

"Clear," Brennan replied. "Confirmed, comply."

He settled the Naga into position, downwind of the *Andros* so that the bigger ship wouldn't risk being dragged into them if she couldn't get the altitude fast enough. It was unlikely; a good handler could play the winds to their favor and launch in almost any direction, but he wasn't about to take a chance on being flattened right before he got to finally put a Naga in the skies.

The deep thud of the *Andros* firing off her projectors swept over them, the thin filament cables glinting in the light. Far above the light projectors the sails snapped into view, and the *Andros* smoothly lifted off the ground.

Brennan frowned. "They only put up four sails."

"So they did," Kennick said.

"Why would they do that? That's going to cripple them."

"Skipper has her reasons. Trust the skipper."

"Whatever," Brennan uttered with a scowl, checking the skies to ensure that they were going to clear the *Andros*. "Launching projectors."

This time the explosive thud was closer and more intense, and in a few seconds the deep ultramarine sails of the Naga burst up above them. Brennan hammered the stick, winching in the cables hard as they pulled heavy and lifted into the skies.

He didn't care. He was already in love.

CHAPTER 15

"Sail on the winds!"

Commander Kim turned, eyes automatically locking on the glint of silver-white light in the distance. It was too far for him to count the sails, but the color matched the *Andros*'s sail frequencies. The *Elemental* was bearing directly down on the ship's position, running as tight to the wind as they could. He was already calculating the intercept chances in his head, but it wasn't looking good.

"They launched early," he growled, grabbing at a pair of long lenses. "We'll never catch them if they head for the desert."

"Yes, sir," his second agreed calmly.

Horace scowled into the lenses. "That's odd."

"What is, sir?"

"Check me," he ordered, handing off the lenses.

His second took the lenses with a puzzled look and put the device to his face. It only took him a moment to notice what his captain had spotted.

"They're flying half-mast," he said, "and they're *not* running for the desert."

Kim nodded, puzzled as he pulled a scarf up over his face. The winds at their altitude were low due to the destroyer keeping pace with them, but the crosswinds were still bitterly cold.

"Maybe it's not the *Andros*, sir?"

Kim shrugged. "It's possible. Maybe they haven't spotted us?"

"*Not* spot an entire legion bearing down on their position while they're in the process of raiding an Imperial depot?"

The incredulous nature of the question made the answer fairly self-evident. Some pirates might have missed the legion, but only the ones who got caught. Delsol was too good not to have an alert watch.

"Just what the hell is she doing?"

"Turning into us, skipper," his second answered, his voice growing even more confused.

"What?" *That* was even less believable than the idea that they'd somehow missed a legion on the move.

"Check me, sir."

Kim accepted the lenses back and did just that. Sure enough the sails had angled into the higher winds and they were clearly pulling south, directly *into* the *Elemental* and her squadron.

"She's insane," Kim said softly, shaking his head.

"Orders, skipper?"

Kim blinked, trying to parse what was happening, but it made no sense at all.

"Orders, skipper?"

The slightly more intense tone of his second's voice shook him from his pondering.

"Battle stations," he said finally. "All hands, all ships. Advise the Bulls that we're preparing to engage the enemy."

"Aye, skipper!"

*

Mira let her hair free as they pulled up through the lower wind shear and climbed for the faster winds of the second-level stream.

Three streams of high-speed wind moved over the land, layered at ten thousand feet, thirty thousand, and finally a hundred thousand. There were plenty of other currents to be sailed in between those, of course, but they were less predictable and generally the domain of master ship handlers and amateurs who sailed for fun.

As the *Andros* pulled up close to thirty thousand feet, the air was thin, enough so that the crew on deck was using breathers and dressed in winter gear. Mira had Cadre-issue gear and a personal warmer looped casually around her neck. She was dressed far more lightly than the others and seemed impervious to the cold as she casually twisted the wheel to bank the *Andros* around.

"We're running half-mast, my lady," Gaston reminded her. "They'll be on us in minutes at this rate."

"That they will," Mira confirmed cheerfully.

Gaston looked so uncomfortably nervous that she chuckled.

"Losing trust in me, Gas?"

"Never, my lady," he swore. "But trust is one thing. Faith is a very different matter."

"Well said," she affirmed. "We have a delivery to make."

Gaston looked out over the rails to the mottled greens and browns below. "The refugees, my lady? But that's suicide!"

"Do I look like the suicidal type?" she asked, amused.

"Do you really want me to answer that?" he asked right back, his brow arched.

"No, probably not," she conceded with a grin.

Gaston sighed, knowing that she was set on her path. "At least put up the rest of the sails. We can be there in seconds and try to skirt the legion . . ."

"We'd never make it." Mira shook her head. "They've spread their lead squadron. We might get a destroyer one time in two . . ."

"My lady!" Gaston looked insulted.

"Fine," Mira chuckled. "Two in three?"

"A little more, I'd say." He sniffed.

"However," she stressed the word, "we'd not take two of them one time in ten . . ."

This time, despite Mira pausing to let him object, Gaston just shrugged. It was a fair assessment. Combined forces were more effective than their individual numbers would indicate.

". . . let alone a full squadron, and at least three would be able to intercept us if we tried that," Mira finished. "So I have a plan."

"You have a plan?"

His tone wasn't *quite* incredulous, but Gaston knew the woman standing beside him well enough to know that those words weren't going to result in anything he personally wanted to be present for. Still, not having much choice in the matter, he just sighed and nodded.

"Yes, my lady," he said.

Mira by then had a predatory look on her face. "Oh, and you might want to tell the crew to secure for maneuvering."

"Yes, my lady," he answered dutifully, reaching for the ship's blower.

"Gas." Mira's voice caused him to pause and glance back.

"Yes?"

"Make sure they're *really* secure."

Oh hell. Gaston groaned. It was going to be one of those days.

*

"She's leading us right into the legion." Brennan scowled as he tightened to the wind, bringing his Naga in within a few hundred feet of the *Andros*, hanging back a little to her port side. "What the *hell* is she thinking?"

"That she's the skipper, and she makes the calls," Kennick said calmly, though inside he was wondering pretty much the same thing.

Brennan, unlike his gunner, didn't have much faith in the former Cadrewoman, but he was now committed. Lydia was on that ship, that corsair, and he'd be damned if he left her to fall into the hands of the people who'd killed the rest of his family.

Damn Lydia and her duty and responsibility streak. He'd kicked most of those feelings aside a long time earlier. Duty had lost him his father and his brother before they'd actually died, and Brennan had little interest in responsibility either. His sister, despite all her rebellions, still held on to those chains deep down, and he'd be damned if he lost her too.

The *Andros* was moving so damned slowly that he had to keep dropping line, using his fighter to drag his sails back and reduce speed. That caused a level of frustration that neared a boiling point when the *Andros* cut to port, turning into the advancing legion.

"What the burning skies is she *doing*?" Brennan growled, adjusting to match speed and course. "If she keeps this up, I'm landing this crate on the deck of that hunk of junk and taking my sister off . . ."

Kennick shook his head, both amused and concerned. Concern was outweighing amusement, though, mostly because he had so many damned things to be concerned about. He didn't know what the skipper was doing either, but he trusted her. He didn't have much trust in the young heir flying the Naga he was currently relying on for his *life*, however, and the boy's lack of cool was a problem.

"Calmly," he said. "It's out of our hands right now. We have to trust the skipper."

"She's out of her mind!" Brennan yelled. "We should be running for the desert. We could easily vanish into the haze and come out anywhere we chose."

"We could"—Kennick nodded—"but that's not what the skipper's decided to do, so we won't. Losing your cool over it just isn't how things are done."

Brennan took a breath, forcing himself to calm down. Kennick was right, of course. The one commandment of flying was that you didn't lose your cool. You didn't panic; you didn't get mad. If you had to, you got even, but that was it.

"All right, fine. I hope she knows what she's doing."

Kennick was glad that the boy couldn't see his face as he looked at the legion they were bearing down on. *You're not the only one, kid.*

*

"The *Phoenix* and the *Thunderbird* are going to make the intercept."

Kim nodded, eyes on the skies. The *Elemental* would come a few minutes late to the engagement, but they'd be able to back up the other two destroyers just in case they needed it. The way the *Andros* was flying, however, made it seem like the current handler of the ship intended to surrender.

There was no other explanation for flying half-mast into a full squadron of destroyers with a ship that had no chance of matching them.

He couldn't, wouldn't, count on that, but that's what seemed to be happening.

"Intercept will happen in three minutes, skipper."

"Location?" Kim asked, eyes flitting to the map.

"Sector Ninety-Eight Aleph."

Kim frowned. "That sounds familiar."

"Refugee camp in the sector, skipper. No armed personnel."

Kim nodded, remembering. He hoped that the refugees wouldn't be caught in anything nasty, but sometimes it sucked to be a civilian.

"Signal the *Thunderbird*. Have them issue the order to heave to."

"Aye, skipper."

*

"Two destroyers on approach, skipper."

Mira nodded. "I see them. Signals?"

The signals officer, Kay Mirran, nodded from where she was standing, her security strap locked tight to a nearby rail.

"Looks like the *Phoenix* and the *Thunderbird*, skipper," she announced. "That means we're up against the Bulls. Hold on. I'm getting a signal code from the *Thunderbird* . . . They're demanding that we heave to, skipper. Do I respond?"

"No."

Mira had a lot of plans in mind, but heaving to for boarding wasn't among them.

"Time to the camp?"

"Almost three minutes, skipper. The destroyers will have us in range by then."

Mira nodded. "Clear. Stand by the projectors."

"Projectors standing by!"

"Gas"—she turned to her second—"make sure the boys below know it's about to get rough, but I need the cargo crew ready to move."

Gaston nodded. "They'll be ready."

"Never had a doubt," Mira said with an oddly peaceful smile.

As Gaston watched, it changed from peaceful to predatory in the blink of an eye as she leaned over her wheel, eager, it seemed, for what was to come.

"Let's have some *fun*."

*

William Everett was pushing his small skimmer as hard as he could, the days of being able to requisition an Imperial reaction craft nothing more than a fond memory. His light skimmer was fast, though, pushing eight hundred miles per hour at the top of the atmosphere, chasing the legion that had just left the central empire a few hours earlier.

At least he now had a name to go with his mysterious arms dealer, or supplier, he supposed.

Mira Delsol.

Delsol was an old family. They'd been with the original Scourwinds when they'd led their people here two steps ahead of the cataclysm. William was more familiar with the Cadrewoman's father, actually. Nikolai Delsol had been a hard man and one of the top strategists in the empire for many years before he passed on. A good man, but one that few people really knew well, including his own family.

Now his daughter was running guns to loyalist sympathizers.

Honestly, William wasn't quite certain how her father would have reacted. The Delsols were long associated with the Scourwind dynasty, despite being occasional rivals in the political arena. Nikolai would have fought tooth and nail against any coup attempts, but the old man had been a long-term strategist to the core.

His daughter's actions were those of a grunt with no view of the big picture.

William wished that he'd pulled her file before he'd destroyed the computers in Cadre command. It would have helped immensely if he could review what sorts of missions she'd been assigned as an operative.

All too often, Cadre personnel became predictable based on the sorts of assignments they drew. In hindsight, even Corian himself had really done nothing more than he'd been trained to do. Most of his assignments had been in the kingdoms downspin of the empire, doing the occasional black work that kept them from building up to strength levels that might challenge the legions.

He'd been *good* at it.

Once he'd become an enemy of the empire, it was without question that he would turn those skills against the Scourwinds.

So what, I wonder, did you do for the Cadre, Mira Delsol?

*

"She's climbing, skipper."

"I see it," Commander Kim said as he watched the opening gambits of the battle play out.

The *Phoenix* and the *Thunderbird* were closing in with a textbook flanking maneuver, tightening their lines while reducing their sails. That would drop their speed but give them more close-in maneuverability with far less concern about blowing each other's sails out of the skies.

By the book, solid, and just as he'd expect from the captains under his command.

It was the *Andros* that had him worried.

She was climbing, scrambling for altitude on four wide sails. Still running at half-mast meant that the ship was already sluggish in the air, but climbing right before an engagement meant that she was intentionally bleeding away her speed.

Speed is life. What is that woman doing?

Both of the destroyers were set to catch her in a cross fire that even the *Caleb Bar* herself couldn't easily weather, and yet the *Andros* was still just climbing.

"Is she heading for the third layer, captain?"

Kim shook his head. "No way she makes it, if she is. The *Andros* is a fast ship, but at half-mast, she'll be in the burning skies before she makes the third layer."

"The *Thunderbird* reports no response to orders to surrender, skipper. Firing solution is confirmed."

Kim nodded, his face setting as the decision was made.

"Engage."

*

The sails of the two destroyers angled out, pulling to the sides of their ships and clearing the chase armaments as they nosed up into the air and locked in on the target skimmer. A blind rat couldn't have missed the brilliant silver-white sails a gleaming hull a few tens of thousands of feet above them as the order came through.

As one, both destroyers opened fire with heavy blasters.

Bomb-pumped lase blasts tore out through the atmosphere, plasma sucked along with the energy lighting up the skies.

A prelude to destruction.

CHAPTER 16

"Kill the sails!"

The order was so unexpected that on another ship a moment's hesitation may have ended them in the next instant, but Gaston acted without thinking, and his hand slammed down on the emergency command even as the horror of what he'd just done struck him.

The *Andros Pak* seemed to hover for an interminable second as the sails died, but it was only an illusion. She entered free fall instantly, and the crew felt their stomachs lurch up into their throats.

Only Mira seemed unaffected, which struck Gaston as both fair and incredibly annoying as she had been the only one who'd known what was coming. She laughed wildly, twisting the wheel in her hand as the nose tipped down and the *Andros* started to pick up speed.

Above them the skies lit up with crossing blaster beams, the red traces drawing a cage in the sky that had been destined to carve the *Andros* to cubes. Instead, Gaston held on for his life and sanity as the mist danced wildly in the distance and the ground appeared ahead of them.

The *Andros* keeled over at the command of her captain. Though she'd never been designed to fly on her own, the ship was built as a lifting wing, with multiple control surfaces to aid in maneuvering. Mira Delsol was making them do things no one had ever intended, laughing all the way.

"Gunners! Fire as she bears!"

This time there was some hesitation, though Gaston supposed it could just be the length of time it took the gunners to get their hands back on the controls. Then one of the blasters fired, followed by two more, and in short order all of the *Andros*'s chase guns were pouring fire down on the *Thunderbird* as the corsair plummeted through the skies, a bird with its wings clipped.

*

On the deck of the *Thunderbird*, a lethal rain began pelting anyone in the open and tearing into the armor like deadly hail. The captain spun the ship away from the attack and his sister ship hard, but with the sails minimized and their speed already killed by the very act of putting her nose up to target the *Andros*, the destroyer was too sluggish to respond quickly enough.

Lase blasts carved out pockmarks in the armor, and fifteen men were killed by direct fire or the spattering molten metal from the armor hits in just the first few seconds.

"Fire! Return fire!" the captain screamed over the sound of the plasma rain tearing into their hull and armor.

"She's dropping too fast! We can't get our nose down quick enough!"

He knew that, actually. He was the one struggling with the wheel.

"Kill the forward sails!"

His second hesitated, shooting the captain an incredulous look.

"I said *kill* the forward sails! Bring our nose down!" he screamed again.

The second slammed his hand down hard, and the *Thunderbird*'s forward sails vanished into the ether. The ship tilted wildly, pitching men around as they struggled to hold on, and the remaining sails suddenly were forced to take up the stress of the big ship.

They would have adjusted easily enough if a lucky shot from the *Andros* hadn't chosen that moment to destroy one of the remaining port-side projectors. As that sail winked out of existence, the *Thunderbird* keeled to port and began spiraling toward the ground.

*

"What is that *woman* doing?"

It wasn't the first time Brennan had asked that question, and he had a sinking feeling that it would not be the last.

I'm not about to watch the last of my family die in a fiery wreck, spread across twenty square miles . . .

He contemplated following them, his knuckles itching as he handled the controls, but Kennick half turned and said, "Don't even think about it, kid. Skipper knows what she's doing." He didn't add the unspoken *I hope* he heard echo in his mind. "She doesn't need you getting in the way."

Brennan ground his teeth but nodded jerkily.

"Clear," he barked, angry and frustrated.

"I'm keeping an eye on them," Kennick said. "Watch that other destroyer. We may have to provide cover when the *Andros* recovers."

"That ship is *not* rated for that kind of maneuver," Brennan gritted through clenched teeth.

He should know. He'd done similar tricks all the time, usually to scare a passenger, but he just did them in a small two-man stunt skimmer and *not* in a 160-foot-long *yacht*. He didn't even want to *think* about the stress the projector stanchions were going to endure.

"It's Imperial shipyards construction," Kennick said diffidently. "They always understate their rating."

*

Inside the *Andros*, Lydia clutched at her mouth and tried very hard to neither scream nor vomit across the entire room.

I hate flying. Why does anyone do this for fun?

Brennan, her idiot brother, had done this to her before. He thought it was great fun, free-falling in a skimmer. His skimmer, however, was a civilian ultralight rated for stunt flying. She doubted *very* strongly that the *Andros* was remotely rated for anything like this.

It was all she could do to just clutch herself tightly and try not to turn into a gibbering wreck.

The only reason she wasn't panicking right then was that she was quite certain if she did, Dusk would completely lose whatever calm the girl had. Disgustingly, Mik was laughing like he was on some amusement ride, but she could see the dark girl's eyes and knew that she was just looking for a reason to freak out.

Lydia sucked in a breath and willed a sickly smile onto her face, even as her stomach rebelled against her and tried to crawl out her throat.

"It'll be fine," she said, yelling. "Brennan was very impressed with the handler on this ship when they landed, remember? And Brennan is the best natural flyer I know. If he says it, it's true."

Dusk managed an equally sickly smile and nodded, but clearly she wasn't feeling up to responding.

That was fine. Lydia didn't think she could maintain a conversation at the moment either.

*

"Festering burning skies and seas!" Kim swore violently as he watched the *Thunderbird* spiral down, even as the *Andros* plummeted past it, still accelerating dead on for oblivion on the ground below. "Sails to maximum! Tighten us to the wind! All flank ahead!"

The gleaming sails of the *Elemental* exploded outward as the ship's projectors were pushed to the max, enlarging coverage to the point where the sails were obscuring some visibility. But the added area increased speed another 10 percent as the lines tightened to bring the destroyer up in behind the light sails to further reduce drag.

Of all the things he'd expected, *that* was not one of them.

Only a fool and a lunatic would even consider a maneuver like that, he thought grimly, knuckles white as he gripped the wheel.

There was an axiom in the military, one he was intimately familiar with: the greatest armsman in the world didn't fear the second greatest. He feared the worst, because he couldn't predict what the damned fool was going to do.

So what in the burning skies do you do when you're dealing with an incredibly skilled warrior who was entirely happy to throw every single rule right out the port lock?

Kim seethed as he watched the sails of the *Thunderbird* flicker and form, her captain clearly trying to recover his stricken ship.

Apparently, if you're not damned lucky, you die.

"New orders to gunners," he called. "As soon as we're in range, open fire on the *Andros*. No quarter."

*

"Passing ten thousand feet."

Gaston sounded calm, but there was an undercurrent of terror in his voice that really made Mira's day. She was giddily working all the controls and throwing the wheel over as she brought the ship back to an even keel across the beam, still pointed too low for anyone's comfort.

"Clear," she acknowledged cheerfully.

A few seconds later, he spoke again. "Approaching five thousand feet."

"Clear."

She didn't have to look at him to know that Gaston was sweating, even in the cold chill of the rushing air. He was secured to his station, as was she and nearly everyone else, so there was nothing he could do but ride it out, and for a man like Gas . . . like most of those on board, that was the true definition of torture.

"Stand by projectors," she ordered as they passed five thousand feet.

"Standing by already . . ."

"Fire."

The *Andros* vibrated with the launch of the four projector rockets she'd kept in reserve.

"Brace!" Mira ordered just before they flared to life thousands of feet aboveground.

The silver-white sails snapped into view, catching the wind and yanking hard on the plummeting ship. A groan was heard through the *Andros* that no one on board had ever heard on a ship before and that none ever wanted to hear again.

They were all slammed down into the deck and against the straps as the *Andros*'s plummet was suddenly turned into a parabola. Vertical velocity converted to horizontal in a bone jarringly short time, the ship like a pendulum at the end of a very long string.

Mira again hit the blower, leaning into it as she called out orders.

"Cargo crew, stand ready to deliver! Projectors, I need those four reloaded! Now!"

Mira smiled, pride filling her as she watched the crew she could see jump to follow her command. She had no doubt that belowdecks the very same was happening.

*

"Thirty seconds to drop!"

The men in the hold of the *Andros* had the supply packets already in place. That had been the easy part. They just loaded them last and put them right on the rails. The hard part had been securing them when orders came down before the engagement and, now, getting them set to launch again.

They professionally ignored the splatters of vomit that decorated the deck and the pallets—not every man and woman on board was made of the sternest of stuff—and trucked everything into place just before they snapped their safety rigs into place.

"Doors opening!"

The whistle and roar of wind tore through the hold as the large doors to the rear of the ship slowly ground open, and they saw for the first time just how far they'd fallen. The ground was whipping past so close in places it almost looked like you could reach out and touch earth.

"Damn. The lady really sliced that one close to the bone."

"Stand by to drop!"

*

"Gas"—Mira smiled—"raise the colors."

"Yes, my lady," Gaston replied instantly, finally getting an order he was eager to follow.

"Gas . . ." She paused. "Best add the Scourwind colors to that."

Gaston nodded. "As you say."

The projectors set into the rear of the ship exploded to life, and a huge black flag with a crossed blaster and Armati rippled in the wind like one made of real cloth. Below it, the Scourwind colors flew as pallets of food, water, condensers, and other relief supplies were rolled off the rails and out the back of the *Andros*.

Mira grinned, glancing over her shoulder as her hair blew wildly in the whipping wind. The supplies were dotting out behind them as they rushed over the camp, but she expected the guidance systems would drop them all close enough.

If not, it's out of my power now, she thought.

The *Phoenix* was still desperately trying to get turned around fast enough to reacquire contact with the *Andros*, but they were out of this fight. The *Thunderbird* looked like it was about to plow into the ground. She couldn't tell if they'd gotten enough control to make the impact survivable or not. She somewhat hoped they had, but Mira could barely bring herself to care anymore.

Having your own armsmen turn on you, choosing instead to follow a mass murderer, had a way of distancing you from any esprit de corps that may normally have lingered.

"The *Elemental* is closing fast," Gaston said.

Mira turned her eyes, spotting the gleaming sails of the approaching destroyer and noting that they were tucked in to the wind as close as she'd ever seen.

"They really want to catch us," she said, moderately amused.

Gaston snorted. "I wonder why, my lady?"

"No clue. Well, let's disappoint them," she said. "Secure the hold; launch the remaining projectors."

"Yes, my lady!"

The *Andros*'s parabola had brought them around under the sails that held them aloft, so that they were now actually threatening to *outrace* their own sails. Since that would mean they'd rapidly lose speed in a situation where Mira really didn't want to lose speed, she let out a tiny sigh of relief as the reimaging four projectors launched out ahead of them.

With eight sails now in the skies, Mira brought the *Andros* tight to their leading four, carefully maintaining tautness on the four they were outracing so as to keep the lines from tangling. The ship began to climb again as the winds caught and all eight sails snapped forward with enough force to jerk the *Andros* hard.

"I see the Bulls, my lady." Gaston nodded off to the side. "We'll clear them easily. The *Elemental* is going to get a piece of our flank, however."

Mira twisted, mentally calculating the vectors even though she was certain Gaston's numbers would be better than hers. She swore when her own agreed, then gritted her teeth.

This was going to hurt.

*

"Clear the sails," Horace Kim ordered sternly. "I want a clean shot at that bitch."

A plume of smoke was rising up in the distance from where the *Thunderbird* had slammed into the ground. He couldn't spare the time to check on the crew just yet, but what he could do was avenge them. Kim was aware that the *Andros* had picked up enough speed with her crazy maneuver that she was going to pull away from the squadron, but at the very least he was going to get his licks in.

The big sails of the destroyer angled out, pulling wider and opening up the range on the chase guns. Kim eyeballed the ranges and did vector calculations instinctively. He doubted that they'd be able to drop the *Andros*, but they could tear a very large hole or two into the smaller ship.

"Fire as we bear," he ordered. "All guns. No quarter."

"Aye, skipper. Firing as we bear!"

Big lase charges were slammed home into the blaster cannons, and in a few seconds the *Elemental* shook as her weapons roared to autofire, spitting beams and plasma across the skies.

*

The first rounds missed clean, but Mira knew that they'd get within range in short order. She hauled in the lines, tucking the skimmer up behind the sails as tight as she could without dirtying her own wind. She angled the *Andros*, using the ship to cover its own projectors, intent on avoiding the fate of the *Thunderbird.*

After that, all she could do was hunker down and wait for the inevitable.

It didn't take long.

The armor of the *Andros* rang like a massive bell as the first blast hammered home, vaporizing a chunk of steel and ceramic and ejecting the resulting plasma out into the air. The ship shook a little but remained stable until the next hit. Another deep ring assaulted their ears. Another crater was dug into the heavy armor of the skimmer.

The next three shots hit in rapid succession.

"We're going to lose parts of the aft cargo hold and quarters at this rate," Gaston warned.

"Evacuate those areas!"

"Yes, my lady!"

*

Kim snarled viciously. He had their range now. With a little luck he might even be able to cripple the skimmer.

"Keep firing! Hammer that ship into dust!"

Kim was leaning over the wheel, eagerly watching the lase blasts strike home, when a shadow passed over the flying bridge of the *Elemental.* He started, looking up and around for the source, and spotted a deep aquamarine sail just as it flashed past.

"Who—?"

He only got the first word of his question out before the deck of the *Elemental* was torn to shreds by a series of hammer blows that tore through his ceramic armor like an ice pick through cardstock. He ducked low just as the mottled green airframe with a wide grinning mouth painted on the front flashed past.

Kim blinked and shook his head. "Where the hell did a Naga come from? A *museum*?"

His second crawled over, keeping low as the Naga spun around practically in place. "Museum or not, skipper, he's packing MACs!"

Kim paled.

Magnetic-accelerated canons (MACs) were antiquated, but they hadn't been retired for lack of effectiveness. Rather they were too heavy and too expensive to deploy to the legion, and over the years the price of maintaining and arming the weapons had just gone up. But for Kim, the question of where the Naga had come from and how the hell it was loaded with MACs would have to wait.

If he weren't careful, that one small skimmer would turn his destroyer to a sieve.

With one last angry glare at the departing *Andros Pak*, Kim gauged the approach of the Naga and flung his wheel hard to starboard. The *Elemental* keeled over smoothly as the Naga flashed past again, MACs roaring, but this time most of the rounds hit low on the bigger vessel's port armor where the thicker plates could take the beating.

"Gunners! Get that thing locked in!"

"No need, sir." His second shook his head. "He's done what he set out to do. He's not coming back around."

Indeed, Kim looked and spotted the Naga already starting to vanish into the distance. Only its sails were still clear, and even they were beginning to fade into the deep-blue sky.

He seethed for a moment, but there wasn't much he could do. He'd lost his window of opportunity with the *Andros*, and the Naga that cost him the chance was pulling away faster than he could pursue. He had a ship down and likely injuries on board.

"Let them go," he said. "I'm bringing us around. We need to check on the *Thunderbird*."

*

Brennan's heart was roaring in his ears, something that hadn't happened to him since he first made a solo flight. He kept twisting around to check behind him, unable to quite believe that they weren't being pursued, but it seemed that the destroyer was actually turning away.

Unbelievable.

"You can relax, kid," Kennick said calmly from the front seat. "They can't catch us and they know it, and now that the *Andros* is clear, they've got other problems."

"It happened so fast." Brennan blinked, confused.

"Battle is like that, kid. Sometimes an hour feels like ten seconds, and sometimes ten seconds feels like a lifetime," Kennick answered. "We lived, we did our job, and we're still flying. Can't ask for much more. Nice flying, by the way. Good approach. You lined me up just right."

"We didn't do much on the second pass," Brennan said, not sure if he should be glad or disappointed.

"We did what we needed to. We made them flinch. Head for the *Andros*. Let's call it a day."

"Yeah," Brennan mumbled, nodding in agreement. "Sounds good."

The stubby Fire Naga rolled a little as he twisted the sails, which spun up behind them and cut into the winds as they headed for where the gleaming sails of the *Andros* were beginning to be obscured by the ever-present mist.

CHAPTER 17

Corian stood on the open deck of the *Caleb Bar*, looking down over the site where the destroyer *Thunderbird* had plowed into the rocky terrain below.

It hadn't been a total loss. Many of the crew had survived the crash. The captain had managed to slow his ship's descent using the remaining sails, but the crash was still bad enough. An Imperial destroyer taken out in the opening moments of battle by a glorified luxury yacht. He didn't care *who* was in command of the damned yacht; it was a disgrace.

"This woman is becoming intolerable," Corian grumbled, half turning to look at the aide waiting behind him. "What of the depot?"

"Our team located the Cadre cache, sire, but it had already been picked clean aside from some restricted but easily acquired equipment."

Corian nodded.

Of course it had. She'd had hours at least, perhaps longer, to accomplish her mission. He needed *intelligence* on this woman, blast it all. He needed the Cadre files.

"Increase the reward on her head, and put a bounty on every known member of her crew," he ordered. "I want them alive, to be tried as pirates and traitors to the empire."

"Yes, my lord. Double her reward?"

"Multiply it by ten."

The aide bowed. "It will be done."

"And have the commander of this pathetic squadron clapped in chains and sent to the palace," Corian said as an afterthought. "This *incompetence* will not stand."

*

Missed them, William thought.

But he wasn't surprised. He'd had late notification while the Bulls had a head start, and even they'd almost missed them.

He'd stashed his skimmer miles away and hiked in to where the legion was still milling about. The dark airborne fortress Corian named the *Caleb Bar* was on site now, floating in defiance of every physical law William could claim to understand. No sails, no thrusters, just . . . floating in the air.

That ship was Corian's trump card.

It was too heavily armored to shoot down, and the weapons it was armed with were staggering. He knew that it had to be the results of a black project backed by Edvard, but by the endless mist he didn't know what the emperor had been thinking. There was no enemy out there that required a hammer like the *Caleb Bar* to put them in their place.

Only the Imperial palace and a few other Redoubts, all controlled by the empire as well, were a realistic threat to the ship.

Why, Edvard? Why would you have such a thing built? You were never that stupid.

It was one question that he would have to get used to not having the answer to, but it was also one that burned deeply within him. Without the *Caleb*, he was certain that he could have turned back Corian's coup.

William shifted his listening equipment, pointing it at different groups he could see through his lenses and picking up bits and pieces of conversations. Some of it useful, most not, but it was all information, and you never knew what information might save your life.

One conversation, however, made him straighten up.

"She was a cocky one," a legion colonel grumbled as William listened in. "In the middle of the fight she dumped supplies to the refugee camp over the ridge. Had the nerve to fly a black crossed guard banner as she did it . . . oh, and the Scourwind colors."

Delsol flew the Scourwind colors?

That didn't make sense. Even the loyalists wouldn't fly the personal colors of the Scourwinds. It wasn't done. Not unless . . .

The twins. She has them, one at least.

William packed away his gear.

Now he *had* to find Mira Delsol.

*

The *Andros Pak* rested along the edge of a cliff, one of the oddly smooth sections where the land jutted up straight and true like it had been cut by an industrial laser. There were several places in the empire like that, formations that no one had ever been able to explain.

The empire and the domain within which it existed was a confusing one for the scientists who studied natural law. There were several things within the kingdom that simply didn't fit within any set of equations they'd come up with to describe the universe they saw, which included oddities like the glass cliffs and the metal floor that ran under the empire in its entirety.

Mira had been privy to a few of the mysteries. In her early days in the Cadre, she'd been tasked with infiltrating a smuggling group. Left to her own devices, she'd attached herself to a well-known researcher and spent a few months learning the ins and outs of the land, eventually using her connections and knowledge to set up a few small trade routes that caught the attention of her targets.

In the process she'd picked up enough to know that a lot about the world just didn't make sense.

The Great Islands, for one, the only source of escape from the burning skies . . . shouldn't exist. They traveled a perfect path through the sky, constant and regular enough to set a timepiece to. They had never faltered, never changed, in all the generations who had observed them, as far back as the Imperial records went.

Everything changed, but they didn't.

No equation that explained gravity could also describe the motion of the islands, and no equation that described the islands could explain gravity.

The world was a confusing place.

She was now faced with another source of confusion, though it was admittedly a little less massive than the mystery of the islands.

The Scourwind twins, the two bratty heirs to the empire—and their friends—were now under her care, which Mira honestly didn't much care for. Oh, she was loyal to the empire . . . after a manner. But that loyalty had been stretched to the breaking point when her own armsmen had fired on her, and it had nearly snapped entirely when the loyalists she'd been helping turned on her for the reward Corian posted . . . but she was still loyal, at an extremely *long* arm's length.

The twins, however, were well within that arm's length now, and frankly she didn't know what to do about it.

The boy, Brennan, had his brother's Bene. No, more than that. He'd *linked* his brother's Bene.

More than loyalty to the Scourwinds, that connection bound her to the boy at least until he was trained. She'd not suffer an Armati to be wielded by a substandard bearer. Her own Elan hummed in her mind, agreement flowing from the ancient weapon.

That was one thing that only wielders of Armati ever truly understood, that they were comrades in blood and history. Even someone you *despised* who had an Armati had to be respected to some degree or another. She would kill Corian, given half a chance, but the man had bonded to an Armati in his time . . . two, if current rumors were correct.

He may be evil, but for his Armati alone he had a portion of her respect.

This brat, however, was another matter.

Oh, he'd linked with his brother's Armati to be sure. She figured that meant he had depths he wasn't showing anyone yet, but, honestly, he'd *have* to soon.

She'd never trained a Cadreman, though.

She didn't know if she even could, but she was going to try.

Bene deserved that much.

Mira turned back to the work being done on the *Andros*, noting that most of the large holes had been patched. The new sections were light on armor. They couldn't exactly pick that stuff up anywhere easily, but at least the ship would be sealed against the cold bitter air of the high skies.

Well, I suppose I have work to do.

Mira made her way back to the ship.

*

Brennan had his head in the old Fire Naga when Lydia and the other two found him.

As usual.

"Skies, Brennan." Lydia sounded exasperated. "What is it this time?"

"Just tuning the controllers," he answered without poking his head back out. "They were a little sluggish."

Lydia grabbed him by a boot and pulled, sliding her brother out from where he'd buried himself in an access panel.

"Hey!"

"Hey, yourself," she scolded. "You've been spending every waking minute in that thing. It's not healthy."

Brennan sighed, grabbing a rag to clean his hands. "Not a lot more to do while repairs are being made. You're the one who decided you wanted to hide out with this group."

Lydia rolled her eyes. "That's no excuse to become a recluse. Besides, she's looking for you."

"She who?" he asked.

"She, the captain of this ship."

The new voice startled them all, and Brennan jumped the highest, as the voice had come from directly behind him. He turned to see the Cadrewoman leaning back against the airframe of the Naga, idly checking her fingernails for dirt.

"Stop *doing* that!" he growled.

"Start noticing me when I walk up, then," she countered, only then raising her head to look lazily at him. "I have no *idea* what Bene sees in you."

Brennan's eyes narrowed. "Who?"

"Really, *really* don't see it." She shook her head, stepping away from the Naga. "Your brother's Armati. Bene, that's her name."

Brennan's hand went automatically to the small of his back, where he kept the last thing his brother had ever given him.

Bene.

He tasted the name in his mind and whispered it so softly that even he couldn't hear it, but he could *feel* the name on his tongue, and it felt right.

"I told you if you came with me, I'd train you to use her," Mira said, "and I keep my word. We start today."

"What? Wait a second . . ."

"No, no more seconds. We start today," she repeated. "The ship lifts off in three hours. Meet me here in four. Don't be late."

With that, the former Cadrewoman walked off, leaving the four teens gaping at her as she left.

"Sorry, Bren. I tried to warn you," Lydia said, shrugging.

Brennan sighed, wiping the sweat from his face. "Yeah, well, maybe she'll have something useful to show me."

"The captain seems very . . . strong?" Dusk offered tentatively.

Brennan chuckled. "She's Cadre. Strong is one of the requirements. I just don't much like the Cadre."

"How come, mate?" Mik asked casually, curious but only mildly interested as he leaned on the Naga.

"We grew up around Cadre personnel," Lydia answered for him. "They took both our father and brother as members. We rarely saw either of them, but there were always Cadre around. They may be great warriors, but many of them were pretty bad people."

Brennan sighed. "Like anywhere else, any other group, they had good and bad in them. But even our brother—I didn't have a lot of respect for him."

"Bren!" Lydia blurted, shocked. "Kayle was a good man!"

"Kayle was Cadre." Brennan scowled. "He was part of that damned brotherhood. Maybe only a few of them were really bad, but the rest covered for them. It took a monster like Corian before anyone would even whisper that maybe the almighty Cadre were actually human. Even Kayle wouldn't speak against his fellows, and you know as well as I do that he saw them do things no citizen would get away with."

Lydia was silent, looking down.

"They're all guilty, as far as I'm concerned," Brennan said. "If you cover up a crime for someone, you committed the crime."

"Aren't you being a little harsh?" Mik asked, puzzled by the anger simmering in Brennan's voice.

Brennan leveled a glare at him that could have killed in another world, another time.

"No."

Brennan tossed the rag down and rubbed his face and hair, cooling down a little.

"Look, I'm sorry. I'm getting all fired up over something that doesn't matter anymore," he said finally, eyes glancing briefly toward Lydia. "I'm just really torn on the Cadre, OK? There's history."

"Apparently," Mik said, holding up his hands. "Not my business. I don't need to know."

Brennan nodded. "Thanks."

"The captain saved us. She didn't have to," Lydia reminded her brother.

"We didn't need her. We could have gotten away clean without engaging a destroyer squadron."

"Not if we wanted to help the refugees."

Brennan sighed. Maybe she had a point. He didn't know.

"Look, I'm not going to insult her or anything," he said finally. "I loved Kayle. He was my brother. I just didn't like what he did with his life. For all that, I want to understand him. I won't put on that uniform, but he gave me this . . . Bene. I'll listen to what she has to say."

*

"It's time."

Kennissey looked up, surprised to see his old friend standing there, but only slightly.

"You've found them?" he asked, leaning forward eagerly.

"I know where they are, one of them at least," William Everett said. "Start the gathering. I'll track them down now that I have a lead."

Kennissey frowned. "Are you certain? It'll expose some of our operations. If you're wrong . . ."

"Mira Delsol has them," William said. "She's Cadre. They'll be easy to find now that I know what I'm looking for."

"How do you know?"

"She flew the Scourwind colors beside her own preferred banner." William smirked, considering how iconic the black banner with the crossed Armati and blaster had become, since the battle had been witnessed by thousands.

It was a black mark on Corian and his new administration. Copies of the flag were already appearing across the empire, fired by the victory over Imperial destroyers as much as by Mira's relief supply delivery.

Dropping the supplies in the midst of a battle at the wrong side of two to one odds was a nice touch, William admitted to himself.

Crediting the act to the twins (or one of them, at least in his mind) had gone a long way to destroying the fragile illusion that Corian was still answering to the Scourwind legacy. People wanted to see the emperor, and the pressure was mounting. In one move, Delsol had accomplished more than he and the loyalists had in months. If William weren't so impressed, frankly, he'd be beyond pissed and frustrated.

He still rather wished that she would check in with someone in the loyalist network and start damned well coordinating with the others. She was making all kinds of waves on her own, but if his allies had a little warning, they could turn those waves into an alluvion flood that would swamp everything in their path.

Particularly as she held the final key he needed to launch the counteroffensive.

"Delsol is a Cadrewoman of some reputation," he added after a moment. "She wouldn't fly the Scourwind colors lightly. She has one of them, at least, if not both."

"Then you're right; we need to find her," Kennissey said, "and before Corian does. He's put a significant reward on her head, if you hadn't heard."

"Last I checked it was ten thousand dinars."

"You're out of date." Kennissey smirked. "He bumped it to a hundred thousand a few days ago, presumably after that stunt. Do you think he knows?"

"That she has the twins?" William considered that, wondering himself. "I think we have to assume that he does."

"Then it's a race."

"One we cannot lose."

*

"Sire, the unrest is growing stronger."

Corian ignored the man. He wasn't telling him anything that he couldn't see for himself. The Scourwind colors had been flown in battle, *against* his forces. That was enough to open a wedge of doubt that he'd been struggling to close.

It's too early for this!

He only had solid support from perhaps a third of the Senate. Another third was still cleanly in the loyalist camp, and their names were on his lists . . . oh yes. The rest were unknowns. Either they were far enough from the center of the empire that he had little intelligence on them, or they were sneakier and more cunning than the rest of their peers.

And one damn woman was giving him more trouble than the combined legions of the empire, the rest of the Cadre, and the emperor himself.

The one thing that gave him some hope, however, was that she'd slipped up.

Oh, she probably didn't see it that way.

No Cadreman would fly the Scourwind colors unless a member of the family was on board. Even he'd not been willing to bend his honor to quite that level, and he'd personally assassinated Edvard Scourwind in the very room he now occupied.

It came from the old laws, a set of guidelines not enforced in generations, because there'd been no need. You didn't break those laws, no matter what else you might do. Not once you'd sworn your oath, at least.

No, she had a member of the family on board her ship.

By revealing that, she'd cracked the surface of his control, but she'd also exposed herself and the heir to the empire's gaze.

Corian had legions scouring the empire for them. They could not hide. He would bring that ship down, personally if need be, and use the heirs to fully legitimize his position.

CHAPTER 18

Brennan threw himself to one side, narrowly avoiding the razor-sharp blade that swept through his previous position.

"Don't dodge," Mira yelled. *"Block!"*

"With *this*?" he asked incredulously, holding up the stubby item in his hand.

The Armatis all had several forms, starting with the one that he was currently holding. Unfortunately for Brennan, that first form was referred to as the sheath. In the case of Kayle's Bene—now his, he supposed—the sheath was little more than a foot long with a slight curve that he pocketed easily in his palm.

Good for common carry, yes, but not great for blocking an attack.

Mira was entirely unsympathetic.

"You've linked once. Do it again or I *will* cut you. Badly."

She backed her promise with a lunge that neatly sliced his shirt as he again dodged out of the way, leaving a swash of fabric floating to the ground in his stead.

"Hey!" He scowled, clutching at the ruined fabric. "Do I look like I have a huge wardrobe? We escaped the palace with just the clothes on our backs!"

"Pfff!" Mira blew him off. "You'll wear coveralls from my crew's supplies, and you'll *like* them."

Lydia laughed outright from the perimeter of the circle Mira had drawn out. The idea of Brennan dressed in anything as close to a uniform as those garments struck her as hilarious.

"Oh, real funny, Lyd—Hey!" Brennan barely skirted a sweep that cleaved the air where he'd been, whistling with the force of the swing. "Come on, crazy lady! I wasn't ready!"

"In a fight, that's code for you're dead."

Brennan had had about as much of that as he was willing to take. He dropped the Armati to the ground with a clatter and turned his back on Mira.

"I'm done."

Mira's eyes narrowed, first at the blatant lack of respect for the Armati Bene he'd been holding and second for the similar lack of respect for herself. She lunged, only stopping the blade just before taking his head off. A trickle of blood ran down Brennan's neck where the razor-fine edge of her Elan had sliced him. He just turned to look at her evenly.

"Are you?" she asked.

Mira seethed inside, though part of her was mildly impressed that he'd not flinched.

The boy has the Scourwind steel, no doubt of that, but he's so anti-authority it sets my teeth on edge.

That, Mira couldn't help but note, was saying something. She'd never been a yes woman herself, and having her own men turn on her and try their damnedest to *kill* her had pretty much soured her on the uniform as well. The boy in front of her, however, made her look like a cog in the machine. She settled back on her feet, sliding the blade along his neck and slicing just a bit deeper before withdrawing completely.

There was some satisfaction in seeing him wince—not very much at all, she told herself, but *some* just the same.

"Fine"—she shrugged casually—"but if I can't cut you, I'm still going to draw *real* blood from someone today . . ."

Mira gave him a moment to consider her words and half turn in her direction before she grinned nastily at him, then twisted and lunged toward Lydia.

Lydia, who'd been watching with disappointment up to that point, was frozen in shock as the gleaming blade sliced the air, heading straight for her head. She flinched back, eyes slamming shut involuntarily, and a clash shook her to her soul.

She opened her eyes slowly, then snapped them wide as she saw Brennan standing between her and Mira with a staff in hand, holding back the Cadrewoman's blade as fury poured off him.

Brennan angled his staff, letting Mira's blade slide off it to the ground away from his sister, then reversed and swung for her head. Mira ducked easily under the swing and countered with a slash to his midsection that was caught by the other end of the staff before he snapped another blow at her ribs.

She laughed, dancing back out of reach.

"Do you hear that? The whispers in the back of your skull?" she asked, blocking another shot with the flat of her blade, then lashing out with a kick that sent Brennan toppling back to the ground in a slide. "Listen to them. They're trying to save your *life*!"

He rolled out of the way as she leapt at him and landed with a potentially bone-crushing stomp where he had been. Brennan tucked the staff in close to his body, rolling for the edge of the circle, but Mira beat him to it, flipping easily over him and landing squarely on the other side. She swung her blade down, making him throw the staff up to block.

Sparks erupted across him as the weapons met, and he grunted under the force of the impact.

This crazy lady is trying to kill me!

Mira grinned down at him over the two crossed weapons. "Taking it seriously yet?"

Brennan grunted, kicking out at her legs from the ground. She avoided the kick easily, but it forced her to let up on the attack, and he used the time to kip up to his feet.

Brennan whirled the staff experimentally, getting a feel for the weight. He'd been trained on a staff, of course, as had Lydia, but somehow the one in his hand felt lighter and yet more solid than anything he'd previously held. It had substance to it that seemed to contrast how light the weapon felt in his hand, like there was a force pushing against him and steadying his hand.

He casually flipped the Armati around, then let the staff roll in his hand and come to rest along his back as he changed his stance and gestured with his free hand.

"All right," he said, glaring at Mira, "let's do this."

*

Lydia watched, heart slowing to its normal pace, as her brother sparred with the Cadrewoman. Brennan had always been competent in the martial courses that were required of all of them, but Lydia could see that Mira's skill was levels of magnitude beyond his. The woman danced around Brennan easily, somehow managing not to inflict any serious injury despite the number of cutting strokes she drove through his defenses.

"They're really good."

Lydia turned, just noticing Dusk slightly behind her to her right.

"Brennan doesn't stand a chance," she told the other girl simply. "He's completely outmatched. She's playing with him."

"Really?"

Lydia nodded. "She's Cadre, and Brennan never really did more than he had to in training. If it doesn't have to do with flying, he's a lazy bugger."

Dusk looked out at the fight between the two, a clearly disbelieving look on her face. "I've never seen anyone move as fast as he did when she attacked you."

Lydia sighed, but frankly she'd also been wondering how the hell he'd done that.

"He's been overprotective in his own way . . . well, for a while," she said finally. "Now that we're the last two of our family left, I guess it's gotten even worse."

"Yeah," Dusk whispered, "I guess I get that."

Lydia saw Dusk sneak a peek across the hold to where Mikael was also watching the fight.

Lydia nodded. "I imagine you do."

*

Metal clashed on metal as blade met staff with ringing reports that echoed off the hold of the *Andros*. Mira had stepped up her attacks as she hammered Brennan with a flurry of blows he just barely managed to knock back. She was grinning the whole time, the entire affair really nothing more than a light workout for her, as the boy wasn't capable of really pushing her capacity. She hadn't even gone enhanced during the whole event, even though she admitted privately that he wasn't a total loss.

Abruptly, Mira broke contact and leapt back. Her blade whipped around her wrist as she flipped it casually, letting it retract into the sheath form before sliding it smoothly into her gun belt.

"Not bad," she said, then added, "for a brat."

Brennan panted as he leaned on his staff, glowering at her.

"You were trying to kill me!"

"Not hardly, kid, though if I'd thought you were slacking, I'd have given you a nice scar to impress the ladies and remind you that a fight is no place to laze about."

Brennan straightened up and lifted the staff off the ground, letting it hang loose in his hand. He was startled as it suddenly retracted into its own sheath, as hers had, and after a moment of looking at it he slowly slipped the Armati into his belt.

"I could hear it," he said finally, "the whispers."

"Good. Then we can really get started," Mira told him with a smile that sent chills up his spine.

Partly out of genuine interest, but mostly in the vain hope that he'd be able to distract her, Brennan blurted out a question that had been at the back of his mind for a long time.

"Is that how you can track and deflect blast bolts?"

Mira paused, her head cocked slightly to one side. "Your brother, I presume?"

Brennan nodded. "I saw him in training."

Mira nodded, understanding. "The short answer is no. We can't track bolts from a lase blaster. That's physically impossible."

"But I've *seen* it!"

"No, you saw something else," Mira said, considering her words. "While a lase blast doesn't quite travel at the speed of light, it's close enough so that by the time you saw the bolt flash and your brain recognized the energy, it would be too late."

Brennan scowled. "Then how?"

"We watch the blaster itself, the eyes of our opponent," she said. "Just before someone decides to *kill* another person, you can read their intent in how they stand, how their eyes narrow. From there it's just math to determine shot vectors. That's an oversimplified explanation, of course, but that's the way we do it. If you aren't already moving to intercept the blast *before* it's fired, then you don't have a chance."

Brennan blinked, not having expected that. "Oh."

He looked down at the Armati in his hand. "I thought it was the weapon."

Mira nodded, face serious now. "I know. There's so much we don't know about the Armati. Even among the Cadre, they're legendary. They were created long before we were born . . . some say before we came"—she looked around the hold of the ship, but her eyes weren't focused on anything in particular—"before we came here," she finished after a moment.

"Here? The *Andros*?"

"No, the empire. This place," she said. "We're not from here. It's not taught much today, as it's ancient history. The legends say that we came from someplace very different. There were no burning skies there, and they say that the sun went away for twelve hours of every twenty-four."

Brennan snorted, then burst out laughing. "That's insane. Where would it go?"

"I don't know. The legends aren't clear on that," Mira said, chuckling with him. "A lot of the old texts were destroyed long ago; most of what we have in the archives are fragmentary . . . unclear. They said that there was a time each day called 'night,' when the sun would vanish and lights called stars would appear. It was a very different place."

"Apparently," Brennan said dryly, not believing it for a moment.

"At any rate," Mira continued, not interested in trying to convince him, as it wasn't relevant to the discussion, "the Armati are a leftover from those days, and a great war. One we lost, and were then forced to flee."

Brennan sobered. He couldn't remember any tales of the empire *losing* a war. They'd been the major power in the region—hell, the *only* real power—for as long as the history books existed, it seemed. There were wars they declined to fight, such as the small kingdoms his father had left to squabble among themselves, but no war that, once engaged, had not ended in the empire's favor.

"The Armatis are, possibly, the finest masterworks in the empire," she said, "and they're priceless relics of our forgotten heritage. Your brother entrusted you with his Bene, and in the absence of any empire I recognize, I don't see fit to question his judgment. Corian, on the other hand, would kill hundreds for less than that weapon on your belt. Guard it well, and it will guard you and yours in turn."

Brennan nodded. "Thanks."

"Don't thank me yet. We've got a lot more work to do." Mira grinned evilly at him. "Now that I've seen what you need to work on, we can get started."

"Oh joy." Brennan rolled his eyes. "And what do I need to work on?"

"Everything."

*

Three days after the repairs had been completed on the *Andros* and two days after Brennan's training had begun, he found himself standing on deck as they sailed the second wind layer, heading up spin along the path tracked by the Great Islands.

Brennan loved the open skies, and though he preferred to be at the controls of a smaller skimmer, there was a lot to say about walking the deck of a large ship under sail. You could see all the way to the edge of the mist in every direction, and even farther if you looked up over the endless shroud that obscured the world.

He was trying to imagine the world Mira had told him about, looking up into the sky and seeing blackness dotted by small lights. It was so absurd.

Above him the sun shone steadily, without the flicker induced by atmosphere in the lower skies, a halo around it obscuring that section of the sky. Beyond the halo, however, he could see the rich blues and greens that made up the real sky. At this altitude, he could even just make out the dark squared-off grid that seemed to measure everything with regularity.

Brennan laughed.

Legends. What nonsense.

The world and the universe were what you could see. Maybe there was something beyond it, but what did it matter? The empire mattered. Family mattered. The endless sky mattered.

Everything else?

None of it was worth the time spent wondering about it.

"You look like someone hung you off the back of a hyper train and left you there for the whole trip."

Brennan turned, relaxing marginally when he recognized Kennick approaching.

"I don't feel much off from that," he admitted. "Haven't seen you around much."

"Been working third shift. You usually sleep then," the former legion man said. "Heard you've been training with the captain."

"Is that what they call it? I thought she was just whaling on me."

"I've seen people she 'whaled' on before, kid." Kennick laughed. "They wind up looking a lot worse than you."

Brennan shook his head, half wanting to disbelieve the man, but knowing damn well that it was true.

"We're a few hours from anywhere in particular," Kennick said casually. "No settlements in the area and certainly no legion outposts . . ."

"Yeah?" Brennan wondered where the man was heading.

"Captain suggested you might like to take your new skimmer out for a run."

"We're in the sky. Is she landing?"

"Hardly. You ever launch from the air before?" Kennick asked, grinning.

Brennan shook his head.

"Oh, you are going to *love* this. Come on, kid. Let's go flying."

*

Lydia sat across from Dusk at the small table afforded her quarters, watching as the other girl worked diligently on a local interface.

"You're skilled," Lydia said finally. "More than I'd expect."

"I grew up with an interface." Dusk shrugged. "It's not so uncommon."

"Maybe," Lydia replied.

It was possible, she supposed. Lydia was well aware that her own experience, while quite rich in some regards, was also grossly disconnected from how the rest of the empire lived. She grew up with interfaces around her, of course, but she'd never had the need to master them to the degree Dusk apparently had.

That wasn't to say she was incompetent with them, far from it. But she'd never learned to push the systems to their limits the way Dusk could.

There was a difference between being very familiar with an interface and being able to make it dance on command.

"What are you working on?" Lydia asked.

Dusk looked up, almost startled by the question, then ducked her head back down and mumbled, "Just making some improvements to the code for the Fire Naga. I wanted to do more, but the captain shut down access to the Imperial network."

Lydia nodded. "There's always a chance of being tracked if someone makes a mistake or lets something slip intentionally." She smiled a little wanly. "Welcome to the life of an outlaw."

Dusk smiled back. "It's not so bad. Better than the camp."

Lydia watched the other girl shudder, but didn't feel it was time to push on that. Instead she leaned in and asked, "Can I help?"

*

"Remember what I told you, kid," Kennick said as the pair sat in the cockpit of the Fire Naga with the canopy still sitting open.

Brennan nodded. "Wait a few seconds after the drop, and then angle away from the ship before firing the sails. Got it."

"You've done free-fall maneuvers before, right?"

"Of course!" Brennan sounded a little insulted, though the question wasn't one with an obvious answer.

Killing your sails in a skimmer was something only the most experienced and daring of handlers tried, and it killed more people than any other ten advanced maneuvers combined. If you misjudged your altitude, you could easily slam into the ground before your sails caught the wind, and that was just the most obvious of threats.

"OK." Kennick accepted the answer, leaning back in the gunner's seat and kicking the canopy pedal.

The armored clear-plast dropped down over them, and a hiss signified the pressure seal locking up. Kennick nodded to the deck crew out beyond the flyer, looping his hand around in the air a couple times. They nodded and strapped themselves in as the big doors at the back of the *Andros* slowly lifted on its hydraulics.

"Drop in three," Kennick said.

The lights outside changed from red to yellow as the flyer shook a little and began to roll backward.

Brennan shifted, twisting in his seat as he tried to see what was happening.

"Settle down. Focus on the controls," Kennick told him. "We'll drop in two."

The yellow lights went out, and green ones lit up as the hold was filled with natural light.

"One," Kennick said in an almost bored monotone.

Brennan stiffened as the back of the Naga lurched, and suddenly he was pitched up and over as the flyer fell clear of the *Andros*. They were in free fall but flying *backward*. Well, more like *falling* backward, really. It wasn't a comfortable feeling.

Brennan automatically began to work the instruments, getting the rear control surfaces open to put resistance on the tail. They wobbled a bit, and then the Naga rolled forward and put its nose down. Brennan breathed a sigh of relief, now in familiar territory as he began working the controls again to bank the craft to the right and away from the *Andros*'s course.

Kennick checked his instruments, then eyeballed the receding vessel for good measure before nodding. "We are clear of the *Andros*. Deploy sails when ready."

"Clear," Brennan intoned. "Comply."

The rockets flared, sending up the filament cable with the projectors attached. He'd set them to hook the second-layer winds and didn't have long to wait. As the aquamarine sails snapped into place, the wind jerked at them, and the Naga was pulled aloft under wind power once more. Brennan's heart slowed as he grinned. "Controlled."

"Clear," Kennick confirmed. "Watch for eddies. Get us some altitude."

Brennan started looping the cable back in, drawing the stubby fighter up into the air. They passed the first wind layer with only a little turbulence, something Kennick appreciated. It wasn't always easy to slip between layers without getting rocked around like a toy in a hurricane, since the different layers moved in different prevailing directions.

The boy is as good as his reputation. That sort of slick handling isn't something you learn in classes.

"All right, kid," he said. "I want you to bring us up to the third-level winds, smoothly if you can."

"We'll lose the *Andros* up there," Brennan warned, even as his hands worked to angle the sails up.

"No worries," Kennick said. "I know where they're going to be, and we can catch them in this heap."

He didn't have to see Brennan's scowl to know it was there. The boy clearly considered the Naga to be his own personal flyer—and, Kennick supposed, it really was. Not many people got to claim a fully armed Fire Naga as their own. In days past, such a thing would have fulfilled his own dreams too.

Brennan angled the sails back, losing forward velocity with the wind angling down off the projected surface and gaining altitude slowly as he checked the air currents.

There were two basic ways to transition between wind layers: The first was to redeploy your sails to the new layer, then pull the fight along with them. It made for a rough ride but was relatively fast. The second was to slowly transition by riding the shifting winds that existed between each of the layers. Those winds could be tricky; they didn't follow the same prevailing directions as the primary layers, and an inexperienced pilot could have his sails blow in on him and easily get the lines tangled.

The Fire Naga made a steady climb, twisting with the winds as Brennan kept the sails full with an instinct that Kennick had rarely seen before. The boy was almost anticipating the wind as it shifted.

"Very nice," Kennick said. "All right, bring us tight to the wind and let's head up spin. The old seabeds are spectacular to fly over."

Brennan confirmed the direction and then wound in the sails until the Naga was almost tucked right into the aquamarine projections, with just enough space below to let them see ahead and to give the Naga's control surfaces something to bite into.

They quickly accelerated to just over nine hundred and fifty miles per hour, well above the speed of sound in the lower atmosphere but just under it where they were flying.

Above the sails, the skies were more spectacular than Brennan could describe. He'd rarely been up this high; his own skimmer wasn't rated above the first layer. The blues and greens that made up the mottled patchwork of the sky were incredible without the atmospheric haze to distort them.

Kennick looked back over his shoulder and noted the direction of the kid's gaze.

"You ever see them through a steady scope?" he asked.

"What?" Brennan looked down.

"A steady scope," Kennick repeated. "You ever see the sky through a steady scope?"

"No, I don't think I have."

"Lakes, forests, and deserts," Kennick told him. "That's what makes up the colors you see. It's unimaginably huge, but the whole sky is full of lands we've never been to."

"Really? But, why not *tell* everyone?"

"Most people don't care, and the few who do . . . they tend to try and get there," Kennick said. "I've seen dozens of expeditions go out. Most never come back. We've measured off the size of our world, you know. It's a little over half a billion square miles . . . almost perfectly square, at that."

Brennan's eyes rose up again and he looked closer at the sky, this time not at the blues and greens, but at the dark-gray-and-black lines that marked them off in a square grid.

"Exactly." Kennick knew what the boy was looking at. The same thing he'd looked at when he'd learned the size and shape of the world.

"How many are there?" Brennan asked, mouth dry.

"Worlds like ours?" Kennick shrugged. "I think the calculation was somewhere around three hundred million. All bounded by the same God Walls the empire and surrounding territories are surrounded by."

Brennan almost couldn't comprehend it. Hell, he *couldn't* comprehend it. He'd learned *so* much more since fleeing the palace than he'd ever been taught inside it.

"The empire discouraged exploration a few generations ago," Kennick said, "mostly due to the loss of people and resources, but also because no one has figured out yet how to cross the God Walls, so there's little point. Small groups still try, usually funded by private concerns, eccentric backers, and so on. Most of those are looking for pockets of resources they can return to the empire with, though, and don't tend to stray more than a few weeks' travel from our borders."

"It seems like such a waste," Brennan said finally.

"It does, doesn't it?" Kennick chuckled softly, but a glimpse of the ground below them caused him to shift. "All right, we're over the flats. Let's tuck and stow the sails and glide in."

Brennan glanced down. "Clear. Confirm. Comply."

He dropped the sails and wound in the lines, getting the projectors ready for the next time he needed them. At their current altitude there wasn't much atmosphere for the stubby wings and control surfaces of the Naga to really bite into, but they were moving fast enough that speed partially made up for that. They held for a while, then slowly began to descend through the layers into thicker atmo.

"Everyone knows about the Great Desert," Kennick said as they descended, "but this is a much more interesting place."

Brennan looked out, waggling the Naga a little to give him a better view.

It didn't look all that interesting to him, mostly just a nearly unending stretch of brown and white. The white was a little startling, though. He'd heard about the area, however, and managed to dredge up the bit of trivia to mind.

"This is where the empire produces salt, isn't it?"

"Righto, kiddo," Kennick said with a laugh, "though it's more accurate to say that this is where we mine salt. All that white you see below is nearly pure salt, just waiting to be processed for the table. It's the remains of an ancient seabed that dried up long before we arrived."

Brennan had only read about seas before, though he knew that they'd existed. The empire had lakes and a few small rivers, but a body of water grand enough to be called a "sea" was something out of children's stories.

"What happened to it?"

"We don't know," Kennick answered. "There're signs that there used to be a lot more water here than there is now, but it was lost somewhere, somehow. One more mystery, I'm afraid."

"Since I left the palace, I seem to be finding more and more of those, and fewer and fewer answers."

"That's 'cause you were taught the basics, which aren't exactly lies, but they're geared for general consumption. The empire doesn't publish everything it *doesn't* know, kid," Kennick said. "I'm sure you'd have learned most of this eventually. Can't imagine the emperor letting you slide, even if you weren't the heir . . ."

Kennick hesitated, then grimaced. "Sorry, kid."

Brennan sighed, but he didn't feel like making a big deal about it. "Don't worry about it. I'm not the heir, and I hope never to be. My brother would have done the job well, but Lydia . . . I think she was born for it."

"I hope you're right," Kennick said honestly. "I really hope you're right."

They glided lower over the flats for a while before Kennick had Brennan deploy the sails and bring them back around.

CHAPTER 19

William Everett stood on the deck of the cruiser, one of the largest skimmers ever built, and looked out over the thick layer of clouds moving in. So far they'd had little luck tracking down the *Andros Pak* and her erstwhile captain, but now it was only a matter of time.

Corian was on the move as well, his eyes spreading out across the empire, and *someone* was going to locate the corsair sooner or later. William only hoped that it would be the loyalists and not Corian's thugs.

"Commander Everett, sir."

William turned and nodded to the attaché who'd stepped up behind him and straightened to attention. "News?"

"Yes, sir." The attaché handed him a modular interface and returned instantly to attention.

William turned back to the rail, looking again at the clouds before he clipped the module into his own system and retrieved the secured message. It was a communiqué from one of his contacts, and for the first time in many weeks, William Everett smiled.

"Tell the captain we have a course and a destination."

"Yes, sir!"

*

Corian scowled from the secure command deck of the *Caleb Bar*, his eyes on the myriad interface displays that circled him. So far the *Andros Pak* had remained undetected, and with it his key to securing his position among all the remaining sides of the conflict.

Having the Scourwind heirs under his control would end most of the infighting and secure the cooperation of the majority of the loyalist supporters. Few from those ranks actually *cared* about the heirs. They just preferred that an unbroken line of succession be maintained. It was partly tradition but also partly useful propaganda that kept the masses in check.

The heirs would also provide excellent figureheads to take any of the ire that his coming plans dredged up. A few years of running the peasants into the ground and he might just be able to do away with the Scourwinds and their name entirely.

First, however, he had to find them.

Mira Delsol.

The woman's very name dripped with venom in his mind, as though even the thought of her was enough to cause injury. It was a name that seared his mind every time he felt a phantom pain in his missing leg and every time someone snuck up on his eyeless left side without him spotting them.

Corian would remember her name until the day he died; he had no doubt.

At every turn, it seemed, she was there to throw a stumbling block in his way. It was a perverse commentary on reality that one woman, no matter how competent, continually stood between him and his goals when *armies* had failed. He didn't know if it were entirely intentional, couldn't see how it could *possibly* be intentional, but Corian somehow knew that, intentional or not, he and Delsol had unfinished business to attend to.

Unfortunately, while his spies and informants had been unable to locate Delsol and her blasted corsair, they had found out that there was a new gathering of loyalist forces being marshaled.

He wasn't particularly concerned. Thus far the loyalists had started off weak and grown only weaker and more disorganized, but it was yet another distraction.

He had to find her, then destroy this latest gathering, and once and for all locate the center of their organization, such as it was, and end it.

*

The *Andros* was cruising a little over four hundred miles per hour just below the second wind layer as Mira stepped on deck and nodded to the officer of the watch. He nodded back and stepped aside from the wheel as she took his place.

Strictly speaking, the *Andros* hardly needed a hand on the wheel. The ship was quite capable of cruising the winds autonomously, so long as they were settled into one of the three main jet streams that roared over the empire. In between those zones, however, you could find more efficient winds for the job, but they could also be less predictable and, for those times, a hand on the wheel was not merely a good idea but a necessary one.

More than that, though, it was custom to have someone at the helm and both a duty and a pleasure to stand watch on a ship in flight.

Mira herself preferred to command from the open bridge, looking forward over the decks and to the sails as they filled the sky above or below the lifting body of the ship. At their current altitude the temperature was chilled, but few people needed more than a light breather and some warm clothes to walk the decks, and she needed even less. Only in the very high atmo did Mira need a breather; part of her training with the Cadre and in mastering her Armati allowed her to more efficiently process oxygen than most.

It was a useful skill, but one a Cadre member and most knights could pull off. Her personal best for functioning entirely without oxygen was almost sixteen minutes, and it was far from the absolute record.

A record held by a civilian, no less.

"Skipper," Gaston said as he walked over.

The engineer was wearing a light breather and heavy clothes and still looked rather uncomfortable in the lighter atmo they were flying through.

"What is it, Gas?" Mira asked, half smiling as she brought her mind back to the present.

"We've an offer on some of the items we pulled from the cache and depot," Gaston said. "Came through loyalist channels."

Mira snorted.

After the last encounter with the so-called loyalists, she wasn't terribly eager to put her crew's head in that particular noose again. Unfortunately, they were going to need hard currency soon, or they'd be forced to *eat* the supplies they'd raided.

Since they'd dumped all the actual food off with the refugees, that would be problematic.

"All right." She nodded. "What's on the list?"

"The expected items mostly," Gaston said. "Lase cartridges in any available caliber; combat tech of basically any stripe. I think they heard about the fight with the cruisers, though."

"Oh?"

"They requested MACs, rounds, the works."

Mira snorted. "Not a chance. We're keeping what we have. The kid probably saved our rears with that Naga and those guns. Besides, we don't have enough to make it worth selling anyway."

Gaston nodded. They'd grabbed cases of the munitions, certainly, but it wouldn't last a unit of any size longer than the opening rounds of a real fight. It would probably keep a single Naga topped off for a while, though.

"The normal stuff we can sell, aside from keeping our own stores in good shape," she said. "Send them a confirmation and get a location for a meet."

"You got it, skipper."

*

Dusk found herself wandering through the cargo hold of the *Andros*, amazed by the near constant commotion.

The *Andros* didn't have a huge crew, but there always seemed to be someone working or training in the relatively large hold of the converted luxury yacht. She wasn't certain what the space had originally been, though the mottled green-and-brown military skimmer Brennan had brought on board looked oddly natural where it was locked down, so she suspected that part of the area had been used for a personal skimmer before.

Now, much of the space had been gutted. While it had clearly been richly appointed at one time, the bulkheads were now bared to the wires, the only hint of the old finish seen around the corners where small bits still remained. The crew now had instant access to the control systems hardwired through the bulkheads, with far less mass weighing them down.

Dusk was looking for Mik. He'd taken to hanging around belowdecks with some of the rougher members of the *Andros*'s crew. He worried her. She'd grown up with him watching over her almost as much as their parents had, but since the . . . well, camp and what had happened before, Mik had been even more obsessive.

She was therefore unsurprised when she found him at the makeshift sparring section drawn off on the composite deck plates, getting fighting tips from one of the less reputable men who crewed the cargo deck.

"Lead with the point," the man said, holding up a wicked-looking knife so that the flat of the blade was parallel to the deck. "But remember to keep the angle so you'll go between the ribs. You'll glance off as easy as not if you grip the blade overhand, not to mention it's easier to spot tells on someone holding a blade that way."

Mik was nodding seriously as he twisted the blade in his own hand and jabbed the air a couple times while holding up his free hand to protect his own face and chest.

"Good, just like that. Practice what I told you, kid, and come talk to me later for more." The man grinned toothily. "But for now I think your sister is looking for you."

Mik looked around and spotted Dusk, waving to her before saying, "Thanks, man."

"No problem. You kids are OK."

Dusk waited for her brother to make his way over to her, eyebrow arched as she watched the friendly camaraderie he seemed to have established with the rough-looking crewman.

Mik had always been like that, though. She was more introverted, but he could make friends with almost anyone. Sometimes it *pissed* her off, honestly, but most of the time she couldn't help but shudder a little at the idea of having people flock around her the way they seemed to flock around him.

She liked her peace and quiet.

Still, she had to worry about how easily he seemed to trust people. Especially in their current circumstances, it seemed like a bad idea.

"Who was that?" she asked, modulating her tone so as not to sound too accusing.

"Hmm?" Mik asked before glancing over his shoulder in slight surprise. "Oh him? That's Burke."

"First or last name?"

Mik frowned. "You know . . . I'm not sure. I saw him with that huge knife on his belt, so I asked him about it, and he showed me some tricks."

Dusk shook her head. It seemed more than a little strange to get knife-fighting lessons from some guy you barely knew, on a known pirate ship no less. Of course, she might be the one who was a little strange in the current version of reality they were occupying. Perhaps, being that they *were* on a pirate ship after all, getting lessons in fighting was the normal thing to do.

It frightened her, just a little, to realize that particular thought made sense to her.

Ugh. I'm starting to think like my brother.

"Do you really think it's smart to hang around . . . them?" she asked, looking askance at the crew as they went about their business.

"Sure, why not?" Mik asked with a shrug. "They're good sorts."

Dusk sighed but knew her brother well enough to know that he wasn't going to be turned from his path.

"Did you come for something, Dusk?"

"Just looking for you, Mik," she told him. "I felt the ship turn and it woke me up."

"Ah . . ." Mik nodded. "The guys were talking about that. Captain has a lead on a buyer for the stuff they raided from the depot."

"The 'guys'?" Dusk asked, amused at how quickly the crew of a pirate vessel—albeit a relatively friendly one—had become "the guys."

"You have a better name for them?"

That, she had to admit, she did not.

*

When Lydia shivered as she stepped out on the open deck, it was only partially from the cold.

The image of the height they were at was so unreal that she didn't have quite the same problems with it as she did when flying with Brennan, but she *knew* just how high they were and that was enough. Even so, she needed the air. It had grown stale within the ship, though she was aware that was mostly in her head.

The winds cut low over the curve of the deck, racing across as the *Andros* tucked in behind the gleaming light sails. The *Andros* was a mid-size skimmer, big for a private yacht but small by military standards. But it was large enough that instead of using wings, the ship was designed as a lifting body in total. It wasn't much, but combined with the control surfaces embedded across the gleaming hull, it allowed the nimble vessel to maneuver tightly in conjunction with, or independent of, its sails.

That meant that there was little shelter on deck, as the lines of the ship were designed to facilitate airflow more than comfort. But the air was crisp and clean, and she'd felt too cooped up inside. It reminded her of the palace at times, only in the worst ways possible.

Lydia was only mildly surprised to find that Brennan was already on deck instead of below with his Naga, but she was more taken aback to find him standing behind the wheel of the skimmer. The goofy grin on his face . . . now that didn't surprise her in the least.

"Please tell me someone is watching him," she begged, not really talking to anyone in particular.

A low chuckle caused her to turn and spot the skipper leaning on a rail. Lydia flushed a little in the cold wind.

"You may relax, Miss Scourwind," Mira told her. "I have Gas watching over him."

Lydia followed the woman's nod and noted that the large man was indeed standing fairly close and shooting the occasional glance over to where Brennan was handling the ship. She couldn't help but let out a little breath of relief.

She loved her brother, she really did. She just didn't trust him to know his limits in a skimmer of any sort.

"We've a sale lined up for the kit we raided," Mira said conversationally.

"Oh?" Lydia asked neutrally, uncertain why she was being told. For all her name was worth at the moment, she might as well be cargo on this run.

"I'm going to have Brennan fly me in for the initial meet."

That caused Lydia to stiffen and pay attention.

"Pardon me?" Lydia's tone was as cold as the biting wind that blew between them, and her gaze had narrowed on the skipper like the focus of a lase blast.

Mira had the nerve to smile blandly at her, igniting a sharp, cold fury in Lydia.

"I need a pilot," she shrugged casually. "And he's willing."

"You need a pilot like my family needs another *former* Cadre member getting us killed, one by one," Lydia hissed coldly.

That got Mira's attention, and the casual smirk was now gone as she pushed off the rail and lifted herself to her full height. Barely into her twenties, Delsol was one of the youngest Cadrewomen ever, but she was still full grown and towered over Lydia as she stepped closer.

"Watch your mouth, princess," she returned flatly. "I'll take a lot from you, but no one compares me to *him*."

Lydia wasn't in a mood to back down, regardless of how much she was outclassed by size or other factors. She stepped right into Delsol's personal space and tilted her head back to glower at the taller woman.

"I am Lydia Scourwind, Cadrewoman Delsol. Whatever the situation we find ourselves in, remember that. I'll not have you getting my brother killed on some whim."

The two glared at each other for a long moment before Mira suddenly grinned and barked an amused laugh.

"Some of the Scourwind steel in you after all, then? Good. You'll need it," Mira said as she stepped back to clear some space between them. "Since you asked so *nicely*, I'll tell you why Brennan's flying me. The sale is to a loyalist group, and the contact man is William Everett."

Lydia settled but looked puzzled for a moment. "Why not take in the *Andros*, then?"

"Multiple reasons"—Delsol shrugged—"including the possibility that maybe it's someone faking Everett's recognition ciphers. I'm not going to risk both of you at the meet without confirmation."

"Then I will go," Lydia insisted.

"You can't fly like it's your second nature, and you're not much for gunning either," Delsol reminded her blithely. "Also, you're the next in line for the throne, not your brother. No, Brennan will fly me in his little Naga. You'll join later at the transshipment point."

Lydia scowled openly again, but she didn't get as angry as she had before. There was, truthfully, a lot of sense to what the Cadrewoman was saying this time.

"Fine, but I do *not* like this."

Mira snorted, clearly amused. "Miss Scourwind . . . what, in all of this, is there to possibly *like*?"

Lydia had no answer for that.

CHAPTER 20

William Everett stood alone in the clearing where they'd agreed to meet, the God Wall looming at his back, all the empire laid out before him—all that could be seen, at least, until the endless mist swallowed it up in the distance.

In most places in the empire, on a particularly clear day you could see over a hundred miles in any given direction before the atmospheric haze swallowed the light. Here, with the wall to his back, it was hard to imagine that the whole of the empire lay in front of him, whether he could see it or not. Few places existed where the sum total of the empire could be laid out at your feet.

His reverie was broken when a section of the sky seemed to move, and he shifted his focus to spot the aquamarine sails of an oncoming skimmer as it closed in on his position.

This must be the Fire Naga the reports mentioned, William thought as he watched the sails grow.

Unlike civilian projector sails, military models had always been shades of blue, gray, or even black in certain specific cases. It was costly to retune the frequencies of the sails, due to the need to maintain a consistent vibrational link between photons, so most military skimmers tended to use variations on blue to match the skies.

Some used browns or greens, but only those that expected to fly low and slow. Darker colors were only used for special operations when a skimmer would pace one of the Great Islands into an area, literally hiding in the shadows they cast across the land.

The Fire Naga's handler approached cautiously, coming in slower than normal and practically standing the old Naga on its sails in an impressive maneuver that held the fighter in one place for several minutes as the occupants scanned the area.

William wasn't concerned. He *was* the only man for some distance, having left his allies at a safe camp several dozen miles away. This wasn't a pickup. It was a meeting that would hopefully settle a good many problems for him in one swoop.

And create several more, of course.

That was the way you made progress, though. You solved the current problems and created new ones to deal with. Movement was only possible through solving one issue after another.

The Naga, apparently satisfied, hauled down on its sails—*hard*—and accelerated in as fast as the winds blew and then some. The stubby fighter swooped in, only to pull up at the last moment and stand on its sails again just a couple dozen feet from William.

He was used to Cadre pilots, however, being one himself, so he didn't flinch.

The handler let out the sail line and settled the Naga into place as neat as could be, then began drawing the sails down by the numbers. William nodded curtly and waited until the lines were secured before approaching.

The Naga's canopy smoothly hissed open on hydraulics as he approached, and William recognized Delsol from her file imagery. He'd read it before the coup, and before he'd destroyed the Cadre files in the palace. But the skimmer handler behind her surprised him. William spotted Brennan Scourwind as the boy let the gunner seat rotate out of his way and unstrapped his restraints.

"Brennan!"

"William." Brennan nodded, stretching out but not dismounting from the aging fighter. "I'm glad you made it out."

The Cadreman nodded. "And I, you. I hoped that Kayle had gotten you out, but when his death was reported, I almost lost hope. Lydia?"

"She and I got out together," Brennan said. "We joined up with the skipper here a few days ago."

William blinked, two things catching his attention: the twins had been on their own for weeks, apparently, and Brennan had called Delsol "skipper."

That wasn't an official title anywhere in the empire, but rather a title of respect generally offered to a ship's captain by her crew and no one else. If Delsol had only had the twins for a few days, then she'd apparently gotten Brennan's attention in that time, if nothing else.

"Well, you have no idea how glad I am to hear you both made it out," he said finally. "The chaos was pervasive in those last hours."

"I know. I was there too," Brennan said dryly. "We had to escape by air, and it was a close call. The rebel skimmers controlled the skies. I had to free fly the city to evade them."

William whistled.

Free flying was a common enough maneuver, of course; it simply meant operating without a sail. Civilian skimmers were designed to be able to glide safely to the ground in case of a failure, but they weren't intended to navigate the artificial canyons of the capital.

"As touching as the reunion is," Mira broke in, "I believe we have business to discuss?"

"Right, of course." William nodded. "Do you have a manifest?"

Mira handed him a portable interface, and he linked to it automatically as his hand closed on the device. William only took a few moments to skim the list, then he whistled again, this time even more appreciatively.

"I knew you'd raided a depot, and I guessed that there was a Cadre stash there," he admitted, "but it must have been one of the newer ones. You've some choice materials."

"I do."

"We'll take them," he said, "all of them."

"I have a crew to pay," she said cautiously.

William chuckled softly. "Yes. I heard about those idiots you turned to fertilizer. Don't worry, Delsol, I'm not here to rob you. We can't pay full value, but then I doubt you expected that?"

Mira shook her head.

While full value would be nice, of course, she was offloading hot and illegal materials. She'd be more than satisfied with a significant cut over market value, and that was before any loyalist discount she might offer.

"I think you'll find our offer fair," William said. "I'll have the list itemized and an offer transmitted. Acceptable?"

"Eminently."

"Good." He turned his focus back to Brennan. "I need to speak with Lydia."

Brennan glanced at Mira before answering, an action not lost on William, but he didn't comment.

"She'll be at the delivery."

William nodded slowly, wondering if he should push for more, but Brennan had always been protective of his sister and distrustful of authority . . . particularly Cadre. William supposed that he couldn't really blame him, all things considered, but for the moment it was problematic at best.

He sighed. "All right. Then I think we're finished here."

Mira nodded. "The *Andros* will be ready to offload wherever you need us as soon as you confirm payment."

"We may want a little more than just supplies," William said, looking at Brennan. "With the heirs found, we can finally move against Corian with a chance of success."

Mira glanced at the young man. "That's between you and them. You'll have your chance to pitch your proposal."

Brennan only nodded in agreement.

"That's all I ask," William said calmly, though he was masking a certain level of disappointment that he hadn't secured a little more enthusiasm from them.

"Excellent," Mira said as the gunner seat rotated back into place and she dropped into it. "We'll see you at the transship site."

"Looking forward to it," William said as the canopy closed.

He stepped back, clearing the area as the sail projectors launched. The aquamarine sails bloomed above them, hooking the deep whirlwinds that existed around the God Wall, and the aging fighter was lifted into the air as he watched.

Godspeed, Brennan. We need you and Lydia now, more than we've ever needed anyone in generations.

*

Flying out from the unpredictable winds around the God Wall took all Brennan's focus, and he didn't have time to speak any of the thoughts swirling in his mind until they were well clear and on their way back to the *Andros*.

"You knew he was going to want to bring Lydia into this," he said quietly, his voice accusing.

"Yes, and you should have known it too," Mira said calmly from in front of him.

Brennan didn't have much to say to that. It was blatantly obvious in hindsight. He'd been blinded by the chance to fly his lovely little toy, but that was a foolish mistake; in the end it was only a toy. His sister was all he had left right now, and he didn't much like the way things were going.

"What do you think we should do?"

Mira smiled slightly, careful not to let Brennan see it. He'd take it the wrong way, of that she had no doubt, but she couldn't help it. She knew that just asking that question must have hurt him, almost physically, but it was a good sign that he was seeking someone else's thoughts.

"Corian is a threat to you and Lydia as long as he lives," she answered honestly, "so you'll need to weigh that long-term risk against the risk of attempting to retake the throne."

"Blast the throne to plasma," Brennan spat. "It's done nothing for us but bring pain."

"You barely can even conceive *pain*," she snapped back. "You lived in the palace your whole life, with every need cared for. The worst thing you ever experienced wasn't even your own pain."

Brennan's breath sharply hissed through his teeth as he sucked it in.

"Oh yes, I know all about that little mess you and your sister stumbled into," she said. "Bad business that. Should never have happened, but don't count that as *your* pain. You were a witness to someone else's pain, which can be bad enough, I'll admit, but it was still theirs to claim."

"What that monster did—"

"Was enough to get him assigned to one of the worst posts in the empire," Mira finished for him. "I understand he froze to death less than a year later. Do you have any idea how long it takes a Cadreman to freeze to death?"

Brennan stilled, the Naga shuddering a little as he lost his focus.

"Oh, you didn't know that bit, did you?" she asked, darkly amused. "Thought he got off, did you?"

Brennan's silence confirmed her guess.

"Your father and your brother did you no favors, babying you the way they did," Mira said. "As emperor, your father had a responsibility to protect the reputation of the Cadre. That's why that scene was covered up. That doesn't mean he let the guilty escape their justice."

They flew on in silence for a time before she spoke again.

"You're not wrong, you know. Corruption is caustic, and it seeps into every crack imaginable. If you don't clean it out, eventually there's just nothing left to save," she said, "and the spirit of the Cadre corps can corrupt just as easily as it can empower. That's why the empress has one of the hardest positions in the Cadre. She has to act to preserve that spirit, yet also keep it in check."

Brennan didn't miss how she'd said "empress" instead of "emperor."

He didn't know what to think now, so he remained silent. He needed more information, information he didn't have access to.

For her part, Mira was happy to sit in silence as they returned to the *Andros*.

She only hoped that she'd given him enough to think about, because she knew and understood where his distrust of authority came from, and he was both right and wrong. He would need to balance his sense of justice with the needs of the empire if Everett had his way, something that was incredibly hard to do without compromising one or the other.

Hard. Not impossible.

She just hoped that he understood the difference. Too many people didn't. They saw the hard decisions in front of them and pretended they were impossible, inevitably compromising their moral foundation on the altar of what was easy over what was *just*.

Do that enough times and justice was just an old joke that had no punch line.

Brennan and Lydia were more concerned with justice than the empire, and she couldn't disapprove of their priorities. Violating your moral foundation might often seem like a solution, but it was illusory. The benefits it gave, such as they were, were inevitably short-term. What you gave up in exchange was the solid bedrock upon which everything was built.

But Mira suspected that the twins would be able to navigate that treacherous passage. They seemed to be more aware of the risks than most. She only wished that her own problems with her former organization were so simply summed up, even if the corrections would hardly be so simple.

She closed her eyes and again saw the blackened barrels of the armsmen's carbines pointed at her from all sides.

*

William watched the mottled fighter as it vanished into the distance, swallowed up by the mist, and for the first time since the night of the coup he felt a sliver of hope.

Without the Scourwind name, even a victory against Corian would be as bad as a defeat.

The political infighting that would result as the Senate and all the various interests started jockeying to take the throne would cause more damage than Corian could do in his worst nightmares. As much as he hated to imagine it, William had come close to throwing in his support and allies behind Corian just to try to keep the empire from tearing itself apart.

Now, however, they had a chance.

It wasn't the greatest of chances, but at least there was now a viable victory condition that could be achieved.

He turned and walked along the smooth metal of the God Wall, back to where he'd hidden his private skimmer. It wasn't as imposing as the Fire Naga, he had to admit, but it was Cadre issue and a fair bit more effective in nearly every margin.

"Well?"

The speaker was a young woman, emerging from under the sealed and masking canopy of the Cadre skimmer.

"Brennan was with her," he said as his gunner rose to her feet as the canopy opened up.

"So we have a chance."

William nodded to the young knight who'd been helping him since this whole mess began. "Yes, Meridith, we have a chance."

"Good. I didn't like the alternative."

"Nor did I."

*

The *Andros Pak* was waiting for Mira and Brennan at the expected location, cruising in the lowest—and slowest—wind layer. The two approached from above and behind, signaling with their lights.

"Pace her," Mira said. "We'll put down and load the Naga manually."

Brennan was a little disappointed but not surprised. Since his first chance to launch from a ship in motion, he'd found a longing to master the art of operating entirely from a ship. However, landing a skimmer on another skimmer was a tricky proposition. In order to not foul your sails, the smaller ship had to come in on a ballistic run.

One mistake could easily take out both ships, so he hadn't expected Mira to allow it.

He still itched to try it, though.

The *Andros* and the Naga slipped down to an isolated stretch of dirt that was empty for a dozen miles in any given direction. Once landed, Brennan let the crew load his Naga and headed straight to his sister to fill her in. Mira let him go. She had her own thoughts to deal with for the moment.

"How was the meet?"

Mira didn't look back as Gaston approached. She'd heard the engineer before he even stepped on the deck. He was not a stealthy man.

"As expected, Everett is offering a reasonable deal on our cargo."

"I have no doubt," Gaston said, amused, "but that's not what I was asking."

She sighed, knowing what he was talking about, of course.

"I don't know, Gas," she admitted. "They're going to want us to join the fight."

Gaston was silent. Mira had changed from the warrior who'd broken him out of the Imperial Redoubt's detention area. She'd been operating on automatic instincts back then, too focused on survival to think about what had happened to her. Since then, the betrayal she'd suffered had eaten at her. Gaston didn't know how much of it she was even aware of, but he'd seen her becoming more hostile to authority, and less trusting. Not bad traits, given the situation, perhaps . . . but potentially troubling. He'd watched her shift after they made it back to the empire, not certain if it was for better or for worse.

"Is that so bad?" he finally asked.

"Once burned, Gas, twice shy . . . twice burned . . . ," Mira said softly. "How much of a fool would I have to be to stick my hand out a third time?"

The big engineer sighed, but he understood. The loyalists trying to claim the bounty on them had brought up barely scabbed-over nightmares again, laying them bare to the air, screaming as they burned.

"Those kids are going to need help," he said.

"They've got help," Mira countered. "Everett is a Cadre legend. He trained the emperor, their brother, and probably half the remaining corps."

"I imagine that's true," Gaston conceded, "but that's not what I meant. The *Caleb Bar* is going to be a problem, Mira. You know what that ship can do."

Mira grimaced but nodded.

The *Caleb Bar* was Corian's ultimate trump card.

It was a floating fortress, capable of breaking armor that should be able to withstand any siege. Armed to the teeth, able to go places no other ship could, it had to be dealt with, or any attempt to retake the palace would be doomed before it began.

And the only man outside of Corian's forces who had any idea how to do that was standing at her side.

"You want to join them, Gas?" Mira asked.

Gaston was quiet for a long time but finally answered. "I don't believe I have much choice."

"You can give Everett the plans."

Gaston's voice was cold and hard, surprising her even though she expected it. "Not even over my own cooling corpse, Mira."

Mira nodded slowly. Gaston had lived to see his life's work turned against him, a monster of his own design wreaking havoc on people he'd sought to protect.

Both of them had their nightmares.

They stood in silence for a long while, watching as the crew loaded and secured the Naga. Only as the hull slowly closed up did Mira speak again.

"Well," she said, "I suppose we'd best get ready for a fight."

CHAPTER 21

The loyalist camp was teeming with men as far as the eye could see, and William's eye could see a long damn way indeed.

This will be our stand. Rise or fall, the fate of the empire will be decided in the coming days by the men and women here today.

"I hope you're right about this."

William turned, his train of thought shattered as he looked sidelong at the field marshal who had stepped up beside him.

"What's the matter, Groven?" Baron Kennissey asked dryly. "I thought you wanted some action."

"What I want is that traitor off the throne," Groven growled. "Not two months ago you convinced me that lying low was the best thing to do, now this?"

"Things have changed, field marshal," William said simply.

"What things? The only change I see is that Corian's had more time to solidify his position."

William was about to respond when a call went up from the nearby spotters.

"Sails coming out of the mist!"

They all turned in the direction indicated, eyes seeking the edge of visibility to spot the sails. The eternal mist of the empire was more of a haze in the distance, really, atmospheric distortion that rendered all beyond it impossible to see. It could range from a dozen miles out to several hundred or more, depending on local temperature variations, but it was always present.

Now, it was probably forty or fifty miles out, and they could see the gleaming white sails even though the skimmer behind them was still too small to spot with the naked eye.

"Are we expecting anyone else?" Groven asked, trying to remember if someone was missing.

"Just one more," William said simply.

The ship closed in quickly, and in a few moments they spotted a second set of sails flying close escort. William smiled slightly, recognizing the symbolism as much as anything else in the action.

Good man, Brennan.

The larger ship sailed straight in, using the second-level winds to power her approach, and closed the distance in minutes. As she spun out her lines, dropping the vessel down and slowing her progress, people got a glimpse of the colors flying behind her.

The black banner with the crossed blaster and Armati made William snort with amusement, but it was the golden banner that flew above it that caught everyone's attention.

"Scourwind colors," Groven whispered beside him.

The field marshal turned to glare at William. "You found them!"

"I did."

The *Andros Pak* settled into a stable hover over the assembled loyalist forces, and William had to appreciate the skill of the handler who was keeping the big ship in place by sail manipulation alone. After several long moments, the corsair slowly dropped into a cleared slot below them and settled easily into place on her skids.

The old Fire Naga, however, kept aloft like a snarling angel watching over its charge. Against the massed forces arrayed around it, the Naga wouldn't last more than a few passing moments, but somehow that made it all the more impressive.

Finally, after the *Andros* had struck its sails and been secured, the Naga too lowered in a show of precision flying that matched the larger ship nearly perfectly.

Very good, Lydia, Brennan. Show them all that you belong here. William had done his part in raising the twins, and while he'd considered them to be brats like everyone else, he always knew they had the potential for more. Now he just needed them to prove it.

"Shall we greet her Imperial Highness?"

William half turned to Kennissey, then nodded as the baron rose to his full height.

"Yes," he said finally, "I believe that we shall."

*

Lydia took a deep breath as the boarding plank was dropped from the open top deck of the *Andros* and the armed men and women of the crew filed off in strict order, lining up on the ground below in two ranks. She was dressed in a modified version of the standard uniform used on board, mostly just a utilitarian two-piece that served to protect the wearer more than making any fashion statement, but it seemed right and fitting.

It had been altered just a bit, including some fine tailoring to make it fit her better than most. She also had the Scourwind colors over her right shoulder, matched off against her brother's blaster in a cross-draw rig off her left hip.

With her hair braided back impeccably, she didn't know if she looked like an empress, but she certainly hoped that she didn't appear to be a child. If she were to do this, she wanted to do it *right.*

"It's time."

Lydia nodded gratefully to Mira as the Cadrewoman took up a position a half step behind her left side. She knew that Mira had chosen that position with forethought, just in case Lydia had to draw her blaster. The weapon would fill Lydia's right fist, leaving her left flank more open, so the Cadrewoman had selected the shield bearer's position.

How many of those watching will recognize that? Lydia wondered idly as she stepped up onto the plank and began the seemingly interminable march down to the ground.

In the distance she spotted the Fire Naga waggle its stubby wings in salute, and she nodded back to her brother. Behind Mira and herself, Mik and Dusk walked in similar dress as the rest of the crew, eyes wide as they looked at the sea of military uniforms that awaited them.

She didn't blame them.

Lydia had grown up in the palace and had only rarely seen this many legion personnel in one place with her own eyes. Generally there were limits on how many legions could be present within a single day's travel of the palace, ostensibly to prevent just what had happened.

She set her jaw as she reached the bottom of the plank and stepped out onto the hard ground. Her eyes immediately sought out and found William, but he shook his head slightly as she walked toward him and flicked his eyes to the left.

Lydia followed the gesture and recognized the man at William's side, adjusting her course.

"Lord Baron Kennissey, I am most pleased to see you here."

The baron bowed from the waist. "Your Highness, as always, I am your servant."

"My family and I owe you gratitude," she said firmly, eyes drifting back to William and then to the man on his right. She didn't know him, but his rank was clear. "Field marshal."

"Groven, Your Highness," he filled in, bowing deeper than the baron had.

Lydia looked out over the shoulders of the men standing before her, to the men, women, and equipment lining the ground as far as she could see.

"You have done well, field marshal," she said, "better than I might have hoped."

"Thank you, Your Highness."

Lydia smiled then, focusing on William finally. "Cadreman Everett, I . . ." She hesitated, and then her smile turned a little sad. "We are most pleased to see you alive. Our brother trusted you with his life."

"I was sad to hear of his death, Your Majesty."

Lydia nodded. "We were stricken to witness it. I believe, Cadreman, that you have a proposal we need to hear?"

"Yes, Your Majesty. If you would come to the strategy tent"—he gestured—"we'll lay out what we have planned."

Lydia nodded, eyes flitting to where Brennan was hanging off the side of his Naga. She wished he would come along, but this wasn't the time. She may never have wanted the position, but she knew enough about it to know that she couldn't be seen needing her brother to help her make decisions.

"Very well," she said. "Cadrewoman Delsol will join us."

The baron and the field marshal started slightly, eyes shifting rapidly to the woman who had silently stood behind the young empress. Only Everett was unsurprised, and he even seemed to hold a slight gleam of approval as he nodded.

"Of course, Your Highness," William said. "Your personal guard is welcome."

*

Corian strode calmly into the central planning room for the legion military, growing frustrated as his eyes flicked over the displays, the information he was seeking evading his gaze. He found the duty officer quickly and glared at her. "Report."

The junior officer gulped, barely refraining from flinching. "All quiet, sire."

That didn't make him happy in the slightest.

"How is that *possible*?" he growled, gaze moving back to the displays. "A rebellion does not just curl up and *die*. The very idea is absurd!"

"There's been no contact with any loyalist force—" She gulped as he scowled openly at her. "Pardon, sire, there's been no contact with any rebel forces in several days."

"What about the bounty we placed on the *Andros* and her captain?"

"Some reports, but nothing that panned out."

He resisted the urge to swear, knowing that there were always false reports. People tried to claim rewards that size just out of their nature. However, *someone* should have seen something they could use by now.

She must be keeping the ship in the upper atmo, away from prying eyes. I would, if I were hiding the heirs.

So he had a missing ship carrying the Imperial heirs, commanded by a woman he personally wanted hung up by her *entrails* in repayment for what she'd done to him . . .

His missing eye still pained him in the evenings, and Corian would swear upon all he found priceless that the new prosthetic they'd fitted to his leg *itched* despite the assurances of all medical personnel.

And on top of all that, he now had an entire rebel *force* that just decided to *vanish*?

He would have said that they were up to something, but that was so blatantly obvious as to make whoever said it aloud look like a fool. *Of course they're up to something.*

The question he had to have answered, however, was exactly *what* were they up to.

"Put all our pickets on alert," he ordered. "I want any legions available to be brought in closer to the capital, and have Captain Jessup alerted. I want her to have the *Caleb Bar* ready to fight on a moment's notice."

"Yes, sire. I'll see to it immediately."

He stared at her for a long moment until she began to fidget.

"Lieutenant."

"Sire?"

"Immediately means right *now*!"

She almost fell back over her heels scrambling to get away from him, then turned and ran from the room. Corian didn't bother watching her go. He was too busy trying to calm himself. He had commanded entire campaigns without screaming at his subordinates, yet here in the palace he couldn't seem to go a day without doing so.

I'm beginning to think that Edvard was a bloody saint. How did he keep from executing these idiots wholesale?

*

"Captain Jessup, ma'am."

Bethany Jessup rose lazily from her seat on the interior command deck. A large and surprisingly well-appointed chair bolted to the deck allowed the captain of the *Caleb Bar* to command from a position of both comfort and authority.

"Yes, you may give your report," she said with cool disdain, eyeing up the young officer who looked out of breath.

"The emperor wishes the *Caleb Bar* to be brought to full alert."

Jessup dropped her façade of disdain, head snapping to the right. "Signal general quarters. I want every crewman to their positions in five minutes, or I *will* know the reason why they aren't."

A soft alarm filtered in a moment later as the rest of the ship became a beehive of activity, but on the command deck a sense of slow decorum remained.

Jessup focused her attention on the reporting officer. "What's the situation?"

"There isn't one, ma'am," the girl said, flushed. "Not that I could see. The emperor demanded a report, but seemed . . . disturbed that all was quiet."

"Quiet?" Jessup scowled.

Of all things that the empire should be right now, quiet wasn't one of them. Oh, certainly if there were any outright fighting, she'd be surprised. Other than a few imbeciles in the Senate, no one wanted to risk breaking the empire along old alliances, but there still should have been distinctive rumblings and maybe even the occasional flare of violence.

"All reports were quiet?" she asked, to clarify.

"Yes, ma'am. No hints of trouble for three days at least. Longer in most areas."

Jessup swore softly.

Someone has an operation in the works, and it's a big one.

"Have the entire squadron rolled up," Jessup ordered her watch crew calmly. "I want a third of our escorts in the air at all times until further notice, and ensure that the remaining forces assigned to the capital aren't being lazy."

With her orders given, she turned back to the young officer and nodded curtly. "You are dismissed."

"Ma'am!"

Jessup had already turned casually away before the young officer could complete her salute, striding back to the bolstered command chair and dropping casually into it.

Now, the only question that remains is . . . are they coming here, or do they intend to strike elsewhere?

On the face of it, a strike at the capital was the cleanest move the loyalist . . . no, the *rebel* faction had available. If they could unseat Corian in one move, most of the current support in the Senate would evaporate like mist in the passing shadow of the Great Islands.

Any other move would require a lengthy campaign, taking out the allies in the Senate one by one along with their territories.

So it seemed clear, to her at least, that they *had* to come right into the lair of the dragon.

Of course, they might see things differently. It depended on who was in charge, and whether they were willing to fracture the empire in the process.

We may not even be dealing with organized "loyalists" any longer, she supposed. *Some members of the Senate might see the current situation as a chance to declare independence.*

That was probably Corian's worst fear.

That his actions would trigger a flurry of attempts at secession among the more opportunistic and less intelligent members of the Senate was the worst-case scenario. They would fail, inevitably, but the chaos they'd cause in the meantime would perhaps be fatal to Corian's rule.

Jessup didn't know which enemy they were dealing with, but she knew her task.

The *Caleb Bar* had to be readied, because whatever was to come, the new Imperial flagship would be at the forefront of the battle.

*

"That's the plan," William said, looking past the central display to each of the observers. "We have to finish this in a single strike. Anything else is unacceptable. As it is, we're already riding too close to the wind on this. Several factions are beginning to think they can declare their own independence. If we lose the empire, we'll be looking at *decades* of war, if not longer."

He glared at every person there. "I would personally *kneel* to Corian before I allow that to happen. Better him than the end of everything our ancestors fought, bled, and died for. We have *one* chance at this, a clean strike and it's over. Am I clear?"

The others nodded, but Mira shook her head.

"It will not work."

Everyone turned to look at her as she spoke, but her eyes were locked entirely on William.

"What won't work?" he asked coldly.

"The plan. There's a fatal flaw," she said, reaching out to the interface display and flicking her finger to highlight a single point. "This."

They all looked to the highlighted image, along with the rather limited information beside it.

"The *Caleb Bar*?" Baron Kennissey asked pensively. "It is indeed powerful, but it's only one ship."

"That is where you're wrong," Mira said. "It's not a ship, not by our standards. It's a prototype, and it's equipped with weapons strong enough to crack an Imperial Redoubt, and her drive lets the *Caleb* sit above any battlefield indefinitely and just *hammer* anything below it. If she sees us coming, Jessup will take the *Caleb* up above the atmo and just sit there."

"That's impossible," Groven objected. "She's a cruiser. A large one, yes, but I've *seen* her sails. You can't sail above the wind layers, not much above them at least."

"Her sails aren't her primary drive," Mira said, correcting the field marshal. "The *Caleb* is how Corian cracked the Imperial palace in the first place."

"There is something different about the *Caleb*," William confirmed. "I've seen her hover over a battlefield, no sails visible. I'd assumed they were just well masked."

"Impossible," Groven muttered again.

"Unfortunately not," Mira said. "I've seen the specifications. I don't know what Scourwind was thinking, but the *Caleb Bar* is a certified nightmare. It uses a prototype quantum-rail system that can generate its own rails in the substrate of space. It has no drive limits, practically speaking, given our current problem."

William grimaced. "So that's what the big secret was."

"William?" Kennissey looked at him.

"I knew that there was a highly secretive military construction going on in the desert Redoubt," William said. "Highly unusual, given that we generally use that as a secure holding facility. However, the isolation that made the Redoubt perfect for holding also makes it perfect for keeping secrets. What was Edvard thinking?"

"We may never know," Mira said. "However, for the moment, that's not our main concern. We need to strike at the *Caleb Bar* before we move in with conventional forces. If we can't bring that ship down, it could turn the wind of battle all by itself."

"Blast! Doesn't that damned bastard have enough advantages?" Groven growled, shaking his head.

"They are what they are," William said, looking evenly at Mira. "I don't suppose you have a plan?"

Mira smiled thinly. "I've had a while to think of one."

"Let's hear it, then," he said tiredly.

Mira nodded and started to explain the plan she'd been working on since first laying eyes on that beast of a ship floating over the capital and the devastation it had wrought in the palace grounds below.

CHAPTER 22

Brennan was waiting when Lydia and the others returned.

He'd swapped off with another of the *Andros*'s crewmen, leaving the Naga visibly "manned" and ready to fly. It was more symbolic than anything. One Fire Naga wasn't going to do much if they were betrayed by the number of troops they'd been surrounded with, but the empress's guard was to always be on alert.

Lydia looked tired, not that he was surprised. She headed for her cabin with barely a word, to sleep, he assumed, but he was surprised when Mira nudged him.

"You'd best pack too."

"Pack?" Brennan asked, confused. "Where am I going?"

"Away from the *Andros*," she said, smiling very slightly. "You can keep your Naga. She won't be needed where we're going."

"Where you're . . ." Brennan scowled. "Where *are* you going?"

"My crew and I have a personal mission," she answered vaguely. "William will look after Lydia and your friends."

"Lydia is going with William?" Brennan asked. "Wait, what about me?"

"I have a mission for you, if you're willing."

Brennan wasn't quite sure what to say. "What sort?"

"Courier," she answered. "Messenger, really, but it's a *very* important message, and it has to come from you or no one."

That wasn't quite true, but Mira knew that Brennan was the least vital of those who *could* deliver the message. He wasn't expendable by a long shot, but he wasn't necessary to what was coming.

"It's that important?"

"Vital, I think," she said. "If you're willing, meet me on the flying bridge as soon as you're packed. I'll have Kennick go with you in your Naga."

She didn't think he'd need a gunner, but it was better to be cautious.

Brennan eyed her warily, wanting to say something about it but not sure what there was to say. He had a gut feeling that whatever personal mission the *Andros* was about to go on, it wouldn't be remotely safe.

"All right."

She watched him head out, then she turned and began walking toward the bridge of the *Andros*, waving to Gaston as she passed. He joined her in her quick step, obviously curious.

"We're enacting the Stone Protocol," she said with determined force.

Gaston smiled, shocked but pleased.

"I thought it was too risky."

"With the assault being planned, it's time to take risks," she said firmly. "Get what you need. I want the crew on deck in ten minutes. I'll ask for volunteers. Everyone else is free to go if they like. I'll do this alone, if I must."

Gaston nodded, then split off as he headed for the lower decks of the ship.

Mira continued on, pausing only to detour to her quarters. She lingered there only long enough to unseal a security safe and disarm the explosives she'd trapped it with. Mira drew out the contents, including a few server blades she'd been holding in reserve for a rainy day.

Originally, she'd intended to copy out a little useful data, then burn the rest in lase fire. However, once she realized that she had the Scourwind twins under her wing, well, that changed the equation.

Blades in hand, Mira made her way to the flying bridge of the *Andros*. Out in the open air, Mira felt a weight lift from her. There were no more decisions to be made now, only a path to follow.

There was a freedom of mind when you no longer had to worry about decisions, and Mira reveled in what she had long considered her mission mind-set. No more worries. Questions of right and wrong were behind her. All that mattered now were the mission goals and the people to her right and to her left.

Those behind her were barely worth a passing thought, and as to those *in front* of her?

May the universe pass judgment on them with mercy, because she would not.

On the flying bridge of the *Andros*, Mira planted a foot on the rail and a hand on the wheel as she looked down over the open deck where the crew—*her* crew—was gathering.

She'd assembled them from some of the dregs of the empire, using contacts from her time in Cadre Shadow Operations. Men and women who couldn't work in the light of the sun under the empire's laws. Some were former legion, others had grown up in the slums that existed in nearly every major city despite the best efforts of both those who wanted to improve them and those who just wanted them gone.

Mira looked on the crew fondly, realizing that it was probably the best she'd ever served with. Perhaps not in individual skill, to be sure, but it was her crew—and a damned good one. Together they'd raided the empire with impunity, and now she was going to ask them to do it one more time.

She waited until she got a nod from Gaston, telling her that everyone was there, then Mira looked them over one more time before speaking.

"Not all of you joined with me because you hated Corian. In fact, I think few of you did," she said. "Most of you don't know him except by reputation. You joined with me because I promised you a paycheck, an adventure . . . or just because I asked."

Mira paused. "Whatever your reason for being here, thank you."

There was no sound from the deck, so she went on without thinking too hard about what she was saying.

"That part of our adventure is over now," she said with finality. "Next, I'm going on a mission that has no payoff in cash or loot, and the risk is very high. This is personal for me, and I will not ask you to follow me. If you feel you're done, just let Gas know and you'll be paid out here and now. If you and I happen to be going in the same direction, however . . . then I'll owe you my thanks again."

Mira paused to let that sink in before finishing.

"You have an hour to choose," she said. "The *Andros* sets sail in two."

*

Brennan looked down at the package Mira had handed him, confused.

"Server blades?"

"And instructions," she confirmed. "Follow them."

He nodded reflexively before realizing he'd done so, then scowled at her for pushing the buttons his brother had obviously installed in him over the years.

"I'm not some errand boy," he ground out, knowing that he was being childish about it but not caring.

"You are if the errand is important enough," Mira countered. "Remember that. None of us are above any job that needs to be done. Start thinking you are, and I'll end you myself before I let you near the throne."

He laughed, almost hysterically. "As if I'd want that job."

"If you did, or if *she* did," Mira informed him, "I'd seriously consider putting a lase round through you both and leaving it to Corian. At least he has experience to go with his arrogance."

Brennan scowled at her again, hating the fact that he couldn't do anything *else* and they were both well aware of it. Instead, he looked down at the satchel again. "It's that important?"

"I said it was."

"Fine." Brennan gave up. "I'll be on my way within the hour."

"Good. Kennick will be waiting for you at your Naga," Mira said approvingly. "See your sister before you go."

He nodded. He'd intended to.

Brennan turned to leave, but Mira's hand snapped out like lightning and pulled him sharply back.

"Trust the whispers," she told him seriously, green eyes staring into blue. "Remember that."

Brennan nodded jerkily, pulling away when she let him go, but said nothing as he walked out.

Mira watched his back as he left, then straightened up. She didn't turn around as she spoke. "Have they all decided?"

Gaston nodded, though she wasn't looking at him, and stepped into the room.

"A few of the lower-deck crewmen, cargo workers, that sort left. None of the officers and none of the boarding crew left," he told her.

Mira closed her eyes and smiled.

That was honestly all she could have wished for.

"Thank you," she said softly, "and thank them for me."

"They know," Gaston answered, "but it wouldn't hurt to remind them when this is over."

Mira laughed. "If we live, they'll drink on me for a week."

Gas shook his head. "You'd better plan on dying, then, my lady. The emperor himself would cringe at the price this lot would command at the taverns."

"That's just perfect"—Mira smiled like a feral beast—"because I fully intend to take the cost out of *Emperor* Corian's pocket."

*

"Lydia," Brennan said, tapping on the edge of the lock that led to his sister's quarters on the *Andros*.

Lydia looked up, surprised but pleased. "Bren. I wish you were coming with me . . . I don't know that I can do this."

"You can do it," he said. "You've always given a damn about people, more than me at least. I just care about flying."

"That's not true, and you know it," she said gently.

Brennan shrugged. "Maybe. Look, Delsol's given me a job."

"You're not coming with me?"

"I'll catch up," he promised, trying to smile as easily as he could to quell the concern in her voice. "It's just a courier job. You know she wouldn't give either of us anything directly dangerous, not if she could avoid it."

"I am leading a fleet into battle," Lydia told him dryly.

"From the most powerful cruiser in the loyalist fleet," he reminded her. "You'll be all right. I should be back before then anyway."

"Promise?"

"I promise to try," he said honestly. "Just have to deliver a message or two."

"What message?" she asked, curious.

Brennan shrugged, pulling a card from the satchel and flipping it open to read.

"It doesn't make any sense," he scowled, tilting his head as if reading the words from another angle would reveal their meaning.

"Let me see." Lydia turned his hand so she could read it, then shook her head. "It's a cipher. Whatever it means, it's not for us. Mira gave you this?"

"And said it was vital," he added with a nod.

"Then it is," Lydia said. "Go. Fly fast, but stay alive and come back, Bren."

"Always, sis," Brennan said with a cocky smile. He saluted sloppily and turned away, heading out the door.

Lydia watched him go, a shadow crossing over her face.

Is this what power means? she wondered. *Watching people march into danger for me? In my name? Who in their right mind would want such a thing?*

*

"Ready to fly, kid?"

Brennan nodded as Kennick hopped out of the gunner's spot and let the bolstered pivot clear. Brennan hooked a foot in the second stirrup and threw himself into place with practiced ease. The second chair now felt natural to him, and he marveled privately that he once felt strange not flying from the front.

Kennick dropped into the gunner's spot and hit the canopy close latch, bringing the armored shield down around their heads.

"Looks like the fleet is ready to move out," Kennick said, looking around them.

Brennan nodded, though Kennick couldn't possibly see him. Somehow, he knew that the other man would know he had anyway.

"A few hours yet," Kennick went on. "The *Andros* leaves in less than one. The fleet will probably follow within six. It's going to be one hell of a fight."

Brennan finished his preflight checklist. "Disappointed to miss it?"

Kennick just chuckled. "We haven't missed it yet, unless you really want me to believe that you're not going to race as fast as this crate will haul to get back to your sister?"

Brennan didn't say anything, as there wasn't much point in lying. He'd finish his mission, and then he'd join hers.

The sail projectors blasted away from the Fire Naga, high up into the air where the aquamarine sails blossomed above them. The Naga twisted and dragged, leaving a deep furrow behind it until Brennan thumbed the winches and the stubby fighter was yanked hard up into the skies.

"Let's break records," he told his gunner.

*

Mira settled her Armati Elan on her hip and secured the armor projector to her left shoulder before leaving her quarters and heading to the flying bridge of the *Andros*. The corridors were unsurprisingly empty, as everyone now had jobs to do. She climbed the ladder to the open bridge and nodded to Gaston, who was standing watch at the wheel.

"The *Andros* is ready to fly, skipper."

"She always is." Mira half smiled. "Has Lydia gone over?"

"She has."

"All right. Let's get this underway, shall we?"

"You got it, skipper," Gaston said, nodding as he reached for the ship-wide broadcaster. "All hands, all hands, stand by for lift."

The corsair's launchers boomed in unison, sending her sail projectors soaring ten thousand feet up. The silver-white blossom bloomed above them, and Mira planted a foot on a bulkhead as the ship lurched. Gaston hit the winches and the *Andros* began to move, slowly at first but accelerating as they drew a deep furrow behind them that grew shallower over time.

Then, in a final surge, the big ship abandoned the dirt and took to the sky. As the *Andros* chased her sails, Mira looked back to the thousands of men and women, and all their ships and gear, and wished the young people she'd just barely gotten to know all the luck they deserved.

She figured fate owed them a good roll or two.

That was all she had time for, as the mission ahead of her swallowed Mira's focus whole. When it was all over, perhaps, she could see them again.

For the moment, however . . .

"Bring us up into the winds and turn our sails to the capital."

"Aye, aye, skipper!"

*

Lydia stood beside William as the *Andros* vanished into the sky, swallowed by the eternal haze that surrounded them. She was moving fast and still accelerating into the wind, and Lydia was almost certain that she had seen the *Andros* fire off projectors to climb to the next wind layer.

"They're in a hurry," William confirmed. "Wind's fortune to them . . . to us all, because we are going to need it."

"Is the situation that bad, William?" Lydia asked softly, uncertain if she wanted to know.

"Maybe. Maybe it's worse," William said. "It depends on how much support Corian truly has. Some will fight for him because they think he represents your father still, others because they're actually loyal to Corian himself . . . and some because they work for people who think they can steal more power from Corian than they could from your father."

"Are they right?"

William snorted. "Possibly. Corian is a battle master of the highest level. He was assigned to command legions in the south of the empire, just to teach the independent kingdoms a lesson they'd not forget. They didn't either. He beat them so badly they've never peeped back in our direction since. A statesman, however, he is *not*. So maybe they could steal power from him, but I wouldn't care to be in their shoes if he caught them at it."

"I see."

"Do you?" William looked at her sharply. "Your father was far from a perfect man or emperor, but he did understand that diplomacy and battle only differed in the nature of the weapons one used."

Lydia sighed, shaking her head. "Right there is what got my father killed, William. He only knew how to wage war, and he died by the weapons he chose to wield. Imperial diplomacy is, in fact, conducted exactly as you suggest . . . and that is a mistake. A victory in diplomacy comes only when all sides involved believe that they've won, but a true victory is when they're all *right.*"

Lydia walked away from him, heading toward the command cruiser that she had an assigned suite on, leaving William Everett with thoughts whirling in his head.

She'll be a great leader one day, if those ideas of hers don't get her killed first.

Someone had to keep her alive until she fulfilled that fate, he decided, and right then William swore that he'd do just that.

I don't know if we deserve her, but maybe someday we will.

CHAPTER 23

Brennan looked at the alley askance, a nervous twitch running down his spine as he considered the directions he'd been given.

She's got to be kidding.

Kennick had stayed behind to watch over the Naga and perform the necessary maintenance to keep the old bird in the air. It was Imperial construction, which meant that unlike many of the more sophisticated ships in modern use, the Naga could be repaired almost literally with a spool of wire and some windburn tape. But even so it needed almost an hour of maintenance for every hour it spent in the air.

Better that than one of the new ones, Brennan thought with a shudder as he started down the alley.

One of the new Savage Warriors required almost ten hours of maintenance per hour of flight time, and really could only be run by government forces because of the costs involved. They were superior machines by many metrics, but Brennan liked to handle his own work as much as possible. It was one of the few things he could get away from his guards to do while in the palace. They figured that if he was in the hangar, he was about as safe as could be.

That life was no more.

He came to a stop, his mind refocusing on the present as he spotted the sign that was almost hidden in the grime and dirt of the old alley.

The Blood and Hunt Tavern. Lovely.

He shoved his way into the place, the ancient door creaking like something out of a damned ghost story. Any decent handyman would have used a silicate lubricant on it and solved the problem permanently, but either that was beyond the abilities of the owner or someone liked the noise.

The general hum of chatter inside dulled to near silence as people looked up and spotted him, but Brennan ignored them. He had a message to deliver, even if he was damned if he understood any of it.

He walked up to the bar, earning himself a glower from the older, balding man standing behind it.

"Kid, I think I hear your mama calling," the paunchy fellow grunted, rolling his eyes. "Best go find her."

"My mother died when I was three, and my father followed her just recently," Brennan told him flatly, "just so you know and don't get any cute thoughts about my dad sounding like a woman."

The bartender stared blankly at him for a moment, then chuckled. "Never thought of that one, kid, but I'm keeping it to use later. All right, what are you here for?"

"Have a message," Brennan said, looking around.

"Oh yeah? For who?"

"Don't know."

The barkeep laughed. "Not much of a messenger, then, are you? Who sent it?"

"Delsol."

The near silence of the bar suddenly descended into total silence, and Brennan slowly turned around to see every face looking at him.

"Where does a brat like you hear a name like that?" the barkeep asked, drawing his attention back.

"I told you, she sent the message."

The man grunted, but held out his hand. "Let's see it."

"Who says it's for you?" Brennan asked, feeling contrary all of a sudden.

The barkeep just laughed at him. "You don't know who it's for. Let's see it."

Brennan sighed, but figured that if the man could read the cipher, then it was for him. If not, well, no loss. He handed him the card.

The keep flipped it open and glanced down at it, eyes widening for a moment before he dropped it on the counter.

"Go on out of here, kid."

Brennan looked up sharply. "I was sent to deliver a—"

"Message. Mission accomplished. Good on you, now get out of my bar."

"Hey!" Brennan tried to protest, only to be cut off by a hand the size of a shovel slamming down on the counter.

"Out!" the barkeep bellowed, making Brennan stumble back.

He heard sounds he recognized and looked behind him to find several lase blasters not *quite* pointed his way. Brennan slowly raised his hands and walked backward to the door. Everyone inside watched him silently until he was gone and the door closed behind him.

The barkeep walked around and over to the door, slamming bolts home to lock it tight.

"What the hell was that about, Yenn?"

The big man shrugged off the badly fitting vest he wore and tossed it aside as he walked over to the painting of the capital hanging on a wall. He plucked it off and tossed the picture aside, then drove his elbow through the wall. He reached into the hole and drew out a silver-and-ivory baton just a little over a foot long.

"Boys," he said as he turned back, "we have some messages to pass along ourselves."

*

Brennan stomped back to the small field that held the Naga, not looking at nor speaking to Kennick as he hauled himself up into the fighter and dropped unceremoniously into the pilot's seat.

Kennick licked his lips for a moment, then decided to risk it. "How'd it go?"

"Delivered the message, whatever the hell it was. Then the jerk *kicked* me out of the place and locked the damn door." Brennan scowled.

Kennick blinked, a little confused by that himself, but he didn't know what the skipper's whole plan was. Maybe it was just to get the kid out of the way in case it all went bad and his sister bought it in the fight. That sounded like something she'd do, but if that was the plan, he didn't think it had worked, because there was no way the kid was going to sit around with family on the line.

"So," he said finally, "what now?"

"Now we get this crate back in the air and fly as tight to the wind as I can manage," Brennan said firmly. "We should be able to catch the fleet before the fighting is over, at least."

Kennick nodded.

Yup, her plan definitely backfired if she thought she was going to keep the kid out of that fight, thought Kennick.

He didn't have any orders other than gun for the kid if needed, so he wasn't stupid enough to get on the wrong side of a potential emperor. Even as it was, thc kid held just a little too much power for Kennick to be comfortable annoying him.

"Your call, kid. You planning on mixing it up with the enemy?" Kennick asked.

Brennan started running the preflight checklist, barely glancing up. "You have a problem if I am?"

"Not as such."

"Let's play it by ear."

Kennick smiled to himself. *This kid would never make it in the legion. Too bad he's too high profile for the skipper to recruit him full time. I think he'd fit right in on the* Andros.

The idea of what was essentially the crown prince of the empire serving aboard a corsair struck him as funny enough that Kennick spent the entire liftoff procedure just barely keeping in his manic giggles.

Above and behind him, Brennan noticed, but decided for the sake of his own sanity not to ask.

Besides, he was too busy climbing for the top wind layer and angling the Naga for the capital.

It was time for a homecoming.

*

In a small house miles from anywhere, a hidden panel in the floor opened and a hand reached in to draw out a gold-and-ebony baton. The hatch was left open, and the house quietly abandoned a few minutes later.

The Cadre were mobilizing.

*

The *Andros Pak* was riding above the top wind layer, her sails extended below to catch the slipstream as they tore through the thin air over a hundred thousand feet above the ground. At the speeds they were running, the lifting body of the ship itself was enough to keep the *Andros* aloft, which allowed them to translate all the strength of the winds to forward motion.

There were minimal hands on deck, as most of the crew operated their stations from the interior. Mira could have done the same, but she enjoyed the cold air and shocking crisp colors that could only be experienced at the edge of the atmosphere.

Her clothes were insulated but tight, and she wore a light breather and tinted glasses to protect her eyes from both the cold and the low pressure. At over nine hundred miles per hour, they weren't quite breaking any records, but Mira would be surprised if there had been another skimmer of the *Andros*'s class that could have touched her.

"We're two hours out from the capital," Gaston announced as he walked up behind her.

Mira nodded, glancing back and smiling as she noticed how bundled up he was, not a patch of skin to be seen. Body control was one of the basic elements of Cadre training, and she was so used to the benefits of it that she often forgot that most people froze in temperatures that she considered mildly chilly at worst.

"Clear," she answered. "How are we looking belowdecks?"

"Crews are ready to go," he said. "Are you sure you can control those?"

"No problem," she said confidently. "The systems are designed to allow them to be slaved to a central control for precision. We don't use them that way often, of course." She grinned wickedly. "We're a contrary lot, Gas."

"Really," he responded dryly, "I never would have guessed it."

At one hundred thousand feet, the air was thin enough, and they were moving fast enough, to whisk her laughter away as the *Andros* sped onward.

*

"It's time."

Lydia looked up to where William was standing in the doorway of her suite and nodded.

"I'll be up on deck shortly."

William nodded and stepped back, letting the door slide shut.

The loyalist forces were preparing to move out, a veritable flotilla of skimmers the likes of which he didn't think he'd ever seen before.

Most legion mobilizations involved escort cruisers running cover support for the ground-based transport. It was a slower process, but usually not by as much as one might expect, since high-speed rail infrastructure was standard in all corners of the empire. It was, in fact, what the empire was known for.

This time, however, they couldn't trust the magnetic rails or the new quantum ones. Both had one weakness in common: you couldn't help but come in from known vectors and be spotted long before reaching your goal. When the enemy held the switches and fortified all the nexuses, you didn't travel by conventional methods.

William made his way to the open deck of the baron's cruiser, the *Pillar of Miogaro*, and the flying bridge. The *Pillar*'s bridge was large enough for the baron to have a section cut out of it for himself and the field marshal to observe fleet actions without disturbing their captain.

As he stepped in, William nodded to Groven and bowed to the baron.

"Your Grace."

"Relax, old friend," Kennissey said tiredly, waving him in. "Here we have no titles."

"All ships have reported they're ready to lift off by the numbers," Groven said. "We're ready."

Kennissey nodded slowly. "Very well. Give the . . ."

He paused, his attention deflected behind William as he saw Lydia Scourwind step on deck. She was wearing the same uniform as earlier, but it had now been altered to the gold-and-black Scourwind colors. The baron waved her on and stood to greet her as she stepped up beside William.

"Empress Scourwind . . ." Kennissey bowed at the waist, joined by Groven, who stiffly matched the motion. "Welcome."

“Please, as you were. I am not empress yet,” she said calmly as she stepped over to a seat that was empty and settled into it.

“An empress in exile is an empress all the same, my lady,” Kennissey said firmly. “I was about to give the order to lift.”

“By all means,” Lydia said. “I am not here to give orders, and if I were, I would not think to give orders on how things should be done . . . merely what those things might be.”

“Of course,” Kennissey said and smiled, nodding to Groven. “Issue the order to lift.”

“Yes, Your Grace.” Groven nodded smartly. “All ships, lift by the numbers!”

“Lift by the numbers, aye!”

The order was repeated across the deck, and they soon heard the distant echoing thumps of projectors being launched.

The first ships rose, catching the first wind layers with their massive sails. Ten, twenty, over fifty in the first wave took to the skies before the second round of launches thudded through the air. Over the next forty minutes the flotilla lifted in waves, until over five hundred cruisers and transports were in the skies, and all you could see for miles from below were the gleaming sails of light that pulled them on to their fate.

*

While it was a bad idea for an invading force to use the magnetic and quantum rails, that little truism didn’t hold for all those intent on visiting the capital.

Across the empire a small handful of men and women simply purchased tickets and took their seats like faithful citizens. Though they were scanned for weapons, as was the norm for most transport to the capital in troubled times, the scanners looked for things like explosives, lase cartridges, and gamma carbines.

None of those turned up, so no one was bothered and the transports all left smoothly and on time.

*

"Skimmer showing on the long-range scans, ma'am."

Jessup walked over to the instrument section and looked over the officer's shoulder. "What kind of hit?"

"Small," he admitted. "Could be any number of private skimmers, I suppose, but the vector is a little off and they're coming in on the third layer."

"Third layer? They're in a hurry." Jessup nodded. "What's odd about the vector?"

"They're not aiming for any of the fields," he answered. "Honestly, it looks like they're just vectored to bypass, heading somewhere else . . ."

"Hmm . . . probably what's going on. Keep an eye on them and nudge traffic control to get an ID."

"Yes, ma'am."

"Let me know when they've been identified."

"Yes, ma'am."

Jessup sighed as she walked away from the station, wishing that they could have based operations out of somewhere with less traffic to monitor. Unfortunately the capital was very nearly the center of all Imperial traffic, for obvious reasons. That had died down in the recent conflict, and things had been quiet for the last couple weeks. They were experiencing a surge in traffic as more transports had to be put on the job just to catch up on lost deliveries.

It was great for the local economy, which had taken a nasty hit, but security was a nightmare.

Unfortunately, with skimmers like the one they'd just tracked, by the time they had an identification the vessel would have blown clean past them or already be settling in for a landing. The speeds involved were such that they needed more tracking centers across the empire, but air movement was still such a small part of traffic, and Imperial resources were largely focused on the rails.

One more thing to address once the situation calmed down.

Jessup knew one thing only: Corian was the man for the job of fixing all the problems the previous corrupt administration had caused.

She had faith.

*

"Drop zone in three minutes!"

Mira heard the call but didn't look up as she cleared the bulkhead and stepped into the now cramped cargo hold of the *Andros*. She took a moment to look over the hive of motion, taking a degree of pride in how well the crews were working. Then she spotted two figures pushing a large pallet into position and frowned slightly.

"I thought you two had gone with the empress," she said casually as she walked over.

Mik and Dusk looked up, startled, and both jumped up straight.

"Skipper!" Mik blurted. "We heard you were short some crew down here, so we volunteered."

"I see." She nodded. "Carry on, then."

"Yes, ma'am!" they both chorused, leaning back into their work.

Mira headed for the back of the hold, shaking her head. She'd wanted them off the *Andros*, just in case, but she supposed they were as safe here as on any of the ships in the loyalist flotilla.

The boarding teams were waiting for her as she walked up, just as the one-minute call went out.

"We ready?" Mira asked coolly, looking around.

The men and women looked bored as they nodded.

Mira smiled, nodding her approval. One rule for prefight talks was to not get excited. It was just another day at the office. There would be time enough for excitement in what was to come.

"Let's get this done, then," she said, activating her projection armor and stepping up to the doors as they rumbled open and the light went from red to yellow.

"Ten seconds to drop!"

Armor bloomed around her crew as they lined up, looking out over the terrain below as the master of the deck called out the last few seconds, and then the light turned green.

Mira went first, stepping into the air and letting the force of gravity take over.

Behind her the rest followed, and the first phase of the assault was officially underway.

CHAPTER 24

Dropping from high atmo was an unreal experience no matter how many times you did it.

At first the air was so thin and you had so few points of reference that, even though you were moving at incredible speed, it just felt like you were floating in place. That didn't last long, though, as the air began to thicken and buffet you around, spinning you above the ground below unpredictably.

That was the first dangerous obstacle to a high-altitude drop. An out-of-control spin could easily cause a person to black out, which might well be the last thing they ever do.

Mira spread her legs, flipping head down and using her limbs as drag to control her fall. As the atmosphere thickened around her, she pulled her arms and legs in, cutting the air like an arrow aimed straight down.

Behind her, the *Andros*'s crew followed suit. They were using Cadre projected armor, slave linked to Mira's own. Without the individual ability to link the armor, it was the best they had been able to work up on short notice. None of the crew was happy with it, but then few men or women of action ever truly wanted to hand their destiny over to someone else.

If they were going to trust anyone, however, they had unanimously elected to put that trust in the skipper.

Below them the world stabilized from the spin, and the thickening air began to whistle and roar around them as they plummeted toward the ground. A little over one minute into the fall, they broke the sound barrier and continued to accelerate.

*

An alert sounded across the bridge of the *Caleb Bar*, bringing Jessup back to the instrumentation station at a dead run.

"What is it?" she demanded.

"Something fell off that skimmer we were tracking," the officer said.

"Fell off? Not fired?"

"No chance. It's unpowered and settling into a terminal velocity of eight hundred and forty-three miles per hour. They're gonna make holes when they hit, but we're not scanning any warheads, so they're not bombs."

Jessup nodded, not that bombs would do much to the palace or the *Caleb Bar* anyway. Still, she puzzled something over in her mind, trying to figure out why that number sounded familiar to her.

"Do we have visuals?" she asked.

"At that speed? No. We're trying to track and magnify, but with velocities like that at this range, we're pretty much stuck picking one or the other," he said. "It'll get worse the closer they get too. We'll have to zoom out constantly to keep them in sight, and as it is, we're just getting vapor trails from the condensate they're causing."

"Great," Jessup growled. "What about the skimmer? Is it damaged? Is the crew calling for help?"

"No to both. The ship's still on course as if they didn't notice what happened."

Damned fools. Probably running some old heap that shouldn't even be in the air, let alone chasing wind three layers up.

She sighed. "All right, where and when?"

"Impact well outside of the city, looks like . . . two minutes and counting."

"Do our civic duty," she ordered. "Put out a heads-up. Tell the authorities to evacuate the area. No chance they'll be able to in time, but at least we're covered."

"Yes, ma'am."

"Now if I could just figure out where I know that number from . . ."

"Number, ma'am?"

"Eight hundred and forty . . ." Jessup trailed off, something snapping into place just before she let out a curse.

"Ma'am?"

"That's the terminal velocity of a Cadre jump team!" she snapped, reaching past him to hammer her hand down on a large button.

Alarms began blaring as the interior of the *Caleb*'s bridge darkened to an angry red.

"Track and shoot them down!"

"Weapon stations booting . . . thirty seconds."

Jessup watched the track intently as the numbers continued to fall as fast as the signals they were tracking. She was doing the math in her head, figuring how long until the guns came online and whether they'd be able to track and intercept the ballistic targets fast enough.

"Targets still ballistic. Weapon stations online. All stations track and calculate firing solution."

The systems on the *Caleb* could do that job in less than a second, but it took the people manning them a hundred times longer to give the order and clear the system to fire. They were tracking the targets for almost two minutes when the first lase blaster opened fire for a ranging shot.

*

The plasma burn off of the lase beam lit up a streak across the air below them like a flare.

Mira had been expecting a response, even one a little earlier than this, so she wasn't perturbed. She checked the chronometer on her armor and then glanced at the altitude to make sure that they were still on track.

"We have maybe fifteen seconds before the *Caleb Bar* plots our ballistic course and blows enough holes in us that we whistle on the way down," she announced calmly. "Stand by to *alter* our trajectory."

She was going to have to slice the maneuver terribly close to the bone; otherwise they'd have to choose between overshooting their target or landing a *lot* hotter than her people could reasonably survive in fighting trim. A real Cadre deployment wouldn't be flying in formation and wouldn't have to worry about how hard they were going to hit the landing zone.

Her team, however, did.

She sent the command to deploy wings just seconds before the traces of red plasma began slicing through the air, and she swore slightly. She could have waited a whole three more seconds and been that much closer to the ground.

Damn.

The armor projectors were unconcerned with Mira's annoyance and slight case of OCD. They functioned as designed, materializing large wings of linked photons behind each of the falling team members, turning ballistic trajectories into guided parabolas that swept them in toward the capital itself.

From below, the red plasma traces continued to track, but Mira's crewmembers were still going faster than sound, and now much of it was horizontal motion.

At ranges under twenty miles, there wasn't a tracker in the empire that could keep up with them.

*

"Plot their landing zone!" Jessup ordered as more of the crew poured onto the bridge in response to the battle stations order. "I want legions mobilized to intercept as soon as we have a location!"

On the displays around her she could see the projected landing area already, but it was based on probabilities and thus was a circle over five miles in diameter. Every passing second shrunk in considerably but also put the Cadre deployment that much closer to their target with no mobilized resistance.

"How many are we tracking?" she demanded of the signals officer.

"At least thirty, ma'am!"

Jessup paled.

Thirty. Burning skies, where did they find thirty Cadremen for this? I thought they'd all gone to ground.

Thirty blazingly fast-moving, living weapons of mass destruction were about to rain down on the capital and all she could do was watch helplessly as the computer tightened the landing zone probability down to a projected circle.

By the time she knew where they were going to land, they would almost be on the ground.

*

Mira banked slightly, altering the angle of her approach just to throw off the tracking systems that were no doubt trying to figure out her landing site. Behind her, the rest of the team followed suit as their armor mimicked Mira's actions precisely through their slave link. They cut through the air in formation, slowing now as air resistance took its cut of their stored energy.

The plasma traces still filled the skies around them, but Mira wasn't overly concerned. She knew they were only in the air for another thirty seconds, and the shots were still so far behind them that not even a lucky strike was likely to score a hit.

The black silhouette of the *Caleb Bar* was looming just ahead and below them now, and she adjusted to a steeper dive as some of the guns opened fire well above them. The team followed, sacrificing altitude for speed again as they raced downward.

A hundred yards from the *Caleb Bar*, they were skimming the city's skyline with the gigantic ship now above them. She could already imagine what was going on in the minds of those on the ship.

Too bad for them, they're wrong.

She abruptly shifted the projected wings she was flying on, tightening her arc into a stomach-curling climb that bled speed in exchange for gaining altitude once more, and the deck of the *Caleb Bar* was suddenly right in front of them.

*

"They're going under us!" Jessup snarled. "That puts their landing zone just inside the palace perimeter! Alert the guards!"

"Captain! Course change!"

Jessup spun back around. "Are they turning?"

"No, ma'am! Slowing and climbing!"

"What? That would ram them right into—" Jessup paled and suddenly jerked her head up to look at the display that showed the forward deck, just as the gleaming armor of the deployment suddenly rose up over the rails of the *Caleb Bar*, all members retracting their wings.

They hit the deck in a slide, guns already out and firing.

Jessup slammed her hand down on the ship's comm channel. "Armsmen to the top deck! All hands, stand by to repel boarders!"

*

Mira hit the deck first, holding her lase blaster in her right hand while she used her left to steady herself. She crumpled down to one knee, skidding along as she fired suppressive fire to keep those on deck from mounting any sort of resistance while her team landed and recovered.

By dumping all their speed in the last climb, Mira had essentially reduced their vertical velocity to a few miles per hour, but they still had thirty or forty miles an hour in horizontal velocity to absorb as they landed. The armor projectors helped, but in the end it was up to the crew themselves to stick the landing.

They did better than Mira had expected, for the most part, the majority landing in a feetfirst skid that almost looked intentional. About half of them even managed to lase the deck with wild, unaimed fire that would keep any sane man's head down.

Despite being guided by Mira's control of their systems, not everyone landed right. The armor prevented major injuries, but from the sprawls she could see, Mira had little doubt that they'd lost at least two to mission-ending injuries.

"Hold the deck!" she called to those who literally couldn't stand any longer. "We need to secure the entry hatches before they're bolted down!"

Together they charged across the deck, still experiencing effectively no opposition. The *Caleb*'s crew hadn't even mustered more than a few watch guards on deck, none of whom had anything other than lase blasters in their hands. Against Cadre armor—even ill-fitting and nonlinked Cadre armor—they were completely ineffective weapons.

In a few moments the deck was theirs, and the entrance to the lower decks of the cruiser was controlled by the injured members of Mira's team.

"Hold here," Mira told them. "No one in, no one out, except us."

"You got it, skipper."

She looked to the others. "All right, let's go."

Once inside, Mira split her team, sending half to the engine room while taking the rest toward the internal command deck.

*

"Intruders on decks three and five."

Jessup growled, severely annoyed that they'd dared set foot on *her* ship. "Get armsmen moving to those locations. I want them dealt with."

"Yes, ma'am."

Jessup was starting to worry. No one had ever really considered the idea of the *Caleb Bar* being boarded, not seriously at least. No one boarded an Imperial military vessel, particularly in flight. It just wasn't done.

She'd heard about the Cadre doing it in some of the outlying kingdoms, usually to plant explosives and destroy the ship in question, but an entire *team*?

Never.

On the displays she tracked the fighting as the boarding team continued to move, splitting their forces and heading for command and engine rooms, as best she could tell. Her armsmen were only now getting their weapons from the armory, other than the few who were on watch and equipped with wholly inadequate lase blasters.

As she watched, however, the first of the armsmen with gamma carbines started to arrive and take cover as they waited for the approaching enemy.

*

Mira ducked back as a sharp crack and whine of a gamma carbine echoed through the hall, the dark-purple plasma trace splattering across the bulkhead just beside her. She held up her hand, fist balled up, and the men behind her froze.

The halls of the big ship were practically custom tailored for defenders, though she knew it wasn't intentional. The bulkheads were solid, with sealed doors that jutted out enough to take cover behind, just like the armsman she was looking at now. Barely the muzzle of his weapon and a sliver of his face and body were exposed, but her team would have to walk right through a door in his plain sight to engage him.

"Hold one," she ordered, holstering her blaster.

"Holding," the team responded behind her, turning to cover the rear as she pulled the Armati Elan from the small of her back.

She shifted it to her left hand and flicked the grip just slightly, the Armati responding to her motion and command and extending in both directions, arcing in a recurve shape as she considered her shot. Mira's fingers brushed the invisible line drawn between the curved tips, and a flare of energy blossomed under them, growing brighter as she drew her arm back and considered the shot carefully.

The photon bolt loosed almost of its own will and raced down the corridor, casting a blue-white light in all directions. It struck the far wall, glanced off, and exploded into shards just before it reached the armsmen.

"Go! Go! Go!" Mira hissed as she drew back another bolt from the Armati, loosing it just ahead of her men's rush, and then rose to charge down the hall herself.

A vicious firefight erupted. The shock of the Armati's assault had stunned the defenders, but they weren't totally stupefied. Those still able fired back, but most of their shots were wild, since the photon bolt had dazzled their eyes. Still, two of Mira's men went down hard, with black burns right through their projected armor, before the fighting was over and her crew secured the corridor.

Mira stood over her fallen people, her link to their armor telling her all she needed to know.

"They're gone," she said softly, hand on the shoulder of a man who'd knelt by the side of his stricken teammate. "The damn carbines . . ."

Another bone she would have had to pick with the former emperor, were he still breathing.

Gamma carbines were basically built to kill Cadre and little else. Oh, certainly they *could* kill just about anything else, but so could lase blasters. Only Cadre wore armor that could deflect a lase cartridge, however, so why in the burning skies the emperor had the gamma carbines developed and deployed, she would dearly love to know.

Probably scared of Corian and what that bastard had managed. Mira sighed as she walked to the edge of the corridor and surreptitiously looked around the corner. Finding no one waiting for her there, she nodded to the lens seated in the corner, near the ceiling.

"Say hello to the watchers," she told her men. "They're waiting for us now."

"Let's not disappoint them, then, skipper."

*

"Barricade the doors!" Jessup ordered, drawing a lase blaster from a wall bracket. "Hold the bridge at all costs!"

The response to the boarding had been fractured from the start, her armsmen caught unawares by the sheer gall of the assault. While Jessup knew she still held most of the ship and boasted superior numbers, key areas were already held by the enemy. The invading crew was now just moments from assaulting the bridge itself.

"Send an emergency hail to any ships capable of responding," she ordered. "We *must not* lose the *Caleb Bar*!"

"Aye, ma'am!"

*

Corian stomped into the tactical situation room of the palace, glaring all around him. *"What in the burning skies is going on?"*

"Sire, a strike team has boarded the *Caleb Bar* and currently has the bridge under siege."

Corian practically choked.

Of all the possible things he thought he'd hear, *that* wasn't among them.

"What? No, never mind, I heard you," he said, cutting the other man off as he began to repeat the information. "What sort of strike team?"

"We believe it to be at least two dozen Cadre members, due to reports from the *Caleb Bar* and analysis of the insertion method, sire."

"Two doz . . . ," Corian sputtered. "Preposterous. Cadre never deploys more than a two-man team. Two dozen would trip over themselves! If a situation needed that many Cadre, the empire would send in the legions. It's *cheaper* that way."

"Sire, I'm just reporting what the analysis group and the watch crew of the *Caleb* reported."

Corian bared his teeth. "Put me on with the *Caleb Bar*."

"Immediately, sire."

Corian turned to the largest display as it snapped into focus to show the command deck of the *Caleb Bar* with Bethany Jessup standing center screen, a lase blaster in hand as she gave orders to secure the access ways to the deck. He knew better than to interrupt her, so Corian waited as patiently as he could for her to finish and notice the screens.

She did a few seconds later, eyes widening in surprise.

"Sire!"

"Forget that. Just tell me what's going on?"

"Two teams, sire," she said stiffly. "The first took engineering with little resistance. Sire, they had to *know* the interior and all our systems. They bypassed security like they had the codes!"

A thud shook the screen and she looked over her shoulder, worry clearly etched on her face.

"We still have superior numbers," Jessup said, "but my teams are splintered all over the ship and they're not going to get here in time to keep them off the bridge. I've called for all available help . . ."

"You'll have it," Corian said firmly, waving his hand at the people to his side, signaling them to do just that.

Jessup dropped to a crouch as the main door to the command deck blew in, and Corian winced as he recognized the sound of a breaching charge. Jessup turned in her crouch, blaster coming up as she started firing. The smoke lit up the lasing blasts more than mere plasma trace, casting red glares around like strobes.

Corian thought he spotted a gleam in the smoke, but he couldn't be sure until an armored form strode out of the veil of smoke with twin blades filling both fists. He recognized that the armor was female and that she held an Armati, but beyond that, the armor was intentionally vague in design to hide identities of Cadre operatives.

It is Cadre, then. Corian shook his head in wonder, still unable to believe it. He'd never heard of more than two Cadre being assigned to a mission before, and even then it normally had to be a pair that was known to work well with one another.

Most Cadremen were jealous of their compatriots' position and honor, and didn't work well with others as equals.

Corian himself was a particularly ideal example of that, if he were to be honest with himself.

The blades twisted in the air, deflecting plasma and lase blasts with easy motions, and more armored forms charged in behind using the first as cover as they opened fire on the bridge with a combination of lasing blasts and gamma carbines.

Jessup came up firing, but her blasts were easily anticipated by the armored form. Blades flashed, intercepting most of the shots, and the armor absorbed the rest. Corian watched as the armored figure spun, flipping the blades together where they sealed into one and melted to staff form. The spin finished with the staff coming up and smashing Jessup hard enough across the jaw to send her sprawling across the deck, a sickening crack filling the air with the sure sign that her jaw was broken.

"Secure the command deck; barricade the doors," the figure ordered, sweeping the staff around again before retracting it back into its pommel and sheathing it in a single smooth move.

"I wouldn't bother," Corian said, making his presence on the display known. "I'll soon have an entire legion boarding that ship, and there's no way you'll gain control soon enough to stop me."

The figure paused, angling its head and looking at the screen. Corian hissed in surprise as the armor vanished to show a smiling face he was all too familiar with.

"Hello, One-Eye," Mira Delsol greeted him with a wide grin. "Ready for a rematch?"

"Any time, Cadrewoman Delsol," Corian gritted through clenched teeth.

"Oh, I think we'll meet up sooner than you believe," she told him.

"Only with you in chains."

Mira winked at him, choosing the eye she'd cost him to do so. "Sorry, I don't play those games with psychopaths."

Corian seethed but knew enough to recognize the psychological war games she was playing with him and took a few breaths to calm himself.

"My legion will be there shortly with your *invitation*," he told her with a tight smile. "Refusal is not an option."

She glanced to one side, a reflexive motion he recognized as her checking the system display her armor was still projecting for her.

"Oh, I think that your legion is about to have their hands full with something other than me."

Alarms chose that moment to start screaming all around him, causing Corian to wrench his attention away and look to the flashing displays. He paled as he recognized incoming tracks being plotted on their long-range systems.

There were so many of them that the display system showed them as a single large track at the current zoom level.

The capital was under attack.

CHAPTER 25

Lydia had never seen so many sails in the sky, and she was no stranger to parades and military formations. Cruisers and destroyers had the lead, with heavy transports filling up the bulk of their formation. Dotted in among the rest were a few heavy cruisers and the baron's personal flagship, the *Pillar of Miogaro*.

The capital lay ahead of them now. They could see the skyline of the city against the backdrop of farmland that stretched on to the mist behind it and below them.

"We've tripped their long-range scanner traps," William said as he stepped up to her side.

The flotilla was in the first wind layer now, just a little over ten thousand feet. It was cool, and a slight crosswind buffeted them, but it wasn't uncomfortable.

"So no turning back, then?" she asked softly.

"Would you, if you could?"

Lydia had to think about it, but finally she shook her head. "No."

That probably wasn't the answer she'd have given a few weeks earlier, and it was certainly not what she'd have said before the coups, but now when the word left her mouth it felt like a weight was lifting from her. Given the choice between standing by and watching other people *screw* things up and actually having a hand in doing what needed to be done herself . . . ? After everything, no, there was no turning back for her. Not anymore.

"Good," William said simply, glancing to where the sky ahead was suddenly lit up with plasma trace. "It's beginning. Someone on the ground got nervous, jumped the gun."

Lydia focused her attention on the plasma trace that began to slash across the sky in both directions, the lead cruisers and destroyers opening fire on the first guns that had fired on them. Explosions tore up the ground as heavy blaster fire superheated whatever it struck. In the case of things like concrete, that often meant flash boiling whatever water was present and causing the material to explode violently.

Some hits were scored on the lead ships, but the initial sporadic fire from different installations had revealed their location before a proper trap could be sprung, allowing the cruisers to pick them off piecemeal.

"Corian will be hopping mad over that," William said with a chuckle, knowing that precision was one thing that the former Cadreman valued over all else. He just wasn't used to wielding a force the size of the one now under his command and hadn't had the time to properly drill them or even get used to the situation himself.

"Will it all go like this?" Lydia asked, hopeful.

"Not likely," William said simply.

Corian, while not experienced with such a command, was a fast learner. He'd have made significant strides, and William had no doubt that the majority of his forces would hold to their discipline. The fighting was just getting started, and it would get far, *far* worse before it even began to get better.

He glanced back at the baron and nodded, leaving Kennissey to issue the order to continue forward.

There really wasn't much else they could do.

*

"So help me, if you don't get your men under discipline, you'll join the late, and unlamented, Captain Kim!" Corian raged, still immensely angry at the missed opportunity blown by the gunners who'd lost their nerve and opened fire too soon.

He took a breath. "Commander, draw them in. Hold fire until you have the bulk of the flotilla inside your kill zone and then eliminate them in one stroke. Focus on the transports. Cruisers are launching from the palace airfield now. They'll deal with the rest."

Corian closed the comm channel and turned back to the display that was still open to the *Caleb Bar*, watching as Mira secured the command deck.

"You are a pain in the ass, Delsol," he said tiredly, shaking his head. "I should have killed you on the train."

Mira glanced back in his direction. "I seem to recall you trying quite enthusiastically. It seems we both missed our coup, back then."

"So it seems," Corian ground out. "You have to know this is insanity. Even if you win, I have too much support in the Senate. You'll split the empire."

"You did already," Mira countered. "We're just making it public."

"You're damn fools," he snarled. "You have no idea what you're doing!"

"You speak like I should care," Mira told him. "You're a mass murderer. Did you really think that this would end any other way? Even if you had succeeded, sooner or later someone would have measured your back for a knife, and you *knew* that when you started."

Corian snarled wordlessly then and closed the comm channel.

He couldn't speak with that woman any longer and still retain any semblance of rational thought.

She flips all my switches like she mapped and installed them herself, he thought, his ire cooling. *I damned well should have recruited her myself.*

*

Mira watched the screen go black with a certain satisfaction, but she knew that the day's work was only just beginning.

"Signal abandon ship," she ordered, "and throw up every smoke alarm, fire alarm, and other alarm you can. I want as many people as we can dupe off this ship, five minutes ago."

"Aye, skipper," her comm tech said as he sat at the instrument console and started putting in commands.

There was a definite advantage to having the ship designer talk them through every step of the mission beforehand, but Mira knew that a lot of it was going to come down to the gullibility of the men on board. Well, that and how dedicated to Corian's cause they were.

A reactor alarm should scare off all but the most fanatical, but this ship was Corian's trump card, so she was concerned that the alarms alone may not be as effective as she hoped. If not, then they'd have to switch to the alternate plan.

In the meantime, with the corridor outside the command deck secured and her second team still holding the engine room, Mira turned to the instrument stations and peeked in on the battle that was just starting to heat up.

Cruisers were launching from the palace air base, a dozen already in the air and probably that many again ready to lift as soon as airspace cleared. Mira knew that they weren't the threat, however. The local air base was deep in secured territory, palace and capital or not, so there just weren't the numbers to really threaten the loyalist flotilla.

It was the ground-to-air defenses that would be problematic.

No one knew how many of them Corian had moved into the area, but it was a safe bet that he hadn't skimped. Until they opened up, there was no real way to find them; the flotilla was about to start what was going to be a *very* bad day, but it was necessary.

Corian still had two legions near the palace, and it had to be assumed that they would be loyal to him. He wouldn't have allowed any wavering loyalties this close to the capital. He wasn't that stupid.

But he's close. Just not quite that stupid, unfortunately.

*

"Sails in the sky!"

William looked out toward the palace and nodded as he spotted the sails now rising up over the city skyline. He looked over to where the baron was watching over the deck. "It may be time to put the transports down, baron. We're going to need the extra sky shortly."

Kennissey nodded. "Agreed."

He nodded to an aide, who bolted off to relay the order to the commodore in charge of the fleet deployment.

"The field marshal will shortly have his work cut out for him," William said, keeping his tone light as he glanced at Lydia.

She didn't seem to hear him at first. Her eyes were focused on the ships around them as the first of the transports began to drop from the formation.

"The dying begins in earnest now," she said softly.

William nodded. "That it does, Your Highness."

The *Pillar* shook suddenly, a hammer blow rocking them hard, and the trio looked out to see plasma trace lighting up the sky around them. The fleet was firing back, almost straight down, but they could see smoke erupting from some of the ships that had taken heavier hits and several dropping along with the transports.

"It would seem that they were waiting for us to deploy ground forces," Kennissey said, holding tightly to his seat.

William shook his head. "More likely they were waiting to box us in a little more, and we forced them to show their hand by landing too soon."

Lydia looked at the two of them, eyes wide. "So this is a good thing?"

"Good?" William shrugged. "Debatable, I suppose. However, it's likely better than what they'd planned for us."

Kennissey nodded. "And in battle, Your Highness, that is often the best you can hope for."

*

Plasma trace was slicing the sky from above and below as the fleet engaged in landing operations among heavy air defenses. Unfortunately for the defense stations on the ground, combat-rated ships were armored more heavily from below for just such reasons as this, which gave the fleet all the time it needed to set down dozens of transports, each loaded with a full century of warriors and arms.

As those men and women poured out, the heavy air defenses came under fire from the ground, which they were poorly equipped to defend against, since they were mobile systems generally intended to be deployed well behind the front of any given battle.

In short order, a ragged line of battle was strewn across the plains outside the city, centuries of armsmen and knights charging fortified locations as the plasma trace shifted from the skies to the ground. Above them, cruisers began providing close air support for each side while simultaneously tearing into one another as the two sides interpenetrated and it became almost impossible to tell them apart in the growing smoke of war.

Skimmers were *not* designed to fly against one another in such tight parameters, and, inevitably, sail lines tangled and ships began to drop from the skies, firing the whole way down.

War—real war—had descended on the capital.

*

"Positions being overrun across our air-defense line, sire!"

Corian snorted but didn't say anything.

Of *course* the air-defense line had been overrun. It was an *air-*defense line. Certainly each of the mobile stations had some security, but they weren't intended to be the first line of defense. The capital wasn't supposed to be under siege by what appeared to be *at least two* legions plus air support.

Where did they assemble a force this powerful? My spies should have seen them gathering.

To Corian's experienced eye, it most likely meant his intelligence service had been compromised from the start.

The fight was far from decided, though, no matter how the initial reports fell. The air-defense line was going to be taken, that was a given, but the city walls were still a formidable barrier, and the loyalists were on the wrong side of them to make much difference. Also, he had nearly a parity of forces, with two legions of his own in the field.

If he still had control of the *Caleb Bar*, there wouldn't even be a question of the outcome.

Delsol had put an end to that, however, and he knew that even if he could spare the forces to retake the ship, it was still out of this fight.

"Direct the Thirtieth to engage the ground forces at the air-defense line," he ordered. "The Ninety-Eighth is to maintain their position within the walls and provide artillery support."

"Orders dispatched, sire."

It would not be a siege, of that he was certain. Neither he, nor the rebels, were in a position to prolong this battle. The rebels were limited by their numbers and supplies. Two legions was a formidable force, and their air support was quite possibly unmatched, but they would run low of consumables in short order without a vastly larger supply train.

As for himself, well, the city had too large a population to bunker down for siege. They had, perhaps, a week's provisions, but more importantly the political implications were potentially far more deadly than the legions he was facing. If certain members of the Senate got word of him and his forces being pinned down . . .

The results of that were quite simply unacceptable.

So both sides had cast their die, and the entire game was riding on the outcome of the roll.

Corian grinned slowly, showing teeth to several frightened aides who abruptly shifted to give him more room.

Whoever you are, you planned this one out nicely. However, let us see if you didn't underestimate the force you would need to succeed.

*

"Kill those alarms," Mira ordered. "Anyone who's going to listen has already jumped ship."

"Aye, skipper."

She checked the status of her team. "Any signs of further resistance?"

"No, ma'am. Most of the resistance ended shortly after the abandon-ship order went out," her comm man said. "I think the ship is ours."

"I hope you're right," Mira said, walking around the command deck and snorting in amusement at the rather ostentatious "throne" that occupied the center deck. "Edvard, you pompous ass."

"Skipper?"

"Nothing." Mira sighed, shaking her head as she tried very hard not to laugh at the high-backed command chair. "Secure the ship, set a roving guard. I want anyone left on board hunted down and *secured*."

"Aye, skipper!"

Taking the ship had been easier than she'd anticipated, likely because no one expected anyone to try something so brazen. Unfortunately she only had a prize crew with minimal training in the ship's systems and barely enough to man the conventional flight systems. Taking the *Caleb* into battle *wasn't* on the docket.

"Step!"

"Ma'am!" Jace Steppard answered, appearing from across the deck.

"The *Caleb Bar* is yours," she ordered, checking her weapons. "Rendezvous with the *Andros* and take Gaston on board as quickly as you can."

"Yes, ma'am," Jace answered, slightly puzzled. "Might I ask what you'll be doing in the meantime?"

She smiled tightly at him. "His Imperial Highness and I have some unfinished business."

"Skipper, I . . ."

"You have your orders," Mira said firmly. "This ship could turn the tide against the empress. See to it that it does *not*."

"You got it, skipper."

Mira nodded curtly and left the bridge as Jace turned about.

"You heard the lady!" she heard him bellow. "Stand by to rig for sail!"

*

The *Pillar of Miogaro* held back from the line of battle, riding the second-layer winds as slow as she could perpendicular to the fighting as the officers on board watched the chaos.

Almost a third of the loyalist ships had gone down, not counting the transports, most due to tangled sail lines. The crews would mostly have survived those impacts, but they were out of this fight for the duration.

The good news, such as it was, was that each of those downed ships had brought down at least one of Corian's ships right along with them. Since the loyalists had the current numbers edge in fighting ships, that was better than it might be, but it still wasn't good.

Their fighting exchange was a little better, though not by as much as William and Kennissey would have preferred. They'd hoped to get close enough to hammer a few of Corian's cruisers before they got aloft, but that hadn't happened. Still, they had been able to get in a few licks while the enemy cruisers were climbing and rigging for battle.

Now the war of maneuvering was over, and tactical combat was the rule of the day.

There were bursts of close, fast, and furious fighting, but then it would devolve into long turns where ship captains gave their foes enough space to ensure that they didn't tangle their sail lines as they lined up the next pass.

Baron Kennissey was using those lulls to move his remaining fleet over the capital, a maneuver that was literally being won by inches.

A roar went up among the crew suddenly, causing the officers to twist and look to see what had happened. What they saw was the black metal cruiser in the distance begin to move, and for a moment William had to admit that he felt a stab of terror that Delsol had failed.

Then he spotted the black banner of crossed weapons flying behind her as the *Caleb Bar* withdrew from battle under sail.

She did it. Burning skies, she did it.

"The Cadrewoman has done her part," Kennissey said, pleased. "Let us complete ours."

William nodded, wishing that he could be in the middle of the fighting where he'd be most effective. However, with Lydia here, his place was decided and etched in stone.

"Mira," Lydia whispered, smiling with genuine pleasure as she watched the *Caleb Bar* climbing as she turned, heading off to the south, "thank you."

*

As the *Caleb Bar* began to move, Mira strode out on deck and activated her armor without breaking stride. She reached the rail and simply planted one foot on the second rung, then threw herself over.

The city below spun for a moment as she spread out her limbs, balancing her fall, and then looked around for a good landing zone. She found what she was looking for within the palace perimeter—the skimmer field on the secure section of the roof—and angled her fall in that direction.

Unlike her earlier jump, this time the rush of air barely had time to build before she activated her projected wings and swooped in a low arc. There were guards on the rooftop, but they were watching the plasma trace lighting up the skies around the battle and never even looked up as she killed her wings ten yards off the skimmer field and swooped to the surface, dropping to one knee and planting a hand to absorb the force of the landing.

The sound of her impact got their attention, but Mira was already rising to her feet as they went for their carbines.

Her lase blaster cleared the photon shield of her armor a full second before the fastest of the guards could have gotten his gamma carbine on target. The blaster barked three times, one for each guard, and then Mira slid it back home as she walked toward the rooftop access to the palace.

You've a lot to answer for, Corian. I don't enjoy killing Imperial armsmen, not even the ones who deserve it.

CHAPTER 26

The Fire Naga was flying tight to the third wind layer, and, unless Kennick was very much mistaken, they were quite close to the speed record.

It was hard to say, because flight speed recorders were notoriously unreliable at altitude, and they'd need ground speed confirmation to make it official, but he had never seen a pilot pull off some of what Brennan had. They were coming into sight of the city now, and already the sails of the flotilla were visible.

"We're late," Brennan said grimly, noting the plasma trace that was visible even from as far off as they were.

"There was no chance we'd arrive before the battle began," Kennick said. "It's a minor miracle that we've arrived this fast, given the message we had to deliver."

"Fat lot of good any of that did," Brennan growled. "No one would even talk to us."

"Trust the skipper," Kennick said calmly as he made their weapons live. "She knew what she was doing."

"She knew she was giving me busy work," Brennan growled.

"If that were the goal, the skipper would still have us running around the empire with phony messages," Kennick told him flatly, "and we'd most assuredly *not* be in a position to fly into the heat of the biggest air battle the empire has seen in . . . well, my memory for sure."

Brennan didn't lose the scowl, but there was likely something to that.

"Fine. I'll stop whining," he finally said. "Do you have an approach course for me?"

"Not yet," Kennick told him. "Orbit the battle at least once. I'll try and get data from the battle networks below. Boiled seas, look at all the ships in the muck . . ."

Brennan banked slightly, looking down himself, and whistled at the sight. There had to be dozens of cruisers and transports lying strewn about the ground under the battle, in a space stretching back for miles. There were fires burning. The composite materials most ships were made of didn't burn easily, but under constant lase fire everything had its limits.

They couldn't see the warriors from their altitude, but flashes of light against the smoke below made it clear that while the ships may be down, the fighting was far from over.

"Get me a vector so we can do some good here," Brennan urged, eyes glued to the scene.

"Patience, Brennan," Kennick said firmly. "This isn't a game. We do *not* rush into this. That just gets us killed, or, worse, someone else killed who doesn't have it coming."

Brennan grumbled but couldn't really do anything since Kennick controlled the guns. And even if he didn't, there was no way to tell by eye friend from foe in the mess under them.

"The *Pillar of Miogaro* is below us, thirty degrees north by up spin," Kennick said. "That's the baron's flagship and where your sister is. They're safe and are directing the engagement while providing long-range fire support."

"Thank the gods." Brennan let out a breath he hadn't even been aware he was holding.

"It gets better," Kennick said, grinning. "The *Caleb Bar* has withdrawn from combat, flying the skipper's colors. I think we're looking at a fair fight."

"Then someone screwed up."

"Yeah, but it wasn't on our side this time," Kennick answered, relieved. The *Caleb Bar* was well known on board the *Andros*, thanks to Gaston being one of the engineers who'd designed the blasted thing. None of them wanted to share the same sky with that monster if it was gunning for them.

At least one thing has gone according to plan so far. We may actually pull this off.

*

Field Marshal Groven directed the charge, not from the front of the pack, but not from the rear either. He'd led enough battles to know that neither actually worked out so well in most cases. If you led from the rear, your troops would learn to mock you, and more often than not you received vital information a moment too late. Leading from the front, on the other hand, was a quick way to decapitate your command structure.

He picked a unit close enough to the front for him to see the fighting with his own eyes, but far enough back to not attract as much attention from the enemy as other active combatants. He also didn't wear his usual uniform. No sense in giving anyone with a lens any ideas.

They were at the city walls now, the first real challenge to the ground campaign.

Even the hastily deployed legion they had been forced to fight through hadn't been much more than a bump in the road. The Thirtieth

Legion was composed of good fighters, but they had been sent into battle barely prepared against an already fighting force twice their size.

Corian should have known better, but I suppose he was sacrificing them to buy the Ninety-Eighth a little more time.

Groven found the action more than a little distasteful, though he'd have done the same thing if pressed hard enough. Now they were facing an entrenched and prepared force, however, and he knew personally that they weren't going to lie down for anyone.

Not even a former commander.

Artillery from inside the walls slammed into their positions, still ranging shots but more than close enough to kill a few, injure more, and throw the whole operation into disarray.

"Get the counter artillery division moving," Groven ordered. "I want those shots tracked back to their source and those guns taken *out*!"

Indirect artillery was rare in the empire, mostly due to the expense of the consumables involved. The empire itself could afford it, of course, but most of the time it was relatively unnecessary due to the Imperial control of the skies. Unfortunately for Groven, that meant that *counter* artillery was a rare specialty indeed, and the few he'd managed to scrape up were going to be hard pressed.

Still, he heard the sound of guns roaring in the distance, the men rising to the needs of the moment.

An explosive shock wave made him flinch, and he looked up to see the cruisers duking it out above him, one he couldn't recognize becoming a blaze of fire as it started to lose altitude.

"Watch that ship!" Groven ordered. "I don't want it dropping on any of our heads!"

This fight is getting out of hand.

*

"I've got a track for you, kid. Check your displays."

About time! Brennan managed not to say anything aloud as he glanced at the numbers Kennick had sent back to him. "Got it. Hang on—this is going to get a little wild."

The Fire Naga banked hard, sails shifting as he cut into the wind and began to use that pressure to push them down. The Naga accelerated as it began dropping from the third layer, nose coming over as the fighter lay out on its side and then pointed down.

The fight below spiraled around the two sitting inside the Naga, along with the entire world, but Brennan didn't even blink as they plummeted down through the second wind layer, still accelerating. Kennick was starting to sweat, but he wasn't about to distract the kid and, frankly, knew that the kid was a far better handler than he'd ever been. He just focused on the targeting reticule and the ships he'd marked as threats to the *Pillar of Miogaro*.

The fight was a scene of aerial chaos, ships from both sides interpenetrated and in some cases intertwined to such a degree that it had taken several minutes for him to figure out who was friend and who was foe. Even the ships in the fight had seemed confused, at least until someone opened fire on them, and at the moment a pair of light destroyers were closing on the *Pillar* from her flank.

The baron's ship could probably take them, but in a fight this intense there was no reason to leave it to chance, particularly since Kennick was well aware just *who* was on board her at the moment.

*

The mottled green-and-brown Fire Naga actually broke the sound barrier as it blew past the *Pillar*, causing most people on deck to flinch and follow it for a moment as its MACs buzzed and tore into the closest destroyer coming in on their port flank.

“Looks like your brother’s back,” William said, keeping his tone as light as he could as his eyes followed the fighter blowing past the destroyer, perforating it with a hundred high-powered magnetic rounds, causing a rapid loss of altitude. The Naga then banked hard to come around for another pass.

“So I see.” Lydia smiled wanly. “Brennan always did surprise people when he was in the air.”

“I remember all the complaints,” the Cadreman said wryly.

“He’s saved us some trouble,” Baron Kennissey said, watching as the fighter came back around and zeroed in on another destroyer. “We’re pressing on to the capital. We need to breach those walls.”

William nodded.

They were about to enter the most dangerous part of the entire campaign. The walls of the capital were frightfully defended. But they *had* to fall for the attack to be successful.

*

The cruisers of the loyalist flotilla pushed through the fighting, closing on the capital as the firing intensified both in the air and on the ground.

Both sides knew that this was where the battle would be decided, with the defense or fall of the capital walls.

Skilled handlers in the cruisers slowed their ships to a crawl as they loomed over the walls, giving their gunners clear shots below, but also opening themselves up to the ground air defenses. The ships absorbed the fire willingly as they hammered down on the defenses; ground forces charged forward, but they couldn’t do so indefinitely.

The *Raven’s Sword* lost control when a direct barrage of fire from the local air defense took out her internal command deck and destroyed the sail controls. She keeled slowly over at first, accelerating as her sails caught the wind the wrong way, and then careened into the *Guardian Hammer*, glancing off on her way down into the walls below.

The crash broke the back of the *Sword*, nearly snapping the cruiser in half as the walls held against the sheer force of the impact.

For the loyalists it was a blow to morale—both the loss of the ships and the sign of just how very strong the walls were, but those who'd planned the battle had known all along that they weren't going to be able to actually breech the walls.

Most of the fighting was centered around the city gates, with loyalist troops throwing themselves into the breach as the defenders held ground with grim determination.

*

Centurion Minas held up his fist as he rallied his troops, which he'd probably lost nearly a third of since they'd started. He waved his gamma carbine in his other hand, a weapon he'd picked up from one of the enemy dead to replace his empty lase rifle, calling his troops in closer under cover of some wreckage that had fallen from the sky. He didn't know what side it had belonged to originally, but for now it was his base of operations.

He laid it out for his men: "We need to take that gate, or this has all been for nothing. And I don't know about any of you, but I've lost too many already to *ever* allow that."

They all nodded grimly. They'd started as a full century of men and were now below seventy, and the fighting wasn't close to being over.

"OK, everyone on my lead," Minas ordered as he steadied himself. "We're *taking* that gate!"

His men roared behind him as he charged out from cover, carbine blasting. Behind him his troops all followed as he led them from cover to cover, firing all the way as the heavy guns at the gate blew through their ranks. Another eight warriors fell to gain them thirty more yards of ground, and then the hammering blasts from the gate gunners drove them to cover again.

"We're never going to make it!"

Minas shot a glare at the man who'd spoken but didn't say anything. The truth was that the gates were *not* soft targets. If they had been, someone would have probably done this before.

"Here's what we're going to do," he said. "There're a few more centuries in this sector, so we're going to team up and take those gunners out before we charge the gate . . ."

"Sir!"

"What?" Minas snarled, twisting around.

"Look at the gate!"

*

It felt as though the heavy mounted guns would shake the whole wall apart as they hammered out a staccato rhythm, the gunners lasing the entire field before them and any warrior who dared charge the gates. It was a slaughter—there just wasn't any other word to describe it. In order to take the gates of the capital, attackers had to walk right into a kill zone that *nothing* could survive.

The gunners on the gates might almost have felt sorry for the stupid bastards, but they didn't have time to think about it as they were mowing down one rank after another.

They were so focused on their grisly task that they didn't notice the shadow on the wall shivering slightly as a dark armored figure stepped into sight behind them. The gleaming flash of light was their only warning as the figure moved, the first slash destroying the mounted gun with a single motion, a sidelong kick dislodging the gunner and sending him flying over the rail and to the ground below.

Across the parapet the officer of the guns went for his sidearm but was silenced by an overhand throw that sent the gleaming blade through his sternum and embedded it deep in the wall behind him. The second gunner saw the motion and twisted, trying to bring his heavy gun around in time, but a single blast from a lazily drawn blaster ended him as the Cadreman surveyed the scene before him.

He stood out in the open, his armor changing from the shadowy form he'd used for stealth to the gleaming iridescent look that was most associated with the Cadre.

Brave bastards, he thought as he walked over to the gate controls and kicked them open.

As the gate fell, the man, who was a barkeep in another part of his life, pulled his Armati from the now dead officer and held it aloft.

"For Scourwind and empire!"

*

"The gate's down! Go! Go! Go!" Minas ordered before following his own advice and bolting toward the gate.

Around him men followed suit, and not just from his century. They closed on the gate, engaging in a fierce but brief firefight with the few utterly shocked and disorganized defenders on the ground level who were caught between fighting back and trying to get the gates closed again.

Minas looked around for the Cadreman after they'd secured the site, but the man was gone. He wasn't surprised; Cadre were like ghosts. He didn't know where this one had come from, but he was grateful he'd arrived.

*

"Gate twelve has been taken by the rebels."

Corian snarled wordlessly, looking over the scene before him as everything he'd sacrificed for crumbled around him. He'd given the lives of his men, his leg, his *eye*, and his *honor* for what was now burning right before his eyes.

"Gate three just went down. We're losing gate seven! *What is going on?*"

Corian knew what was going on. He could see the armor easily enough and knew that his former comrades had chosen the precisely worst moment to emerge from hiding.

I don't know how, but somehow the loyalists found them.

The skies knew that *he* had tried to find the missing Cadre members, but when Everett burned the servers, he'd effectively destroyed all leads Corian could have used.

Cruisers sailing over the capital were now hammering his defenses with near impunity, the air-defense stations were already smoldering ruins, and a flood of rebels were charging into the city through the fallen gates. The fighting was devolving to door-to-door and block-to-block skirmishes that would be vicious and hard fought . . . but the outcome was written.

Corian calmly walked to a command station and picked up a secure comm line.

"Order my personal units to fall back and prepare to retreat," he said quietly. "No, just my own men. The rest will buy us time; maybe they'll even kill someone valuable. But I want *my* men out of the capital within the hour."

Corian flicked off the comm channel and looked over the people monitoring the battle, catching the eye of one of his men and nodding silently.

Then he turned and simply walked out.

The capital may be lost, and with it the throne of the empire, but his campaign was far from finished.

*

Brennan was slammed back in his seat as he flipped the Naga end for end and caught a reverse air current, using the sails as brakes to kill his speed in a bone-crushing maneuver. The sudden reversal sent the much larger destroyer that was chasing him flying past, probably as much out of sheer shock as the more significant momentum of the larger ship.

"Coming around," Brennan gritted out. "Shoot those bastards!"

Kennick, who was shaking his head to try to clear the stars he was seeing, managed to mumble in agreement and get his hands back on the gunnery controls.

Brennan again flipped the Naga end for end, bringing her guns to bear on the destroyer right on cue.

The MACs buzzed as Kennick jammed his thumb down, sending a thousand rounds of magnetically accelerated metallic death into the destroyer that was only just starting to come around in an attempt to bring her guns to bear.

The gargantuan craft took the hits amidships as she turned, the line of rounds cutting a gash almost fifty feet long in the ship's side.

"Watch out!" Kennick blurted as he spotted the destroyer's broadside cannons spit plasma trace.

Brennan worked the controls, but they were going too slow now, and the sails weren't even close to a wind layer he could use to do much more than stay aloft. The lase blasts and plasma trace etched a cage of light around them, and for a moment it seemed like they were going to escape.

A shudder and a screaming sound put paid to that thought as one of their projector moorings was blown clean off and the Naga twisted in the air, dropping in a parabola under their one remaining sail.

"We're going down!" Brennan called.

"We've got company," Kennick said, eyes on the smoking destroyer that was also losing altitude quickly.

The problem was that the bigger ship still had some control and, it seemed, a death wish for the little Naga that had taken it out.

"They're lining up another shot!"

"I can't maneuver," Brennan swore. "We're helpless here!"

Kennick swallowed but continued to watch as the Naga swung under their one remaining sail as they descended to the ground below. "She's firing!"

The cage of plasma trace etched around them again as Brennan slapped his hand down and the Naga lurched, Kennick's stomach jumping up into his throat.

"Did they hit us?" he wondered out loud.

"No. I killed our sail," Brennan answered, sweating as he worked the pedals to bring the tail back up and the nose down. "I'm going to glide us in."

"Is this thing rated to a glide landing?"

"Not even close."

CHAPTER 27

Corian walked into the late emperor's private hangar, heading for his personal flyer, but he stopped about halfway there. He drew the Armati from his belt and casually extended the blade to his preferred length before turning around.

Mira Delsol was standing behind him, her own weapon in stave form.

"Well now"—Corian smiled—"you are a credit to the Cadre, Delsol. I will offer you that much respect. However, you've crossed me one time too many."

Mira looked at him with cold, almost haunted eyes. "You turned my men against me, then set them to murder me and Stephan."

"Who?" Corian asked, honestly puzzled.

"Exactly."

Corian was still trying to figure out who the hell Stephan was when Mira attacked, but the question didn't dent his reflexes even slightly; he easily parried her blow and casually lashed out in a kick. He knew he'd cherish the look on her face forever as the blow lifted the woman clear off her feet and sent her flying back more than twenty yards, then tumbling and skidding across the floor another fifteen into the wall.

"Prosthetics have certain advantages," he admitted as he calmly began walking toward her, "and while I can't say I'd have chosen to *lose my leg*, I believe that I've made the best of a bad situation, don't you?"

Mira rolled to her hands and knees, shaking her head to clear it. She cast about, trying to spot her Armati, but she didn't see it and couldn't remember actually losing it. She was struggling to get to her feet when another kick from Corian lifted her clean off the deck and sent her flying back into the wall again.

"Pah!" he spat on the ground. "I slew Scourwind with a single motion. You aren't even close to my old friend's level, Delsol. You're one hell of a Cadrewoman, and maybe in fifty years you'd be my equal, but you're not going to have the chance to prove it."

Mira spit blood, spattering the deck as she gasped through the pain in her ribs and went for her blaster.

Corian's boot slashed out, catching her wrist and sending the weapon clattering across the deck. Mira flipped over onto her back and stared up at him in shock.

"Surprised? Really?" Corian asked as he stood over her. "I suppose few people ever really learn just *how* powerful a Cadreman can become . . . we're a secretive lot, Delsol. I doubt anyone, even the late emperor, *really* had any idea of our limits."

He drew back his weapon, a thick, long two-edged blade with an ornate hilt, and sneered down at her.

"You should have signed on with me," Corian said as he struck.

Mira's eyes widened and she threw up her hands in a useless defensive gesture. In the corner of her gaze, as time slowed, she saw the gleam and ivory of her own Armati. So close, yet beyond her reach. Mira looked back up at the descending blade and closed her eyes, wishing she had the comforting weapon in hand.

Elan!

The Armati shone briefly on the deck, fifty feet from the fighting, then vanished from sight and reappeared in Mira's hand. Mira's fist closed reflexively over the contoured weapon as her eyes opened and time sped up again.

Sword slammed into stave with enough force to throw sparks across the deck and into the faces of both shocked warriors, who stared at each other for a brief instant.

"What?" Corian managed to blurt. Mira didn't blame him. She was wondering the same thing, but her body didn't have time for that nonsense, and it already knew what to do.

The Cadrewoman curled up, rolling onto her shoulders as she held off the sword, then kicked out with all the strength she had in two good legs. The blow didn't pack the force Corian's kick had, but it was enough to lift the big man off the ground and throw him into the air as Mira spun on her shoulder and kicked out to bring herself up to her feet.

She snapped out with her stave as Corian started to come back toward her, connecting with enough force to deflect his approach and slam the Cadre traitor down onto the deck. She adjusted her footing, twisting as she surged to the attack again.

Corian rolled away from the strike, coming to one knee in time to meet the next. A flurry of blows descended on him, and he was forced to grip the blade of his sword to give him more speed and control as he parried them. His mind was racing as he tried to work out what the hell had just happened, but he couldn't think clearly while she was raining blows down on him like a machine.

Corian parried one blow to the side, then dove away from the next, hitting the deck in a roll that brought him back to his feet a dozen yards away. He turned just in time to meet the next series of strikes as he backpedaled away from her, trying to regain the upper hand against the fury of the assault.

Mira ducked under his slash, lashing out with a sweep for his legs that Corian was forced to jump over, since the stave could easily break the bones of his good leg if it connected. He shifted his blade to an overhand strike and brought it down on her position as he descended from his jump, only to have the weapon batted aside by the stave as it came back around in a smooth continuous circle.

He snapped out a kick at her, but Mira bent to one side as his mechanical leg hammered past her. She let go of the stave with one hand and curled it back before driving out in a knife-hand strike that hammered his inner thigh above where the prosthetic attached to his leg. A sickening crack of bone signaled that she'd struck home.

Corian hissed in pain as he fell back, suddenly unable to put any weight on his mechanical leg.

"Funny thing about prosthetics, Corian," Mira said as she rose to her full height, "it doesn't matter how powerful they are. They can't be stronger than what they're connected to."

Corian hopped back, his sword weaving a pattern intended to keep her at bay as she advanced on him. Mira simply struck out with her Armati and destroyed the pattern easily, leaving his hand stinging and barely able to hold on to his own weapon.

"It's over," she said as her weapon shifted, becoming shorter and wider. Just as the wickedly curved blade of Mira's Armati Elan came up to strike, a series of shots rang out across the deck and sent her diving to the ground.

"Kill her!" Corian snarled as his guard arrived, the besieged commander hopping furiously toward the flyer that was warming up just a few dozen yards away.

Mira brought her Cadre armor back up. Now that she wasn't engaged in an Armati battle, it would actually serve some use. She scrambled for cover as gamma bursts burned the air and the deck around her. She angrily flicked her wrist, and the weapon in her hand smoothly shifted form again. Mira then brought her free hand up to draw back the photon bolt that appeared on command.

The first bolt ricocheted off the deck and nailed an armsman in the leg as he was trying to get a clean shot at her. The bolt took his leg clean out from under him, sending him face-first into the deck as his fellows gaped at him momentarily.

That was enough of a distraction.

Mira rose from her cover, another bolt already drawn back, and loosed it in under a second. Three more followed in the next second, dropping the rest of the guards. Before the last had hit the ground, she was already turning, bolt drawn, toward Corian.

The hatch to the flyer slammed into place as she loosed her bolt, and she watched it slam into the flyer's armor, leaving a deep gouge but not penetrating. Mira began walking toward the ship, drawing and loosing bolt after bolt as the reactor engine on Corian's flyer whined and the thrust kicked up a wind around her.

The flyer lifted off the deck and turned slowly in place. She saw Corian glare at her for an instant through the armored cockpit before the main thrusters roared. Mira covered her face with her arm as the flyer charged out of the hangar. She chased him out, still firing as the reactor craft continued accelerating away.

"You lucky bastard," Mira swore as she let her arm drop and watched.

The skies above her were filled with smoking cruisers, many barely aloft. She couldn't tell which side any of them belonged to anymore, not that it mattered. They were all Imperials, both sides. There would be no enemy forces dead when the tally was counted, just brothers and cousins to send on to the burning skies.

The Scourwind banner fluttered above her as a large cruiser slowly sailed over the palace, and Mira just hoped it would all be worth the cost.

At what cost, empire?

*

The Naga had dug a deep furrow in some poor farmer's field, but had mostly remained in one piece, much to the surprise of its occupants as they pried themselves out of the craft.

"I can't believe you glide landed an armed Naga," Kennick mumbled as he held his head.

Brennan was just barely holding the giggles at bay and couldn't really relay just how surprised he was himself.

Of course, calling it a "landing" might have been a bit of a stretch. More accurately he'd managed to crash the vehicle without turning the whole thing into a cartwheeling death trap.

"We're alive," he said after a moment. "I guess it's technically a landing, then."

Kennick looked at him incredulously, and then both of them lost their composure and broke down, laughing hysterically, a hard edge to their laughs that would have made anyone overhearing the two question their sanity.

In the distance, the capital was ringed with dense black smoke and the burning wrecks of three dozen cruisers—and the bodies of men and women who had yet to be counted.

*

"Resistance is dying out, Baron Kennissey."

Kennissey nodded. "Good. Bring the *Pillar* down on the Imperial field."

"Yes, sir."

The baron watched the aide leave for a moment before turning to William. "Are you certain? It's not going to be entirely safe yet."

William glanced at Lydia, who nodded firmly, then he sighed.

"Yes, my lord," he said. "We need to end the fighting before more lives are lost. Only the Scourwind can do that now."

The *Pillar of Miogaro* settled down on the field, planks already extending as she shifted into place.

The honor guard that led the way was more of an invasion force, but they were all flying the Scourwind banner as they huddled around Lydia at their center. William Everett was at their head, leading the charge into the palace.

"Lady Delsol," he blurted as he recognized the first figure standing there to greet them, shocked both by her presence and by her appearance. It appeared that someone had worked her over quite severely, though he didn't see any signs of gamma burns or lase blast injuries.

"My Lord Everett," she returned, then bowed slightly to Lydia. "Your Highness."

"Where's Corian?"

Mira shook her head. "He escaped. The bastard had a bolt-hole and a plan."

William swore but wasn't really surprised. He glanced at Mira's injuries again. "You tried to stop him?"

She nodded.

"It's a miracle you're still alive," William said. "You shouldn't have tried one on one."

"I owe him."

Lydia spoke up. "We need to finish this, William, Mira. *Now.*"

"Of course," William replied and nodded. "We need to take the control center."

The group got moving again, carving a path through the palace as they cut straight to the command and control center of the empire. Few who crossed their path actually put up resistance, most likely because they didn't expect to have to fight for the palace itself—and due to the Scourwind colors the group flew.

Those who did were dispatched swiftly.

Once they'd secured the control room, Lydia sat gingerly on the throne her father had used when overseeing Imperial military operations.

She hesitantly opened the secure comm line to all Imperial ships, set it to repeat on all frequencies, and took a breath before speaking.

"This is Lydia Giselle Scourwind," she said slowly, "seated empress of the empire. All ships, all warriors . . . cease fire. The battle is over, the palace secured. I will grant amnesty to those who cease all fighting *as of right now*. Anyone still fighting after this message will be arrested, tried, and . . . executed. I am Empress Scourwind. This is my command."

William stepped up behind her, straightening as he took in a breath to speak. "So says the empress! So says the empire."

EPILOGUE

Lydia was seated in the throne room of the empire, trying not to fidget uncomfortably as she remembered all the times she'd been in that very room trying to gain her father's approval or his attention.

Brennan was standing off to the side, smiling in her direction. She supposed that he thought he was being comforting, but at the moment she didn't think much of anything would comfort her. The fighting had all ended a week earlier, for what that was worth.

Repairs and funerals would take the rest of the cycle, at least, and it seemed that war wasn't entirely behind them.

Corian had escaped, and his allies in the Senate, while likely not happy with him, had bound their future to his. She supposed that they were terrified that she would take her revenge on them, and honestly Lydia couldn't say for sure that she wouldn't if she got the chance.

Unfortunately, the result was what they'd all tried so hard to avoid.

Corian had split the empire; several senators had seceded their provinces and were already reportedly building up a military force to repulse "Imperial aggression."

So she had no choice but to order her own military constructions to heighten their pace, which frustrated her to no end but seemed to please most of the remaining Senate. She supposed Imperial construction contracts would go a long way to please their base, but she also knew that she had to be careful where constructions were issued.

Not all of the remaining senators were entirely trustworthy, so she couldn't pay them to build anything critical, but she also couldn't ignore them for fear of driving them into the arms of Corian's alliance.

The politics were dizzying and disgusting, but they were for another time.

Before her were the heroes of the loyalist revolution. A centurion who'd led his troops in a desperate bid to take the gates, a Cadreman who had rallied his fellows to provide support from within at a critical juncture in the battle, the captains of many of the destroyers and cruisers that had secured the city, and even her brother, who had, along with his gunner, personally downed four cruisers and destroyers in the battle.

One person was notably absent.

Mira Delsol had vanished immediately after the battle had ended, leaving only a record of the fight from her perspective and a "gift" of the plans of the *Caleb Bar*. Plans she apparently had had all along, which explained quite a lot.

Lydia had already ordered new constructions of that class of ship, and modified plans for new variations were in the works.

She had little doubt that Corian would do the same.

The actual ship that defined the class remained at large, in the hands of known pirates.

Lydia couldn't help but smile ever so slightly at that.

*

Corian looked out over the shipyard bays, his expression as angry as it had been ever since the defeat at the capital.

In one fell swoop he'd lost everything he had sacrificed for and had likely *caused* more harm than if he'd done nothing in the first place.

He knew what was coming, and it wouldn't be met with diplomatic words and patronizing smiles. It would be met with force, or it would meet them with death.

Looking over the six bays before him, Corian saw the only hope for the empire.

Six black ships sat there in various states of construction, warriors in the making for the hard times ahead.

*

The *Caleb Bar* and the *Andros Pak* sailed the second wind layer along the northern stretch of the empire, transferring materials and people as the captain of the black ship stood out on the deck and smiled, the wind blowing her hair around wildly. She looked over the crewmembers going about their business, securing the ties and prepping the ship for a prolonged flight. Across the deck, the two youngest of her crew caught her eye and she nodded to them as they waved.

The young Dusk and her brother, Mik, were skilled for their age in useful disciplines, and they'd shown themselves willing to work. It certainly didn't hurt that neither of them were shy of hard labor either. She'd offered to let them off, of course, and to send a message to the empress to come pick them up. There was little doubt that they'd find a place in the capital, likely the palace itself, but they'd wanted to stay on the ship; the skies called to some people.

She herself had had her fill of civilization for a time, of orders and of rules. Authority set her teeth on edge, and she'd been burned too many times now to fully trust the empire, even under an empress she rather grudgingly liked. It was time to see some of the world hidden from them all.

Mira Delsol walked the large deck of the black strato-cruiser, nodding to Gaston, who was standing watch at the tiller wheel as she approached. He stepped clear as she took the wheel and took position just behind her.

"Supplies have been transferred from the *Andros*, skipper," he told her.

She nodded. "Excellent. So we're almost ready."

Gaston nodded, almost hopping on his heels, he was so giddy. "We are. This is what I built her for."

Mira grinned. He didn't need to tell her that. He'd been regaling them all with the story of why he'd built the *Caleb Bar* ever since she'd met him. It was a *good* story.

"I've been thinking," she said, interrupting him before he could continue.

A good story, but one she knew by heart.

"Oh? About?"

"About the name of the ship," she said. "I don't think I want to sail the *Caleb Bar*, Gaston. Not after everything."

Gaston frowned but nodded. "I suppose I can understand that. What do you want to name her?"

"What do you know about history?"

"Depends on how far back and what sort, I suppose."

"Very far back and military history."

Gaston shrugged. "Not much."

"I would be very much surprised if you did," Mira said. "In the days before the empire there were great warriors who had fought an unspeakable war . . . They were masters of their craft, which was death, but also masters of many other things."

"I . . . see?"

Mira smiled, eyes out on the sky ahead of them and the God Wall to the north in the near distance.

"These warriors each constructed weapons, weapons that to this day bear their names," she said, patting the weapon on her hip. "My Elan, the young Scourwind's Bene, all of the Armati in fact."

"I had no idea," Gaston said honestly.

"No reason you should. Few do. It's ancient history now."

"You want to name the ship after your Elan?" he asked, thinking it sounded like a good idea.

Mira laughed cheerfully. "No, though that is a pleasing thought. I was actually thinking about Caleb Bar, one of the greatest warriors of his time . . . legend has it he was the lover of Elan."

Gaston blinked. "I don't understand."

"I believe that we should christen this ship after the weapon that bore his name," she said sadly. "One of the Armati that was lost to history, before we came here . . . I suppose it is probably lying out there somewhere, alone in the dirt and waiting to be rediscovered."

Mira smiled softly, wistfully. "I like to think that our wayward brother found worthy hands and made his own mark on history . . . or perhaps will, someday yet to come."

She looked around the deck of the black ship and nodded, liking the idea more and more. The whispers in the back of her mind seemed to agree, and she imagined she felt a shiver run through the weapon strapped to her side. Mira's hand dropped unconsciously, caressing the ancient weapon as she remembered the single moment of clarity in her fight with Corian.

She should have died then, she knew. Armatis were powerful weapons, versatile like few things in the known world, but they could not simply vanish from one place and appear in another.

Or, at least, she had never heard of one doing so until that moment. Until her weapon saved her life—apparently of its own accord.

There is more to my Elan and the others than even I knew. She was now certain of that, and she was equally determined to learn more. However, for the moment, there were more pressing matters.

Mira looked around at the crew, some close enough to be paying attention, and some not having noticed the conversation. It mattered little. It would get around to them all soon enough. Rumor traveled faster than reaction jet after all.

"From now on, as the captain of this ship," she said boldly, attracting attention, "I christen her after the weapon whose creator she was named for . . . From today on we sail the *Excalibur*."

Gaston considered it for a moment, then finally nodded.

Excalibur. He liked that.

"Ready the quantum-rail drive," Mira ordered, eyes rising to where the God Wall climbed up and out of the atmosphere. "It's time to see what's on the other side of that wall."

"Aye, aye, skipper," Gaston said enthusiastically.

The *Excalibur* was, for the moment, the only ship in the empire that could cross a God Wall. Hell, it could reach the Great Islands themselves!

And now Gaston and the ship had a captain who would do just *that.*

ABOUT THE AUTHOR

Evan Currie is the bestselling author of the Odyssey One series, the Warrior's Wings series, and more. Although his postsecondary education was in computer science, and he has worked in the local lobster industry on the Magdalen Islands steadily over the last decade, writing has always been his true passion. Currie himself says it best: "It's what I do for fun and to relax. There's not much I can imagine better than being a storyteller."